Praise for
RACHEL
LEE

"Lee is an evocative writer with the ability
to effectively build suspense…a series
that will stand out."
—*Romantic Times BOOKreviews* on *Shadows of Myth*

"A suspenseful, edge-of-the-seat read."
—*Publishers Weekly* on *Before I Sleep*

"Rachel Lee deserves much acclaim
for her exciting tales."
—*Midwest Book Review*

D1019706

"Le…
—Publish… …w in September

RACHEL LEE
SHADOWS of DESTINY

LUNA™

www.LUNA-Books.com

LUNA™

SHADOWS OF DESTINY

ISBN-13: 978-0-373-80261-6
ISBN-10:   0-373-80261-7

First printing: January 2007

Author Photo by: Kim Doner

This edition published by arrangement with Harlequin Books S.A.

® and TM are trademarks of Harlequin Books S.A., used under license.
Trademarks indicated with ® are registered in the United States Patent
and Trademark Office, the Canadian Trade Marks Office and in other
countries.

www.LUNA-Books.com

Printed in U.S.A.

To Holly, for the song of Anahar.
And to Matt, for the courage of the Anari.

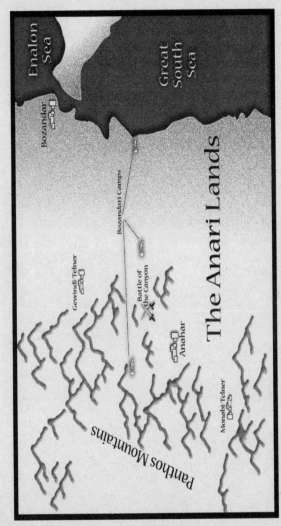

Enalon Sea

Great South Sea

Bozandar

Bozandari Camps

The Anari Lands

Gewindi Telner

Battle of the Canyon

Anahar

Monohi Telner

Panthos Mountains

Copyright Cris Brown, 2005

Chapter One

"And be ye faithful always, one to the other," the priestess intoned quietly.

"And be we faithful always, one to the other," Tom Downey and Sara Deepwell responded.

"The grace of the gods be with you always," the priestess said. "You are now one before this company, before the gods, in this world, and in every world where you may travel."

Tom and Sara kissed. Cilla Monabi could feel the radiant glow in her sister Ilduin's heart, and her own heart shared Sara's joy. Yet this time of joy would be fleeting. Sara met her eye, just for an instant, and nodded. She, too, knew.

But for tonight, they would celebrate.

The stones of Anahar did not sing in celebration, though Cilla could feel the joy of the gods as she walked through the temple. A precious love was joined, and even in a world fraught with war and the black hatred of Ardred, that precious love was worthy of joy.

The marketplace before the temple was adorned with the trappings of a wedding, for in the wake of the war that had taken so many of their number, the Anari longed for just cause to wear their finest, cook their best, sing and dance beneath the stars. Cilla found Ratha at the edge of the crowd, his iridescent blue-black face impassive, his obsidian eyes unreadable.

"Dance with me, cousin," she said.

"I cannot," he replied quietly, almost with shame.

Cilla placed a hand on his strong, muscled, scarred arm. "Look around you, Ratha. The men and women of Monabi Tel are dancing. Giri was their kin, and my own as well."

"He was my brother," Ratha said. "We had endured so much together. I am not whole without him."

They had endured much, Cilla knew. Ratha and Giri Monabi had been betrayed by Cilla's brother, captured by Bozandari slavers and sold on the block, until Lord Archer Blackcloak had gained their freedom. Their hardships had not ended then, for as they rode with Archer they had found themselves drawn into the lives of warriors. When they had finally returned to Anahar, at the dawn of winter, it had been to kill their betrayer, and then to train and lead the Anari in war.

Ratha had atoned for killing Cilla's brother, for she had witnessed that act, and her brother's confession, and pronounced it justice. Such was her right as an Anari priestess and judge. But Ratha had sojourned in the desert to cleanse his soul, and he had returned a different man. Still a warrior, but no longer with a thirst for blood. He had hoped that Giri, too, would find that redemption. Instead, Cilla knew, Ratha had watched as Giri was cut down in the savage battle of the canyon that had destroyed the Bozandari invaders.

And Ratha had not been whole since.

"Dance with me," she said again, softly, insistently. "Dance with me as Giri would have, with joy in his heart and a jest on his lips. That was your brother's magic, Ratha. Do not let it die with him."

He moved as if his limbs were stiff with frost. But he moved. Cilla took his hand and led him to the dance.

Tess Birdsong, too, patiently tried to draw a man to dance. But like Ratha, Archer Blackcloak seemed to find little room for joy in his heart. Guilt weighed upon him like a mantle of lead, and Tess knew it was a guilt neither she nor a wedding could push aside. Yet somehow, she must.

She was no longer the terrified, confused, lost woman who had awakened in a field of blood and death those many months ago. But enlightenment had borne a steep price. Though she had not chosen it, destiny had chosen her, and she was as shackled to its whims as an Anari slave in a Bozandari market.

And still, she did not know who she really was. Amnesia had stolen most of her memory, and while the Temple of Anahar had revealed moments of her past to her, it had failed to fill in all the empty places.

Tonight she had worked to look her finest, her blond hair, longer now than it had been when first she had awakened with a mind as bare as a newborn babe's, was threaded with blue ribbons and golden trinkets Cilla had loaned her. Her dress, blue rather than the white she usually wore, had been made for her from a fine, glistening fabric found among the spoils of the army they had defeated. Golden ribbon wound it about beneath her breasts, across her middle and around her waist. On her feet she wore fine golden slippers.

Dressed, she thought, like a queen, for a moment of joy that carried the shadow of death.

For death would come. She knew that to the core of her being. Too many had already died and too much evil yet remained.

She avoided touching the walls of the temple. Tonight she needed it to yield no secrets to her, and she feared the stones might do just that.

Outside she sought Archer with her eyes. Something about him remained always apart, even from his closest companions. Hence it was no surprise to find he had stationed himself in shadows at the edge of the square. He leaned against the corner of a rainbow-hued building, one arm folded over a broad chest cased in black fabric. Of all the people present this night, only Archer wore black. He was the quiet mourner at the edge of the celebration, the one who knew better than any of them all that lay ahead.

His gray eyes missed little as he watched the dancers, jugglers and musicians. He even smiled as Tom and Sarah emerged from the temple, wed at last.

But it was a smile that didn't reach any further than his face.

Feeling a pang for him, Tess made her way through the crowds to his side, and reached for his tanned and battle-scarred hand.

He looked down at her as she gently squeezed his fingers.

"'Tis a fine night for a wedding," he said.

"Aye, but you look less than joyful. Come, dance with me and allow your heart to lighten for just a brief while."

"Is yours lightening?"

After a moment, she looked down, away from his perceptive gaze. "We all know what has passed, Archer," she murmured finally, her words barely audible above the music and laughter. "And we all know what lies ahead."

"I very much doubt anyone knows what lies ahead. 'Twill be far worse than what we have so far faced."

"Aye," Tess nodded. "I have dreams, such dreams...." Her face shadowed, but then she looked at him with a determined smile. "However it may be, and whatever looms ahead, the gods have decreed that we must live. So let us live this night."

After a moment, he acquiesced and led her into the square to join the other dancers. She had never, to her memory, danced before, but it wasn't long before Archer had helped her master the simple steps and she was whirling with him in the outer circle of dancers that surrounded an inner circle moving in the opposite direction.

When the feet and body moved to such happy music, it was impossible to remain sad. Before long, Archer smiled and his feet seemed to grow lighter. Tess let go of the pall that always shrouded her heart and let laughter flow freely.

Regardless of what the morrow might bring, life had granted a respite, and she felt it would be wrong, very wrong, not to savor these precious moments of joy.

Topmark Tuzza, the Bozandari commander, could hear the rejoicing in Anahar halfway across the valley where he and his men were imprisoned behind fences, watched by Anari guards. They had been defeated in battle three weeks before by the Anari, and they were still licking their wounds.

The topmark had been invited to the wedding, but had refused the honor. His men were not yet ready for what he was about to ask of them, and he was not about to anger them by attending the wedding as an honored guest. He could not afford to lose his authority over them.

Yet even after all this time, he could still not think of a way to broach the subject. Many of his men, *most* of his men, thought of the Anari as a slave race. They had set out to conquer a rebellion against the authority of the Bozandar Empire.

How was he to persuade them that there was a greater evil, and a greater cause? That they now must switch allegiance, but yet would not be betraying their own families and people?

Tuzza was no dull man. Sharp wits more than family connections had raised him to the heights. He was related to the emperor, yes. But so were many others. It was only through achievement that Tuzza could stand directly behind his emperor at important events, could offer words of advice directly into his emperor's ear.

He would be seen as a fool and a traitor when his intent became known. Either one would be enough to make his men turn on him.

Closing his eyes, he listened to the distant sound of reveling, and leaned back in his camp chair, seeking yet again the words that would persuade.

His men, of course, had seen the many healings the Ilduin witches had caused. Many of the more severely wounded had benefited greatly from the Ilduins' touch…as had he himself. Some had even outright marveled that after a battle so bitterly fought, the Ilduin, who had fought beside the Anari, had been so willing to heal their enemies.

Perhaps that was the place to start. Perhaps he should speak of the Ilduin and the Lord Annuvil, he who was the

First Prince of the Firstborn King, long before Bozandari and Anari had ever walked the face of this world. Perhaps he should remind them of the tales of old, and of the nearly forgotten prophecies that foretold such a time as this.

Of course, if he had not himself seen the Ilduin and their powers, had not seen the Lady Tess lead troops into battle, then with one word from her mouth cause the conflict to cease…Tuzza himself might not have believed the dark man who had come to him and said, "I am Annuvil."

The Firstborn Immortals had vanished so long ago, so many centuries in the past, that it was hard to believe one of them yet survived. Two of them, actually, according to Lord Annuvil.

Yet Tuzza could not deny it. He had seen what he had seen, and he was still alive only because of it.

These times had been foretold. The outcome was unwritten, but the return of the Ilduin and the Firstborn King were writ in more than one prophecy. They were writ on the fabric of every soul, every mountain and stream, every rock and tree, every bird and bear, serpent and snow wolf. They were writ by the gods themselves, and Tuzza knew better than to dispute such a destiny.

His mother had schooled him thus from the time of his birth. His mother and the old Anari woman, each of whom had sat beside his bed and told him stories when he was too ill with fever to rise and run and play. The same two women who had patched his wounds when he fell, ensured that his bedding was clean and that his pillow bore the fresh scent of spring flowers. Looking back, he could hardly remember where his mother left off and the Anari woman had begun, could hardly distinguish which of them had performed which graces in his youth.

They had taught him to respect the old ways, and some-times—when she was sure no one else could hear—the Anari woman would speak in the Old Tongue. Fragments of words floated into his consciousness, and though he knew not their meaning, he felt once again that sense of wonder, of contact with life, with light, with the gods themselves, which had filled his heart in those bygone days.

But in his childhood that wonder had been bright and beautiful, song and light. It was a dark wonder that now filled him. Fear and grief and a bottomless, aching loss for the men who had died under his command, and the many more who would die in the war to come.

It would be Tuzza who would lead those men—the same men who now sulked sullenly under the eyes of their Anari captors—once again into battle. He would lead them into battle with an Anari host at their sides and a Bozandari host before them.

And more would die at his hand.

Chapter Two

They danced until their bodies were weary, yet their minds did not tire. At last, Archer and Tess slipped away from the revelers and into the quieter night beyond the city of Anahar. Above, the stars looked cold and unforgiving, and beyond the warmth of Anahar's walls, the wind held a bitter bite.

The unnatural winter, which to the north had left so many to starve and freeze to death, now at long last was reaching the normally warm lands of the Anari. Never had snow been seen in Anahar, but Tess suspected that would soon change.

"His breath still blights the land," Archer murmured. Lifting his cloak, he drew Tess within its warmth, against his side. "Can you tell yet how many Ilduin he has subverted?"

Tess shook her head, grateful for the warmth Archer shared with her. "Other than the two I have already found, I cannot yet tell for certain." Her hand lifted to touch the pouch of colored stones that hung around her neck. Each stone belonged to one of the twelve living Ilduin. When she held them in her hands, she could draw on the power of her sisters, or communicate with them. But some yet remained out of reach, beyond her ability to call. Two she was certain belonged to Ilduin who had fallen into Ardred's clutches. But others remained a mystery to her.

"I am sorry," she said after a few moments. "If I knew all the other Ilduin, it would be easier. But so far I have met only Cilla and Sara. Some of the others I can reach, while others yet remain untouchable to my mind. It may be that they themselves have not yet discovered their powers."

"Indeed. Many believe the Ilduin long dead and gone from this world. Why should not some of the Ilduin be among the nonbelievers?"

He sighed. A gust of wind at that moment snatched his cloak and lifted it, blowing its icy breath inside. Tess shivered.

"I fear," he said presently, "that Ardred must claim more than two of your sisters. This winter he inflicts on us is a sure sign of his growing power."

"I fear it, too."

"With the Bozandar Empire lying between us and the lands to the north, it is impossible to learn how many others he and his hive-masters have drawn in. We will need Tuzza's help to pierce the veil and glean information."

"I know."

"A relief army will be leaving Bozandar soon, to come look for Tuzza's army. There will be a terrible battle. But Tuzza has not yet found a means to convince his men to fight beside the Anari against the greater evil, especially since it may require fighting their brothers-in-arms."

"It is essential we gain the cooperation of Bozandar."

"Aye." He looked down at her, his face unreadable in the starshine. "I would hear any suggestion you might have."

That was when she realized that he had at last begun to trust her. Always before there had been a sense that he doubted her real purposes. It was a doubt for which she could not blame him. After all, she could remember nothing before the horrific day the past autumn when she had awakened among the slaughtered caravan, knowing not even her own name.

Sometimes she wondered if she should trust herself. At times she had felt the touch of the Enemy, Lord Ardred, like a dark shadow in her mind, seeking, always seeking, something from her. It had been a while, though, since she had felt that chilling, oily touch in her mind, and for that she was grateful.

"I wish I had a suggestion," she said finally. "I don't think asking those soldiers to become traitors is going to be easy for anyone, no matter how silver-tongued."

She felt, rather than saw, his agreeing nod.

"Yet," he said after a moment, "they will not be traitors, but saviors. Saviors of all men."

"So go in and tell them who you are. It worked with Tuzza."

A sigh escaped him, barely heard before it was snatched away by the wind.

"How many will believe that I have lived for so long, hidden among them?"

"I find it hard to believe myself. Has it been as awful as I suspect?"

"It has been a curse. Death would have been welcome countless times. And yet it is a just punishment. My deeds led to the end of the Firstborn. Why should I not wander the world, a stranger among strangers, for the rest of eternity?"

"Not your deeds alone." She turned to face him, allowing the icy wind to come between them. "Just because you have a conscience does not mean that you alone are responsible. I have looked into the past in my dreams and in the old stories, and what I see is that many were responsible in different ways. Say what you will, Annuvil, the guilt is not yours alone."

"Mayhap not. What does it matter? I have been preserved for this time, these events. Perhaps if I acquit myself well and do what is expected of me this time, the gods will set me free."

She tilted her head back to better see him. "You would wish your own end? Are you sure that is a good wish for a man who will lead us in the war against Ardred?"

Surprising her, he chuckled. "There are many ways a man can be set free. Perhaps at last I will be free to be mortal. Perhaps it will be something else. How should I know? The minds of the gods are ever opaque."

"I am coming to know that well." She felt a wave of relief at his laughter, though she couldn't have blamed him for being bitter about his lot. Nor could she imagine how awful these centuries must have been for him.

"It's a wonder," she said slowly, "that the years did not drive you mad."

"Sometimes they did. I am grateful that I have little memory of those times, however. They are blurred in my mind, and all sense of time was lost. I sometimes lived like a beast in the forest, I believe."

"I'm sorry. Sorry and awed, for I cannot imagine surviving such a thing. How did you make yourself go on?"

"I was promised," he said slowly. "I was promised that someday my Theriel would be returned to me."

She stepped back even farther, and ignored the cold wind. For some reason she could not readily name, she felt…hurt. "Who promised you?"

"Elanor. She came to me after…after the destruction. She promised that if I served her well, in the end I would see my wife again. I have clung to that promise."

"Are you sure you can trust Elanor? Or any of the gods?"

He shook his head. "No. I freely admit I cannot. Their purposes are not ours. But…it is all I have. My heart died with Theriel, and the remaining ember is all that I have left. I *must* believe."

"I can see that." She turned from him, letting his cloak fall away, letting the wind sweep over her and chill her to her very bones. She spread her arms as if to embrace the winter night. A snowflake, such as had never fallen in this valley in the memory of men, drifted down and landed on one of her fingertips.

"I don't know who I am," she said slowly, watching the flake melt. "I don't know where I am from. I have no promises to uphold me. Yet here I am, and I do what I must."

"Then perhaps your burden is the greater by far."

She turned suddenly and faced him. "What do they mean when they call me the Weaver?"

"It is said that one day an Ilduin would come who could touch the warp and woof of reality, and bend it to her will."

"And they think I am that person?"

"You wielded the Weaver's sword in battle."

"Anyone could have wielded that sword."

He shook his head slowly. "Not as you did."

She closed her eyes, remembering the moment when Tom had placed the sword in her hand and told her what it was. After that, everything had become a great blur. She had little memory of the battle afterward, and knew only what she was told: that she had led a force of men against a flanking attack and had saved the day. That later, with one word, she had caused the battle to instantly still.

A great fear began to tremble in her, colder than the cold that surrounded her. "What does it mean? What is expected of me?"

"I know not."

"The prophecies. If the Weaver is mentioned in them, there must be some hint, some clue!"

"Have you not realized by now how prophecies are more riddles than foretellings? I cannot tell you what it is you are to do. I cannot tell you how to do it. You must trust, my lady, that when the time comes you will know."

"There is too much call for trust."

"I know." He looked past her down the valley to where the fires burned in the prison compound. "They too must find a way to trust. For trust, I believe, is all that will save us from the wiles of Ardred."

She turned from him and looked down the valley, too, thinking of the men who must be huddled around those fires, despairing and perhaps even bitter in defeat, a taste that no Bozandari had known before. "Aye," she said, her heart heavy with dread. "They, too, must trust. And perhaps that will be the most difficult thing of all."

That night, in her dreams, the white wolf came to her again, as he had twice in reality. He howled, a mournful, spine-tingling sound, then seemed to gesture for her to follow him.

Through the mists of her dream, she slipped after him. As was the way of dreams, she never wondered why she followed, or what the wolf wanted of her. Nor did she feel any fear.

Gradually the mist softened, then faded until she could see the woods through which they traveled. Always the wolf was just ahead of her, pausing in his easy, long-legged lope when necessary to let her catch up.

At last they emerged into a clearing. Above, the sky glistened with a carpet of stars thicker than any she had ever seen. Then, around her, she heard the murmur of voices. She could not make out the words but sensed that she stood in the center of some invisible gathering.

Until now, she had felt nothing, but as she stood there, her discomfort grew, because she felt as if she were being judged by some unseen jury. The wolf remained at her side, but his presence offered scant comfort. She began to think of fleeing from this haunted clearing. At that instant the voices fell silent.

Then a woman stepped out of the shadows, her face concealed by a hood that cast it in darkness.

"Many," the woman said quietly, "are your sisters who have gone before you. To none of us fell the burden that now befalls you. Yet each of us, in her own way, has prepared your path with promises and prayers. We cannot tell you what is to come, for the gods make a game, and we are bound by their rules. But we will be with you, little sister. If you hear a whisper on the air, listen for our voices. All that lies between is a veil, and that veil can be pierced."

Before Tess could question her, the woman had vanished

back into the shadows. For a second or two, she could hear the quiet murmur of the voice again.

Then she was alone in the clearing with only the white wolf.

He nudged her hand with his cool, damp nose and she blinked.

And gasped. For she no longer stood in the clearing at all, nor was it any longer dark.

Dawn was breaking over the mountains to the east, wreathed in red and pink and orange, the globe of the sun not yet visible.

Nor was she in her bed. She stood halfway between Anahar and the compound housing the Bozandari prisoners of war.

The frigid morning air made her cheeks sting, but she was still surprisingly warm. Looking down at herself, she saw that she had dressed in her fine white woolens and boots, with her cloak about her shoulders. Had she done that in her sleep?

A sound behind her made her swing sharply around, and she gasped as she saw the wolf was still with her.

What was going on? Had she been dreaming? Or had she been awake in some netherworld? Had long-dead Ilduin really spoken to her?

Or was she simply losing her mind?

But then the wolf came toward her and shoved his big, soft head beneath her hand. Instinctively she scratched him behind the ears, and marveled at how silky his coat felt.

She must have been sleepwalking, she thought. Thank goodness she had dressed before setting out from Anahar. Else she would be frozen and dead right now, it was that cold.

She was about to return to the city on the hillside when

the wolf tipped back his head and howled. It was a beautiful sound, music unto itself.

And it was answered. Tess felt her scalp prickle as wolves howled back from the awkward, hardy trees that made life for themselves in the green desert that was the Anari lands. The sound was eerie, as eerie as anything she had ever heard. There must have been dozens of them.

But then they emerged from the trees, still howling, a harmony among their voices that reverberated until it sounded as if they numbered in the several dozens. But there were only seven more of them, all as white as the one that stood beneath her hand.

She should have been terrified. She should have fled. She should have tried to call on her powers for protection. Instead she remained rooted to the spot as the wolf pack ran toward her, their yellow eyes bright, mouths relaxed in smiles, as if they were coming home.

When they reached her, their howling stopped and they began to make quiet whimpers and whines as they swirled around her legs, sniffing her as if to learn her. Then, as if by silent order, all seven sat on their haunches and looked up at her.

She spoke, not knowing what else to do. "What do you want?"

The only answer she received was from the pack leader. His head moved from beneath her hand so that he could tug at her robe with his mouth.

He pulled her gently.

Toward the prison compound.

And all the others followed, as if they were tamed beasts at her beck and call. But she knew otherwise, and wondered what it all meant.

* * *

Ras Lutte, formerly overmark of the Bozandari army, approached his ruler slowly, as if hoping to avoid notice. He had news to bring, and bring it he must, for such was his duty. But he knew the meaning of the dour visage upon the throne, a face that seemed to bear the weight of the gods themselves upon its features. Lutte was all too familiar with that expression. It had been months, it seemed, since his ruler had borne any other.

Yet the ruler was still an astonishingly beautiful man, fair of complexion, golden of hair, blue of eye. To Lutte and others, it seemed he might even be the spawn of the gods, for never had a man so handsome and charismatic ever been seen before.

Until this brooding had begun.

But at least no one died from these silent broodings.

"My lord," Lutte finally said, after placing his right fist to his heart and bowing at the waist. "I pray that I disturb thee not, yet the woman has spoken."

The man on the throne looked up slowly, as if all of his strength were required simply to lift his head. Lutte could not be certain, but he thought he saw tears in his ruler's eyes. Immediately, Lutte lowered his gaze to the floor. Such things were not to be seen.

"What is it, Overmark?" the ruler asked, each word seeming to wend its way from the bottom of a deep cavern.

"The Weaver summons the wolves, my lord. Soon, the woman says, the Enemy host will march."

The man's eyes closed for a moment, then he nodded. "Just as it was foretold."

Lutte knew little of prophecy and trusted less than he knew. He was loathe even to trust the woman who sat in her room like the shell of a human being, hardly taking even food or drink, her body nearly as desiccated in life as any Lutte had seen in death.

He was a man of science and mathematics, the science and mathematics of war. Born into the Bozandari peerage, trained in the Academy of War, tested in battle, proved in a half-dozen campaigns. His exile after an affair with a topmark's wife had not changed his nature. It was possible to take the soldier out of the army, but never to take the army out of the soldier. Now he had found another army, and he had taken to the task of training the ragged band of outlaws and exiles into a smoothly functioning fist to be wielded at his will.

But not his will. The will of his ruler. And the will of his ruler was guided by prophecy and the mumblings of the woman. It was, Lutte thought, a shaky foundation upon which to base a campaign. But he had learned loyalty in the academy, and his personal dalliances aside, his professional loyalty was a matter of pride.

He relayed the woman's words as if they were those of the most accomplished spy, not because he trusted her or her ramblings, but because it was his duty to do so.

"If this is so," Lutte said, "then our agents in Bozandar must be at their task. Surely Bozandar can crush the slave people and end this rebellion."

"Bozandar will not be our ally," the ruler said. "In the end, it will come to us and us alone. It will come to me. For only I can slay my brother."

Again he is on about his brother, Lutte thought. As if the rest of the world were mere pawns in this sibling rivalry. Lutte had heard the whispers, that his ruler was in fact the second son of the Firstborn King, but he did not believe them. The children of the Firstborn were long dead, if ever they had existed. Lutte needed no ancient good or evil to empower him. The evil of the human heart more than sufficed to afflict the world. And only the good of the human heart could bring it comfort. The rest were tales, legends, myths told to fortify the sheep against the hardness of life, and make the sheep compliant within it.

"Is there anything else?" the ruler asked.

"No, my lord."

"Then go," the ruler said. "Tend to your numbers and your geometries. And pray that you never stand on a field where straight lines bend and twice two is not four."

He did not read my mind, Lutte thought as he bowed and turned to leave. His face had betrayed his skepticism, and his ruler knew of his reputation. It was nothing more.

What a pity, Ardred thought as Lutte left. What a pity that such a talented young mind should lack the most essential of all knowledge: the numbering of the gods, the geometry of the soul.

Lutte was a good soldier, but poor counsel. What he lacked, Ardred most needed. For no man can make war upon his brother with lightness of heart, whatever their past. Once, Ardred had laid siege to Annuvil. Now Annuvil would come to lay siege to Ardred.

Lutte thought he knew what danger lay when two men loved a woman, for such had been his crime. But he knew nothing at all.

Ardred must kill his brother. The world could not be stitched back together until Annuvil was dead. Only then would the glory and true power return.

And all this for the love of a single woman.

Theriel.

Chapter Three

The rustle began at the edges of the Bozandar camp. Muted gasps and movements filtered through the camp as if through the muscles and sinew of a waking giant, slowly willing it into motion. Tuzza put down his pen and emerged from his tent, his senses alert for any hint of danger or malice. He felt none, and slowly made his way through the gathering throng of soldiers at the eastern fence.

"It cannot be!" one man whispered.

"They cannot live so far south!" another added.

"My eyes deceive me, for they bend to her!"

Tuzza shouldered his way through until he could see for himself what had caused such a stir. And his mouth dropped open.

There stood Lady Tess, a semicircle of snow wolves arrayed behind her, silent yet alert, their eyes fixed on her as if she were their pack leader. One of them, however, stood beside her, golden eyes searching among the soldiers

until at last they fixed on Tuzza. A shiver ran through him
as he made eye contact with the beast, a recognition of
something preternatural and unexplainable.

So it was true.

Tuzza instinctively lowered himself to one knee and
bowed. He had no need to speak, for his men were still
soldiers, whatever their current lot. They knelt with him.

"Rise, Topmark Tuzza," the woman said, her voice quiet
but firm. She spread her hands behind her, indicating the
wolves. Then the fingers of one hand returned to rest on
the head of the snow-white beast beside her. "Rise and
make way for your Lady and her court."

"Fall in!" Tuzza commanded.

Some, those whom fortune had placed at the rear of the
battles and who had not needed her healing touch,
grumbled. But they were the fewer, and the looks of their
comrades shamed them into obedience.

"Dress ranks!" Tuzza said.

Even in those who grumbled, the first act of obedience
had rekindled the training and drill that countless hours
had transformed into automatic responses. The men adjusted their spacing, and soon stood in lines so straight that
they might have been set down by a surveyor.

Tuzza faced Lady Tess. "My men stand ready, m'lady. We
are at your service."

"Very well," Tess said, now striding toward them as if she
were gliding on air, the wolves in her train.

She marched to the front of the formation, then turned
to face them. Once again the wolves took up their places
behind and at her side. When she spoke, her voice was clear
and strong, a bell ringing in the soul itself.

"I am she who was foretold," Tess said. While she

loathed the words and what they meant, she knew their truth. She could not hide from herself any longer. "Believe, or disbelieve. But disbelief will be your doom, for you will disbelieve that which you now see for yourselves. Topmark Tuzza stands at my service. Where stand you?"

For long moments, the host stood frozen. Tuzza stepped forward and ranged himself beside the lady. Now, perhaps, he could quell the unrest in his ranks and refashion from them an army. He spoke quietly, yet pitching his voice to reach even the most distant of ears among his men. "The days we learned about as children, the days we thought were mere tales fashioned for our amusement, have arrived. While we may have to fight our brethren, our purpose is not to bring about the fall of Bozandar, but her salvation. For the Enemy we fight would bring the death of all.

"Stand with me, my men, for the sake of your families, for the sake of your children yet unborn. For if we do not stand now, we shall face the fate of the Firstborn, and never shall our names be heard again."

He could see his men wavering, uncertain in their loyalties. Outside the walls of the compound, however, the Anari guards bent their knees and made signs of fealty toward the Lady Tess. Then the wolves began to keen, a sound that made the hair on the back of a man's neck rise, that sent a tingle running along even the bravest spine.

With a simple movement of her hand, the lady silenced the wolves, a sight so shocking that many doubtful hearts were swayed.

"Brave men of Bozandar," she said, "declare yourselves now, for your entire future is writ in this moment."

A ripple of movement ran through the ranks, and when stillness again returned, every soldier had knelt.

The lady opened her arms and turned her face heavenward. To those with eyes to see, she almost seemed to glow a pale blue, an aura that enveloped the wolves at her feet. Then snow began to fall, gently, sparkling in the rising dawn light, looking almost like blood. Above, gray clouds churned, marked red here and there as the sun rose above the mountains.

"He brings the snow," the lady said. "He seeks to destroy you with cold and hunger. He would murder your brothers and leave barren the wombs of your sisters. He would strike from the fabric of time your very existence. I will not let this be."

Reaching up with one hand, she appeared to grasp something in the air and twist it. A sudden wind sprang up, strong enough to make men lean. As it blew, it drove the clouds away, clearing the sky until it was the perfect blue of dawn.

The lady lowered her arm and looked at all the men kneeling before her. "Rise," she said. "You have chosen wisely this day. I will arrange better accommodations for you as swiftly as I can. May Elanor bless you and your families."

Then she turned and exited the compound, the wolves a protective phalanx around her.

In the Bozandari compound, the murmuring and even arguments continued throughout the day. Some refused to believe what they had seen. The vast majority, however, believed their own senses, and eventually argued the dissenters into silence.

The strongest voices among them were the voices who had seen Tess on the battlefield, those who had seen or experienced her healing and that of her sisters.

Such magicks had long vanished from the world, and had long been thought to be silly tales. Now those who had seen with their own eyes no longer could deny the truth of the stories.

Tuzza chose to remain mostly out of sight this day, while the discussions raged outside his tent. His men had elected to offer fealty to the lady, and he never doubted that they would keep that oath. Honor was held in the highest esteem by the Bozandari army, and these men would not go back on their words. Yet still they might argue about what they had seen and what it meant.

Toward evening, as the sky reddened again to the west and the camp began to settle for another cold night, Archer Blackcloak, he who was Annuvil, came to the prison camp to speak with Tuzza.

The first thing Tuzza noted was that Master Archer, as he preferred to be called, seemed to have grown somehow since last they spoke. It was as if in shouldering the burdens left to him by his heritage, as if in announcing his true identity, Archer had grown physically as well as figuratively. The lines of care and suffering still carved his face deeply, but they only enhanced the sense of power about him.

Tuzza offered him wine, and the two of them sat at the wooden camp table, the map of the Bozandari world between them.

"I heard," Archer said, "that the lady paid you a visit early this morning."

"Aye, she did. With eight white wolves."

Archer's mouth lifted in a smile. "That must have commanded attention."

"I am not certain what commanded the most attention—

the wolves or when she stopped the snow and drove away the clouds." Tuzza, who had believed himself to be the most unsurprisable of men, nevertheless sounded awed as he spoke of the lady banishing the storm.

Archer nodded and sipped his wine. "She is full of surprises, that one. Nor does she yet know all she can do."

"A wild talent?"

"At times. For some reason, the gods deprived her of all memory when they brought her to me and my friends. Whatever she may have known before, all is lost. She knows only what she learns with each passing day."

"Then she has learned a great deal."

Archer nodded. "Quite a bit in such a short time."

"I hear the Anari guards referring to her as the Weaver. Do they mean the one foretold?"

There was a glint in Archer's eye. "What think *you*, Tuzza? Did she reach out and cast away a storm?"

"I saw it with my own eyes." He looked down into his wine and breathed, "The Weaver. I never thought to see such a thing."

"Few of us did. I do not mind saying that living in the times foretold by prophecy will bring little joy to most of us."

"No. These will be hard times."

"The hardest. We will all be sorely tested. Sorely indeed." He caught Tuzza's gaze and held it. "All we will have, brother, is trust in one another. I cannot tell you how important that will be."

"You call me brother?"

"Aye, for you are about to share my burden. And no joyous road it will be."

"I am honored, my lord."

"Speak to me of honor when we have passed through

this shadow and can clasp hands on the other side." Archer shook his head. "I have known for centuries that this time approached, yet I am no more ready to face it than I ever was. And it grieves me that others must share my burden, for if I had chosen to act differently long ago, this would never have come about."

"And I might never have been born and never have seen my children grow to adulthood."

Archer smiled faintly. "You are very positive."

"One must be positive to lead an army."

"Aye, it is so."

They sat quietly together for a while, sipping their wine, a silent camaraderie growing between them.

The first to break the silence was Archer. "Do you trust your men?"

"Aye. We regard honor very highly."

Archer nodded, then leaned closer. "Watch them nonetheless, brother. For *he* has ways of taking over the minds of men. You have heard of the hives?"

"Aye, but I have never met one."

"You will, before this is done. He draws men into his sway, then bends their will to his. He can even occupy one of them if he wishes. It is as if they have only a single mind, and it is strange to see how they work in concert. That is how *he* controls his armies."

Tuzza looked appalled and took a deep draft of his wine. "That will worry me."

"It should. Once he takes them over, they even lose their fear of mortality. It is unforgivable that he uses them thus, but he does and you must be prepared for it. And you must ever be wary that he might take control of some of your soldiers. For he will certainly try."

"How can I guard against it?"

"I know of no way to stop it. But when it happens…Ilduin blood judges harshly. Be wary and tell your men to be wary. And know this. While your men may hesitate at the thought of battle with other Bozandari, those whom he holds will not hesitate to cut your men down like chaff."

After a few moments of clearly pained thought, Tuzza refilled their wine goblets. "Then tonight, my lord brother, we must enjoy the fruits of the earth and the gifts of the gods, for we cannot know when our hour will come."

Archer raised his goblet in toast and took a deep drink. "We need information about what is happening to the north of Bozandar. Since the rebellion, your armies have made it all but impossible to send scouts in that direction. If there is any way you can get news, I will be grateful. It is never wise to march blind to meet an enemy."

Tuzza nodded. "I will find a way."

"I'm sure by now an army marches to your rescue. Ponder on this, Tuzza, for I would not engage them in battle and waste lives needlessly. We must find a way to prevent the fight and convince them to join us."

"That will be even harder than today was."

"Aye. I have some notion of the stiff spines of the Bozandar army. And whether you believe it or not, the Anari are every bit as stiff-spined. I would avoid the bloodshed if we can. We are going to need every able man to fight the evil that comes."

Tuzza's mouth framed a wry smile. "And apparently we will need some Ilduin as well."

"Aye, for he has corrupted at least two that we know of, and there may be more."

"Fire must be fought with fire."

"Sad to say. I would not corrupt these women in any way, had I the choice."

Tuzza sighed. "I think they will not be corrupted, my lord. They will see what they should not see, and perhaps do things they will regret, but they will understand why the choices were forced upon them, as any good soldier does."

"I hope you are right. The three who are with us seem somehow steeped in unassailable purity. I fear it will not last."

"War carries a heavy toll. But perhaps Lady Tess can travel with me to meet the advancing army. If she could do for them what she did for us today, my job of persuasion would be ever so much easier."

Archer lifted a brow. "You will not ride alone regardless, Tuzza. For I will not have you called traitor and carried away in shackles. You are no traitor, and we need you."

"Treason is in the eye of the beholder, Master Archer. My emperor will not see my actions as anything other."

"Then we need to enlighten him as well."

Tuzza almost laughed. "He is not an easy man to persuade."

"Perhaps he has never been swayed before by an Ilduin."

"Certainly not by the Weaver."

Archer's expression grew grave. "She must be guarded at all costs, Tuzza. Ardred will stop at nothing to claim her. The mere fact that prophecy predicted her appearance is no guarantee of safety. The days and weeks to come hold no guarantees. At this point, the future is no longer writ, even for the most gifted of prophets."

Tuzza's answering nod was grim. "I understand, my lord."

"Tomorrow I would take you into Anahar with me to meet my lieutenant Ratha. It is time for us to forge bonds between us, and we must forge them like the finest steel if we are to withstand the onslaught to come."

"It will be no easy task."

"No part of this task will be easy. The faint of heart may as well flee right now."

"There are no faint hearts in this camp, my lord."

"Nor in mine. But we will come across them, just as we will come across enemies stronger than you now imagine."

"I have seen what the lady can do, Lord Annuvil. Trust me, I can imagine."

Chapter Four

We should listen in, Cilla thought, an impish smile on her dark features as she met Tess's eyes.

Without a doubt, Tess agreed, meeting her gaze. She was still sometimes surprised at the ease with which she and her Ilduin sisters could touch each other's minds, and remembered the first time she had noticed this ability, as Sara and Tom had demonstrated their love for each other.

Ahem! Cilla and Tess immediately looked to Sara's window, where Sara was glaring back at them with a mock stern expression. *Can a girl have a bit of privacy, please?*

Cilla put a hand to her mouth to suppress a laugh, mirth dancing in her eyes. *But sister, you are the only hope we have!*

Get your own man, Sara thought with a toss of her head, followed by a wink.

I'm trying, Cilla thought. *I'm trying.*

Tess laughed aloud and drew Cilla aside. "Come,

sister. Let us walk together and leave sweet Sara to enjoy her new marriage."

"Of course," Cilla said. "'Twas only sport."

"And pleasant sport at that," Tess said, her smile fading. "But as our men have gone to discuss things manly, perhaps we should take the opportunity to advance our own knowledge."

They walked toward the temple slowly, as if reluctant to end the celebratory mood and resume the hard work that lay before them. Even Tess's visit to the Bozandari camp had seemed almost a royal visit, born of a dream. The snow wolves had slipped away into the hills around Anahar, and now, even with Cilla beside her, she felt very alone as she walked to face the gods.

"Have you any news of Ratha?" Tess asked.

"He has withdrawn within himself," Cilla said, shaking her head. "I try to tell him it was not his fault that Giri fell, that it is not wise to grieve alone, but he will hear none of it."

"Do Anari believe in life after death?" Tess asked. For all the time she had spent in the temple at Anahar, she knew little of their religion.

"Yes," Cilla said. "Of a sort. Giri is beyond the veil now, in the garden of the gods, but his life there—if life it be—is nothing like life here. Those who pass beyond the veil become all and nothing, united yet unique. All of those beyond the veil can feel one another's thoughts as we Ilduin can, if thoughts they have at all."

Tess nodded, ghosts of memories flitting through her mind, wispy and unapproachable.

"You do not remember what your people believe," Cilla said.

"No," Tess replied. "Although my heart tells me it was not far different from what you have said."

Cilla smiled. "Why did you ask?"

"We grieve not for those who have passed," Tess said. "Their pain has ended, their struggles complete. We ought not to be sad on their account, for the life they have now— whatever it may be—is better than any they have known. No, we grieve for ourselves, for the holes that are left in our own lives by the passing of those whom we loved."

"This we are taught as well," Cilla said. "It is as if a piece of flesh has been cut from one's arm. We do not feel the pain of the flesh which is gone. We feel the pain from the flesh that remains, raw and open and torn. Until the body can repair it, the pain remains. But it is never fully repaired, for the scar we build is not the same as the flesh it replaces."

"Exactly," Tess said, squeezing her sister's hand.

"You are saying that Ratha needs time to build a scar over the hole that Giri's death has left."

Tess nodded. "And until he can do that, dear sister, he will be too pained to feel your love for him. Or his for you."

"Give me not false hope," Cilla said sharply. Then, after a moment. "Forgive me, my lady. I did not mean to scold you."

"There is nothing to forgive," Tess said. "And I am not your lady, but your sister. I must have someone in my life who pays me no homage, but simply shares with me this journey of life."

Cilla nodded. "Yes, sister."

"And I give you no false hope," Tess said. "Trust not in what you see on Ratha's face just now, nor hear in his words. Ratha cannot look upon you, nor hear you, nor speak to you. Only his grief sees you, hears you, and responds. Grief cannot love. But Ratha can."

Tess sighed and looked down at the colorful, rainbow-hued cobbles beneath their feet, trying desperately to recall the song that the stones of Anahar had sung when they had summoned the Anari. That song had seemed to open doors within her, to fill her with a sense of awe that had been good, unlike much of the awe she had felt since awaking with no memory.

"Grief," she said, "is not a gentle thing, Cilla. It claws at us like a ravening beast, and is loathe to release us from its grip. Worse, we find it hard to accept that someone we love is lost to us for the rest of our days. 'Twould be easier for Ratha had Giri left on a long journey with no intent to return. For at least then he would have known his brother still existed somewhere within this world, and that eventually he might hear Giri's voice again in this lifetime. He has no such hope now. But eventually he will find acceptance, and with acceptance he will return to you."

Cilla squeezed Tess's hand. "I pray that you are right, sister. For my heart both leaps and aches every time I see him. Long did I gaze upon him in my childhood, when I hid among the rocks and watched him play. Longer, it seems, was he lost to me after he was taken away into slavery. Then he returned, and it felt as if I had found the missing part of my own soul. And now…"

"Now he is gone again," Tess said. "For a time. But only for a time, sister. You have been patient these many years. Let not patience fail you now."

"Listen to you two! Gloom and sorrow!"

Tess and Cilla turned to see Sara, running to catch up with them. Her face shone with the glow of a new bride.

"And why aren't you in your room with your husband?" Tess asked.

Sara giggled. "Men, it seems, lack…stamina."

Cilla held up a finger. "You asked for privacy, if I recall? Now you will tell us what we could have heard for ourselves?"

Sara shook her head. "No. I have said all that I will. But a woman cannot live only in her husband's arms. Not this woman, at least. I need time with my sisters as well. So scold me not for my presence, nor if I should leave you. Tom will not sleep all day, and I will be there when he awakens."

"I'm quite sure you will," Tess said, laughing. She turned to Cilla. "Come, let us hurry to the temple, while he sleeps, lest Sara's…needs…call her away before she can learn anything."

"Somehow," Cilla said, "I think she is learning quite a lot. Just not of Ilduin lore."

Sara smiled. "With sisters such as you, a bride needs no groomsmother. Perhaps the gods will be more delicate."

"That," Tess said, sighing, "would truly surprise." And deep within her, she felt the stirring of anger, anger that her sister's joy must be overshadowed, anger that they all grieved so much, not only for the past, but for the future as well.

No one, she thought as her steps carried her closer to the temple, should have to grieve for that which had not yet passed. But that sorrow, it seemed, was the fate of the Ilduin.

"The young prophet emerges," Erkiah said with a smile as Tom entered his chamber. "Although now that you are wed, I suppose that 'young' no longer applies. Pray, Tom, tell me why you lie not in the arms of your bride?"

Tom blushed behind the leathern mask that covered his eyes, leaving only slits for him to see through. Ever since

Tess had healed him from fatal wounds received in a Bo-zandari ambush along the road to Anahar, his irises had grown so pale that he could no longer bear bright light. The mask Tess had thought to make for him had saved him from being virtually blind. "I pretended to sleep. I love her like a fish loves the river, yet we have been so busy these past days in preparation for the wedding…and I found myself missing my studies."

Erkiah waved a hand at his young charge. "Apologize not, my friend, neither to me nor to her. Apparently she waited only minutes after your ruse before scurrying off to meet her sisters at the temple and continue her own work. In other times, lovers might pale at such a thought. But you both know there is much to be done and little time in which to do it. The shame is only that you could not speak openly of it, one to the other."

"I fear I am not yet accustomed to marriage," Tom said. "Nor is Sara, I suppose."

"I pray that you will have time to grow into it," Erkiah said, sadness on his features. "For all that has happened, the greater burden lies before us."

"And Lord Archer's strength will fail," Tom said.

Erkiah nodded. "Sadly, yes. Thus it is foretold. It weighs upon us to ascertain how, and when, and stand ready to fortify him."

"Show me those prophecies, please," Tom said, walking to the shelves on which Erkiah's scrolls lay. "Nothing we have learned together will matter if in this we err."

"You speak truth," Erkiah said. "If my memory fails me not, that text is on the second shelf, third scroll from the right."

"If ever your memory fails you," Tom said, reaching for the vellum, "the gods themselves will quake with fear."

"You do me too much credit," Erkiah said, laughing. "I am but a man, and like any other I am prone to error."

"But not in matters of consequence." Tom met his eyes, then unrolled the top of the scroll. "*Eshkaron Treysahrans.* Your memory does not fail."

Erkiah nodded and watched as Tom stretched the scroll over the table and weighted the corners with candlesticks.

He shuddered and spoke. "I would that I had forgotten. This is a text I have not read since I was a young man. It frightened me so that never again have I touched it, save to pack it for my journey here, and unpack it upon my arrival."

Tom studied him gravely. This was not the Erkiah he had come to know, eagerly seeking knowledge as a hungry man at morning. "I would ask why it frightened you, but I know your answer already. You will tell me to read it, for then I will know."

"That is true," Erkiah said, "though hardly prophecy."

"Of course it was not prophecy," Tom replied, smiling. "It is simply what you always say."

"Prophecy," Erkiah said, "would be to tell me why I say those same words each time."

Tom shook his head. "No, it takes no prophet to see this. If I simply commit to memory all that you say, I can never be more than your pale image in the mirror of time. Your wish is that I will be greater than that, and thus you compel me to read for myself and challenge you."

Erkiah smiled weakly. "I would that we had met in happier times, my son. Were it such, we might spar thus hour upon hour and take joy in the sparring. Alas, we have no such luxury."

"We will," Tom said firmly. "We will."

* * *

The *Eshkaron Treysahrans* was the most difficult of the prophetic writings, but Tom slogged through it with a determination that Erkiah found both admirable and almost frightening. While the name of its author had been lost in the sands of time, Erkiah considered it to be among the oldest of the prophecies, and the one least changed by the pens of the intervening scribes, in large part because few had chosen to transcribe it. His copy might be the only one still in existence. If not, he doubted there were even a half-dozen others.

The title of the work—*The Death of the Gods*—gave little clue as to its meaning. Unlike the titles of most prophecies, this seemed to have been chosen by the original author, for reasons that had little to do with illuminating the text itself. In fact, the author had gone to great lengths to avoid precisely that sort of illumination.

The text was divided into three sections. The first was a series of riddles without either answers or, it had seemed to Erkiah, any connecting subject line. The second part was a fragmentary chronology, beginning with "the death of the last of the First" and ending with "the birth of the first of the Last," without any context to identify what beings, or even what kind of beings, were referenced. The few scholars who had appended notes to this section had served only to muddle the issue, with interpretations ranging from the gods themselves to the Firstborn to the Ilduin and even, among the last scholars to attempt, to the Bozandari nobility.

It was the third section—*Aneshtreah,* or "Admonitions"—which had struck fear in Erkiah those many years ago. In the style of a stern master writing to a recalcitrant young student, it was a series of warnings, each more dire than the last. Its central message was one about trust, or, more aptly, suspicion. It began:

Trust not your mother.
In pain has she born you, in hardship sustained you,
And great her resentment, though hidden it may be.
Trust not your father,
For first when he spawned you was last as he fed you,
And greater his wrath at the end of the day.

And so it continued, admonishing the reader to trust neither man nor beast, friend nor foe, neither wife nor children, neither master nor servant, neither god nor priest. The cold dissection of each relationship left no room for honor, commitment or even love. The final stanza banished all hope:

Trust not the Shadow,
For shadow must fail in the presence of light,
The Dark One must yield to the Fair in the fight.
Trust not the Light,
A dagger he wields for the heart entombed,
While cruelty unbounded his soul attuned.

"By the gods," Tom whispered as he sat back from the scroll. His face was ashen. "It cannot be."

Erkiah nodded. "So I thought as well, my friend. And yet, thus it is written."

"Do I read this right?" Tom asked. "Lord Archer is the Shadow, and the Enemy the Light?"

"The legends say that Ardred was the fairer of the

brothers," Erkiah said. "And surely it does not surprise you that Archer would be called the shadow. From his hair to his visage to the way he has slipped through this world almost unseen for all of these years."

Tom shook his head slowly. "But if that is true, then Archer will fail us."

Erkiah simply nodded.

Tom's face fell as he completed the thought. "And our future rests in the hands of Ardred."

Chapter Five

The temple seemed troubled, Tess thought. All of the joy she had felt in its walls yesterday was gone, replaced by an aching sense of loss. She tried to avoid the statue of Elanor, hoping that perhaps some other niche, some other graceful curve of stone, would speak to her this time. Yet it was as if the stones had fallen silent, save for a grief that threatened to crush Tess's heart beneath its weight. It was as if the temple had chosen this moment to mourn the loss of every fallen Anari.

"It hurts," Tess said softly.

"Yes," Sara said, tears in her eyes. "Why must it be thus? Cannot we have joy in our lives? Has all of the joy left this world?"

"Perhaps the world was never a well of joy," Cilla said. "Perhaps joy is something we must bring into it, as an act of will."

Tess shook her head. Anger grew within her, anger at the

way death had stalked her these past months. It was an anger that seemed to spring fully formed from the grief she felt in the stones around her. She had been set onto this path by powers she did not comprehend, impelled and enabled by the death of her own mother, into a game whose rules and objectives were unknown and unknowable, and where the only certainties were blood, sorrow and horror. And death, death, always more death.

Her jaw ached from clenching it as she tried to fight down the surging rage that swelled within her. Losing the battle, she reached for the statue of Elanor, not with the hand of a supplicant but with the hand of an interrogator.

"What foul-tempered god," Tess asked coldly, "would create a world of pain and misery, and lay upon its frail children the burden of creating joy and hope?"

None, my child.

The voice coursed through her like the shock from a cold stream, and for a moment Tess nearly yanked her hand from the statue. Then, as if steeling herself for battle, she placed her other hand on it.

"Then make yourself known," Tess said, a firmness in her voice that shocked even herself. "The times are too dire and our hearts too troubled for more riddles. We grow weary of your games. Make yourself known!"

With a crack like the opening of the world itself, the temple flooded with a light so intense that Tess had to turn her face away. Elanor's presence filled the room, causing the hair on the back of Tess's neck to rise and her heart to thunder.

You have wielded the sword of the Weaver, but do not dare challenge me!

"I dare and I do!" Tess shouted. "Look at my sister, in

tears on the day after her wedding, when she ought to be lying in the arms of her true love, coming here to learn more of that which we need for our journey! Look at my other sister, her heart filled with love and longing for one who cannot know love through the scourge of battle. Look at us and tell us that we have not bled and wept and walked in this path that you have set for us! Look at us and tell us that we are not worthy of even the barest comfort!"

Worthy? Elanor raged back. *Would the worthy have rent the world asunder at the start? Would the worthy have set upon this world a race too weak to protect their sons and daughters from the slaver's block? Would the worthy have gone into the service of Chaos? You speak to me of worthy? 'I dare and I do,' you say? Then dare it and do!*

"Tess," Sara said urgently, taking her hand. "Tempt her not."

"No!" Tess cried, jerking her hand away. "This must be! Too long have we watched our brothers and sisters slain, our hopes dashed against the rocks like so much worthless pottery. Too long have we quailed before gods, only to see those gods leave us to the wrath of our own kind. We sisters, cursed to see the deaths of our own mothers, that we may become pawns in the games of those gods. No more! No more, I say! I command you, make known yourself!"

You command me?

"Yes," Tess shrieked, her voice rising above the rushing roar around her. "I command you!"

In an instant it felt as if all of the air had been sucked from the temple. The light swirled and compacted, growing brighter moment by moment, until it distilled into the form of a shimmering snow wolf.

"It cannot be," Sara said, aghast.

"Aye," the wolf replied, amber eyes flashing. "Tell me of commands now, Weaver. Tell me that I have not walked beside you, seen what you have seen, borne what you have borne, and more, more than you will ever know? Tell me that my sisters and I have not succored you in your need, from your first battle with the minions of Glassidor to your battles in these mountains to your entreaty to the host within your midst just this morning. Tell me that I have left you alone, and that alone you have faced these hardships. Tell me that I have not guided your steps to this day. Then, and only then, I will attend to your commands."

Tess, shaken to her core, fell to her knees. The rage and anger born of danger and fear gave way to racking sobs. "I did not know. I did not know."

The wolf stepped closer, and its muzzle nudged her cheeks, its delicate tongue drawing out her tears. "Faith is found when we do not know, my child. Faith and courage alone can carry you through this time of trial. Never would you have found it had you known."

Tess nodded, shame and anguish rolling through her in equal measure. Finally spent, she felt her sisters' hands upon her, stroking her shoulders. The wolf sat before her, its face impassive, patiently waiting.

"You must not tell any other of this," the wolf said. "None but Ilduin blood may know it, and none but Ilduin blood would believe. You must find your sisters, those whom the Enemy has not yet taken. You will know them when they see me."

"And you will stay with us?" Tess asked.

The wolf smiled. "We are of different worlds, my child.

I can no more stay with you than can the wind. I—we—will be with you as we have always been."

"May I never see another snow wolf pelt," Sara whispered, remembering the trappers in the mountains around her native Whitewater.

"We forgive them, for they do not know," the wolf said to Sara. "Do likewise. Always."

And then the wolf was gone as if it had never been, save for a single, snow-white hair on the statue of Elanor. Tess, as if bidden by an unknown force, took the hair with trembling fingers and tucked it into the pouch with the Ilduin stones.

Rising unsteadily to her feet, she took a moment to gather her determination and will once again. "Come, sisters. There is work before us. And hope."

"One thousand, three hundred and sixty," Topmark Tuzza said, looking across the table at Archer. "Twelve strong companies, enough to form a single regiment. That is how many men I have fit for battle. Perhaps another four hundred could be ready in a month. The rest…"

Tuzza sighed. He had brought six thousand men into the Anari lands. More than half now lay in unmarked graves along his route of march, victims of disease, hunger, the incessant Anari raids, and the final battle in the canyon. He had presided over the worst disaster in the history of the Bozandari Empire.

As if reading his thoughts, Archer said, "And your men are willing to follow you again."

Tuzza shook his head. "They are loyal to the Weaver, because they have witnessed her miracles. They are loyal to their Topmark—whomever that might be—because of their training. But I have no illusions of their loyalty to my person, Lord Archer. Whatever loyalty I might have inspired was bled white along their journey here."

"Personal loyalty is a fickle thing," Archer said. "Only our Enemy can rely on absolute loyalty, and only because his magicks have broken the wills of his minions. No man should ask for such."

"That much is true," Tuzza said.

"What of your officers?" Archer asked. "Do they still trust in your judgment?"

Tuzza nodded. "What few remain, though I worry of them as well. Too many of my best officers—those inspired by their deeds rather than their words—fell with their men. And too many of those who remain have come to me petitioning for promotion. They assert claims of noble blood, spin tales of their courage, and whisper against their comrades."

"Such men are not fit for command," Archer said.

"And well I know it," Tuzza replied. "Yet I have not enough officers as it is."

"Your men would not serve under Anari officers," Archer said. It was neither a question or a criticism, but simply a statement of fact.

"No," Tuzza said. "They would not."

Archer sat for a moment, as if pondering the dilemma. Twice he made as if to speak, bringing Tuzza forward in his chair, before shaking his head and drifting again into his thoughts. Tuzza could well sympathize, for many long hours had he spent on this same question.

Finally, Archer spoke. "We have already decided that your men will establish a new camp, alongside the Anari."

"Aye," Tuzza said. "I will go this afternoon to look at possible sites, and draw up plans."

"Do not," Archer said. "Rather, use this as an opportunity to test and select those who would serve as your officers. Simply assemble your men and direct that this be done. Your real leaders will emerge."

"Yes, they will," Tuzza said, a smile working its way across his features. "I will see who can talk and who can act, who can say 'go and do it thus,' who will say 'follow me,' and whom the men will follow."

"And always with an eye toward those who will enlist the aid of their Anari brethren," Archer said. "For in our time of need, we need to turn to one another."

"That," Tuzza said, sighing, "may be a sticking point for some. I need leaders, Lord Archer, and not merely men who will be puppets of the Anari."

"Certainly," Archer said. "And you should demand no less. But one need not be a puppet to ask where water may be found, or where wood or stone are at hand for building. There are Anari who still do not trust you and who would lead you astray. You must have leaders who can discern whom they can trust, and enlist their help without giving undue offense to those Anari who would object."

Tuzza could see for himself the truth in Archer's words. "The campaign before us will be unlike anything we Bozandari have before conducted. We have never fought beside an ally. We have never needed one."

"But now you do," Archer said, nodding. "This will call for leaders who can meld their actions with those of their Anari brethren."

Tuzza drew a breath. Long had Bozandari command been rooted in bloodlines and patronage. He himself was a minor noble, and a beneficiary of the very system he was now compelled to overhaul. "There are some among my officers and men who will resist and resent any change that does not recognize their heritage. They may resent even more those whose positions remain unchallenged."

"Such as your own?" Archer asked.

"Precisely," Tuzza said. "It is not enough for me to direct my men, and then stand above them, testing them. I must put myself to the test as well."

"Then do so," Archer said. "For I have no doubt that you will pass this test, and perhaps in the passing of it, restore your own confidence."

Tuzza shook his head. "No mere test can erase the stain I bear, Lord Archer. Still, there is no other way to prove myself to them. And prove myself I must."

As Archer left Tuzza's tent, the problems of the coming war weighed heavily. In its own way, this would be a far more challenging task than those they had faced thus far. Not only must Tuzza find officers who could work with the Anari, but Archer must find Anari officers who could work with the Bozandari. And this promised to be no mean task, especially when one of his chief lieutenants—his longtime companion, Ratha Monabi—was still dark with fury and grief over the death of his brother Giri. Worse, Ratha had watched Giri die, at Tuzza's own hand.

It was to Ratha's home that Archer was now going, and he found himself turning over the question of how to broach the topic of Tuzza's force serving alongside Ratha's. Ratha was certain to have heard of the events Tess set in motion this morning with her visit to the Bozandari camp. The entire city of Anahar seemed to be abuzz with the news, and the reactions were not wholly positive. Too many Anari had seen their kin enslaved or killed by the Bozandari to forgive easily.

Ratha's decisions would sway many, Archer knew. And he could not count on a shocking dawn visit by Tess to sway Ratha's heart, as she had done for the Bozandari. He would have to do this himself, man to man, friend to friend.

Chapter Six

"You cannot ask this of me!" Ratha thundered the words at Archer, his usual deference to the man totally gone. "He killed my brother!"

Archer listened, unmoving, offering no response. Ratha had withdrawn for the *telzehten*—the ritual grieving period—and had come to the wedding only because custom demanded it. Otherwise he remained in a small tent in the foothills at the edge of the Monabi Tel section of Anahar, alone, staring at the scarred and dented armor that had been Giri's. Such was not unusual among the Anari. They were a long-lived people for whom death had not been an everyday companion, and a period of communion with the soul of the departed was not only accepted but honorable.

It was in Giri's tent—pitched on a craggy, windswept hilltop—that the two of them stood now, faced off as if they were enemies, rather than friends of many years. The cold of the unnatural winter beat about them as if it would hammer them to the ground. Neither man yielded an inch, and only Archer spared a fleeting thought for how pleasant Anahar should be at this time of year...except for the machinations of Ardred, he who was called Lord of Chaos.

Ratha was clearly past remembering such things. Grief had rent his spirit and soul, had blinded him to the evil they faced, and had left him a husk filled with nothing but pain and fury.

Before Archer's unwavering, expressionless stare, however, Ratha's rage could not stand its ground. Muttering an oath, the Anari stormed out of the tent, not stopping until he stood at the edge of a ravine. Ratha kicked a rock over the edge. The wind soon swallowed the clatter of its fall.

Archer had followed Ratha, and now he spoke. "Your brother was my friend, too, Ratha. And if he died by the sword of Tuzza, he died at the hand of the Enemy that stalks us all, the Enemy that brought this war upon us. Will you forget your people and misdirect your rage?"

"Misdirect?" Ratha swung around and glared at him. "My people have been enslaved by the Bozandari for generations. Would you have me forget all that?"

"You cannot forget. I will never ask that of you."

"What then? Unlike you, I am a mere mortal, and I have lost the other half of myself to the man you now ask me to trust, to march beside with an army of my kinsmen, into battle with other Bozandari."

"Aye, 'tis true. If blame you need, then blame me. I and my race created yours, and in that act of hubris sowed the seeds for your enslavement. Blame me, Ratha, for I bear more the stain of Giri's death than Tuzza ever could."

Ratha's head jerked back, almost as if he had been

slapped. When at last he spoke, his voice was rough, almost hoarse. "You saved Giri and me from slavery. You made us your friends and companions. Am I to forget that?"

"You may as well, as you are determined to forget the Enemy still before us. As you seem determined to forget that we cannot win this war alone."

Ratha groaned, a sound of anguish and anger that bounced off the nearby rocks. He appeared about to kick another stone over the edge, but his foot paused midswing, as if he were recollecting the bond between his people and the rock. The Anari, and the Anari alone, could hear the voices in the stone. Because they could hear those voices, they appreciated rock as the truly living thing it was. Kicking that stone as he had earlier was a sin among his kind, and he was not about to repeat it.

Instead, he fell to his knees and picked up one of the larger stones that lay scattered about the ledge, having fallen from higher up. He raised it to his cheek, near his ear, and closed his eyes. Tears ran down his dark face, glistening like ice, and one fell upon the rock he held.

"I am sorry," he whispered.

The rock he held responded, glowing faintly.

Archer squatted before him. "You see, Ratha? One must grieve, but one must never forget who he is and the duty he owes to those still living."

Ratha's black eyes opened slowly, wet with tears. "You would know, my lord," he said slowly.

"I have had many years to learn. You have had only a handful. Stay for your *telzehten*. I would not deny you that, and would expect no less from a brother whose bond I shared. But then you must return to us, for our days of calm are short. Rescuers for Tuzza's army must already be on the way. Tuzza will send out scouts to find out how long we have. But it will not be very long."

Ratha nodded slowly as he gently set the rock down. It still glowed, as if his touch had brightened its life. He stroked it with one finger, then looked at Archer.

"I will come," he said. "Soon."

"That is all I can ask."

"Stay with me, my lord. As you said, you shared my bond with Giri. Anari share *telzehten* only with family, and I have none save you."

Archer shook his head. "I would that I could, my brother. But the Enemy gives me no time to grieve. There is much to be done, and much that only I can do."

"I understand," Ratha said quietly.

"But you do have family apart from me," Archer said. "Your cousin, Cilla, also grieves for Giri, and for you. I have not asked her, but I am certain she would be honored, and heartened, to share *telzehten* with you."

"She has other designs," Ratha said. "Designs for my heart."

"Aye," Archer said. "I will not deny that. And I have designs for you as well, for your mind and your skill as a commander. Yet you would share with me and not with her. Whose designs threaten you more?"

Ratha smiled for an instant. "Hers, my lord. The battle you ask of me is one with which I am familiar. The battle she asks…"

"I cannot deny the truth of that, my brother," Archer said, his face mirroring Ratha's smile. "The battle she asks risks more than your life. Perhaps it is better that you are fully healed before you face that."

"I will rejoin you soon, my lord," Ratha said. "And please

tell Cilla that I cannot return until I am whole. She will know of what I speak."

"I will, my brother. I will."

Archer rose and left him, picking his way down to where he had left his mount. He hadn't the heart to tell Ratha that grief never ended, it merely yielded.

For a moment, his own shoulders slumped, as if the weight of his burdens were bending him low. Then he straightened himself, refusing to give in. Despair was a luxury none of them could afford.

At the temple, the three Ilduin walked in a slow circle around the central chamber of the round building. This chamber held the statues of twelve women, presumably the original Ilduin, and it was toward these they looked, as if the statues might somehow tell them where to find their still-missing sisters.

Tess had avoided this chamber since that first visit when she and her sisters had felt the horror of the Ilduin destruction of Dederand. Instead, they had focused their work on the anteroom, with the statues of the gods. It was Sara who had suggested that perhaps Elanor had revealed all that she would, and they should shift their studies to this room. The temple at Anahar was a living being in stone, and this chamber was its heart.

"There must be some of our sisters among the Bozandari," Sara said, an edge of distaste in her voice. The only ones who liked the Bozandari these days were the Bozandari themselves.

"Of course," Tess said slowly. "But at present we cannot reach them. We cannot go to Bozandar."

Cilla spoke. "The two of you could. No one would remark you in Bozandar."

"Mayhap not," Tess replied. "But what are we to do? Go from door to door asking if an Ilduin dwells within? I think not."

She reached out and touched the cool, rainbow-hued stone of the temple wall. "I wish Anahar could sing for them, calling them as she called the Anari...." Her voice trailed off as a thought struck her.

"The stones!" Cilla and Sara said on a single breath.

"Aye!" Eagerly, Tess drew forth the leather pouch she wore always around her neck. Walking to the center of the room, she spilled the stones upon the floor. "We know two of them have fallen under the Enemy's sway."

"These," Sara said. She pointed as she watched two of them roll apart from the others and begin to make their ways across the floor, toward two of the statues. One of the stones was beryl, the other yellow quartz.

The three of them stared dubiously at the remaining nine stones. Cilla reached out, removing the opal, which was Tess's, the sapphire which was Sara's, and the emerald which was her own. That left amethyst, ruby, carnelian, topaz, garnet, jade and turquoise. Those, too, then began to roll across the floor, drawn by an unseen force.

"Should we do this?" Sara asked, her voice hushed. "We don't know how many may belong to Ardred."

"Nor do we want Ardred to know we are summoning them," Tess pointed out. "Although I am not certain we can avoid it. He has Ilduin serving him."

"And we know at least two of them," Cilla said, pointing to the two stones that had begun to roll toward their statues before turning away from them and coming to rest near each other. The other stones had seemingly scattered themselves around the room.

Cilla continued, "Even so, Ardred's Ilduin will know we are doing something. How can they not? We seem to be joined tightly to one another, all twelve, in some way."

"And those who have no notion that they are Ilduin might not even understand the contact," Sara said.

Tess had fallen silent as she stared at the stones. For a time, no sound passed among the women. "There is a riddle here," she said finally. She placed her stone onto the floor. "Place down your stones, sisters."

The three stones rolled across the floor, coming to rest in a tight cluster, apart from the others.

Tess's brow furrowed. "It is as if they mimic where we are in the world. Almost as if they form a map."

Tess found her mind drifting back to a time before she inhabited this world, to lessons she had studied. How to find her way across a landscape with the barest of tools. She could not pull the whole of the memory into focus, and yet she knew that it would help her resolve this mystery.

"If they are a map, there are no landmarks," Sara said, looking at the floor. She pointed to the cluster of their three stones. "We know we are there, but where is that in relation to anywhere else?"

"We need to know where Ardred is," Tess said. "That will give us an orientation, and perhaps even a scale."

Cilla looked at her strangely. "You speak of things I do not know, sister."

"And I hardly remember them myself," Tess said. "It angers me that my own past must bear on our journey, and yet most of it lies behind a veil, unknown to me."

"But not all," Sara said. "You spoke of, what was it, orientation and scale. What are they?"

Tess closed her eyes for a moment, hoping that perhaps this past would emerge fully formed, and yet it remained clouded in impenetrable mist. Still, she had spoken the words, and she knew their meaning.

"A map must give us direction and distance," she said. "If we know the orientation of a map, we know which way to walk to reach a destination. If we know the scale of a map, we know how many days it will take to get there."

Tess pointed to the three stones that represented them and then to a looser cluster of four others. "If the stones are indeed a map, four of our sisters live near one another, there. But we don't know what direction to walk in order to reach them, nor how far away they might be."

"You said that if we knew where Ardred is, we could know this," Cilla said, pointing to the beryl and quartz stones. "You think those two will be with him?"

"I would be surprised if they were not," Tess said. "He relies on the power of the Ilduin. He must keep them near at hand, lest he find himself caught without them."

"But surely he cannot control the whole of his forces with only two Ilduin," Sara said.

"No," Tess agreed. "He cannot. Glassidor's hive was small by comparison to the Enemy's. The Enemy would reach to his other Ilduin through the two he keeps at hand."

The three women stared down at the scattered stones, trying to find some clue that would give them direction. Presently, Tess began to walk around them, viewing them from all directions, seeking any hint they might give her. Hoping the arrangement would speak to her on some level.

"All we need," she said slowly, "is one other point of reference. If we knew where just one of these Ilduin was located, other than ourselves, the map would become clear."

Cilla pointed. "These four that are near one another. Surely they must be in a large city? Bozandar, perhaps?"

Sara answered. "Mayhap. Or mayhap they have been drawn together by him whom we fight."

"Aye, that concerns me," said Tess slowly. "But they may also have come together as we have, finding one another by chance as they seek to fight the Evil One."

"Even so," Cilla said, "they must be from different bloodlines, as we are. Four such women, together in one place, speaks of a city where people gather from all over. Surely Bozandar is such a city."

"I agree," Tess said. "It is likely that they are in and around Bozandar. But we must assume that at least one of them is in the Enemy's thrall. He could not master the Bozandari otherwise."

"Aye," Sara said. "And perhaps all four."

Tess nodded. "We must proceed with caution, then. But has this not been our watchword since we began this journey?"

"I would never approach Bozandar otherwise," Cilla said. "But I see no choice."

Tess nodded, her face drawn. *I see no choice.* That had been her life for too long.

Chapter Seven

Tuzza was surprised, both at the progress that had been made in constructing his army's camp and in the men who had risen to the forefront in the process. Some were experienced officers who had shown themselves willing to follow Tuzza's lead in stepping in to share the manual labor, and in reaching out to the Anari for help. But some were men he would never have known by name, but for their exceptional performance in this exercise.

One such man stood before him now. Denza Grundan was a mere filemark, serving his second term of conscription. By all accounts, Grundan was a capable and brave soldier, well skilled and respected by the men of his file. He was also one-quarter Anari.

Given his heritage, and it was apparent from his deep, burnished brown features, his accomplishments shone even brighter.

Even Grundan's rearmark had stepped out of the way

over the last week, content to let Grundan organize the accommodations for not only his own file, but the entire company. What at first had seemed like sensible leadership had become something else when Tuzza had asked after the rearmark, and after some searching had found him drunk in his tent. That, combined with the rearmark's reputation among his men and his fellow junior officers, had made Tuzza's present decision an easy one. If Tuzza was to rebuild his command, this was an ideal way to begin.

Tuzza stood and spoke with a voice that would have rung through the company camp, even if the company had not been formed in ranks before him. "Filemark Denza Grundan, you have excelled in your duties, demonstrating not only strength of mind and will but also humility and attention to the needs of your men in the highest tradition of the Bozandari legions. Your character and commitment are above reproach. It is for this reason that I now appoint you a Rearmark, an officer in this legion from this time forward. Will you kneel and accept the oath of commissioning?"

"Aye, my lord," Grundan said, kneeling and presenting his sword to Tuzza.

Had this ceremony occurred in other times, Tuzza would have asked Grundan to swear fealty to the emperor. In the present circumstances, Tuzza had rewritten the oath of commissioning.

"Do you swear by your life to serve these your men with your full measure of loyalty and honor, to obey all lawful commands of your seniors, to devote your whole mind and strength to your duties, and to respect and bear upon yourself the proud history and traditions of the Bozandari legionnaires and our Anari brethren?"

"Aye, my lord," Grundan said, "upon my honor and my life itself, I swear myself thus."

Tuzza smiled. "Then stand, Rearmark Grundan, and receive your company."

Grundan stood and pivoted smartly, sheathing his sword and holding out his hands to receive the company's battle standard. It was not the spotless pennant that had been carried out of Bozandar months ago. It was like Tuzza's legion, tattered and soiled by the campaign, save for the radiant image of the white wolf, which had been stitched into the pennant by one of the men. Tuzza felt tears in his eyes. This company standard reflected the trials these men had borne, their defeat, and their hope of redemption under their new allegiance to the Weaver.

As Grundan grasped the staff that bore the standard and lifted it above his head, the men erupted in a cheer. In another time, in another legion, it would have been no more than a formality, a change-of-command ceremony, little noticed and less remembered. At this time, in this legion, it was so much more. It was the start of a new tradition, a beacon of hope to those with the talent and commitment to serve with honor, and a warning to those who thought their status guaranteed by patronage.

"For the Snow Wolf!" Grundan cried.

"For the Snow Wolf!" his men replied.

The word of Grundan's appointment spread quickly, and in the days that followed, as Tuzza visited other units, he found that each had added a snow wolf—the prophesied companion of the Weaver—to its pennant.

"Your men speak of themselves as the Snow Wolves," Jenah Gewindi said, walking beside Tuzza.

Jenah, alongside Ratha and Giri Monabi, had been one of Archer's three chief lieutenants in the campaign against Tuzza's men. Giri had fallen in the battle of the canyon, and his brother Ratha was still observing *telzehten*. This left Jenah as the only Anari commander on hand to forge a command coalition with the Bozandari, and at Archer's order he had spent the past two days with Tuzza in the Bozandari camp, observing their training and the appointment of new officers as needed.

"Yes," Tuzza said. "It began with the commissioning of one of your brethren. I have since been told that it was the decision of Rearmark Grundan and two of his fellow filemarks to add the Snow Wolf to their pennant. But it has served to rally my men, to give them a new sense of shared identity."

Jenah nodded. "This is important, Topmark. Even now there is talk of doing the same among the Anari."

"Your men would share the symbol of a Bozandari legion?" Tuzza asked, incredulous.

"Perhaps," Jenah said. "Perhaps we both share a symbol of and allegiance to something greater than either of our peoples. It is this that I have suggested, when I have been asked for my view on the issue."

"Very politic," Tuzza said, smiling.

"An alliance cannot be formed without such," Jenah said with a faint shrug. "My people are no more eager to fight beside yours than your men are to fight beside us. Yet necessity commands it, and it falls upon men like us to make it possible."

"How many are you?" Tuzza asked. "We never knew, for certain, during the campaign past."

"We were never more than five thousand under sword, and fewer still in the end," Jenah said.

"Between us we are barely a legion strong," Tuzza said, his brow furrowed.

"Perhaps," Jenah said. "But even if we were thrice thus, we could not count on weight of numbers in the march to Bozandar. And in our very weakness may lay strength."

"How so?" Tuzza asked.

Jenah smiled. "Consider how your emperor would respond if three legions marched out of Anahar."

"That would seem nothing less than an invasion," Tuzza said, nodding. "They would see no option but battle."

"Precisely," Jenah said. "But an understrength legion, composed of Bozandari and Anari marching side by side. That can seem like a peace envoy."

"Let us hope," Tuzza said. "My men have no desire to slay their brethren. However committed they may be to the Weaver, to lift swords against men they have known and fought beside before would be very difficult."

"Aye," Jenah said. "Thus it would be for Anari also. No, our strength will lie not in numbers, but in the gifts of our Ilduin, and perhaps your own gifted tongue."

Tuzza looked at Jenah. "If our future rests upon my gift for clever speech, I fear we are all in graver danger than I knew."

"It will come to all of us to give what we can," Jenah said. "Whether that will be enough rests on shoulders larger than our own."

Tess sat beside an icy stream, her feet bare and pink in the cold. The need to escape to quiet and privacy had driven her into the mountains by herself. She could still see Anahar's beauty below, so she was in no danger of becoming lost. But the hike had made her feet tender, since it appeared her new boots were better made for riding than walking. She had soaked them in the stream until she could bear the frigid water no more.

As she turned her ankle to one side, she noted again the tattoo of the white rose, still as fresh-looking as if it had been done within the past year or two. How did she know that about tattoos?

For a moment, she closed her eyes, reaching for the information, but as always when she sought her past, it was as if the doors closed even more impenetrably. A small sigh escaped her, and she shivered a bit as the icy breeze caressed her feet. She should put her boots on again, before her bare feet sucked out all the warmth that her woolen cloak preserved.

But instead she looked again at the tattoo, knowing in some unreachable part of herself that it was more than a pretty decoration. It said something about her past, about who she was. Perhaps it even said something about her destiny.

Gingerly she poked a hand out from the shelter of her cloak and touched it. Within, she felt no reaction to it at all. At this moment, it was nothing but a pretty little bit of folly.

But it was her only true link with her past, that and the memory of holding her dying mother in her arms, a memory that Elanor had returned to her. An unhappy, unwanted, inexplicable memory. It told her almost nothing, and she had a crying need to know *something*.

If she was a pawn of the gods, and it appeared she was, then why must she take every action in blindness? Why was she permitted to know little of any real use?

Her own powers, powers that had been steadily revealing themselves, terrified her. If she was capable of so much, 'twould be better for everyone if she knew how to control this wild talent. Instead she discovered her abilities in moments of dire need, and so far as she could tell, other than healing, she had little say in what she did.

She lifted her fingers from the tattoo and studied it for another few seconds, then sighed and pulled her white leather boots on again.

For some reason, nearly every piece of serviceable clothing she owned, from the very first clothes given to her by Sara so long ago at the Whitewater Inn, was white. When she had asked the bootmaker to make her a fresh pair, he had made them white. She was quite certain she had not asked for that. The same had happened with every other item that she requested.

A little smile curled one corner of her mouth. Only her gown for the wedding had been a different color, and now that the wedding was past, she had no excuse to wear it. It was as if some silent conspiracy existed, insisting she wear only the color of the white wolves, the White Lady, the Weaver.

Shod once again, her feet numbed enough that she did not feel the mild irritation of her new boots, she resumed her hike, now heading toward Anahar. The quiet and solitude had allowed her to relax, a luxury she rarely knew. For a little while she had stopped worrying at the temple for more information, she had escaped councils of war, and the cacophony of voices that accompanied the crowding of the city of Anahar by Anari summoned from far and wide to battle.

A snatch of music danced across her mind, and she recalled the day that Anahar had sung. The rainbow-hued city had gleamed from within its every stone as the music had emerged from them, sending out a call to every Anari, a call that could be heard nearby with the ears, but elsewhere with the heart, according to the Anari.

And the Anari had come from far and wide, dropping every task to answer the summons. They had become the army that had defeated Tuzza's legion.

Now Tess wondered if Anahar would sing again, for it seemed they were about to march again, this time toward Bozandar.

The chill that passed through her then had nothing to do with the weather. She could not imagine that the remains of the Anari army, even allied with the remnants of Tuzza's legion, could withstand the might of Bozandar, be it only one fresh legion strong.

Yet march they must, for more than their own lives hung in the balance. It was a somber, sober burden, one which weighed more heavily with each step toward the city.

Again the snatch of music danced across her mind, as if trying to tell her something, but before she could reach for its meaning, it was gone again.

Perhaps Anahar was calling *her,* telling her it was time. Even as the thought crossed her mind, she realized this was not Anahar calling her. No, this was something else, something far darker than Anahar could ever be, even in the silence of the blackest night.

Yes, Tess. You will come. But not for their sake. You will come for me!

Tess slammed down the walls within her mind, even as she began to run toward the city. Blisters bedamned. She knew she had not the strength to withstand this attack alone. She needed her sisters.

She needed them now.

* * *

Archer had been looking for Tess, to confer with her about the army's departure. She was, whether she knew it or not, the only true unifying point for the two groups who would march toward Bozandar. Not even his own birthright, Firstborn Son to Firstborn King, would unify in the way the Lady Tess's mere presence seemed to.

Nor did he begrudge her that, though he still wondered about her origins. For his part, he had no desire to be the rallying point for what was to come. He would simply do his duty and use his expertise as needed. Having once heard his name used as a rallying cry, and having seen what followed, he never wanted to hear it that way again.

'Twas then that he spied Tess hurrying out of the wood at the far end of town. The way she was racing and stumbling concerned him, and he spurred his mount toward her, his heart suddenly hammering.

When he reached her, he saw terror on her face. He slipped at once from his saddle and reached for her, swinging his cloak around her to cover her even as he assumed a protective stance, hand on his sword hilt.

"Are you pursued?" he demanded roughly. "Has someone hurt you?"

"No…no…"

He relaxed, but only a little, as he felt a shudder rip through her.

"It's him," she whispered hoarsely. "It's *him*."

"Him?" In the deepest part of his heart he knew who she meant, but he didn't want to accept it.

"*Him*," she whispered again, as if afraid to speak his name. "I feel him again. He is near in my thoughts, his touch so cold…colder than ice. He wants me."

At once he wrapped his other arm around her, as if he could shield her from the assault. As if anything could. "Tess," he said. "Tess…" It was all he could say. He had no idea how an Ilduin might fight such an assault on her mind. No idea how to protect her. All he could do was give her the sound of his voice and the touch of his arms for her to cling to lest she be swept away.

She shuddered against him, as if from great cold or great effort. "He knows," she said, her voice trembling.

"Knows what?"

"He knows you are here. He knows we are coming. And he wants *me*."

He hesitated only a moment, then with one easy movement lifted her onto his saddle. An instant later he was behind her and they galloped toward the city.

"Take me to my sisters," Tess begged. "He wants *all* of the Ilduin! And none of us can withstand him alone."

I could have, Archer thought grimly as his mount devoured the distance in hungry strides. He had had countless opportunities to deal with Ardred, when they were children or even young men, before the evil had taken root and transformed his brother into his enemy. He had missed them all. But not again. *I could have, and this time, I will.*

Chapter Eight

Ratha looked at Cilla, uncertain of what to say. She had been with him for two days now, though she had yet to speak a word beyond their brief opening greeting. Nor had he. The initial stage of the telzehten was observed in silence, apart from the customary prayers, and in silence they had remained. But now they had completed that stage, and were supposed to move on to the celebration of a life well lived. And while Ratha knew his brother had lived life well, he also knew that in the end of Giri's days, an awful bloodlust had consumed him.

Worse, Ratha knew that he, too, had fallen victim to that bloodlust before his sojourn in the desert, and now was perilously close to succumbing again. To openly discuss these things risked falling into the pit that yawned beneath him like a gaping maw. And yet he knew he must face his demons eventually whether alone or not.

Even so, his tongue felt leaden in his mouth, and the

concerns he most needed to share were the very things of which he must not speak.

Still, as the closest blood relative, it fell upon Ratha to speak first. At last the silence grew too oppressive to bear, and he drew a breath. "Giri was a man of honor."

"Aye, cousin," Cilla said quietly.

"More than once did he risk his life for those whom he loved, and in the end he gave his life for the freedom of the Anari," Ratha continued.

Cilla nodded. "He spared nothing."

"Not even his own soul," Ratha said, tears forming in his eyes. "I have prayed that the gods will forgive him for what he became."

"He became hardened," Cilla said gently. "War is a cruel undertaking, cousin."

"That it is," Ratha said. "Perhaps if we Anari had been more suited for it…"

"I fear that no one can be truly suited for it," she replied. "Or perhaps that no one should. I fear that any people truly suited to war would be too cruel and horrible to bear imagining."

"Perhaps that is true."

Cilla let a moment pass before speaking. "Giri was a man of laughter."

"Oh, yes," Ratha said. "And some of the stories he told…I could not repeat in the presence of a woman, not even my cousin."

Cilla smiled. "Of that I am certain. There was nothing about which Giri could not laugh, even those things at which most of us would blush."

Ratha closed his eyes, recalling the long days riding with

Archer, when he and Giri had often passed the time with jokes and songs.

"He liked to tell a story of a woman who was out in the field gathering wheat when she came upon a red desert adder. The woman asked of the adder, 'Why do you have fangs, and venom that kills?' The adder replied, 'It is only to defend myself, or to kill prey that I may eat.' The woman was unconvinced, and said, 'I would never use venom to defend myself!' The adder simply smiled. 'Why must you lie, woman? For I have heard you speak to your husband!'"

Cilla laughed, a rich, hearty laugh that seemed to unlock something within Ratha. His own laughter and tears burst forth in equal measure, each riding upon the waves of Cilla's laughter, but continuing long after as he recalled the times that he and Giri had combined to make even Archer turn red and cover his mouth.

This was the Giri that Ratha could celebrate. The brother who, no matter how long the days or how rocky the journey, could bring even the stones to laugh. The brother who had hidden pebbles in Archer's boots, so tiny and placed so well that with every step Archer felt a tickle between his toes.

It had taken Archer half a day to find the pebbles, and three days more to plot his revenge on Giri, carefully weaving a string of nettles into Giri's breeches that left him hopping and howling until he could find and break open a soothing reed.

For his part, Ratha had laughed along with Archer at his brother's discomfort, for such were the just desserts of the prank Giri had played, and he knew the nettles were as harmless as the pebbles Giri had employed for his own amusement.

As he told Cilla of these times, and many others besides, her peals of laughter echoed through the rocks below, and the stones themselves seemed to respond with a quiet glow that spoke their approval. She told him of one of her cousins who had been the happy, if unsatisfied, host of Giri's first clumsy kiss. Her description, doubtless embellished in the telling, left Ratha holding his sides and wiping the tears from his eyes.

"Giri was a gift to us all," Ratha finally said, when he could catch his breath.

"Yes, he was," Cilla said. "And whatever he became, dear cousin, he became it only because he never lived by half measures."

Ratha nodded. "That he did not. Whatever he was, in whatever moment he lived, he lived it fully. And if he lived war no less fully than he lived all else, I pray he did so not from malice but from the same completeness with which he gave every day of his life."

Cilla reached out and took his hand. "If we can see him thus, my cousin, how could any just and merciful god not see him likewise?"

Ratha did not withdraw his hand, for in that simple touch he felt the beginning of something he would not have imagined possible only days ago. He felt the beginning of healing.

"I will always miss him," Ratha said.

"As will I," Cilla said. "But he lives on in our hearts, and in our memories. And I dare say with surety that he lives on beyond the veil, and even now plots his mischief with the gods."

"If that be," Ratha said, "then I pity the gods."

"Share a meal with me, cousin," Cilla said. "You have fasted enough."

Something in the quietness of her voice, in the softness

of her touch, in the laughter they had shared, and even more, in her having come to share his grief, reached through the anguish that had plagued his soul from the moment he had seen Giri fall. To spend time alone was an honorable thing. But to return to his people, and his duty, was no less honorable, and all the more so in this time of need.

"Yes, cousin," he said. "Let us return to Anahar and eat together. For duty weighs upon us both, and to duty we must return. But first let us feast in honor of Giri."

"Long have I waited to hear those words," Cilla said, rising with him.

"And others that I cannot yet say," Ratha added, a wry smile on his face.

Cilla laughed. "Tease me not, cousin! Come, strike your tent before I smite your heart!"

Ratha joined in the laughter as they made their way back to Anahar.

Many days and hours of sorrow still lay ahead, but a glimmer of acceptance had at last eased Ratha's heart.

It was terrible, thought Tess, to rip Sara from the arms of her groom yet again, but it could not be avoided. *Come,* she cried to her sister in her mind. *Come to the temple at once and bring Cilla!*

The answer was not one of words, but one of feeling. She felt Sara's startlement, followed by a burst of fear. Then: *Cilla is in the mountains, with Ratha.*

Then summon her now!

Archer continued his gallop through the streets of Anahar, his mount's hooves striking fire from the cobbles, though it was forbidden to ride this way in the city. As people scattered before them, they were recognized, and their haste awoke fear.

He drew his steed to a skittering halt in the square before the temple. "I will find your sisters," he said as he slid down from the saddle, then set Tess on her own feet.

"I summoned Sara already. She says Cilla is still with Ratha, but she will call for her to come."

"Then Cilla will find her way back swiftly." For a moment he looked deep into her eyes while giving a squeeze to her upper arms. "Fight hard, my lady. I will seek what help I may find."

Inside the temple, Tess found no comfort, but then comfort had been a stranger to her since wakening alone in this land. Nor had the temple itself ever offered her anything beyond grief and warnings of her destiny.

Still, thinking the early Ilduin who had directed and supervised the construction of this place might have had protection in mind as well as teaching, she sought the very center of it, the very heart of the temple. There she sat on the stone floor and waited.

Whether her fear and anger had driven him back, or whether the temple provided psychic shelter, Tess could no longer feel the oily, icy touch in her mind, nor hear the snatches of music that had heralded it.

She closed her eyes, chilled to the bone from her time outside, although the winter's fury seemed unable to penetrate these walls. The music, she thought. The music. Had it been meant to enchant her? To open a way to her deepest mind? Or had it been something other?

It had certainly been beautiful. As beautiful as the singing of Anahar. Hadn't Archer once said that his brother had been fair and beautiful, and had used that beauty to bring about strife?

Her mind whirled in circles, unable to settle on any particular thing, almost as if she feared that if her thoughts slowed *he* might find his way in again. Where was Sara? And why could she not warm up, even when every part of her was burrowed into her cloak?

She thought of a fire, thought how nice it would be to be sitting before one right now. The flames seemed to dance before her eyes, and almost as if by magic, she felt the heat of them stinging her cold cheeks.

Her eyes popped open and she gasped. Before her, on the stone floor with no fuel to feed it, a fire burned, emitting heat. Did she need only to visualize something to have it occur? The thought terrified her.

But then she saw Sara sitting across from her on the other side of the fire. How long had she been distracted? How had Sara come without being heard?

Fearing that she was imagining everything, she opened her mouth to speak Sara's name, when a chant began to emerge from the shadows around the fire. Tess's head snapped up, and all of a sudden she saw the clan mothers, every one of them, in a circle around the fire and the two Ilduin. Their hands were joined as if to make an unbroken ring, and they intoned a prayer that sounded as if it were as old as time, chanting words Tess could not understand.

Sara smiled at her. "Cilla is on her way. She will be here soon. Archer said the Enemy is assaulting you."

Tess nodded jerkily. She felt stiff, as if she had been sitting here for hours, not just minutes. But given what she saw around her, she must have dozed off…or gone somewhere else for a time. Some place she could not now remember. Too much time had elapsed.

She drew a frightened breath. Was she still losing her memory? Was she about to forget these past months as she had forgotten her earlier life? The terror that pierced her then had no equal.

How could she go forward if she could not trust her mind not to forget?

All of sudden, Sara slipped into her mind. *He is attacking you now, sister. He seeks to make you doubt yourself.*

He was certainly succeeding, Tess thought.

If you doubt yourself, he will find you easier prey. Seek your strength.

What strength? She felt cold, frightened and very much alone, as alone and frightened as when she had wakened among the gore of the slaughtered caravan.

Still she felt no touch in her mind. That was a good thing, because if there was anything she was certain of, it was that the Enemy wouldn't be able to reside within her mind without being detected. His presence was too alien to be missed, as recognizable as a fingerprint.

A fingerprint? Where had that come from?

For an instant she feared she might simply dissolve into hopeless tears, unable to cope any longer with the weight of things forgotten and the weight of things to come.

But then her spine stiffened, and she drove away the despairing thoughts. Those, she thought angrily, would only serve *him*.

A whisper passed through the room, and the circle of clan mothers parted, allowing Cilla to enter. She looked cold and windblown, but in her hands she carried a tray of food.

"I am sorry that I was delayed, sister, but tradition dictated that Ratha and I feast in Giri's honor," she said, placing the tray between Sara and Tess. Then she squeezed Tess's shoulder. "I ate quickly and brought the rest for you. Eat and rest, sister. You are guarded now."

Tess looked around at the ring of aged faces, at her two Ilduin sisters, and finally understood.

She was not alone.

Chapter Nine

Archer joined Jenah and Tuzza in the large tent that served as a temporary headquarters for both armies. As it was set on neutral ground between the two camps, no one could see a purpose in raising a building here yet, because they were planning to march very soon. The work on a camp and buildings for the Bozandari had been born of an effort to establish a sense of purpose and permanence for the erstwhile captives, and to help build relationships between them and the Anari.

So far there had been few problems. It had helped greatly when the Anari army had sprouted banners sporting the white wolf as well. Just as helpful had been the amazing gifts of the Anari stoneworkers who assisted their former foes in building the camp.

But now the real dangers approached, ones that might not be so easily solved. Would Tuzza's men be able to stand against another Bozandari legion if necessary? Or would they lay down their swords?

No one could say for certain, oaths aside. All had sworn fealty to Tess, but that did not necessarily mean they would kill their own comrades-in-arms.

Tuzza grew more uneasy about the difficulties ahead with each passing day. So did Jenah, who often had a nightmare vision of the Bozandari troops laying down their weapons, leaving the Anari who marched beside them to be slaughtered and taken into slavery. Both men were wary, even as the friendship between them appeared to grow.

Archer was acutely aware of the tensions, though he seldom mentioned them. "Time," he had said to both Jenah and Tuzza. "Time is needed. This is all new to our peoples. We must gently carry them along with us for as long as we possibly can."

But tonight, as he stood at the fore of the tent beside Tuzza and Jenah, he noted that the Anari and Bozandari officers stood apart from one another, almost as if there were an invisible wall between them. Denza Grundan, the quarter-Anari soldier who had recently been promoted to rearmark, alone stood between them like a bridge. Archer was relieved to note that neither side seemed bothered by his presence so near them.

When everyone had settled, Tuzza stepped to the fore and held up his hand. "The time approaches," he said. "We have received word from both Anari and Bozandari scouts." He paused then, weighing the import of his words. He paused to choose more carefully. "Let me say that otherwise. *Our* scouts have returned with information."

Throughout the tent, heads nodded, noting the distinction he was making. Faces, however, offered no clue as to what lay behind them.

"A legion has marched into Anari lands presumably to rescue us." This with a nod toward the Bozandari officers. "We must go forth to meet them, but we must try at all costs to meet them peacefully."

Murmurs of agreement from the light-skinned officers, no sound whatever from the dark-hued faces of the Anari.

Jenah stepped forward then and looked directly at his fellow Anari. "The same applies to us all. We must win allies, not alienate them. All of us face a threat bigger than our past problems. We face a threat to our entire world, as my lord Annuvil can well tell you."

"Annuvil…" The whisper passed among the Bozandari who had not yet heard Archer's true identity. The Anari, who had long known, remained stoic. Archer, however, did not speak. Standing with his arms folded, he merely lowered his head and looked downward.

Finally, someone called out, "Where is the lady? It is to her that we have sworn our fealty."

Only then did Archer lift his head. "She is at the temple," he said heavily. "The Enemy assaults her. Thus, her sister Ilduin stand guard at her side, as do the clan mothers."

The silence grew profound at that, and men shifted uneasily.

Archer tilted his head a little to one side and scanned all the faces before him with his gray eyes. "I am sorry," he said, "that it has come to this. And yet, awful though the days ahead may be, none of you ever would have been born had not we Firstborn made so many mistakes. Learn from our sins. Do not repeat them."

After a few moments during which men murmured and

then stilled, Tuzza spoke again. "From the banners our scouts have observed, it is my cousin Alezzi who comes to us. He is a good man, my cousin, and close to my heart. If for no other reason, we must do all we can to avoid a clash. I will speak with him."

A Bozandari officer called out, "Are you certain you can persuade him to join us, Topmark?"

"I must," Tuzza answered simply. "I must. Still, we have but tomorrow to complete our exercise, and not even all of the one day. We do not want to fight, but we will have to when we find Ardred's force, if not before. Anari and Bozandari must be able to fight together, or his army will defeat us in detail."

"And this will be difficult," Jenah said, continuing their prepared remarks. "We Anari prefer night action. It caused confusion among you, which multiplied our numbers."

"The Anari never had even a full legion arrayed against us. And the column that harassed us on our march was less than one thousand strong," Tuzza said. Murmurs of surprise spread through the Bozandari officers, but he silenced them with an upraised hand. "It is true. The harassing column steered us into that canyon, where we could not deploy our full strength and would be forced to frontally assault their prepared defenses."

The memory of that bitter defeat darkened their faces. Archer could see that this could quickly transform into something else: resentment of the Anari who had defeated them, and the commander who had led them into that defeat.

"However, remember that the Anari had many advantages in that campaign," Archer said.

"This is true," Jenah said. "We had Ilduin to help our

communications, and we were fighting in our own lands, among the rocky hills and mountains. It was not difficult to find terrain that favored us, and Topmark Tuzza had few choices as to his route of advance. While we will still have Ilduin among us in the next campaign, our Enemy will as well. And we will not be fighting in Anari lands, but in the open spaces of the Deder desert. That which we have done before will not avail us twice."

This seemed to mollify the Bozandari somewhat.

"Our tactics are also different," Tuzza continued. "The Anari threshing lines are better suited for attacking an enemy. They maneuver more quickly than we do, but the threshing line also gives way to exhaustion more quickly. Our tactics are more stable in defense, and if we are less mobile in attack, we can sustain the action longer."

"Thus," Jenah said, "our exercises will seek to take advantage of our differences. We will cooperate as hammer and anvil. The Bozandari, more stable and resilient, will be the anvil. Anari mobility will provide the hammer."

"Is that not the role of cavalry?" Grundan asked.

"Aye, Rearmark," Tuzza said, "if we had it. We do not. What few horses we have must be used in draft. But our Anari brothers can move as swiftly on foot as mounted cavalry." He pointed to the map they would use for the exercise. "The Bozandari must fix the Enemy in place, and apply constant pressure to maintain his focus and wear down his strength. The Anari must strike him from the rear, crushing him against us. This makes the best use of our respective strengths."

"This plan of battle calls for great coordination," Archer said, seeing the doubts reflected in the officers of both armies. "Each arm must trust the other. The Anari must trust the Bozandari to be strong and steady in their role as anvil. The Bozandari must trust that the Anari hammer will strike, at the right time and with sufficient force to shatter the Enemy before the Enemy's pressure is too much to bear."

"And," Jenah said, "we must train to strike at dusk, rather than at dawn. The Bozandari will deploy and move to contact in the final hour of daylight, while the Anari deliver our blow in darkness."

Tuzza again held up a hand to quiet the murmuring among his officers. "I am well aware that we are used to giving battle in the morning, when our men are more rested. We must change our habits, pausing on the march so that our men have time to rest and eat. This will be difficult, but we will have many days to practice the new ways along the road to Bozandar."

"In this way," Archer concluded, "we will strike the Enemy when he is tired, ready to make camp and prepare his supper. We preserve the greatest strengths of each of our proud traditions, and forge a new tradition."

Archer lifted his mug, and Tuzza and Jenah did likewise. Their officers took their lead.

"To the Snow Wolves!" Archer said.

"To the Snow Wolves!" the men replied.

Ras Lutte watched his men drill with a growing sense of dismay. Lord Ardred's army—a collection of brigands, thieves and rogues—was proving to be a much greater challenge than any he had faced in the service of Bozandar. Ardred could control them as a hive, but Lutte knew that no mere swarm would survive in battle against even a small force of well-trained men. That had been made clear in

Lorense, when scores of Lantav Glassidor's men had fallen to Ardred's brother and two Anari slaves.

Lutte would have much preferred a proper army, comprised of trained, disciplined men who would stand by one another and continue to perform their duties under the harshest of conditions. But men built of such stern stuff were far more difficult for Ardred to bend to his will.

Thus Lutte found himself at the helm of what was little better than a mob. His officers were a mixed bag, a handful of other Bozandari who had fallen from favor like himself and the rest nothing more than the strongest and the cruelest, those willing to murder rivals and control their men by force of terror. Such men enjoyed giving orders, but were ill-suited to taking them.

Worse, men like these were the least affected by the witchcraft of Ardred's enslaved Ilduin. Lutte could hope for little more than to point these men in the direction of an enemy, fire their hearts with the prospect of looted treasure, and release them as one would a pack of wild and hungry dogs.

No, he could count on one hand the number of officers he could rely on to rally their men after a local defeat, or reform them as they plundered an enemy camp, and offer a cohesive unit that was prepared to return to action. Men he had in abundance, for there were many who had bristled under Bozandari or any other rule. But men without leaders were little more than grist to be ground down and scattered in the winds of battle.

Given the force at his disposal, Lutte's options were limited. He could not hope to conduct complex maneuvers, and most of his units were little more than arrows in a quiver. He could aim them, draw the bow and loose them. After that, he must consider them spent. The handful of comparatively reliable units he would keep in the rear, both to preserve his greatest strength and to act as a bulwark against those in front who might otherwise flee.

Battle, he decided, would be much like a hand pushing forward piles of sand, with his more skilled officers the fingers and the rest a mass to be pressed forward against the desired target. Some of that sand would inevitably slip through those fingers, and Lutte knew he must discount his numbers accordingly. Once the sand had worn down the Enemy's line, Lutte would look for opportunities to use the fingers to punch through and deliver the critical blows.

These were hardly the elegant, precise tactics he had learned in the academy. They were little more than the application of brute force. He would have to depend on Ardred and his witches to sustain the army's mettle, and his own observation and timing to transform the crude cudgel into a dagger to the Enemy's heart.

It was not a proper way to make war. Lutte saw little hope that his men could withstand a determined assault by Bozandari legions, let alone deliver a riposte that would deliver into Lutte's hand the imperial scepter his lord had promised. For that to happen, the Bozandari must be divided, scattered, their allegiances torn, their officers pitted against one another.

Certainly there were rivalries aplenty among both the imperial court and the officer corps. The task of fueling those rivalries fell upon Ardred's spies and minions in Bozandar. If they were equal to that challenge, then Lutte would be equal to the challenge on the battlefield.

And he would be Emperor of Bozandar.

Chapter Ten

Ratha carefully rolled Giri's sword in the bedroll Giri had carried on campaign, and tucked it within his own pack. He could not have said why, save that it felt as if the sword were his last connection to his brother. He felt a presence behind him, and turned to see Tom standing in the doorway.

"Welcome back," Tom said quietly.

"And my blessings on your marriage," Ratha replied. "I am sorry that I could not share more at the wedding."

Tom extended his hand, and Ratha grasped it. "There is nothing to forgive, my friend. Sara and I were honored that you interrupted *telzehten* to attend. She and Cilla are with Tess at the temple now. Archer and Jenah are preparing for tomorrow's maneuvers, and Erkiah seems to need more rest with each passing day."

"And so you came to me," Ratha said.

Tom nodded. "I would have come regardless. I sense there is much that we can learn from each other."

Ratha smiled. "I am no prophet, Tom Downey."

"Perhaps not," Tom said. "But you can be much more than a mere prophet. You can be a priest."

Ratha paused for a moment, then laughed. "Unless much has changed since last I undressed, I am not eligible to join the ranks of the priesthood. Or have you forgotten that all Anari priests are women?"

"I have not," Tom said. "But not all priests serve at the temple. Your women, bless them, know less of war than you. And in these ill times, the fate of the Anari, indeed the fate of the world, lies on the field of battle. But the war will end, my friend. And what then?"

"If we are defeated, nothing," Ratha said.

Tom nodded. "Aye, but if we are not? Must there not be those who can create peace in hearts hardened for war? Who can be among men who have shed blood, who have swum in anger and fear, and coax them to the shores of forgiveness and hope? Your men have followed you into battle, Ratha Monabi. More will follow you into battle again. Will you not lead them into peace when the battle is over?"

Ratha shook his head. "That is too heavy a burden for any man, my friend."

"Yes," Tom said. "It is not the burden of a warrior. It is the burden of a priest. But will men who have walked with a warrior suddenly turn to a priest who has not known their pain and horror, of one who has not seen in the night the faces of those he has slain? They will not, friend. They cannot. They will need a priest who has borne their burdens and who carries their scars."

Ratha felt the truth in Tom's words, even as he doubted his strength to fulfill them. This war would not, could not last forever. And if the gods should bless them with victory, then he and his men would have to return to their homes, to the stones of their Telner, and find again the beauty and joy in the simpler things of life. They would have to bear the daily trials of life with the warmth of husbands and fathers, and not with the cold hearts of warriors. They would have to step out from under the dark cloud of war into the sunlight of peace.

Could he lead them thus? How could he himself emerge from that darkness and be a man of peace, when he had never known the life of hearth and home, of wife and child, of sowing seed, nurturing field and gathering harvest? It was as if Tom were asking a blind man to teach color to those who had shut their eyes from too much.

"I am not the priest you seek," Ratha said. "Call instead upon Jenah, who at least has lived among the Anari all of his days."

"Had this war ended in the canyon, that might be," Tom said. "For that was Jenah's war, the war of the Anari to shake off their shackles and live as free men. But this war to come is more than that. It is a clash of brothers, of Annuvil and Ardred. The Anari will look to you, because you have walked beside Annuvil longer than any among us. You must be that priest of peace, my friend. For if you cannot, I fear the Anari can never again be as they were."

"And how would I do this?" Ratha asked. "It is not enough to be willing. I doubt that I am able."

"The power of one is the power of many," Tom said. "And the power of many is the power of one. Begin with the one, my friend. Begin with yourself."

When Tess emerged into the morning sunlight surrounded by her sisters and the clan mothers, she felt a lightness of spirit that had long been missing. It was as if spending the night surrounded by protectors had lifted her out of the dark place into which she had been steadily slipping since her battle with Elanor.

The sunlight seemed particularly clear and bright this day, paining her eyes until they adjusted. It seemed to her that she was seeing the beauty of Anahar afresh, almost as if she had never seen it before. Everything looked cleansed, almost purified, as if by a heavy rain.

Yet it had not rained.

She lifted her gaze to the cloudless skies, feeling the touch of Cilla's and Sara's shoulders against her own, and waited to see if anything would happen.

Something had changed. She felt it now in the chilly air. It was not only as if the darkness within her had vanished, but as if it had been driven out of this part of the world. Only in its absence did she realize how much Ardred had overshadowed everything.

She turned to look at the clan mothers who were arrayed behind her. Their dark, aging faces revealed fatigue, but a kind of shining joy as well.

"Thank you," she said. "Thank you all."

As one, they bowed to her. Then, as they straightened, Jahila, the youngest of them, spoke.

"Long have we awaited you, my lady. Your burdens are heavy and many, and what little we can do to help is gladly given."

Tess returned the bow, but could feel her cheeks heating with embarrassment. Despite all that had happened, she didn't believe she was even *half* what these people believed of her. She was certainly no savior, although they seemed to think otherwise.

"I am," she said quietly, "only a woman like all of you. I hope I will not disappoint your hopes."

She turned to walk away with Cilla and Sara. Behind them, the clan mothers drew bells from within their robes and shook them. A tinkle of almost unearthly music followed the three Ilduins' departure.

"You look ever so much better, Tess," Cilla commented. "I did not at all care for how you looked when I arrived yesterday."

"Nor I," Sara agreed.

Tess felt herself smile for the first time since the wedding. "Something has changed. Can you not feel it? Anahar is cleansed of his presence."

Her sisters paused, closing their eyes as if sensing their surroundings. Then they, too, smiled and linked arms with Tess.

"If it be for only a short time, still will I enjoy it," Sara said. "For tomorrow the armies march, and we with them."

"And our most important task at the outset," Cilla said, her voice tinged with foreboding, "will be to keep the peace among them."

"We shall," Tess said, feeling more positive than any time in a long while. "We shall."

That night Cilla and Sara disappeared with Ratha and Tom. Tess sat outdoors in the gardens of Gewindi Tel, deeply wrapped in her cloak, entranced by the stars above. So many stars, more stars than one could count in a lifetime, she thought. In the cold air they shone brightly, illuminating the bare branches of the trees around her, silvering them with light. No moon filled the sky tonight, but the stars were beauty enough.

Ordinarily at this time of year, Cilla had told her, this

garden would be full of blooming flowers and shaded by a leafy bower of trees. But the evil winter had browned everything, and what it had not been content to brown, it had killed.

But tonight Tess had no thought for that. Instead she lifted her head to the beauty that the Enemy could *not* smite, and drank it in. It was almost as if the pale light from so far away filled her and illuminated her within.

She felt as if a transformation were taking place, a transformation that had begun with the protective circle the clan mothers had created around her yesterday. The feeling was a good one, so she let it happen.

But she also found herself thinking absently of the gods. There were how many? Nine? Twelve? For some reason she could not remember the children's poem that she had heard months ago, a poem that listed the gods.

But their number did not matter, she supposed. What mattered was that if Elanor was helping her, then Ardred probably had a god helping him.

Playthings of the gods. An apt description. Dragged into some inscrutable diversion as if they were but chits on a game board. An answer, perhaps, to an eternity that would otherwise be intolerably boring. Or even pawns in a power struggle of some kind.

But how could a mere mortal ever know? All a mortal could know was that the survival of this world and all that was good in it depended on the outcome of their struggles over the next few weeks or months. The gods could always create another world for their own amusement. The people of this one could not.

A small sigh escaped her, but her spirits did not diminish. The shift taking place deep within her was filling her with something warm and good, something hopeful, and she wanted to cling to it.

A sound alerted her and she looked quickly to her left. Archer was approaching, clad in his usual black from head to toe. He looked tired, and very much worried.

"My lady," he said, approaching on swift, light feet. "How do you?"

"Much better." She smiled, and was glad to see an answering smile appear on his weathered features. "For a little while I have been granted peace."

"It pleases me to hear so." He sat on the stone bench beside her. "Are you not cold?"

"The cold cannot touch me tonight. Little can. I wish this would last."

"As do we all. You know we march on the morrow?"

"Aye. Thus begins another stage in a journey that seemed so small when first we left Whitewater in pursuit of a few thieves who had slaughtered a caravan. Did you guess this awaited us?"

"I am not so prescient. Yet with each step, this moment has drawn closer."

"So it has." She tilted her head back again and looked up at the stars. "Have they changed much since your youth?"

"What?"

"The stars?"

He looked upward. "A bit. The constellations have slowly shifted, but only someone who studies them would note it."

"Or someone who has lived as long as you."

"Aye."

She looked at him, saw that he was studying the

diamond-studded sky above. "I am sorry your life has been so hard."

He turned toward her. "I earned such a life. Perhaps now I can finish paying my debt."

Impulsively, she reached out and clasped his hand. "I think you have already paid a thousand times over."

"I doubt it." He shook his head once, quickly, and squeezed her hand. "But you are enjoying a respite, so let us speak of happier things. I would not destroy your mood, my lady. Tomorrow will bring us enough difficulty."

"Aye, that it will."

Once again she tipped her head back to look at the stars. "I have been thinking, Archer, and it seems to me that the gods would be bored if we were perfect. I think they enjoy making a game of us, and part of that game is for us to make mistakes."

"You may be right."

She glanced at him with a smile. "Can you think of any other reason?"

At that he chuckled. "It makes sense in our terms, but who can know what gods think?"

"Or perhaps we know better than we think. You were made to be immortal. How can you think you are so different than they? You even helped create the race of Anari."

"It was that which brought about the fall," he reminded her. "It was the sin the gods would not forgive."

"Or perhaps it was the sin the gods provoked."

He turned his body so that he faced her directly. "What do you mean?"

"You had warred, and wanted to create a race that would never war. Instead you created a race that became enslaved until they learned how to fight. Now the Anari will be free, but through the horror of war."

"Do you say the gods think war is good?"

She shook her head. "No. But I think they will not abide perfection."

Chapter Eleven

Ratha sought out Cilla in the wee hours, well before dawn, while most slept. He could not sleep, nor could she, evidently, for he found her sitting in the gardens of the Monabi Tel, wrapped warmly in cloak and blankets. He joined her on the stone bench and stared at the blackened stumps of frost-slain shrubs.

"It begins," he said.

"Aye." She sighed and leaned into him. He felt no urge to draw away. "I hope our children will not know such evil times."

He squeezed her and let out a small laugh. "You leap ahead of me, cousin. You have me fathering children with you, and we have not yet even kissed."

A little chuckle escaped her. "I spoke in general, cousin, not in specifics. Although I cannot say that I have not often thought of such things with you."

Ratha smiled. "I would that we could focus only on such dreams, cousin."

Cilla nodded. "Yet without such dreams, how have we the courage to press on? Without a dream of the dawn, how would we endure the night?"

"You are right as always, cousin," Ratha said. He winked impishly. "It seems that I must grow accustomed to being wrong."

"But of course," Cilla said. "It is the way of things that men must learn to be wrong in the presence of their women. The gods have decreed that your fate in life."

Ratha burst into quiet laughter. "What cruelties they work on us."

"Yes," Cilla said, smiling. "But tender cruelties they are, my cousin dear."

"Unlike the greater cruelties we face."

Cilla nodded. "Yes. I will say again, we must make the world better for *all* children."

"'Tis an honorable task."

"Aye, but a pity we must go about it this way."

Ratha nodded. "The cost will be high."

"I have decided, cousin, that the cost of anything we hold dear is high. Else we would not hold it dear. What we purchase in blood will be the dearest of all."

"You sound like Tom Downey," Ratha said.

"I am a priest," Cilla said. "Not a prophet."

"And I am neither priest nor prophet, but rather a warrior. Yet Tom tells me that I must become a priest." He saw the look of surprise in her face, and quickly continued. "He said that not all priests serve in the temple, and that I must be as ready to lead my men into peace as I have been to lead them into war."

"He speaks the truth," Cilla said.

Ratha shook his head. "How can I do this, Cilla Monabi? How can I soften the hearts of men who have known war, and lead them back to their hearths, when I have known nothing but struggle and war in my life?"

Cilla seemed to consider this for a long moment before she replied. "Do you know what it is to kiss a woman?"

"No," Ratha said. "I do not."

Cilla leaned in and pressed her lips to his. Ratha fought down the urge to flinch, and let her lips linger for an instant. When she broke the kiss, she looked into his eyes. "Now, cousin, you know of something more than struggle and war."

To Ratha, lost in the sensations and wanting more, her words seemed jarring. In the instant of that kiss, he had put thoughts of battle out of his mind. Now she not only revived those thoughts, but reminded him of the task that Tom—and apparently she as well—had set for him.

"One kiss cannot a priest make," he said.

"Would you like another?"

The divergent streams of desire and inadequacy swirled through him. "No…I mean, yes, but…"

"But?" Cilla asked, smiling, her face nearly touching his, her deep eyes holding his gaze without flinching.

"I do not know if…"

She kissed him again, just for a moment, then held his face in her hands. "Ratha Monabi, I am sorry, for I know it must seem that I toy with you. And yes, I am. But also I am not. For yes, I long to kiss you, and for no other reason than that your lips taste of morning dew in my heart and stoke a longing in my loins. Yet I am also trying to show you that what you have known of life need not be all that you ever know. It is our challenge to learn from each day the lessons it offers us. Your lessons can change, my cousin. Your past is not your fate, but only what brings you to this moment."

She kissed him again. "And it is in this moment that you must live, Ratha. That is all we have."

Her words danced lightly through his mind. His lips like morning dew? Her loins longing? Her other words, however true, melted into the background as he felt his own stirring, and drew to mind the taste of her lips. Was this what love felt like?

"Speak no more," he heard himself say. "Only kiss me again, please."

Again their lips touched, and this time all thoughts of duty and destiny were lost in the soft contact, the taste and scent of her, the sound of her quiet sigh, the brush of her fingertips on his cheek. His arms drew her closer and he felt the softness of her breasts pressed to his chest, the gentle hollow of her waist, the fullness of her hip, the warmth of her, spreading through him, filling him, as if the entire world were reduced to tingling nerve endings and an urge deeper than any he had ever known.

Somewhere in the kiss their lips had parted, oh so slightly at first, but then more, as tongue sought tongue and that graceful, gliding dance began. He heard a moan, whether hers or his he could not tell, for in this moment it was as if they were one being. Her fingers tightened against the back of his neck, her body turned even more into his, the blanket having found its way around them both as if by its own strength. When finally she paused to draw breath, he saw the pinpoints of starlight reflected in her eyes, the entire universe living in her, offered to him.

"Oh, my," she whispered softly.

Ratha moaned softly. "More…"

But Cilla touched a fingertip to his lips. Her soft eyes and tender smile cushioned him as he felt himself tumbling back to earth.

"I tease you not, love," she said. "I wish for nothing more than to lie in your arms and kiss you until the end of days. But we cannot, and that pains me more than any hurt we have borne so far."

Ratha felt the sting of tears in his eyes as he saw them grow in hers. He knew the truth of what she said, and the hurt as well. "Promise me, Cilla Monabi, that we will find a time that is ours."

"I promise you that," she said. "On my heart do I swear that we will find that time."

In that moment, in her eyes, he saw the faintest glimmer of hope that life could bring beauty. He saw the hope of dawn.

Leagues away in the capital city of the empire, Bozandar, a slave named Mihabi slipped silently through an elegant house. He had come from the slave quarters in the rear yard, but the high walls with their many spikes could not be climbed, and the only gates from the yard were barred and bolted. He could not open them without waking everyone.

But to escape through the front entrance of the house would be comparatively simple. The house was not yet barred to the slaves, although there had been outbreaks of violence caused by other slaves since the news had arrived that a Bozandari legion had been defeated by an Anari army. Those who had never considered hope now whispered of their deliverance. And Mihabi dreamt with them.

But this family trusted its slaves. Or perhaps more important, this family could not begin a day without slaves to make them their first meal and tend their young.

As slave owners went, Mihabi felt this family was better than most. Mihabi had never felt the bite of the lash or the weight of chain on his wrists. But the Anari were still their *slaves*. It was a condition that burned its way into the soul no matter how well treated a slave was. He felt the weight of chain on his heart, and that weight wore heavier than any shackle.

Mihabi had been born here in this household. All he knew of his people were other slaves and the tales his mother told him of his kind in the lands to the south. Yet those tales had fed in him an innate need to be free, to learn to commune with the rock, to stand tall and proud as only a free man could.

He paused in a tiled hallway, listening. Nothing. He took another silent step forward.

The news of the defeat of the Bozandari legion had upset his masters and all the Bozandari including the emperor, whose beloved cousin had led the defeated troops. The general outcry for a rescue mission had overborne even the fear of the restless slaves who grew more and more threatening. The mothers and wives of the missing soldiers wanted their men home, and the emperor wanted his favored cousin back safely.

So a legion had marched forth. Other legions were being recalled, but for this brief space of time, the capital city was relatively lightly protected.

And the growing restlessness and anger among the slaves had turned into a plot. All who could were to meet tonight, and the uprising would begin with the dawn.

Mihabi slipped toward the door, a sliver of torchlight from outside lighting his way through an uncovered window. Soon he would be free, and if that freedom came in the form of death, then so be it.

Suddenly an arm grabbed him from behind, wrapping tight under his chin. He felt the prick of a knife against his side.

"Mihabi!"

It was the voice of Ezinha, his master.

For the first time since deciding to join the revolt, Mihabi was glad he carried no weapon. He could claim innocence in his passage through the house.

"Master." Mihabi spoke the word, though never had it burned in his throat more.

At once Ezinha released him. The Bozandari, a tall, pale man, was clear to Mihabi's gaze, while Mihabi must have been nearly invisible to his master. Between them the knife glinted red from the torchlight, but Ezinha made no threat with it.

Ezinha spoke. "You go to join the rebels."

Mihabi wanted to deny it, but suddenly found it impossible to lie.

Ezinha nodded. "I thought this would come. How can you do this? Your mother nursed us both and raised us as brothers. We played together as children. I have always treated you well."

"You have done such," Mihabi said. "But I have always been a *slave*."

Ezinha stiffened. "I have loved you as one of my own family."

"Yet still I have had no freedom."

"I thought you loved me as well."

It was then that Mihabi felt his determination waver, as

his chest suddenly tightened and his eyes began to burn. Now, truly, he was facing in the depths of his being what he was about to do. It no longer seemed exciting. It only hurt. His voice was hoarse when at last he replied. "I have loved you, master."

Ezinha looked down at the knife in his hand, then slowly lowered it. "I would not hurt my brother."

Mihabi swallowed hard. "I have never been your true brother. Had I been, I would have been as free as you. I could choose my own place in life, rather than having it chosen for me. I could have chosen to love and serve you."

Ezinha nodded slowly. "You will die out there, Mihabi."

"Perhaps. But I will die free."

Ezinha stepped swiftly forward. Before Mihabi could react, his owner used the knife to cut a slash through the slave brand on Mihabi's arm. It was the mark of a freed slave. Blood ran down from it onto the tile floor.

"You are free now, my brother," Ezinha said. "Do what you must as a free man. But mark my words, Mihabi. If you threaten me or mine, I will treat you as I would treat a thief in the night."

"I would expect no less."

"Then, I pray you, do not come here again. For your life's sake. For if I see you again I cannot trust you."

Mihabi turned toward the door, still dripping blood, but then he paused and faced his owner once more. "You have never trusted me. Our stations have forbidden true trust. If we meet again, let it be as equals. And if we both survive, then perhaps trust will be born."

Then he slipped through the door, into the night. Aye, he was free now, the stinging wound on his arm protecting him from any roving night patrols. But the blood price of freedom paled beside the ache in his heart. For what did it mean to be free when he had lost the only brother he still had?

As he walked through the city, tears stung at his cheeks. Tears and blood were the currency with which freedom was purchased. And he knew the cost was not yet paid in full.

More tears, and more blood, would be shed.

Dawn barely limned the eastern mountains as the armies set out in the morning. Given the latest reports from their scouts, it was determined that the Anari should lead the way through the mountains, then circle around until they were in the rear of the rescue legion. The remnants of Tuzza's legion would approach head-on.

Most of the Anari felt better about approaching in this manner than approaching head-on with Tuzza. Trust between the groups was still tenuous, and neither group cared to be in a position where they must rely on the other.

It was also a good tactic, a "hammer and anvil" as Tuzza called it. The Bozandari had been successfully applying this tactic for generations, and the Anari had only just used it against them for the first time.

At the head of the column rode Archer, Tuzza, Jenah and the three Ilduin. They had hardly traveled half a league when Archer saw Ratha galloping across the plain to catch them. As soon as he saw the lightness in Ratha's face, he knew something had changed.

"Welcome, brother," he said as Ratha rode up beside him. "It is good to have you at my side again."

"Thank you," Ratha replied. "It is my honor to march with your company, Lord Archer."

"My company?" Archer asked.

Cilla laughed. "He speaks of me, I think, Lord Archer. Though he would never say as much."

"But you would," Ratha said, trying to fight the smile that spread across his face.

"Of course she would!" Tess said with a chuckle. "But fear not, my friend, for whatever she has said was spoken genuinely and with kindness."

"And we did not believe the rest," Archer said.

"What did you…?" Ratha began, before Archer put a hand on his shoulder.

"Fret not," Archer said, laughing. "We jest at your expense, my friend."

Ratha nodded, joining the laughter. "Three kisses and I am the talk of the camp, it seems."

"I had not told them about all three," Cilla said.

"Good that you did not!" Ratha said. "Or they would have dragged us to the temple at sword point!"

"Now, cousin," Cilla said, squaring her shoulders. "Let us speak no more of this."

Archer laughed again, and moved his horse to Ratha's other side, placing Ratha beside her. "Let me not be between you."

"Perhaps it is better that you are," Tess said. "It sounds as if they need a chaperone."

"Sister!" Cilla cried.

"You sowed this seed," Tess said, shaking her head. "I merely note the harvest."

"Enough," Ratha finally said, his expression one of mild embarrassment. "We are an army on the march, and not children."

But, Archer noted, Ratha took Cilla's hand as he spoke and did not release it. That small gesture warmed Archer's heart. And he would take any warmth he could find on this march, for he feared there would not be enough.

Archer saw that Tuzza kept silent throughout. While he had noted Ratha's arrival, he seemed to feel no impulse to greet the brother of the man he had killed. This did not surprise Archer, but neither did it please him. There were too many in this column who had shed one another's blood. He hoped that they would shed no more of it, but he knew too much of men to take comfort in that hope.

Nor did he take comfort in the way both Anari and Bozandari expected him to lead this campaign and somehow quell the inevitable stirrings of anger. The weight of military command was heavy enough without the added burdens this placed upon him. Sooner or later, he knew, the impulse to peace must come from the Anari and the Bozandari themselves. He could not impose it from above.

"You are troubled," Tess said, having moved to his side as if she had read his thoughts.

"There is trouble afoot," Archer said. "And we are marching into it. There can be only so much laughter in such times."

"Aye, that is true. But it is the laughter which buoys our spirits and renews our courage."

"Only to a point," Archer said. "When the true test comes, it will not be laughter that carries us forward. It will be each man's implicit trust in the men next to him. And this we do not have yet."

"No, we do not," Tess said. "But we will."

After a long moment, Archer set his jaw.

"We must," Archer said. "Or all is lost."

Chapter Twelve

Ezinha Tondar had not slept since his slave Mihabi had slipped away into the night. At first he had tried to sleep on a sofa in the drawing room, but failing in that he had gone to the kitchen to make himself his first meal. He had abandoned that plan when Ialla—his cook and nanny—had awakened to his stirrings and insisted that she prepare it for him. On any other day, he would have seen this as an act of kindness by a woman who had been with his family for nearly forty years. On this day, however, he saw it for what it was: the act of a slave who feared she had disappointed her master by not rising in time to have the meal ready.

Ordinarily he would have left her to the task with hardly a word spoken between them. On this day, he found he could not. He sat at a table in the kitchen, searching for the right words to open a conversation he knew Ialla would find uncomfortable at best, if not insulting. Failing an elegant approach, he opted for directness.

"Have I been a good man, Ialla?"

She paused in whipping the eggs that would be his breakfast and looked at him. "You have been an honest and fair master, sir."

She had obviously chosen her words carefully, and the mere fact that she had done so said much. He thought for a moment before continuing. "That is kind of you to say, Ialla, but that was not my question. I have striven to be a fair and honest master, for you and your kin who are in my household. And I believe I have done such. But have I been a good *man*?"

"I am not sure what you ask, master," she said.

"Mihabi left in the night to join the uprising," Ezinha finally said. "I was shocked that he would do so, for I had considered him a brother. Yet I now wonder if I truly had. You raised me as much or more than my own mother, yet you do not think of me as a son."

Ialla said nothing while she poured the eggs into a hot skillet, one seemingly frail but sinewy strong arm shaking the skillet to spread them in an even layer. Only after she had set the skillet over the low flame did she finally turn to him.

"No, master. You are not my son. The time has long past when I could scold you, and even in your youth I could do so only because your mother entrusted you to my care."

"Did you love me?" Ezinha asked, cringing inside as he asked the childish question.

Ialla smiled. "Of course I did. How could I not? You were a good-hearted child, and if you were prone to mischief, it was a mischief you shared with Mihabi and his cousins rather than playing against them."

"I remember," he said. "We tried your patience far too often, I fear."

"No more so than any child, and less than most," she said, now using a flat instrument to press the edges of the eggs as they solidified. She sprinkled a handful of chopped onions into the pan, seasoned with snippings of fresh brown peppers from his garden. "That your mother left was not your fault, master."

"Oh, that I know," Ezinha said.

He had long since come to terms with the bitter day when she had walked out the front door with nary a word to anyone, never to return. Rumors that she had taken up with another man were rife, but Ezinha's father had never found her or the man. In the years after, Ezinha had come to realize that his father was a very hard man. Surely his mother had grown weary of his father's dark moods, rages that Ezinha himself had felt the sting of more than once. Ezinha had felt more relief than sadness at his father's funeral. He had sworn that he would never be his father's likeness, yet had he not done exactly that with his cold words to Mihabi?

"I told Mihabi that if I ever saw him again, it would be as an enemy," he said.

Ialla froze in the act of turning his eggs and looked at him. "Surely you did not, master."

"He has gone to join the rebellion," Ezinha said. "Anari are slaying Bozandari in the night. Could I doubt that he would do the same to me?"

Ialla kept her silence as she served his breakfast. While her cooking was nothing short of outstanding, on this morning he could barely taste his food. She cleaned the skillet and bowl as he ate, and finally he pushed the plate away.

"Speak to me, Ialla. Not as a slave to her master, but as a wise woman to the man she raised."

"You were a fool, Ezinha," she said. "Mihabi would no more harm you than I would. Are you a good man? Do you want me to tell you that Mihabi and I and your other slaves think of you as one of us? How could we? You own us. You sold Mihabi's brother to another man, because you had no work for him. Would you have sold your own brother?"

Ezinha's face fell as he remembered that day. He had not considered it a great thing. Bozandari often offered Anari on the auction block when they had more slaves than their work required. That he had separated two brothers seemed to him little more than what would happen if two Bozandari brothers chose different employers. But now, as Ialla confronted him with the reality of what he had done, he saw that it was something else entirely.

"How could I have been so blind?"

"You were raised to think of us as property, master. Individually, you may have loved Mihabi as a brother. But he was still Anari to you. Still a slave. Still property that you inherited from your father, as you inherited this house and your gardens."

"And you, Ialla, who have always been my truest mother…" He paused, nearly choking on the words. "I took from you your son."

Ialla folded her arms across her breasts and stared off into space. "Do you truly want me to answer your questions?"

"Help me to understand who I am, Mother!"

Ialla's face softened then. Reaching out, she touched Ezinhar's hair as she had often done in his childhood. "Then I will tell you. You will not like it."

"I already do not like any of this."

"Then hear me. When I was but a young woman of scant

more than twenty winters, I was seized by slavers. They are ugly people, engaged in an evil business. Their only purpose is to enrich themselves. At the time I was taken, Mihabi's brother was little more than two years old, and I was heavy with child. They took me from my husband. I know not what happened to him, not even to this day. I fear they killed him."

Ezinha bit back instinctive words of sympathy.

"The day I was taken to be sold, your father sought a wet nurse, for you were about to be born. My eldest son was proof that I could amply provide, and so we were bought. I still do not understand why your father troubled to buy such a small, useless child, nor yet to allow me to raise him. Often, I learned since, once the older child has proved that a woman can produce sufficient milk, the older child is slain. Your father, for all he was a hard man, did not do that. Perhaps he thought I would be kinder to you if he did not exact that evil."

Ezinha nodded, head bowed. "Instead I did it in a different way."

"You did what slave owners do. I was able to learn that my son lives, though in a household where he is beaten for even small mistakes. I suspect that he has already joined the rebels. Perhaps that is why Mihabi left."

Ezinha looked at her. "And you, Ialla? Will you also join them?"

The woman shook her head. "No. Who else will look after you and your children?"

The question pierced him because she was right. He and his family had become dependent on their slaves. The Anari were a background to their lives, rarely noticed. Yet, in their absence they would be sorely noticed. Little, he suspected, could function without them.

"You humble me," he said.

"You have humbled us. But ever it has been thus. It is the revenge of those forced to serve: to make ourselves indispensable."

Ezinha sat in silence for a long time, pondering as his self-assessment shifted to one far less flattering. He had been blind to his sins for no better reason than that it was easier not to think about them.

"I am not a good man," he said finally. "You have answered me truly."

"Nor are you all bad," Ialla said. She reached for the food he would not eat, but before she touched the plate, he grasped her wrist gently. Then, pulling his knife from its sheath on his belt, he cut a slash through the brand mark on her arm. "You are free, Ialla."

She stared at her arm, then looked at him. "Do you want me to leave?"

He shook his head, fighting the tears that threatened his eyes. "I do not. But to stay or to leave is your decision. As it should always have been."

She straightened, leaving the plate, and reached for a towel to press against her bleeding arm. Then she kissed his forehead. "I will stay, my son. I fear you will need a mother in the times ahead."

Near Anahar, a hawk soared on the morning's rising thermals. The armies reached the mouth of the pass where they had fought each other so bitterly only weeks before, and it was as if a lurch passed through the columns. The memories of these soldiers, men and women alike, was still fresh with memories of comrades slain, of ugly killing and maiming done.

In an instant the air began crackling with tension. Not a soldier, not even an officer, failed to feel a thirst for revenge. There was no one in either army who had not seen his fellows fall, no one who could honestly deny a desire to turn on his former enemy and exact retribution.

The Ilduin were the first to pick up on the change. Where at the outset the troops had been joking among themselves to avoid thinking about the dark journey ahead of them—to avoid thinking that they might never return from it—now all thoughts grew dark with memory.

None of the three women failed to notice the encroaching darkness or the feeling of barely restrained violence. At once they brought it to the attention of the commanders.

"We must take care," Tess said. "There may be trouble at any moment."

Archer rubbed his jaw. "I feared this. The wounds are still too fresh, and passing through this canyon will only rip barely formed scars."

"Is there no other way?" Sara asked.

Cilla shook her head. "Not for an army that wants to leave the valley."

"Then we must find a way to separate the two columns or distract everyone."

"Or a way to keep control," Archer said, looking at Tuzza and Ratha. "If we lose control now, 'twould be best to abandon the campaign, for there will be no hope."

The two officers nodded, and without further discussion spurred their mounts back toward their separate armies.

"And that is the problem," Archer said. "Making one of two."

"'Twill be easier once we have passed through the canyon," Sara suggested hopefully.

"The entire route to Bozandar is littered with the slain, buried though they be. These men will never forget. We can only urge them to overlook anger for the greater good."

"They understand that," Sara said. "Have they not sworn fealty to Tess?"

Cilla viewed matters far less positively. "Half of them previously swore fealty to the Emperor of Bozandar. I fear they are remembering that even now."

Archer looked around. "Where is Tom?"

Sara answered. "He said he would ride in the rear for a while. I asked why, but he did not answer. Mayhap he felt an omen. But what could he do?"

Tess spoke. "All of the men of both sides know Tom is a prophet. Word of that spread swiftly. Mayhap he can do more than any of us might think."

Archer caught her eye. "You can do something, my lady."

Tess raised a brow, suspecting she would not like what he was about to say. "Do not ask me to use my powers. They are wild and I cannot guarantee the outcome."

"They are less wild than you think. But no, I do not ask it. I ask only that you ride up to that cliff." He nodded toward a promontory that would be easily visible to the marching columns. "Take a standard bearer with you. Let them see you. It will remind them."

Tess felt quite certain that she was not the sort who liked to stage a show, certainly not one that placed her at its heart. But she had long since realized that events moved her as much as she moved them, perhaps more. If this would help prevent trouble, then she would do it.

Archer signaled to the nearest standard bearer, one carrying a flag diagonally divided into the red of Bozandar and the gray the Anari had chosen for their color. Atop the triangles a white wolf with golden eyes looked down on the world.

Tess nodded to her companions, then with the standard bearer, an Anari of very few years, headed up to the cliff Archer had chosen. When she reached the crest, she looked down into the valley below. The awful memories of that last morning of battle flashed through her mind. The heaps of dead, lying in windrows where they had been cut down. The cries of Bozandari who had fallen into the Anari pit traps, pit traps that later became mass graves and still showed as freshly turned earth.

The magnitude of their mission hammered her with renewed force. "Raise the standard," she said.

"Yes, m'lady," the boy said.

The boy planted the butt of the staff in the ground, using his foot to brace it, and held it upright. Tess knew what she needed to do, and almost in the thought of it, a gentle breeze came across the crest, lifting the pennant to its full length.

"Look upon me, Snow Wolves!" Tess cried in a voice that rolled down the slope and cut through the valley like rushing water. "Look upon your new standard! Fail it not, or Ilduin blood will judge!"

Chapter Thirteen

Mihabi found his older brother, Kelano, in a darkened wood that lay within a huge city park. Normally a place for Bozandari children to play with their mothers, the park had been all but empty since the bitter winter had fallen upon them. Now its winding paths and secret hollows were an ideal base for the Anari rebels.

"It is good to see you again, brother," Mihabi said, grasping Kelano in an embrace. "I feared we would never again meet face-to-face."

"It would be a cold fate that we should not," Kelano said. "A fate the gods have spared us. How is mother?"

"She is well," Mihabi said, "though she remains in Ezinha's house. I did not tell her that I was leaving."

Kelano nodded. "We must get her out. Ezinha will kill her, as many other masters are doing to the families of those who leave. As if by spilling the blood of our mothers and sons and brothers, they can break our will."

Mihabi considered that prospect. He had heard that some Bozandari were exacting reprisals, but strangely he had not considered that possibility when he had made his decision to leave. Surely Ezinha would not kill the woman who had nursed him? Yet he had sold Kelano, had he not?

"You are unsure," Kelano said, reading his eyes. "Have no doubt of the evil of slave owners, brother. You may have played with Ezinha in your youth, but he is no better a man than any Bozandari. We must get mother out of his house, and quickly."

"I cannot believe Ezinha would kill mother," Mihabi said, trying to imagine his former owner's arm falling, the glint of a blade plunging into his mother's throat. He could not force the image into focus. "He could not."

"He would and he will," Kelano said. "He is his father's son, and his father was a cruel man. Cruel to his wife. Cruel to his children. Would his son not show the same cruelty to a mere slave?"

Mihabi remembered the stern warning Ezinha had issued before he left. If he returned to Ezinha's house, he would be treated as a thief in the night. While Ezinha had freed him, there had indeed been a hardness in his eyes. Perhaps Kelano was right. Perhaps even now his mother lay dead, her body flung through the doorway of the servants' house as a brutally plain message to any of the others who might consider leaving.

Kelano held Mihabi's gaze until finally Mihabi nodded.

"You see the truth of my words," Kelano said. He put a hand on Mihabi's shoulder. "Come, brother, and quickly. We must gather a company of our brethren and forge a plan. You know Ezinha's house and grounds better than any, and we owe our mother a debt that only this can repay."

* * *

Tess had watched the army's march through the valley with a mixed sense of sorrow and hope. Each company, both Anari and Bozandari, had saluted her standard as it passed. But the anger still simmered as they made camp north of the valley that night. More than a few fights had broken out, the largest because a group of Anari had wanted to return to the valley to offer prayers at the graves of the fallen, while the Bozandari had no desire to see Anari both in front of and behind them in that valley of death. While the senior men quickly quelled the disturbances, the sense of fracture was imminent.

It was Cilla who had come to Tess with the germ of an idea, although Cilla had known that she lacked the means to make it happen. Now, as Tess approached Ratha's tent, she wondered if her powers of persuasion would be any better.

"Come in," Ratha said when she announced her presence.

"Hello, my friend," Tess said.

Ratha quickly gathered maps and other papers, tucking them into his knapsack, then invited her to sit on the low bench that functioned both as his cot and his map table. He sat beside her, the strain of the day evident in his dark eyes.

"What can I do for Lady Tess?" he asked.

The formality of the question left little doubt that he had some inkling of the reason for her visit. She chose not to evade the issue. "There is trouble in the camp."

He nodded. "Yes, I know. I cannot say that I am surprised. These men slaughtered one another in this same valley only a few weeks ago. Such memories burn deeply in the belly, m'lady."

"Both Anari and Bozandari look to Archer, and to me, to make peace between them."

"I envy you not that task. I know in my head that we must march together or fall to the Enemy. I think both of our peoples understand this." Ratha pointed to his chest. "But here, in our hearts, there are wounds that cannot be ignored. And the chasm between what we know and what we feel is…all the wider as we see each other arrayed as for battle."

Ratha knotted his hands together and Tess reached out to cover them. "I am so sorry, Ratha. But unfortunately it seems the gods will not give us time to grieve and lick our wounds. We must bring this army together swiftly."

His face tightened yet more, then with visible effort he relaxed. "Aye. What would you have me do?"

"There must be some way you and Tuzza can be seen by everyone to unite and put aside your past wounds. Everyone knows Tuzza killed Giri, and everyone knows that he did so because Giri killed an officer for whom Tuzza felt a great deal of affection. You have both suffered grievous harm…but pray do not misunderstand me, Ratha. I do not seek to minimize the loss of Giri. It is still a knife in my heart as well."

"I believe you." He closed his eyes tightly, as if to deny his eyes access to the world. Or to memory. "I can still see him killing my brother. It is etched in my brain with acid. The sword swinging, glittering in the sunlight, and my brother's head…" He shuddered, keeping his eyes closed. "You have no idea what you ask of me. Ask me to make peace with any other. But with Tuzza…" He shook his head.

"I understand, Ratha. Believe me, I understand. All our

minds are filled with horror since the battle. Not a person among us escaped the loss of someone we loved. But the future demands that we ignore our hurts for now, else there will be endless war."

Her gaze grew distant and she rocked a little, as if she were caught in a vision. "Few of us have any idea," she said in a voice barely above a murmur, "how awful it can be. And it can be so much worse than anything you have yet seen, Ratha."

He stared at her, tugged from the sorrow that angered him as much as it hurt him. An eerie feeling settled over him, as if he could sense that the woman beside him was bridging the veil somehow. As if she were seeing beyond this world.

Then she looked at him, and her blue eyes were dark. "You can make peace with any man you choose, but only peace with Tuzza will make a difference."

A chill crept along his spine, reminding him that there were far greater forces at work in this world, and in these events, than he had allowed himself to think of since Giri's death. The rightness of what she said filled him as much as his grief. Still, the internal struggle continued. It was a time before he could bring himself to make the promise.

"Much as I am loathe to make amends with Tuzza, it must be done for the greater good of all. So give me a while, my lady. A while to think on this. Then I will go to Tuzza and we shall make a plan."

"Thank you, Ratha." Tess squeezed his hands. "These times demand so much of us, my friend. I fear that in the end our hearts will be nothing but worn-out husks." She spoke as if she knew, as if she had seen.

Slightly unnerved and worried about the way she

looked, Ratha unknotted his hands and clasped hers. Yet still she rocked, as if caught in the grip of something beyond herself. "If that passes, then the Enemy will win. We must keep heart. We must always care. Even if we must at times numb our pain so we may do all that is needed, we must never sacrifice it. Armies will fight in the next weeks, but our spirits will wage war also."

"You speak wisely, Ratha. Very wisely. And only with unity can we sustain each other."

He sighed. "I will think of something, my lady. The stakes are far too high to allow hatred to rule us. I have buried Giri. Now we *all* must bury our dead."

Outside Ratha's tent, Tess sagged on legs that didn't want to hold her. She had seen, and what she had seen had shaken her to her very core. She did not know if she had glimpsed the future, or glimpsed the past, but either way horror gripped her.

She steadied herself against a tent pole, trying to clear her head enough to think. She needed to be alone, to absorb what she had just seen in her mind's eye, but finding solitude had become ever more difficult. Her sisters were very often with her, and since both armies had sworn fealty toward her banner—to *her*—everywhere she went someone wished to speak to her.

Strange how it was that the wounded hearts of these men seemed to want a few words from her, or a moment of her time to mention someone who had died. She understood their need, but she felt wholly inadequate to the task. She was the Weaver, but she was no healer of wounded hearts. The only gift she had lay in healing flesh, and causing terrible death.

Finding some strength, she headed for the edge of camp,

thinking that somewhere in the no-man's-land between the farthest tent and the sentries who had been placed as a screen to alert them before any attack could come near, she would find a place of solitude.

She was wrong. No sooner did she leave the edge of camp when the phalanx of Bozandari who had first sworn themselves to protect her, surrounded her. Since she had been moving through the Anari camp, she was even more surprised.

"Odetta," she said to their commander.

He bowed deeply.

"I need solitude."

"We will ensure you have it, my lady. We will position ourselves far enough away that you shall not know we are there."

As he spoke, he made a gesture with his hand. At once the men around her melted into the darkness. "You have only to lift your voice, m'lady," Odetta said. He saluted her smartly, then also vanished into the night.

In spite of herself, Tess smiled. Alone but not alone. It was undoubtedly the best she could hope for now, when they were two days' march from another Bozandari legion, one more likely to attack them than to talk first. Their scouts would likely be ranging out well ahead, and contact could be made at any moment.

She found a flattened rock of just the right height to serve as a seat. Her trembling legs were glad of the relief, but it only seemed the anxiety she felt moved from them into the rest of her.

She was not accustomed to having visions outside the temple, yet this one had seemed exactly like those she saw within the temple walls. Even with her eyes open and the stars casting their silvery light everywhere, giving the rocky desert a beautiful argent sheen, she could still see the horrific images.

Weapons that flew and sprayed fire, bodies hewn open in ways no sword could accomplish, in ways the mind could scarcely believe. A screaming roar, and then earth erupting around her, scattering men and women and children in parts around her, torn remains sticking to her clothes and her face and her soul.

Was this her past or her future?

Perhaps solitude had not been a wise choice. There was no answer to her vision, nothing that she could pick out of it to point a way to either her forgotten past or the dreaded future.

Rising, she started back toward the camp. Moments later the phalanx surrounded her again. This time she found them comforting.

Past or future, what difference did it make? she wondered finally as they approached the nearest tents. One way or the other, it was part of her.

Much as he hated the company of the crone he kept secreted in his fortress, Ardred needed, at times, to avail himself of her powers directly. He entered the Ilduin's small cell and tried to ignore the odor of decay that hovered in the air. The woman was nearly a walking corpse, yet she seemed unable to die, much as she might wish it.

Or perhaps, he thought grimly, she was *afraid* to die. The punishments of the gods, as he himself knew, could be as diabolical as their games. The quarrel between Elanor and Sarduk played out here in this world, and for all they were the cause of everything, they freely punished those who displeased them.

Elanor's punishment of both Ardred and Annuvil had

been harsh, but Sarduk had saved Ardred from the worst of it. And so he should have, Ardred had always believed. After all, it was the creation of the Anari that had so infuriated the gods. The war that led to it, between Annuvil and Ardred, had merely been a part of the game.

But the creation of a new race...that had been treading into territory the gods reserved for themselves. And Annuvil had been part of that, while Ardred had not.

Ardred's lip curled as he thought of his older brother. The folly, the sheer arrogance, of thinking any being could escape the wiles of the gods only showed Annuvil's failings. And as a result of those failings, the world had been rent asunder, Annuvil left here on this plane to wander like the lost sheep he was, and Ardred on another plane under Sarduk's protection. Ardred had used the time to learn what he must do to reunite the world.

While Annuvil had simply waited for events to unfold.

Well, Ardred thought, staring at the living husk of the Ilduin, events were certainly unfolding now. Rebellion in Bozandar—that must be quite a surprise to his brother, who had wanted the Anari to be peaceful to a fault—a legion marching toward Anahar to rescue its brothers, an emperor who was losing control of his empire though he did not yet know it, a people weakened by famine and harsh winter, all in turmoil....

Now it was time to wake his hives. The stupid overmark he had hired to train his ragtag army had no idea what other tools lay at Ardred's command. Nor did Ardred want him yet to know. If anyone looked, they would think Ardred weak, not worthy of concern.

It was good. It was as it must be. For out of this turmoil, the worlds would be reforged.

But far more important than that, the Weaver would be brought to heel. *His* heel. Only that, he knew, could avenge the way his brother had stolen Theriel those many years ago. White Lady for White Lady.

When he at last spoke to the woman he had come to see, he actually smiled.

Chapter Fourteen

"Snow Wolves, form ranks!" Archer cried.

His voice echoed off of the canyon walls, booming with an authority that made hearts quiver and muscles respond with trained precision. The host had returned to the site of the battle, the Anari along the eastern face of the canyon, the Bozandari to the west, facing one another with wary eyes. Between them lay the mass graves of those who had fallen.

Ratha and Tuzza received the salutes of their men, then turned and marched toward each other, moving between the graves. Murmurs rippled through the ranks as the two men stopped two yards apart. Above, on the rim of the canyon, Tess watched with growing concern.

"Surely they are not planning to duel?" she asked.

"I do not know, my lady," Archer said. "Ratha came to me, asking that the men be formed thus. I assumed that he and Tuzza had reached some accommodation."

Tess nodded, trying to force her eyes away from what was happening beneath her on the canyon floor, but she knew she could not. This had been her idea. Now she could do nothing but watch, and trust in the essential goodness of Ratha's soul.

Mihabi moved with three Anari through the quiet back gardens of Ezinha's estate. Kelano, he knew, was moving around the other side with three more. Unless Ezinha had changed his household routine, his wife would have taken his children to the market, leaving Ezinha at home alone to work on his ledgers. The Anari would be in his home before he had an opportunity to react.

If everything went well.

Mihabi looked up, shielding his eyes. The sun was nearly overhead. Soon the bells would ring, calling those few Bozandari who still honored their gods to their midday prayer. That would be their signal to move.

Mihabi was not happy being here. He had a promise, and whatever Ezinha might be, he would be true to his word. Mihabi would be nothing but a common thief in his former master's eyes. That thought troubled him more than any other. He had seen anger in Ezinha's face more than once. He had seen it the night he left Ezinha's estate. But it had always been the anger of a brother. An anger that he had known would pass.

This would be something else.

In the distance, the bells pealed midday.

Mihabi and the three Anari moved quickly and silently toward the kitchen door. As he stepped through the door, Mihabi froze.

Ezinha was in the kitchen with Ialla.

And he had a knife in his hand.

* * *

Ratha studied the eyes of the man who had killed his brother. The brother who had not only killed but had also mutilated Tuzza's cousin. It had been a calculated act of brutality that Ratha could not imagine Giri ordering, and yet he had. Giri's soul had grown much darker than Ratha had believed. Whatever pain Ratha had felt as he watched Giri fall, Tuzza's anger had been all the greater. Ratha considered how difficult his path to this point had been.

Ratha wondered if Tuzza was capable of the task that now lay before them. He was not certain that he could do it himself. And Giri had not been mutilated.

Ratha placed his hand on the hilt of his sword, watching as Tuzza grasped his own. As they drew their weapons, a gasp passed through the watching men.

But Ratha did not hear it. He could hear only the pounding in his own chest.

"I warned you, Mihabi," Ezinha said. "Had you come alone, perhaps I could have forgotten our last words. But to come like this, armed, and with your brethren. You are no more than a common thief."

"We come for my mother," Mihabi said. "You know what has happened in other households."

"And you think I would harm the woman who nursed me when I was a babe, and loved me ever after?" Ezinha asked.

"Why would you not?" Kelano asked, having crept through the house and who now appeared in the doorway behind Ezinha. "You sold me to a man who has done thus."

Ezinha nodded and looked down. The sight of the brother he had sold, the scars of the cruelty that this brother had borne, sickened and shamed him to his very soul. "I did, Kelano. I was a fool, though the cruelty you felt is no less for that. I was wrong. No one could judge you for wanting to strike me down. But look at your mother's arm before you do."

Mihabi saw the wound first, a wound that matched his own. Ezinha had freed her. And yet she remained here, in Ezinha's house.

"Mother…" Mihabi began.

"This is my home," she said.

"You are a fool," Kelano said, bitter anger in his voice. "Why would you remain with the man who sold your own son?"

"Because he is also my son," Ialla said firmly. "You are all my sons, and yet you stand here with daggers drawn. A mother can feel no worse pain than that."

"We are your *blood*," Kelano said.

"And my blood has been spilled," Ialla said, pointing to the scars on Kelano's body. She took the knife from Ezinha's hand and held it to her wrist. "Will a greater pool of my blood make old wounds heal? If so, then let me shed it."

"Mother, no!" Mihabi shouted. "You have done no wrong!"

"Have I not?" she asked. "I raised Ezinha, and more than once did I scold him when he erred. But never did I scold him on the greatest error of all. I spoke not of the evil of one man owning another. I spoke not of the anger that simmers when men are property. I warned him not of the danger that some day—*this* day—a vile crime that he thought normal would rise up and smite him. How can you say I have done no wrong, when I did not teach my child that most important truth?"

Ezinha heard her words as if through a cheesecloth

soaked with bile and guilt and sorrow. "You could not have spoken thus. My father would have beaten you, or worse."

"Aye, he would have," she said, tears rising in her eyes. "And fearing that, I said nothing while my own son was taken away to the auction house like a pig to the market. To spare my own pain, I let one son hurt another. What kind of mother does thus?"

"A human mother," Mihabi said, his knife lowered, his voice gentle. "A mother as flawed as her sons, yet no less loving for her flaws."

Ezinha gently took the knife from Ialla's hand and placed it on the table. "Mother, spill no more blood on this day. Nor will I."

He looked at Kelano. "As to whether you will spill my blood, Kelano, I cannot decide that for you. I pray that you will not, for I believe I can help your people in their time of need. But that is a choice you must make."

"How could you help us?" Kelano asked, his own dagger still clutched tightly.

Ezinha spread his hands. "You brought armed men into my house. Have I called for the city guard?"

"You have had no chance," Kelano said, eyes narrowed.

"Oh, yes, my son," Ialla said. "He did. Did you think your mother a fool? I had heard of the reprisals against the families of Anari who joined the rebellion. I knew you would fear Ezinha's vengeance. I told him you would come for me. We watched through the window as you stole onto his estate and waited in his gardens. He knew. I knew. He could have called for the city guard. He chose not to."

"But why?" Mihabi asked.

"Wherever you are hiding," Ezinha said, "the Bozandari will find you. Even now, a legion marches from the north

toward the city, to crush your brethren here. They may not
arrive for days or perhaps even a fortnight, but what of the
people in the city who have taken to the streets with swords
and bells to summon the guard? How long until they track
one of your parties back to your base, and fall upon you
with red in their eyes and black in their hearts?"

Ezinha paused to let the question sink in before continuing. "You need sanctuary, and I have both a walled estate
and good standing in the community. Neither guard nor
mob will assail this place."

Ezinha walked over to Kelano and stood before him, his
arms at his sides, his hands open. "Shed my blood if you
will, Kelano, but waste not the blood of your people. This
was once your home. Let it be so again."

"And how do I know that you are not merely drawing
my brethren in so that they may be slaughtered?" Kelano
asked.

"Because he swore to me," Ialla said. "He swore to me
on pain of *keh-bal*. And I will hold him to his oath."

Tuzza's hand rested on the hilt of his sword and hesitated
there. He knew what must be done, yet he couldn't quite
bring himself to make the first movement. The laughing
face of his young cousin floated before his eyes, then dis-
solved into the mutilated corpse he had last seen.

The man before him was the brother of his cousin's
killer. In keeping with customs of *ahwesa*, Ratha's life
should be forfeit for his brother's deed. Not the slaying in
battle. That was battle. The mutilation was not, and for that
a penalty should be paid.

But this was not a time for ancient customs and honor
claims, he reminded himself. He could, with a mere swing

of his sword, exact his family's due. It would be so easy that his heart rebelled at his refusal to do so.

Yet…not only was he aware of his army ranged behind him, but also he could read the face of the Anari facing him. Ratha found this no easier than he, yet Ratha had been the one to come to him and suggest this, that they end not only their own bad blood, but the bad blood between the armies.

A greater threat awaited them, one they could not afford to ignore, and certainly not for a few moments of satisfaction.

From behind him he could feel the pressure of anticipation, and he spoke quietly to Ratha. "They think we are about to fight to the death."

"Aye." Ratha's voice was heavy. "And it is that specter that we must end. I understand your reluctance, Tuzza, for I feel it as well. But for how long can we stand here and postpone our duty?"

"Are you eager?"

Ratha looked down at the ground. "Nay," he said. "I still grieve. But not only for my brother's death."

"No?"

Ratha looked at him. "My brother was as close to me as if we had emerged from the womb at the same time. He was my other arm, my other half. He is gone. It is where he is gone that I fear."

Tuzza felt his brow crease. "What do you say?"

"I saw that my brother was caught up in the lust of battle. I knew what he did to your cousin. My cousin Cilla swears that in his last moments, Giri recognized the wrong in what he did, that in the last moments of his life he regretted his errors."

Tuzza nodded, careful to keep his expression neutral.

"But, Tuzza," Ratha continued, clearly finding it difficult to speak of something so personal, "I have a fear."

"Fear?"

"What if Cilla is wrong? What if he did not have time to repent? What if, instead of crossing the veil, he wanders this world as a dark shade, forever barred from comfort and rest?"

The muscles in Tuzza's neck jerked, and he felt something chilly run along his spine. "Those who die in battle are guaranteed to cross the veil, for they have died bravely and in service."

Ratha shook his head. "Those are your beliefs. Ours are different. I cannot say who is correct. But I do know one thing. There is a difference between fighting for a cause out of necessity, and fighting because one gains a personal satisfaction from it. Giri began to thirst after blood. That was his sin. Did he repent it? I pray so, else he will never cross the veil, and I shall never see him again."

"Then let me offer you some measure of comfort," Tuzza said. "You have no reason to trust me in this, and many reasons to think me a liar. But listen, I pray you. Your brother's mission was not an easy one. He could not risk open battle with my legion, nor was that his task. And so he was reduced to pinpricks, drawing me along the path you had chosen, watching his men die, and exacting what revenge he could.

"A war such as that can produce no heroes, Ratha. It is too cold and too cruel. It produces cold, cruel men. The gods will know this when they meet your brother. They will look at how close you and Giri were. They will look at him. Then they will look at you. They will see that the differences in your hearts lay in the different battles you were forced to fight.

"And they will forgive him," Tuzza concluded.

"It would be blessed if that were true," Ratha said.

Tuzza nodded. "My people have a saying. The gods are gentle when the devils are cruel, and the gods are cruel when the devils are gentle. The devils were cruel indeed to your brother, Ratha. The gods will be gentle."

Ratha looked down for a moment, blinking away tears. "Many have spoken to me of Giri's life and his death. My friends. My kin. Even my beloved cousin. None of them spoke as you speak, Tuzza. And only in your words have I found the truth that reaches my heart."

Tuzza extended his free arm and grasped Ratha's shoulder. "One warrior to another, my friend."

Ratha shook his head. "No, my friend. One man to another. Men who long for an end to war."

"Yes," Tuzza said. "One man to another. Let us make peace, Ratha."

"Let us make peace," Ratha echoed.

They sheathed their swords and knelt to pick up two shovels Ratha had laid in this spot during the night. Wordlessly, for there was no need of words, they dug in the freshly turned earth. When they had dug a hole almost half the height of a man, they put the shovels aside and drew again their swords.

They brought the blades to their foreheads in a salute as old as time.

Then they tossed their swords into the hole.

Neither heard the gasps or the cheers that spread through their men. Neither heard Tess's quiet tears, high up on the rim of the valley, nor Archer's oath of wonder. It was as if a veil of silence had descended around them.

They heard the muted *chunk* of spade digging into earth,

and the *thud* as that earth landed in the hole. They heard each other's quick caught breaths. Later, each would swear he could hear the other's tears wetting the soil.

In a final gesture, each snapped the handle of his spade over his knee. Their swords were buried, never to be unearthed.

Tuzza considered whether to embrace Ratha, and finally decided upon a crisp, formal salute. Ratha returned it. Each spoke only one more word.

"Brother."

Chapter Fifteen

"Uneasiness everywhere," Ardred told Overmark Lutte. "The crone sees all, and it is well."

"Well?" Lutte looked at his new liege and pondered the word. "Well would be victory. Uneasiness is naught."

Ardred smiled, superiority in every line of his face.

"You doubt me, Lutte."

The overmark felt a distinct chill run down his back. He still had not taken the full measure of his new emperor, and he often had the feeling that the man had powers no Bozandari emperor had ever claimed. "I merely do not understand," Lutte replied.

"Nor would you." Ardred's smile broadened. "My plan proceeds. The capital of Bozandar is in the grip of a slave revolt that is spreading to outlying areas. They are thus weakened. The only threat marching their way is a small band of survivors of the battle between the Anari and Tuzza's legion. They will be crushed when Alezzi's legion meets them."

Lutte stiffened. "Alezzi is cousin to Tuzza."

"Do you think that will make a difference when Alezzi learns Tuzza has thrown his lot in with the *Anari*?"

Lutte knew enough of Bozandari officers to answer quickly. "No."

"Exactly. And most likely Tuzza will seize the opportunity to rejoin Bozandar regardless of whatever promises he may have made. So either way, that annoying little group will be eliminated. Then we will move."

Lutte thought of his own army coming up against a Bozandari legion, and he didn't like the assessment he reached. "We are not ready, my lord."

"You are ready enough, Lutte. Do you think I count only on you?"

That stung a bit, but Lutte managed to conceal his response by bowing his head. Yes, he supposed he had considered himself essential. Or at the very least he had wanted to think so. Why had he thought it should be any different here than it had been in Bozandar? He quelled the disappointment and annoyance he felt.

Ardred hummed for a moment, an unfamiliar tune, and rocked back on his heels, while clasping his hands together behind his back.

"They are doing exactly as I want, Lutte. Soon my brother will pay the price of his transgressions."

Ezinha's house had filled steadily over the past few days. His wife and children had gone to visit his wife's family in the country some thirty leagues away and were not expected to return until he sent for them. He had wanted his children to be away from the capital city at this time, to be at her father's large country estate where a private militia would be able to protect all of them.

But never had he imagined the threat would venture this close to his own door. Or that he would be risking his life—and ultimately those of his sons—by protecting rebels. And yet, he could not escape the justice of it. He had been blind to too much that he should have seen, and now he would pay the price. In the balances of eternal justice, he suspected that he owed a very heavy price indeed.

As the number of Anari within his walls grew, however, he noticed that many of them were children and women heavy with child. As if the rebels themselves were reluctant to overtax Ezinha. As if they wanted his offer of shelter and protection only for those who most needed it.

Which was not to say they didn't have any armed men and women standing secret guard. They weren't trusting *him* to provide all the protection they might need. Nor could he. Other than secrecy, he had little to offer. He had never had his own militia, nor felt the need for one. As physician to the emperor, he was nearly untouchable. As a man of influence, few would think of crossing him.

But now he was crossing his own people, and rightly or wrongly, he felt uncomfortable about it. Since Mihabi had first left, Ezinha had undergone a radical transformation in his outlook and identity, and it still sat uneasily on his shoulders. Helping these Anari escape Bozandar, he realized, would have felt less like a betrayal. But instead he was harboring people who might well set out to kill others.

And there things began to stick in his throat.

Troubled, he went to the kitchen to find Ialla, and there he found Mihabi as well. Ialla had just finished directing a number of the women in preparing a meal, and relative silence reigned throughout the large house as everyone within dined. Everyone except Ezhina, who ignored the plate Ialla put in front of him.

"Mother," he said finally. "Brother."

They both looked expectantly at him.

He spread his hands on the table and looked at them. Like every Bozandari male, he had taken military training and was expected to retrain several times a year. But despite the nicks and scars, his hands retained the look of a healer's.

"My son?" Ialla prompted.

Ezhina sighed. "I find myself torn. I feel a strong need to help your people gain freedom, but if one of you should go from my house to kill my people…how am I to live with that?"

Mihabi stopped eating. After a few breaths, he said, "I feel much the same, Ezhina. When I heard the song of Anahar and made my decision to leave, I was full of anger and hatred toward you and your people. Now, in the light of day, that anger dims, and the hatred seems misplaced. I do not know if I could kill Bozandari, and yet Anari blood runs in the marketplace. How am I to live with that? Anahar has called to us. My people must be free."

"Aye, you must. I agree. But I would that I might think of a means to do so without more bloodshed. I am sure there are those among both sides who deserve to die, but I am equally certain that there are even more among us who do not. But how is this thing to be stopped?"

Ialla sat on the bench facing both of them. "It cannot," she said simply, looking at Ezhina. "The Bozandari enslaved the Anari. We want our freedom. There are those among the Bozandari—many of them, in fact—who want things to stay as they are. We cannot petition your emperor or your judges to set us free. Already they have declared that it is legal to kill Anari slaves who flee their masters. We have no choice but to shed the blood of those who would keep us enslaved. And it is folly to wish it were otherwise. The Bozandari created this trouble. If the emperor will not end it, we must end it in blood."

"Mother," Mihabi said. "Surely you have not become so hardened that you can see no other path to peace?"

Now she turned to Mihabi. "Surely you are not so naive as to think we can simply put down our swords, plead our case, and be set free? Ezinha is a good and brave man, but he cannot speak for all of Bozandar. He knows this."

"Our mother speaks the truth," Ezinha said. "We have no choice but to be soldiers now. Our only choice is under whose banner we will fight. As for me, I will fight for my mother. I will fight for the Anari."

The army of the Snow Wolves marched north through the winding valleys. Tom found himself keeping his distance from Archer, looking at Archer with a suspicious eye, as if he were waiting for Archer to fail them. Yet Tess and her sisters, Cilla and Sara, walked with Archer every step of the way. Only at night, after they had made camp, could Tom spend time with his wife.

Even then, there was little time for talk. It was inevitable that some should be injured in the course of a day's march. Each evening, the Ilduin tended to those, as well as to those who had taken ill. By the time Sara could come to their tent, she was exhausted by the day's march and the evening's duties, ready to fall into sleep. While Tom recognized the necessity of their situation, it was not a proper honeymoon. Nor was it what he had considered when he had thought of marriage.

Now he was pitching their tent again, working alone as she and Tess and Cilla moved through the camp. The mood in the army had changed since their march through the canyon, and the reconciliation of Ratha and Tuzza. Distrust no longer dominated, and only a handful of brief scuffles had marred the peace of the past days. This, Tom thought, ought to have given him greater confidence in their cause. Instead, he simply felt alone.

"Sara stays busy."

Tom turned to see Archer at his side. "Aye. There is much work for the Ilduin."

"Aye," Archer said. "Let me help you pitch your tent, my friend. I have lacked for your counsel of late."

Tom simply nodded his assent, trying not to let his thoughts wander back to the dark warnings of the *Eshkaron Treysahrans*. And yet he could not escape them as he stood in Archer's presence.

"You are quiet, Tom," Archer said.

Tom nodded. "I am, my lord."

Archer's brow furrowed for a moment. "Have I hurt you in some way, Tom Downey? For you are ill at ease with me, and have been since we left Anahar. If I have given you any cause for offense, I know it not, but I offer you my apology regardless."

"You have done nothing," Tom said. "It is I who should apologize."

"Accepted," Archer said. "Still, I know you, young Tom Downey, and you would not act thus without reason. I entreat you, not as your lord, but as a longtime friend to your father and, I hope in these past months, to you as well. Tell me what darkens your face, prophet."

"You have been a staunch friend to my father, and to

me," Tom said, choosing his words carefully, mindful of Erkiah's admonition that Tom not discuss the prophecy with anyone. "Fear not that you have failed in that."

"If I have failed not in that, then in what have I failed?" Archer asked.

Tom looked up at him. "Do you need my blessing, Lord Archer? You know you are a strong and good man. You have fought to liberate the Anari, and even now we fight to free the world from the icy grip that your brother has wrought. For time out of legend you have traveled this world, doing right wherever you found yourself. You are Firstborn, yet now you come to the lowly foundling son of a gatekeeper, seeking forgiveness for wrongs you have not committed?"

Archer seemed to study him for a moment, as if stung by Tom's words. Finally he spoke. "Yes, Tom Downey. I, Archer Blackcloak, Annuvil of the Firstborn, come to the lowly foundling son of a gatekeeper. For no man is lowly, save for the man who thinks himself or others to be so. I think not thus. Do you?"

"No," Tom said, looking down. "I am sorry, Archer. I miss my wife and spill frustration on you. I am sorry."

"Trust not your wife," Archer said. "For in hope did she take you, in hope to remake you, and great her regret in the dark of the night."

Tom's jaw dropped as he heard the words. "That is…"

"The *Eshkaron Treysahrans*," Archer said. "It is an old poem, thought by some a prophecy, though many a wiser man has deemed it merely the bitter rambling of a bitter soul. It speaks nothing of your love for Sara, nor hers for you. It foretells no betrayal by her, nor you of her. It speaks only the darkest anger of a man who cannot feel even a glimmer of hope or love or goodness in his soul."

"You have read it?" Tom asked.

"As have you, apparently," Archer replied. "And now I know why you feel ill at ease."

"The final stanza—" Tom began.

"Is no more to be trusted than those before it. The bitter rambling of a bitter soul, Tom. Nothing more."

"You did not read it," Tom said, realization dawning. "You wrote it."

Archer paused for a long moment, then nodded. "Yes, Tom. I wrote it in a time when I could see no good in the world, and even less in myself. I have not always lived the life of my legend. Often, I was less than the lowest beast, drowning in sorrow and pain and shame. It was in such a moment that I put quill to parchment and wrote those words. I have long wished I could find every copy ever made and destroy them, for too many have sought wisdom in the ravings of a madman."

Chapter Sixteen

The camp had settled into quiet by the time Archer and Tom finished erecting the tent and Sara's few conveniences. Then Archer did something that sent a shiver through Tom.

Squatting beside a stack of wood and kindling prepared for the night's fire, Archer didn't bring out his flint and striker to ignite the tinder. Instead he passed his hand over the wood, murmured a few words, and in the blink of an eye a fire arose, burning as if it had been so for hours.

Tom gasped. Archer looked over his shoulder. "I wondered if I could do that again. It seems I can."

Tom edged closer and squatted beside him. "You have magicks?"

"I used to have more than such simple ones. After the great war, I lost the abilities. Not that I much missed them. I can build a fire without it. I can do many things without the old lore. And perhaps that was part of the lesson."

"That may be."

"Or, perhaps, the world is changing in such a way that magicks are growing more powerful again."

"I thought the Ilduin were the only ones who could do such."

Archer sighed and sat with his legs crossed on the cold desert ground. "They always had the greatest magicks. But in the first times, many of us had minor powers. Powers that helped lead us into trouble."

"What else can you do?"

"I know not, nor am I sure I want to." He frowned. "You do realize, Tom, that if the world is changing in such a way that my powers begin to return, my brother's powers will return as well."

Tom felt another shiver of fear. "What powers did he have in the past?"

"Have you ever met someone who, when they spoke, could persuade you to believe almost anything?"

"Not really. I have met some with great powers of persuasion, but not such that they could overcome my sense."

"Ardred could persuade you the sky was green if he bothered."

Tom turned that around in his mind, trying to grasp that kind of ability. "And you? Could you not?"

"No. It was not my gift. Nor am I sure that much would have changed had it been. The gods know I have had ample time to think on it. Ardred's persuasion helped lead us to paths that divided our people and our cities, but I am not sure that had it been otherwise the outcome would have been so very different. The Firstborn were inherently flawed."

"How so?"

One corner of Archer's mouth curled, and he reached for

a stick to poke at the fire. Sparks showered upward toward the inky sky, where an unexpected flash of lightning explained the lack of stars. Rain in the driest of Anari lands? Surely that was remarkable.

"Well," Archer said slowly, "I allowed myself to engage in war with my brother, to the detriment of all. And many joined both sides. Is that not a flaw? And of course there were others, lesser ones, but flaws all the same."

"And thus the Anari."

"And thus the Anari."

Tom stared into the leaping flames, trying to imagine all the things that must have led to the attempt to create a perfect race in the Anari. Trying to imagine how awful it would be to find oneself in a war against one's brother. Trying to imagine even a small part of the horrors Archer had been through.

Horrors that must have changed him, some little voice in his head whispered. *Horrors that gave rise to the* Eshkaron *you just read. Were they not an unguarded glimpse into this man's mind?*

A shudder passed through Tom, like a frosty wind passing through dessicated leaves. He was not at all happy with the direction his thoughts were taking. "So if you and your brother regain your powers, what will that do to the rest of us who have none?"

Archer's gray eyes, reflecting the dance of flame in the eeriest way, settled on Tom. "I wish I had an answer for you, Prophet. But I cannot see beyond the dark veil of the next moment in time. Had I been gifted with prophecy, none of the evils that befell the Firstborn might have happened. Certainly I would not have contributed to them."

He turned his attention back to the fire. "Theriel…" he

murmured quietly. "My Theriel. The first White Lady so pure of heart and soul. She warned us. She warned me. She begged me not to yield to my brother's provocations, nor to try to create a better race. She asked me, *If the gods could do no better than us, what makes you think you can do better?* But I was so convinced we could make a world without war."

He gave a bitter laugh. "You see how well I succeeded. Theriel would have no part in the creation of the Anari, save to bless them with long life and the gift of great art. Then she walked away and told us we must come to our senses. It was her death in the end that provoked the final battle. That caused her sisters to blast Dederand, the Second City, into a plane of glass."

Tom shivered again. "So terrible."

"There are not words for it. Theriel's death…I know the stories say my brother killed her. But he did not. He captured her, and sought to make her his own, just as he now seeks to enslave the Weaver, Second White Lady. My Theriel died by her own hand rather than break her vows to me. And with her died our son."

"I am so sorry…." Everything in Tom constricted as he thought how he would react if such happened to Sara. He doubted he could remain sane.

"I lost the best part of myself when I lost Theriel," Archer said. "I have heard many say that, but it was most certainly true in my case. Her gentle hand and words ever sought to guide me to righteous paths, to the good that I could do. I should have heeded her better. Instead I fell into the pit my brother set for me, allowed myself to become angry, and once I was angry it was but a small step for him to provoke me and my fellows into the war that he wanted."

"But why did he want a war?"

"Of that I am not certain. I suspect the gods had a hand in that. Certainly our father treated us as equals. He was the high king, and I was the firstborn son, but he gave us each dominion over our own city and lands, and while one city was called Samarand, the First City, and the other Dederand, the Second City, they were merely names. But, of course, he desired Theriel. Perhaps that was the thing that most insulted him, when Theriel did not choose him."

"But doesn't the story say she chose neither of you?"

One corner of Archer's mouth lifted in a bitter smile. "Our father would have been a far wiser king had he not hidden Ardred and me where we could hear the lady's words when he asked her which of us she would marry."

"I remember the words from the story," Tom replied. "She said, 'If I marry Annuvil, Ardred will kill him, and I cannot marry Ardred.'"

"Aye, 'tis as she spoke. The words are graven on my heart as if by a hot brand. The joy that filled me that day made me blind to the insult my brother felt. And yet, as I repeated her words over the years, I have realized the wisdom they evinced. Had we not been able to overhear her, my father might have simply let her go on her way, and ceased pressing her to wed either of us. In that, as brothers, we would have shared an equal loss, and perhaps that would have eased matters between us. Instead we heard, and knew, her preference. What had before been difficult, thereafter became impossible."

"But yet, should that not have been simply between the two of you?"

"As I said, we were flawed. Ardred had long built a faction to support himself. It gave him weight in council, and made it clear that if anything happened to end our father's reign, he would be the one to take the role of High King. I thought I did not so much care, for Samarand was quite enough to occupy me. As was my beautiful wife, once we wed. But my father, unbeknownst to me, had noted Ardred's desire for the high throne, and because Ardred desired it, my father felt him unfit. So it was that another faction was raised at my father's behest, though I did not know it. Many gathered around me, and added the weight of their words to mine. We soon found ourselves at odds over many public projects.

"Then Ardred persuaded the people of Dederand that Second City did not simply mean that it was the second city the Firstborn built. No, with his silver tongue he persuaded them that they were considered to be second in every way, that their influence was less than that of Samarand, that their wishes meant less…. Need I go on? Before long, jealousy and envy became the bane of the Firstborn. And between them they led to wars. At first the skirmishes were brief, a handful of fighters here and there trying to make a point. But as the conflicts became more common, it was as if the Firstborn developed a taste for them. Or if not a taste, at least a numbness to the horror."

Tom nodded. "I hope that never happens to me."

"I pray it will not, Tom. For men become worse than the worst of beasts when they no longer care how they slaughter others. War grew like a fevered illness, fed by unreasoning jealousies and resentments, and eventually by revenge. And I was no better than the rest."

"I think you undervalue yourself."

Annuvil shook his head. "I have learned my lessons

painfully, Tom. And I learned them when it was too late. Theriel argued in councils, telling us how foolish we were. She tried to persuade us back to sanity, but no ear seemed to hear. I even think…I even think I lost a part of her then." He shook his head as if to drive out a pain. "I know I failed her. I was not the man she thought."

Impulsively, Tom reached out and gripped Archer's forearm. "How many times have you and the others kept me from bloodying my own hands? Sometimes I wish still that I were a warrior, for I feel so useless with nothing to offer but an occasional riddle of prophecy. But you must not count yourself less than others, for we have all made war in our own ways, have we not? To this day the fight goes on. And now we have a chance to right a very old wrong."

"Time will show us. But rest assured, Tom, I am not the man I was meant to be. Nor am I certain that I can become that man, a man who would have been worthy of Theriel."

Rising, Archer strode away into the night, just as a misty rain began to fall, hissing and spitting on the fire. Tom stared into the flames, the slits of his leather mask making their light tolerable, and had the uneasy feeling that he could see a laughing face within the fire.

His mind drifted back to the horrible images in the *Eshkaron Treysahrans*, and once again he knew unease. A mind that could create those images, and hold forth such despair and bitterness, and even hatred… That wasn't the Archer he thought he knew now, but yet that was still Archer.

It would be wise, he decided finally, to watch very carefully. At this time he could not guess who would be the betrayer he foresaw in his dim visions of things to come.

It might well be Archer.

* * *

During the night, heavy sheets of rain fell. Men who had no tents huddled beneath shields and any other protection they could find. The desert rarely saw more than an occasional light rainfall, and this night's storm, crackling with thunder and lightning, caused a lot of uneasy comment.

The desert thirsted, of course, but not even its dryness could suck up the torrents, and soon small rivers and pools had formed in every hollow.

Together in Tess's tent, the three Ilduin listened to the hammering rain on the cloth above and bent their heads together, trying to sort through a welter of feelings and images that had begun to flit into their minds.

"I feel others reaching for us," Sara said. "Other Ilduin. I cannot tell if they are corrupt or not. Yet I feel that they are being stirred by events."

"I, too," agreed Cilla. "I wish there was some test we could apply, for if we ally with the wrong sister, we could abet the evil that comes."

Tess nodded, and poured a hot, bitter herb brew into stone cups for her sisters. It reminded her of something she had forgotten, but as usual she could not summon the memory. She had virtually given up trying to remember, certain only that Elanor would reveal what she chose when she chose. Until then, she, Tess, was a pawn in a game the gods played.

"This rain is unnatural," she said as she put the pot down on the folding table. "Do you feel it? It is no more natural than the winter has been."

The other two nodded.

"But it is more than unnatural," she continued, folding her hands and closing her eyes. "It is…" She trailed off, caught by some sort of strange image. "I see something."

Rising, she went to the door of her tent and stepped out into the deluge. Raising her gaze to the heavens, watching the flashes of lightning, she tried to grasp what it was she was sensing, seeing.

"Tess?" The other two had followed her and now stood beside her, their robes growing drenched. "What is it?"

"I see… I see…"

And indeed she did see something, though exactly what it was she could not be sure. It was as if a golden net were cast over the sky, but while it should have been even and beautiful, it was blackened and twisted in places. Some part of her rebelled violently at the ugliness, and she tried to imagine it whole and beautiful again, unscarred by whatever had damaged it.

Because in her deepest being, she knew those scars were unnatural.

"Tess?"

She hardly heard her companions. The part of her that had healed so many wounds seemed to leap from her heart and reach out to that scarred web. As she stared at it, it gradually began to heal, growing golden and straight once again.

The rain stopped. She didn't notice. The sky cleared. She didn't see. She saw only the web above her, and suddenly knew she had revealed herself. A blackness began to spread out from the far end of the web, to the north, approaching…approaching.

Terror filled her and her essence snapped backward, returning to her physical form, seeking to hide therein from whatever sent that blackness crawling toward her.

Weakness filled her and she began to sink to the ground.

"Tess?" Sara and Cilla caught her, their grips painfully tight. "Tess? Talk to us!"

The bite of their fingers kept her conscious just long enough to say, "I have seen the warp and woof. I have seen how he blights it. I have seen that he comes for me."

Then blessed darkness claimed her.

Archer arrived as soon as he received Cilla's summons. With him came Ratha and Tuzza. "What ails the lady?" Archer demanded as he stepped into the tent.

The rain had ceased abruptly, but the skies, which had cleared so suddenly, now dumped their endless burden once again. A river ran under the tent now, and at this rate would soon wash it away.

"I am not sure," Sara said. "We saw her step into the rain and stare up at the sky. We felt...power emanate from her, although it was unlike anything we know. Then she collapsed."

"Did she say anything?"

"Something about seeing the warp and woof, and that he is coming for her."

Archer's head jerked. "She spoke of the warp and woof?"

"Aye."

Ilduin and commanders alike stared at him. It was Cilla who spoke first. "You know what it means."

Archer knelt swiftly beside Tess and touched her cheeks. "More blankets. She is wet and growing cold."

The women immediately obeyed as best they could. It wasn't as if this army carried huge supplies with it.

"Archer," Sara demanded, "what did she mean?"

"She is indeed the Weaver."

"Most of us already knew that."

He lifted his face and looked directly at his four companions. Every line of him was stamped with anguish. "She has seen the warp and woof. The fabric that underlies our world, the fabric upon which the gods built all of this."

"And?"

"Of course Ardred wants her. If she can manipulate the warp and woof, then she is as powerful as the gods themselves."

Sara hastened to shake her head. "I think she stopped the storm, then she collapsed. She is limited by her own strength."

"But what if her strength grows? No one would be able to stop her, not even the gods themselves."

Silence filled the tent, except for the renewed drumming of the rain. Archer bent and brushed his hand gently against Tess's cheek before rising to face the rest of the group.

"Hear this and obey," Archer said. "Whatever else is at risk in the days to come, *she* must never fall into the Enemy's hands. *Never.*"

He scanned their faces and saw horror, discomfort, a mixture of unpleasant feelings.

"I repeat," he said, "she must never fall into the Enemy's hands. Not even should it cost her her life."

Then he strode from the tent, leaving the others to exchange looks and wonder if he was right.

Or if he could even be trusted.

Chapter Seventeen

The morning dawned clear and cool. The air, denuded of dust by the nighttime rain, was unnaturally crisp, and even with aging eyes Tuzza could pick out details in the column of men descending from a distant ridge. The gold-and-black lion's-paw pennants were clearly visible.

"They are Alezzi's men," Tuzza said.

Beside him, Ratha, Jenah and Archer stood silent. The Bozandari relief force was traveling faster than they had anticipated. Though contact was still a day away, it was clear that their final preparations would have to be made quickly. Too quickly. But such was too often the nature of war.

"I had hoped to meet them three leagues farther north," Jenah said, pointing at the map he had placed on the ground, each of its corners held by a rock. "There is a pass where we could have held a defensible position. But they are already descending from that pass."

"Alezzi would have seen the same situation on his map,"

Tuzza said. "He is a gifted commander and not to be under-estimated. Do not expect him to walk into any defile with his main body in the lead. He will have scout patrols ranging far to the front, as well as on his flanks."

"And we can't use his patrols against him as we did with you," Jenah said. "We want to avoid combat if at all possible."

Tuzza nodded. "We cannot afford to contact his patrols. His patrol commanders will have authority to make probing attacks, to determine our strength and positions. We must parley with him before that happens."

"You fear your men will not fight, brother?" Ratha asked.

Tuzza studied Ratha's face. There was no indication that the Anari was speaking with contempt. If he doubted the courage of Tuzza's men or their loyalty to him, there was no sign of it. He simply recognized what they all knew: whether Tuzza's Snow Wolves would be willing to kill their Bozandari brethren was an open question, and one best not put to the test.

"There are likely many in my legion who have blood brothers or cousins in Alezzi's legion," Tuzza said. "He himself is my blood cousin. I would grieve at his death, and whether it was my sword that felled him would matter not at all in my heart. To slay his own is not a weight I would wish upon any man."

Ratha seemed to study him before nodding. "You are right, my brother. Such a battle would offer no hope of victory, for there would be no victors. There would be only the dead and those whose souls have died while their bodies remain alive."

At this, Archer visibly winced. "I need to consult with Lady Tess," he said before walking away.

Tuzza exchanged looks with the two Anari who remained, but their faces were unreadable. Either they knew not what lay in Archer's mind, or they declined to share it. And it mattered not which at this point. Tuzza studied the map, trying to estimate how many patrols Alezzi would send out, and their likely routes of march.

"In terrain this rugged, Bozandari doctrine would call for Alezzi to break one of his foot regiments—a quarter of his force—into patrol groups of one or two companies. That would yield six such groups. Our standard practice is to have one to the rear, one each on the flanks, and three fanning out to the front."

Jenah nodded. "He would not use his horses for such?"

"He would if he were campaigning in the Adasen Basin, to the north," Tuzza said. "But he will have learned, as I did, that horses cannot move swiftly in these rocky lands. Too many of my men's mounts had to be put down with broken legs. However, he will have several mounted couriers with each patrol group. One or more of them will break off immediately when the patrol makes contact, to report the news to Alezzi."

"So we cannot risk even to ambush a patrol," Ratha said, his brow furrowed. "I must tell my men to avoid them completely. This limits their capacity to scout for us."

Tuzza nodded. "That is precisely the purpose of our patrol doctrine, my brother. There is a saying in our officer academy—'He who wins the skirmish wins the main.' And now we are forced to concede the patrol skirmishes, to retreat and evade, even at the risk of permitting him to find and calculate our main body. If we cannot carry the parley, I fear for our prospects in battle."

"We must disperse our main force," Jenah said.

Tuzza shook his head. "We risk too much. Alezzi can fall upon each camp and defeat us in detail."

"You have forgotten the Ilduin," Jenah said. "That was our advantage in the prior campaign. We separated our columns then, and communicated through our three Ilduin. Thus were we able to coordinate our columns, and bring them together quickly when needed."

"My brother is right," Ratha said to Tuzza. "You say that we cannot win the skirmish, but we can if we create an illusion for his patrols to report. We must evade them for only one day, yes?"

Tuzza nodded. "Yes. By tomorrow his main body will be close enough that we can approach for a parlay."

"We withdraw now," Ratha said. "We withdraw in three separate groups, each far enough that his patrols cannot reach us until nighttime. Then we tell each squad to pitch three tents and build three campfires."

Tuzza smiled. "Alezzi's patrols would not attack so large a force. Instead, they will report to him that he is outnumbered. We both avoid the skirmish and give him more reason to avoid the main. It is a brilliant stratagem."

"Then it is agreed," Jenah said. "Let us issue the orders. The Snow Wolves will not fail."

"No," Tuzza said, feeling more comfortable than he had in some time. "We will not fail."

Ezinha's hand gripped the sword tightly, betraying the tension that filled him with dread. While he had served his required time in the Bozandari army, he had done so as a healer and not as a soldier. He had never killed a man, and he was not certain that he could. Yet on this night, he knew, he might well have to do just that.

Count Drassa Langel, the emperor's minister of war, had urged the court to declare the Anari rebels guilty of treason. All rebels now lay under sentence of death, and in the absence of the rebels themselves, the sentence was to be carried out on their families. The emperor had issued a declaration of martial law, and Langel's troops were now moving through the city with brutal efficiency, rounding up Anari whose kin were suspected of participating in the rebellion.

The rebels had until tomorrow at noon to surrender themselves. If not, well over a thousand Anari—including women and children—would be impaled on stakes throughout the city, to die slowly of thirst and exposure and agony, their bodies left for birds and then animals to pick clean, as a symbol to anyone else who might consider challenging the Bozandari throne. Not a single street corner in Bozandar would escape the screams of the dying, nor the stench of the dead.

Ezinha had long known Langel, for the count had been a friend of his father's. And, like his father, Langel was a cruel and hard man. This was no idle bluff. Nor, Ezinha suspected, would the surrender of the rebels forestall the executions. If the Anari would not be docile and loyal slaves, then Langel meant to exterminate them to the last.

Mihabi and the other rebels knew this. They would not surrender themselves, and Ezinha had not challenged their decision. Nearly three hundred now sheltered on his estate and he knew there were at least five other Bozandari homes that held an equal number. Their leaders had convened at Ezinha's house for a council of war. He could see no other option. Better to die in battle, fighting for their lives and freedom, than to hang for days, dying by inches on a wooden stake.

Lacking military training, the rebel attack plan was born of simplicity, aided by the dispositions of Langel's troops. They had established a dozen camps throughout the city, each with a hundred or more Anari prisoners guarded by a company of Bozandari legionnaires.

But not all of the Bozandari would be guarding the prisoners, all of whom were bound and helpless. Instead, many were busy erecting the stakes upon which the condemned would be placed, rounding them so that the victims would slip slowly down onto them, screaming as the unyielding wood pushed up through their bowels until, days later, the pressure would make it mercifully impossible for them to breathe.

It was the most brutal form of all the Bozandari methods of execution, and Ezinha was ashamed that his own people were capable of such cruelty. He could almost grasp how the legionnaires themselves, hardened by the privations of battle, could perform their tasks. What he could not fathom, and what truly sickened him, was how other people could bear to watch such a horror. And yet he knew they would come out by the thousands, fueled by a blood-lust that repulsed Ezinha, jeering at the victims, cheering at their agonized screams, groaning with disappointment when death finally relieved the suffering.

He had overcome his qualms about fighting such a people. They might be his own in blood, but he could not place himself among such men. If his choice was to stand with the crowds and delight in the pain of innocents, or to take up a sword and join the Anari in battle, it was an easy choice indeed.

The rebels had split into groups, each group assigned one of the compounds where the Anari prisoners were held, each man carrying two swords, one with which to fight and another that he might arm those he freed. Then rescuers and rescued together would fight their way out of the city, taking with them any other Anari who sought freedom and were willing to join the march. They would assemble on a hilltop two days' march west of the city, and there they would prepare to march south to their homeland.

Although Ezinha was no soldier, he believed it was a good plan. He also recognized that it was the only path left open to them. Now—as he crouched in the darkness and watched two legionnaires joke between them as they slathered suet over the end third of the stake, explaining to a young Bozandari boy that they were making it slick to ensure that, once impaled, its victim could gain no purchase with his or her feet—he realized it was also the right path. The boy was nodding eagerly. Ezinha had never felt hatred until this night, watching these two men. He felt it now.

Mihabi grasped his arm and nodded into the darkness. Ezinha could barely see the three Anari in the alley across the way, hiding in the shadows, waiting to pounce.

Ezinha looked in his brother's eyes and saw the same fury. Boys should not be taught such hateful skills, and whether these legionnaires themselves were taught as boys did not matter. They were men now, not merely performing but rejoicing in their duty to inflict agony and death, passing their twisted hearts on to a child who could not be more than six years of age.

If there was ever to be peace, if the Bozandari were ever to return to their noble roots, such legacies must end. And this one would end tonight.

The sound of hammer against cymbal, beginning in the

center of the city, was too faint to hear at first. But it spread quickly, as a woman at each signal post stood poised to repeat it as soon as she heard it. Within seconds, the sound of clanging cymbals had rippled through the city, to be joined immediately by the sounds of battle.

Ezinha leapt from the alley where he had crouched, with Mihabi at his side, both with swords at the ready, closing on the two legionnaires with shouts of fury. The Bozandari, suddenly outnumbered and surrounded, had no choice but to fight and die where they stood.

And die they would.

They were trained, while Ezinha and his companions were not, but training can go only so far. Ezinha saw an opening as one of the Anari slashed the back of the man in front of him. The man turned, for an instant, his focus on Ezinha broken. The instant was long enough.

Lifting his sword with both hands and swinging with all his might, Ezinha caught the legionnaire in the side of the neck. The force of the blow carried the sword down through the man's shoulder and into his chest, but the deadly damage had been inflicted almost immediately. Blood geysered from the man's throat, spraying Ezinha's face with its thick, coppery taste. Ezinha lifted a foot and pushed the dying body off of his sword, then turned to the other legionnaire. But the other soldier was already falling to the ground, Mihabi's sword buried in his chest.

Only then did Ezinha see the head of the young boy, rolling past his own foot. Part of him hoped it had been hewn off by a stray blow. And part of him did not care.

"Come," he said. "There are more and we must work quickly."

The Night of the Black Sword had begun.

* * *

"Ratha's scouts have identified a Bozandari patrol west of his camp," Tess said, repeating the information that Cilla had sent.

Tuzza smiled. They were sitting in Archer's tent, a map spread below them, a dim lantern the only light. Tuzza placed a wooden disk on the map, indicating the location Tess had described. "That is the second of Alezzi's three forward elements."

"If indeed there are three," Archer said.

"There will be, my lord," Tuzza said, his voice full of confidence. "Alezzi will not rest this night until he knows, or believes he knows, the precise location of each of our bodies. Indeed, he will not rest then, for once he has that information he will hold a council of war with his senior commanders. They will finalize their attack plans, issue their orders, and prepare a report to the emperor, to be dispatched by rider at first light. Then, and only then, will he allow himself a few hours' sleep."

"First the horse, then the saddle, then the man," Tess said, instantly wondering whence the phrase had come. Yet another grain of dust from her past, blown into her present consciousness.

Tuzza looked at her, surprise etched on his features. "That is a saying among our cavalry, my lady. Its meaning is plain for them, for that is the sequence in which they care for their mounts and themselves at the end of a day's march. But I can see how you apply it here. Our academy instructors would say 'Duty before comfort, and comfort before sleep.'"

Tess smiled sadly. "In many respects, the ways of war are universal, Topmark. Those who forgo duty accomplish nothing. Those who forgo comfort, in the form of hot meals and dry clothes, will quickly fall ill. But those who forgo sleep for too long are no less useless than the rest when the time of battle comes. And we have forgone much rest on this march."

"Aye, my lady," Tuzza said. "But I would not rest if I lay there wondering about Alezzi's plans. The third of his patrols will be spotted soon. Then I can rest with the peace of a commander who has done his duty."

"Then let us use the time wisely," Tess said, "and not simply sit here waiting. What do you intend to say to your cousin on the morrow?"

"I will speak of justice," Tuzza said simply.

Archer looked at him. "Not of the Weaver?"

Tuzza shook his head. "My cousin is a brilliant overmark, but a very practical man. From the time he was a child, he cared naught for the games of the gods and those who professed to know them. But he is a just man."

"Tell me more about him," Tess said.

Tuzza laughed. "Where to begin? With the boy who could work his numbers before I could count? Or should I tell you of the young rearmark who knowingly took his men into the teeth of a bandit ambush in the Deder desert, to draw away their strength so that his regiment could cross a gully and form ranks before its final attack?"

"Both," Tess said.

"And I will say much of neither," Tuzza replied, "for neither is the measure of the man. The former was a gift, albeit a gift to which he dedicated himself. The latter was an act of desperation, assigned him by an overmark who lacked the discipline to patrol properly on the eve of battle and looked upon his enemies with scorn. Too many of

Alezzi's men did not live to see the fruits of victory, and forever after he swore never to repeat that mistake."

"Too many of life's lessons are purchased in blood," Tess said.

Tuzza nodded. "And worse, too few even learn those, so we must purchase the same lessons again and again with new blood. And in this, perhaps, I can come closest to sharing the man who is my cousin, Topmark Alezzi. He has no room in his life for the ways of court. Since he joined the army, he has spent fewer days in Bozandar than any of our topmarks. His place is in the field, with his men, and never has he taken a single luxury that his men lacked."

"And thus you will speak of justice," Tess said, now understanding the beautiful simplicity of Tuzza's plan.

"I will speak of truth," Tuzza said. "There are men who believe they are born to a life of ease. They purchase that life of ease with the sweat and the blood of others. But no man was born to live thus. This dark greed—this will to enslave others—is the work of the Enemy. Some have resisted that darkness. My cousin is one of those men. His father owns slaves, or did when I left Bozandar, but Alezzi did not accept the gift of them when he joined the army. Lest you read too much hope in that, he made that choice simply because his men would not have servants, and he did not believe himself entitled to anything more than the lowliest soldier in his command. And while many junior officers believe thus, rank and its privileges change most of us. They did not change Alezzi."

Archer drew a breath. "The question is whether he will believe the way of the soldier should apply in the estates of Bozandar as well. Has he ever spoken against the keeping of Anari as slaves?"

Tuzza shook his head. "If he has, it was never in my presence. But I must confess that there was a time when I kept slaves, a stain on my soul that perhaps he wished not to call to mind. I am two years older than he, and thus I was always his senior in the army. Moreover, my family ranks above his in the list of court. These are barriers that one does not cross in Bozandar, however strong the bond between cousins. And ours was strong indeed."

"I pray that it is still strong," Archer said. "And I pray that your cousin truly is a man of justice. For no man of justice can doubt the rightness of our cause."

"Jenah's scouts have found the third patrol," Tess said. "But his scouts were also found. And there was fighting. Three Anari and two Bozandari were slain, and Sara is now treating the wounded."

"We have shed blood," Tuzza said, shaking his head sadly as he placed the last of the three disks on the map. "This will make tomorrow much more difficult."

"We could not hope for a bloodless campaign," Archer said. "But we can hope that this is all of the blood that will be spilled before the gates of Bozandar."

"Yes," Tess said, fighting back tears as she watched Sara move among the bodies. Tess tried to lend her power to Sara's, but some men were beyond Ilduin touch. "Yes. We *must* hope."

Chapter Eighteen

Mihabi moved swiftly, Ezinha at his side. They and their companions had taken the four execution stations assigned to them, and were now moving toward the compound where the condemned Anari were being held. Blood flowed from a wound on Mihabi's hand, but that was a trifle when placed beside the blow Ezinha had taken. Mihabi had heard the harsh crack as the hilt of the Bozandari sword had crashed into Ezinha's side. That his former master, now his brother, had suffered a broken rib was beyond question. That he continued to fight, however, left Mihabi in awe.

The stealth of their earlier attacks was no longer a viable strategy. The whole of Bozandar had been awakened by the sounds of cymbals and swords, and lanterns glowed in every window, torches flickering in every street. There would be no surprise when Mihabi and his comrades fell upon the prison compound. The legionnaires would be ready and waiting, bolstered by citizens who had flowed out of their houses to join their ranks. More would die, and not all of them Bozandari. But the die was cast, and on this night, Mihabi had no fear of death.

"You must rest, brother," he said to Ezinha, whose wheezing sounded ever more labored with each step.

"No," Ezinha said. "I will rest when we are free."

"You were free when this war began," Mihabi said.

Ezinha turned to him. "How can a man who treats other men as chattels be himself free? He is but in the thrall of a greater and darker master, whether he knows it or not. I will be free when all are free, Mihabi."

Mihabi heard the pain in his brother's voice, and knew that gathering the extra breath to speak must feel as fire in his rib cage. "Speak no more, brother. Rather save what strength you have."

Ezinha nodded.

With each block their number grew. Slaves who had quailed at the thought of rebellion had slipped out of estates bearing makeshift weapons, and the once-scattered rebel attack groups were assembling on the march. Mihabi was surprised by how well the untrained army had performed thus far. He was also concerned, lest overconfidence give way to panic when the fight at the compound began. For it would not be as easy as what had come before.

Already he could see the makeshift prison up ahead, little more than a ragged but effective stockade within which bound Anari shouted encouragement to their rescuers. It was what lay in front of the stockade that gave Mihabi pause: nearly a full company of Bozandari legionnaires, drawn up in battle order, eyes full of cold fury.

Mihabi knew there would be no subtlety, no craft in this

attack. The Bozandari streets, however wide, gave too little room for maneuver. Nor could the rebel army have performed such maneuvers; there simply had not been time or opportunity to train in the arts of war. No, this would be a headlong charge, fury against fury, sword against sword, will against will.

Mihabi lifted his sword as they closed with the Bozandari. From the corner of his eye, he saw that Ezinha could barely hoist his sword to waist level, yet Ezinha did not retreat. The clang of metal against metal, the battle cries of enraged men, and the screams of the wounded soon filled the streets around the compound.

Mihabi slashed across the throat of the legionnaire before him, hardly pausing to notice the man fall before wading deeper into the melee. The street was slick with blood, and more than once a man died because his footing gave way in the midst of what might otherwise have been a killing blow to his enemy. The air was foul with the scent of killing, and Mihabi fought the urge to gag each time he drew breath.

Still, the Anari now outnumbered the legionnaires by a considerable number, and while some Bozandari citizens had thought to join the battle, many paled at the action and quietly slipped out of harm's way. Generations of pent-up rage spilled out as Anari slashed with swords, daggers, kitchen knives, spades, scythes, axes and simple clubs. Heads split open with sickening hollow cracks, and limbs and chests were hewn with the wet *shuck* of a butcher's blade cutting meat.

And then there was silence, save for the moans of those for whom death would be a mercy.

Mihabi wiped blood from his face, though in truth he

merely smeared it, for his arms were even slicker with the coppery milk of battle. Many Anari had fallen around him. Many within the compounds would be rescued, only to grieve at the deaths of sons and brothers and fathers. But they would be free, for the Bozandari lay in the streets to a man, ragged, groaning, or with voices forever stilled.

Mihabi was the first to reach the compound, and he hacked at the heavy chain with which the Bozandari had secured the gate. Sparks flew as his sword fell again and again, his muscles moving in a brutal, incessant rhythm, his voice screaming rage and freedom with every stroke, until the chain gave way and the gate sagged open from the weight of those behind, once condemned, now free.

But not yet free.

For they still had to make their way out of the city, and Mihabi had no doubt that the Bozandari would not lie down and let them walk out unopposed. He turned, looking for Ezinha in the seething mass, but Ezinha was nowhere to be seen. Perhaps he had finally given in to pain, sagging in an alley. If so, Mihabi knew he must rescue his brother as well, for the Bozandari would doubtless wreak the cruelest vengeance on those among them who had aided the rebellion. The thought of Ezinha dying slowly on a stake filled Mihabi with dread, anger and determination.

As his comrades cut the bonds of the prisoners and thrust swords into their freed hands, Mihabi walked the street, calling his brother's name, searching the faces of the fallen in the guttering torchlight.

Somehow he heard a familiar moan among the hundreds of other moans, and followed that sound as a dog might follow a scent, turning his head this way and that to locate the source.

While he knew he was drawing closer, the moan seemed fainter with each step he took. And when he reached the recessed doorway of a bakery along the street, he realized why. His brother lay in the doorway, blood dripping from the stump of an arm, the rest of which lay somewhere in the carnage of the street.

"Ezinha," Mihabi said, kneeling at the side of the man who had been his friend, his master, his protector, his comrade in arms and his brother. "We will get help."

Ezinha's eyes found focus as he searched Mihabi's face. "I am beyond help, my brother."

"No," Mihabi said, tears stinging his eyes. "No, I will find a doctor."

Ezinha lifted his arm, grimacing at the pain, and placed it to Mihabi's cheek. "I am a doctor, Mihabi. I know what the body can endure, and what cannot be cured by any medicine we have."

Blood bubbled from Ezinha's mouth as he spoke, and Mihabi dabbed it away.

"Yes," Ezinha said. "The rib has pierced my lung. There is no healer in all of Bozandar who can treat that. But it is no matter."

"No," Mihabi said, tears now joining the blood that trickled down his ebony face. "No. You cannot die."

"It is no matter," Ezinha said, his voice almost too faint to hear. "For I will die a free man. As will you, my brother. And for that, I will go to the gods with joy."

"Stay with me, brother," Mihabi said, cradling Ezinha's head in his arms. "Stay with me."

"Elanor asks for me," Ezinha whispered. "Only hold my hand, I beg you, as I go to her."

"Yes," Mihabi sobbed. "Yes, I will. I promise."

Mihabi took Ezinha's hand in his, holding it to his brother's chest. He kissed his brother's forehead, willing himself not to close his eyes, nor even to blink, lest Ezinha feel alone in that last instant. Ezinha's chest struggled to rise one last time.

And it could not.

Mihabi wept.

For all of the hardships his life had known, none approached that moment. The moment when his brother's body, the body that had chased him through the woods of the estate and hidden with him under Ialla's table, the lips that had spoken in whispers and giggled as their mother searched for them, the eyes that had shone with the joy and promise of childhood, then darkened with the weight of adulthood, only to shine again these past days, the arms that had wrestled with him, the heart that had beat with glee and with sorrow…

…the moment when that body became only dead flesh.

"Go to Elanor," Mihabi whispered. "May she welcome you as a brother of freedom and truth. And, I beg you, prepare a place for me, where we will once again hide under mother's table."

Mihabi rose, hefting his brother's body onto his shoulders. He would not leave Ezinha to be a cruel signpost of the Bozandari, even in death. He joined the ranks of the Anari walking out of the city.

He joined the ranks of the free.

The morning sun glittered harshly, as if the air had turned to crystal. The sound of marching feet seemed a sharp counterpoint that might shatter the morning like a rock tossed through glass.

At last silence fell, broken only by the flap of banners on the breeze. With a plain between them, the Black Lions of Bozandar faced the Snow Wolves of Anahar.

Alezzi's scouts had told him of the banner this army carried, and in the quiet of the night, when no one was about, he remembered stories he had heard from his Anari nanny. Stories she claimed were true, some of them about the history of the Firstborn, some about the Anari, and some that had been more like prophesies. He had dismissed many of the latter as the hopes of an enslaved people.

But the Snow Wolf…that story had captured his child's imagination. The Snow Wolf, it was said, had broken with its kind to serve one person in history, the White Lady of the Firstborn. It was said that when she died, the snow wolves had disappeared into the mountains, far to the north, at the headwaters of the Adasen. It was so rare that a single snow wolf pelt would sell for enough to make a trapper wealthy for life.

It was also said that the snow wolves would return one day, no longer hiding but walking with a woman, she who would be called the Weaver of Worlds.

The old Anari woman had assured him the Weaver would come to save her people from oppression, but she hadn't told him that more than twice before his father had beaten her into silence.

But Alezzi remembered that story now, and a chill ran down his spine as he looked through his glass and saw that the banners of the legion facing him were all of a white wolf rampant. Including, to his horror, the Bozandari who stood at the very heart of this abomination of a formation.

Bozandari fighting *with* the Anari? The rumors had come to his ears, but he had dismissed them. No Bozandari soldier could be guilty of such treason. And most certainly not his cousin Tuzza. He had been convinced that what his scouts had seen was nothing other than their brethren being marched as prisoners, possibly as hostages.

But what he saw arrayed before him now he could not mistake. The survivors of his cousin's legion were arrayed for battle, ready to fight their own kindred.

Alezzi had been hardened by many years of service, but he was not hard enough to look at this without feeling betrayed to his core. He had been sent to rescue his cousin's legion, and his cousin who was so dear to the emperor. Instead he must now fight them as enemies.

He was about to lift his arm and signal his army to descend from the hills and meet the Enemy on the plain below—for what other option did he have?—when a sight stayed his gesture.

Descending from the facing hills came three riders: a Bozandar by whose posture in the saddle he recognized as his cousin, a man all in black with a gleaming sword at his side and a quiver and bow on his back and—most striking of all—a woman clad all in white who, to his disbelieving eyes, seemed to gleam as if she were part of the morning light itself.

They carried a parley flag with them, overlaid squares of black and white. He could have ignored it and simply attacked, but his cousin was out there, and curiosity was too strong to ignore.

"It is a trick," his lieutenant Malchi said.

"It is my cousin. I will go to meet him and see what he has to say."

"They are using him."

"Perhaps. And perhaps he uses them."

Malchi's brows lifted. "I had not thought of that."

"Which is why I command this force and you do not."
It was a harsh statement, but Alezzi had always found
Malchi to be of less use than trouble, a man who had risen
to his present position simply by connections and money,
having earned none of it himself. Alezzi's family, and by ex-
tension Tuzza's, had always scorned those who failed to
understand that wealth and position carried with it great
responsibility. They were not merely toys for the lazy.

"Who will you take?"

"Why, you, of course," Alezzi answered, as if there could
be no doubt. In truth, he would rather have the man at his
side than behind him where he could make mischief. "My
standard bearer and one swordsman."

"Only one?"

"Aye. I can protect myself, but you might need some protection."

Malchi's face turned a deep hue of red, and anger flared
in his eyes. Had Alezzi not already known what a powerless
toad the man was, he might have become genuinely concerned. As it was, while Malchi had his faction within the
legion, they numbered far fewer than Alezzi's supporters.

A short while later, he and his small band ventured forth
to meet his cousin and companions. Alezzi, however, did
not carry the parley flag; he carried his own black lion. Let
them know that they were not safe from attack should he
consider it necessary.

Tuzza watched his cousin's approach with mixed
feelings. The two of them had been closer than brothers
most of their lives, though the demands of their positions
had often carried them hundreds of leagues apart.

It was good to recognize his cousin riding toward him. It was not good to see the banner his cousin's standard bearer carried, for it was a message of no mercy, a message of readiness to attack. They were not to be granted the ancient rule of protection for this meeting.

"It is not good," Archer murmured. "Tess, you must head back to the army. We cannot afford to lose you."

"You will not lose me." Her voice carried not a shadow of doubt.

Archer sighed exasperatedly and wondered how it was he had let the woman talk him into joining them. Hadn't he only yesterday said she must not be taken, even if it meant her life? Yet here he was, allowing her to expose herself in a way that might very well require him to slay her to keep her from capture.

But somehow it was impossible to ignore the decree of an Ilduin when she drew herself up and fire flashed from her eyes. So like Theriel, he sometimes thought, yet even greater in power, for he had, to his own sorrow, ignored Theriel too often.

Tuzza looked at the two of them, one on each side of him, then shrugged and shoved the parley banner's staff into the ground so both his hands would be free. The wind lifted it and flapped it, that dull sound that fabric made, a sound that had accompanied most of his adult life. It was rare, however, to hear it in the kind of silence that swathed the plain right now.

At last the sound of the hooves of the approaching horses could be heard. Tuzza did not misunderstand his brother's message in bringing an additional swordsman. The beginning of this talk would be difficult indeed.

Alezzi reached them and reined his steed. His eyes, very

like Tuzza's, scanned the two men and the woman before him. "Who commands here?"

Tuzza answered, "In what way, cousin?"

Alezzi's brow lifted. "Who commands this army?"

Tuzza signed toward Archer. "Annuvil. Firstborn son of the Firstborn king. And the Lady Tess." He gestured toward her. "The Weaver who was foretold."

Alezzi's face reflected shock, then scorn. "Are you maddened by your losses, cousin? You listen to children's tales? You are seeing things?"

"The things I have seen I have not imagined. I was close to death, but this lady saved me. She saved hundreds, friend and foe alike. She walks with the white wolf."

Again the chill passed down Alezzi's back. "And you have become a traitor, cousin?"

Tuzza shook his head. "I have much to tell you and show you, Alezzi. But give me the time. Then, if you are unpersuaded, you may kill me and join the battle. But it is a battle you will not win, for this army is guarded by Ilduin."

Again the chill ran along Alezzi's spine, even as his mind tried to rebel and tell him that clearly Tuzza had lost his mind. He glanced toward Malchi and saw that his lieutenant would gladly draw his sword right now and begin the fight.

Perhaps it was Malchi's expression as much as anything that made Alezzi hesitate. He never respected the wisdom of bloodlust.

He looked at the lady again, and saw a light that seemed to shine from within. Then he looked at the large, silent man in black, the one his brother had called Annuvil, and sensed something of great dignity and patience. What he did not see on any of the three faces before him was the hunger he saw on Malchi's face.

"We will talk," Alezzi said.

Malchi started to object and Alezzi turned to the swordsman he had brought with them. "Guard Malchi from all harm," he said to the man. "But at the same time, make certain he stays here and talks to no one."

The swordsman, one of the strongest and most trustworthy in the legion, a strong supporter of Alezzi, nodded. "Aye, Overmark. So it shall be."

Then Alezzi looked at his cousin. "I will give you the remainder of the day to persuade me why I should not condemn you as a traitor and wipe your misbegotten army from the face of the world."

Chapter Nineteen

Within an hour, a huge bonfire had been lit in the center of the plain, a sign to both armies that a parley was taking place. As long as that fire burned, none would take action against their foes.

Alezzi, and even Malchi, as it happened, learned something very important in the building of that fire. While soldiers had gathered the dead wood from the surrounding hills (and much there was, this being a desert) and laid it, it was a wave of Annuvil's hand and a few murmured words that set it ablaze.

Alezzi, sitting on a camp stool, felt awe creep into his every bone. All knew the Ilduin had possessed magicks, and one Ilduin worked for the Bozandari emperor, a woman who, to Alezzi's way of thinking, accomplished very little that couldn't have been done as well with a few spies.

But since the First Times, no man had possessed magicks

of any sort. He looked at the one who claimed to be Annuvil, and began to wonder.

Then Annuvil, he whom the others called Archer, pulled from his scabbard a sword so beautiful that Alezzi wondered what mortal could have forged it.

"This is Banedread," Annuvil said. He lifted it, and in his hand it began to hum, making a sound not unlike the most beautiful of crystal chimes. "In my hand alone will it sing, and to my command alone will it come. It has accomplished awful deeds in the past, Alezzi. It alone can kill me or kill the Enemy who faces us. It alone can murder the Firstborn."

He thrust it point down into the sand and let it stand for all to see. "It alone can be used to kill me," he repeated. "If you think we play you false as we talk, take it and pierce me. I will not see another dawn."

The Lady Tess gasped, and made to move as if she would shield the sword, but then she sank back on her small stool and sighed. "Trust we must have."

"Aye," said Annuvil. "And we must have it now, or the Enemy will triumph and turn all the world to his evil ways. Only through trust can we triumph against the coming dark."

Alezzi looked at his cousin. "Speak to me, Tuzza. Tell me why you have turned against your own kind."

"But I have not, cousin. The threat facing Bozandar is greater than that of a slave uprising, or a war for independence by the people we have oppressed. What lies ahead of us if we fail now will be an oppression beyond any we have inflicted on others."

"But how can you know this?"

Tuzza looked at the Lady Tess. "She walks with the Snow Wolf. It is the time prophecy has foretold."

"You have seen this?"

"I and my entire legion, or what is left of it. The white wolves came with her like an escort, and the biggest walked beside her."

"I find this hard to believe. Those tales…they were but cautions for the nursery!"

"Would it were so," said Annuvil. "Would it were so."

Tuzza kicked at a pebble with the toe of his boot, as if to unleash a frustration beyond words. "Have you any idea what happens in Bozandar, cousin? I would have turned about to go to the city's aid were it not that our emperor loves you so much. Were it not that the mothers and wives of your legionnaires demanded their bodies be returned. The streets run with blood. A messenger has come but recently to say that the Anari slaves have revolted and killed hundreds, if not thousands. That even now they flee the city and head toward my legion. What do you expect me to do?"

"Let them flow through you as water flows around rocks. When they meet their fellows, they will know why they were called."

"Called?" Alezzi looked up. "By the gods, who called them?"

"Anahar," Tess said quietly. "Her stones sang, and her song reached the heart of every Anari. Those who were free to do so came and joined our army to withstand Tuzza's attack. The rest…apparently the rest have answered Anahar's call in the only way they could, by gaining their freedom."

"How can there be any good in so much bloodshed?"

Tess's gaze turned steely. "How can there be any good in slavery?"

Malchi snorted, ignoring the order he had been given to remain silent. "Some are meant to be slaves. It is right that the powerful should use them."

"So power makes right?" Annuvil asked, looking at Malchi.

"Aye, that it does. The strongest arm, the deadliest sword. These are what grant authority, and those who do not have them are fated to serve beneath the heel of the strongest."

Annuvil nodded slowly. "Then I am the most powerful man you will ever meet, Malchi, and it is only just that you should lie beneath my heel."

Malchi's face reddened and he took a threatening step toward Archer. The man set to guard him moved to block him, but Archer waved him back. "No, we must settle this now. This man misunderstands true power."

"I do not!"

"Aye, you do. If the ability to deliver death is power, then I have more power than you will ever have in a lifetime. If it elevates, then it has elevated me to near godhood. I have helped destroy entire cities in my time. I am the one who caused the creation of the plain of Dederand. Have you seen it, Malchi? Have you looked upon the leagues and leagues of black glass where nothing will ever again grow? That happened because of me. So let us talk of power."

Malchi stepped back, his eyes uncertain.

"Aye, think about it, Malchi. True power lies with the Lady Tess. Power beyond your imagining. Perhaps you should place her heel upon your neck right now. But the most interesting thing, Malchi, is that she would not let you do so. For all her power, she wishes none to bow to her. And when she calls upon her power, it is to save and almost never to destroy. For she understands power, Malchi. The real power is the power to help."

Malchi spat. "That is weakness, not power."

Annuvil shook his head. "I pity you."

"You pity me? You are a madman whose mind has been bent by ancient tales until you think you are immortal. There are no immortals, and you are but a pale shadow of a true man. As for her…" He looked at Tess. "She plays tricks with her white dogs. They are not the snow wolves of which prophecy speaks."

Tuzza spoke sharply. "Malchi, you do not know of what you speak. Be silent!"

But Malchi had other plans. Before anyone could stop him, he leapt toward Tess, grabbed her and held a knife to her throat. "Power? If she has power, let her save herself now."

The men had risen to their feet, as if they would act, but the knife blade pressed too close to Tess's throat.

"Let the woman go, Malchi," Alezzi barked. "Let her go or I will see you drawn and quartered and left for the buzzards."

"Then so be it, but at least you will no longer consider turning traitor to your people! You will see that these three lie to you, that your cousin is deluded."

"Malchi." Tess spoke quietly. To the surprise of the others, her eyes showed no fear, only sorrow. "Malchi, cut me not, for my blood judges."

"Tripe!"

"I have seen it," Annuvil said. "Let her go. If you so much as prick her, you will burn in a fire beyond your imaginings."

Malchi glared at him, his knife still pressed to Tess's throat.

"Malchi," she said again. This time her tone was less sorrowful, more steely. "I pray you, do not do this thing. Save yourself. Spare me, spare all of us, the horror of what my blood will do to you."

With those words, she began to glow faintly, a blue aura that crackled. Malchi was startled but did not release her. "Soft words and pale magicks. They may fool ignorant Anari, but they will not fool me."

Then, as if to prove he was not intimidated, he moved his knife, drawing it down Tess's cheek and laying it open.

Tess cried out once, but her cry was nothing compared to the shriek that issued from Malchi's throat as her blood dripped on him. Alezzi stared in horror as Tess's blood spurted freely onto his lieutenant, and everywhere it landed he began to burn. It was not a natural fire, but one that burned inward, blackening deep holes in his flesh. He dropped his knife and backed away, still screaming.

"Oh, Elanor, I cannot save him!" Tess cried, recoiling from the horror of what her blood had done. She reached out as if to lay hands on Malchi, who now rolled in the dirt in agony, but Annuvil pulled her back.

"No, my lady. You must not. Your blood has judged him. He is beyond the power of anyone to save now. You will only bleed on him more."

She turned swiftly away, covering her ears, trying to close out the gruesome scenes and sounds. Alezzi stared both in horror and amazement as the drops of her blood fell to the desert sands and small blue flowers appeared almost immediately. Behind her, Malchi's cries weakened, and finally died.

He noted, too, that where Tess's blood fell on Annuvil, it did not burn. Truly the woman's blood was a judgment. He knew then for certain: She was who they claimed she was.

In his entire life, he had bowed to no man or woman save the emperor, but he bowed now to the Ilduin. He had seen all the proof he needed.

Annuvil nodded his way, then swept Tess into his embrace, covering her shaking figure with his black cloak, holding her as if he would suck the pain from her if only he held on tightly enough.

"'Twas not your choice, my lady," he murmured. "You did not choose this. It was not by your will that Malchi died, but by his. You warned him."

She shook with sobs now. "Why must I be so cursed?"

"You must be protected until the Enemy is defeated. It is for this reason that your blood judges. And it will judge whether you will or no whoever seeks to harm you. But it is not for you that it protects you. It is for all of us."

She lifted her tear-stained face to search his eyes, and Alezzi saw with awe that the wound on her cheek had already healed, leaving nothing but the thinnest, finest of scars to tell the tale.

Tuzza caught his eye. "What think you now, cousin?"

Alezzi steadied himself. "I think we must talk. And I am fully prepared to listen."

Alezzi ordered Malchi's burial first, calling down a squad from the hills to deal with it. He made a point, though, of refusing Malchi even the smallest of military honors. If anyone else in his legion was thinking about disobeying an order, the message should be plain.

Senior officers from both sides were also summoned, and soon a dozen men, both dark and light-skinned, faced one another, some seated on camp stools, others on rocks. Denza Gruden, the officer promoted by Tuzza, once again sat almost like a bridge between the two groups.

The distrust among Alezzi's commanders was evident in

every gesture, in every look. They eyed Tuzza, Odetta and Denza with something like scorn, and the Anari Ratha and Jenah with outright hatred.

But Alezzi carried enough of their respect that they opened their ears, if not their hearts.

Tuzza faced Alezzi's officers, standing in the pose of an orator. The pose signaled that he commanded nothing from them except a hearing. No Bozandari would deny him that much.

"You are wondering," he said to Alezzi's men, "what it is we are discussing here, why my legion arrays itself in those hills with the Anari. Against you."

A murmur of agreement answered him.

"We are not against you, my brothers. Not unless we must be. But we are on an important mission, one more important than any ever undertaken by a Bozandari army. We have all known our conquests over the years. The history we repeat to our children is rife with tales of glory."

Again murmurs of agreement.

"There is no soldier of Bozandar who cannot hold his head high in memory of those who came before. There is no soldier of Bozandar who does not feel the deepest of commitments to emperor, empire and people. Each and every one of us is willing to die for that commitment."

Nods of agreement answered him. But questions remained on every face.

Tuzza lifted a hand, indicating those arrayed behind him. "You are wondering at the companions I choose now. You wonder why I would join with those who so recently attacked my legion and killed so many. One might ask the same of these Anari and their companions, the Lord Annuvil and the Lady Tess, for they suffered mighty losses of loved ones at the hands of my men."

Now satisfaction chased over the faces of his listeners. He had given a good account of his legion, while reminding them that the losses had not been Bozandar's alone.

Reaching back, he motioned Ratha to step forward. "This Anari beside me watched me kill his brother, just as I watched his brother kill my young cousin. Yet we have buried our swords rather than pursue revenge and bitterness, for there is a greater enemy who threatens *all* of us.

"But before I speak of that, let me remind you of equally important matters. You worry because there has been a slave rebellion at home. Some of you may have lost family in that rebellion. I have no doubt that in the army of the Snow Wolves behind me, many have lost loved ones, both Anari and Bozandari. So why should we end the fight here? Why not carry it on and seek a hollow victory right now in our foe's blood?"

Some heads nodded and others murmured agreement. Even Alezzi seemed to find that idea appealing.

"I will tell you why," Tuzza said, his voice quiet. "Because if you do that, you will not be fit to fight the greater evil. And to fight the greater evil, you will need everyone, Anari and Bozandari alike, to stand together as brothers, for in this fight we *will* be brothers. Failure to unite now will leave us easy prey for the Enemy who even now plots against us. An enemy that will makes slaves of Bozandari as surely as we have made slaves of Anari. Think on that, my brothers. Think on how you have treated the Anari and ask yourselves if you would like your families to be treated in the same way.

"For you must decide and you must decide now. Joining us will be no betrayal of Bozandar, but instead will be its salvation."

One of Alezzi's officers spoke. "Who is this Enemy? We have seen no one."

"You will," Tuzza said. "You have heard of the hives."

The man nodded reluctantly. "But I have not seen them with mine own eyes. It is rumor."

"Not rumor," Ratha said, folding his arms. "We fought one. They are possessed by the Enemy, and they care not if they die. They act as with one mind. Have you tried to stomp out all the ants in an anthill? You cannot do it. The hive is much the same."

The Bozandari exchanged looks.

"The Enemy," continued Tuzza, "makes this winter unnaturally cold and bitter. He has caused crops to fail and thousands to die of hunger and cold. You know of this. You have heard of it or seen it. What you do not know is that it is being caused by the Enemy. He seeks to weaken us before he takes us over."

"Who is this Enemy? Where does he get this power?"

Archer stepped forward. "It is he who was foretold and called the Lord of Chaos by some. He is my brother. Ardred."

Gasps ran through the assembled Bozandari, who had not heard all. Every one of them had heard the old tales and prophecies, for all were educated men. But none had ever expected them to be real.

"These are the foretold times," Archer said. "I will fight him alone if I must, but he has armies and hives, and he will use them to gut your cities and homes all while I struggle to reach him. The only way you can protect all that you cherish is to make it impossible for him to sweep unopposed through your lands."

This comment brought murmurs of agreement, for the argument made sense.

"But how," one of them finally asked, "do we know the truth of this?"

"Is not my word enough?" Tuzza asked simply.

Everyone among them knew Tuzza's reputation and importance, but they were being asked to commit an act that might well turn out to be treason. Loyalty to their emperor demanded that they die before allowing such a thing to happen.

Many appeared almost swayed to Tuzza's side, but it was as if that last step was just one too many. They hesitated, and while they hesitated, one of them cried out and pointed to the west.

Brilliant in the afternoon sunlight, glowing white as the creature of myth it was, a snow wolf came running. He crossed the plain like the wind while every eye fixed on him in disbelief and awe. Murmurs of wonder escaped several throats. Only one man even thought of touching his sword hilt, and he was stayed by Alezzi.

"Wait," Alezzi said. "I have already seen a miracle today. I would not object to seeing yet another."

The wolf loped toward them with all the ease of an animal accustomed to running league after league. It slowed only when it came within a spear's throw. Then it walked toward them, its golden eyes bespeaking ancient wisdom.

When at last it halted, it stood beside Tess, leaning against her side as she sat on her stool. Reaching out, she buried her fingers in its thick white ruff. Then she looked around at the gathered circle. "Do you need more?"

"That is no dog," murmured one of the Bozandari.

"Nay," agreed another. "'Tis the Snow Wolf. I saw one once as a boy in the northern forest, but I thought they had long since died out."

"It is not yet their time," Tess answered. "What more do you need? Tell me, and I will try to show you. Would you like me to turn the sand to glass right before your feet? Shall I shoot a thunderbolt into the air?"

"Tess…" Archer spoke cautiously. "You must not use your strength for a mere display. These men must believe in what they do, not be cowed into it."

She looked down, then nodded. "Let them decide, then." She rose and scanned them all. "I am done with councils, done with trying to persuade men to do what is right and good. If you cannot see the way, then perhaps you deserve all that will befall you."

With that she turned and walked back toward the hills. Beside her went the Snow Wolf.

Chapter Twenty

On the whole, Tess was pleased. The Snow Wolves had spent the past two days encamped with Alezzi's Black Lions. Once again, there was tension in the camp, for there were some among Alezzi's legionnaires who could not countenance marching alongside Anari. Alezzi offered amnesty and an honorable discharge to all who could not march with him, and perhaps one in ten of his number had done so.

Still, their combined host numbered nearly eight thousand, and while the commanders lacked confidence that they could fight together effectively, Tess believed they could at least march to Bozandar without too much friction in the ranks. The more time they spent together, sharing the inevitable hardships of an army in the field, the more they would bond as a unit.

"My men do not wish to adopt your pennant, lady," Alezzi said quietly, watching the activity in the camp.

"Nor would the Snow Wolves wish you to," Tess said. "The Snow Wolves fought together, and even if they fought against one another in that battle, they share the memory of those dark days. They might resent granting their banner to men who have not yet been tempered together with them."

Alezzi nodded. "You are very wise, lady. And perhaps that is for the best. Would it not be better that we enter Bozandari lands not as one army but as two—one from each of our peoples—marching side by side?"

Tess smiled. "Yes, that might well spare us much trouble along the way. Once we near the city, though, I wonder what we can expect."

"I would not hope for arms opened in friendship," Alezzi said. "Sadly, I do not believe that can happen."

"You think not?" Tess asked, not in challenge but because she was curious as to the mettle of the man with whom she now stood.

"Have you never been to Bozandar?" he asked.

Tess shook her head. "I don't know. If I have, I have no memory of it."

She quickly told him what she knew of her story, from waking in the carnage of a butchered trade caravan, her rescue to Whitewater, her journey down the Adasen River, the horrible famine and death in Derda, her captivity in Lorense and the battle with Lantav Glassidor's hive, then through the desert into the Anari lands and on to Anahar.

"The rest you know," Tess concluded. "And I know only little more than you of my life before that."

"That must be…frightening," Alezzi said.

Tess smiled. "Yes. I know too much of who I am, but too little of who I was."

"I can scarcely imagine, lady. If I am a good officer and a good man, it is because I remember the mistakes of my past. How can you avoid the mistakes of your youth if you cannot remember them?"

Tess considered that for a long moment. It was a question she had not yet pondered, and the more she thought on it, and the man who had asked it, the more she saw of the depth of that man.

"I suppose I can only trust myself," Tess said. "Trust that the choices I make are born of those lessons, even if I cannot recall them."

And yes, she thought. That was frightening. Alezzi had put his finger on the fear that hovered always in the back of her mind, the reason she so often doubted every decision she made.

"I would not fret on this too deeply, lady," Alezzi said. "I can clearly see that you have earned the trust of all who know you, and not only because Ilduin blood runs through your veins. My cousin has spoken of your courage and wisdom, as has Lord Archer and his Anari commanders. Whether you know from whence comes that courage and wisdom is of little account. That you possess them is without question."

"Thank you, Alezzi," she said. "You are a comforting counselor."

"If I am," he replied, "it is only because the truth favors you."

"And if it did not?" she asked.

Alezzi replied with an almost unreadable smile. "I am an officer, lady. My life is governed by the harsh truths of time and distance, hunger and fatigue, fear and death. I cannot afford to lie to myself, nor to my men. Nor would I lie to you."

"If all officers saw their duty thus, there would be no cause for war," Tess said. "Yet fight we do. And, you say, we will again at the gates of Bozandar."

Alezzi shook his head. "I did not say that, lady. I said only that we cannot hope to be greeted as friends and brothers."

Tess looked at him, the unspoken question written on her face, waiting for him to continue.

"The Bozandari are a proud people," Alezzi said. "And with good reason, I think. For many generations, we have brought security and prosperity to the people of the Adasen Basin. We provided a common currency and a system of roads and markets. We provided both a body of law and the courts in which that law is applied. The city of Bozandar is the sparkling jewel of the Enalon Sea, a beautiful, safe and orderly city where peoples from east and west, north and south come together for commerce and banking."

"I dare say that your home is not so beautiful, safe or orderly right now," Tess offered.

He nodded. "Perhaps not. Though perhaps once those Anari who wish to leave have done so, it will be even more beautiful than ever. I say that not to criticize them, but simply from my belief that to own a slave poisons the owner as much as the slave."

"You oppose slavery," Tess said.

Alezzi lifted his head, as if searching for an answer in the wispy feathers of cloud that floated high above in an otherwise clear azure sky. "Yes, I suppose now I do. I have not opposed it in the past. I merely rejected it for myself, leaving for others their own choices to make."

That rationale, Tess thought, had been a seductive yet incomplete justification for keeping silent. Such thoughts were likely common among the citizens of Bozandar.

"And yet," Tess said, "in leaving for other Bozandari their own choices to make, you stood by while choices were denied the Anari."

He met her eyes. "You speak truth, Lady Tess."

Speak truth to power. The phrase bubbled up into her consciousness, and for a moment she waited, wondering if the words would find context in some as yet buried memory. But none came. Still, the meaning of the words was plain in her mind, and she decided to continue.

"And if Bozandar has given so much to the people of these lands, do not forget that those gifts were offered at the point of a sword."

Now Alezzi closed his eyes, drawing a long, slow breath before he spoke. "If that is true, it is only in part, my lady. Yes, we conquered. But in most of those lands, our conquest brought the first peace their people had ever known. Darkness more than light was often their fate, and clans fought clans, slaying people in their beds or in the streets. And do not forget that most of the more lawful peoples joined Bozandar willingly, paying taxes and swearing fealty to the emperor in exchange for the security and commerce we could provide."

"I cannot forget what I never knew," Tess said, wondering how much of this explanation was true, how much Alezzi believed to be true, and how much was yet more facile justification. "But your treatment of the Anari makes me…skeptical. Perhaps too much of your glorious history has been washed too clean."

"That may be true," he said. "But if so, I played no part in the scrubbing of it. What I have shared with you is what I was taught. Until these past days, I had not thought to challenge it. My duties and my focus lay with my men."

Tess nodded. "I appreciate that, Alezzi."

He let out a brief, silent chuckle, almost a sigh.

"What?" Tess asked.

"No one calls me by name except my wife and Tuzza, lady. And I have seen little of them in the past months. It sounds strange to hear my own name."

"I am becoming too familiar with that," Tess said, smiling. "Too often now, I am 'lady' or at most 'Lady Tess.' Whatever others may think of me, I have not yet become entirely comfortable with it."

"And I would feel disrespectful calling you anything else, Lady Tess," he said, smiling. "Please do not take that amiss. It is a sign of honor."

Tess sighed. "Sometimes I feel I receive too much honor. I did not ask for this gift, if indeed a gift it is. I did not ask for blood that causes men to burn and die a horrible death. I hate it."

"And well you should," Alezzi said. "What an awful burden to carry. And yet, you also heal men. I have heard of it from the Snow Wolves, of horrible wounds made whole, so that men who would otherwise have died could live."

"Many of them only to die in the battles ahead," Tess said. "What gift is that, to enable a man to experience that agony and terror yet again?"

Alezzi ran a knuckle along his chin, studying the rocks for a long moment. "And yet you press on, my lady."

"What choice do I have?"

"We always have choices," Alezzi said firmly. "Those who believe they have no choices panic and do nothing, or worse. You may not have wanted this road you walk, but you choose it each day when you put one foot before the next."

"If I saw another road, I fear I would walk it," she said. "I fear I would leave all of this behind and return to whatever my life was before. I would never again burn a man with my blood, or heal the horrible wounds of a war that is fought in my cause. I would never again see men suffer so horribly under my care. Yes, Overmark. If I saw another road, I would flee this one, no matter how much I might loathe myself for doing it, rather than bear another day of battle and death."

She hated herself even for saying the words, and for a moment her lip trembled, her vision blurred. She turned away, repulsed by her weakness, revolted by what she had admitted. She was no Weaver, save for a weaver of death.

She felt a hand on her shoulder, gentle but firm, and soon her back felt warmer, the nerves alerting her that he had stepped closer. When he spoke, his voice was quiet and soothing.

"Lady Tess, you have no idea how often I have heard those words. I have heard them from my officers. I have heard them from my men. I have heard them from my own lips, too many times to count. No soldier who is also a good man could think otherwise, for no good man could take true pleasure in war. Those who do are dark men, evil and not to be trusted, for they have a lust that all the blood in the world could not slake. What you say does not make you a coward. It makes you a woman worthy of respect, worthy of the blood you carry."

Tears trickled down her cheek but she kept her face averted so that Alezzi could not see them. She still did not know this man well enough to show weakness with him. Certainly not weakness of this kind.

Salvation arrived in the form of Archer. "Alezzi, Tuzza,

Ratha and Jenah seek you. A council is being held to determine our strategy for the next few days."

Alezzi's hand dropped from Tess's shoulder. "I will go at once. Do you come?"

Archer shook his head. "This is a decision for the commanders of the armies. I would not take their place."

Alezzi bid them both good-night and clattered his way down the rocky slope, disappearing into the inky night. Soon even the last of his sounds trailed away.

"I did not hear you come," Tess remarked.

"I can be as silent as a desert mouse when I choose. I felt you needed me."

She turned toward him then, her face wet with tears, and offered no argument when he wrapped her in his embrace. Somehow over the past months, even with the shadow of her forgotten past hanging over her, and despite Archer's occasional doubts about her, this embrace had become her only haven, the one place in all of this world where she actually felt safe. Safe enough to lay down her burdens. Safe enough to just be.

"I wish you had left me in the woods to die with the child I held in my arms."

His embrace tightened. "Do not say that, my lady. This world needs you as it has needed few others. I know how hard the journey is, and how it often wounds you, but there is ever a price to doing good things."

This was one man she could truly believe when he said he knew how this wounded her. Within him she sensed wounds every bit as painful, and some far worse.

"It is useless to ask for reasons," she finally murmured, her wet cheek resting against his shoulder. His heartbeat was strong and steady beneath her ear, and she found herself noting the aromas that lingered about him, the smell of horses, not unpleasant, the odor of the leather he wore, a faint hint of desert sage, and more...more. Man. She almost caught her breath, for in all these months she had never allowed herself to think of him that way, not even when she had teased him into dancing with her.

The man was not merely a man, he was an immortal on a hellish mission to mend what he claimed he had once rent. Often she thought he was too hard on himself, for no one was so perfect that they never made mistakes, and the worst mistakes were always made with the best of intentions.

The Anari, for example. She spoke now, saying something that had preyed on her mind for some time. "You say you were wrong to create the Anari."

"It was sheer hubris. How could we hope to create better than the gods? And it angered the gods, causing more trouble in the world."

"Aye, I know, you and others have said so. But I want you to think of something else, my lord Annuvil."

"Aye?"

"I want you to think of how much poorer this world would be without the beautiful Anari. And they *are* beautiful, their skin so rich in its blue-blackness, their eyes such deep, dark pools that can reflect so much gentleness. How sad if Anahar had never been built, if no one had ever heard the songs of the rocks and mountains."

She felt, rather than saw, him nod. A sigh escaped him. "Even in your sorrow you offer me comfort, my lady."

"I think we must comfort each other, my lord, for it becomes increasingly apparent to me that we each bear burdens only the other can understand. My sister Ilduin are good women, and their hearts shine pure. But they are not the Weaver."

His hand gently caught her chin and tilted her face up so he could try to read it in the starlight. "What are you saying?"

"Before all is done, the Weaver will be stained in ways they will not."

"You cannot know this!"

"I sense it. We are going to face a great wrongness. I will not say evil, though others call it such. Either way, it will not leave me untouched. Nor you."

Reaching up, she touched his cheek. "I have one wish for you, my lord. Whatever we face in the days and months ahead, I pray you are freed of your guilt and sorrow from the past."

"I would wish that for everyone."

"I know." She smiled then, her tears still glistening on her cheeks. "I wish we could walk away from this task. I freely admit it. But that is not to be."

He shook his head. "I know that I cannot, for it has been bearing down on me since my first misstep."

She nodded and once again leaned into him. "Hold me close, Annuvil. Only in your arms do I find safety."

He obliged gladly, and looked up at the heavens, wishing the stars would speak and promise that all would come out well.

Then, overpowered by her nearness, he swept her down with him onto a soft bed of flowers that had sprung unexpectedly from the desert in the recent rain. There he held her tight and pretended that he was just a man like any other man, holding close a woman he had come to deeply care for.

* * *

Cilla found Ratha in his tent after the conference ended.

"Greetings, cousin," he said pleasantly. He was bent to maps on his camp table, attempting to read by the light of candles that flickered too much. Cilla waved her hand and was delighted to see the flames steady.

Ratha chuckled. "So you Ilduin *do* have some useful talents."

"One or two," she agreed saucily. But being a coquette was not a natural part of her nature. Cilla had risen to be a judge of her clan, a woman with great power, a priestess, and had even trained as a warrior. Like Ratha, she was not a trifler, nor was she to be trifled with.

"We get close to Bozandar," she remarked.

"Aye. Our patrols are beginning to find escaped slaves and we are bringing them into the army. Those fit to fight, anyway. The rest we send back to Anahar."

"I know it."

He chuckled. "I keep forgetting you are Ilduin, cousin. We played too often among the rocks as children, and you were not above pelting me with stones when it suited you."

She arched one brow. "I seem to recall you were not above it, either."

"Certainly not. And remember our little stone house? The very first time the three of us attempted to make a structure of our own with the skills our elders had taught us."

"Aye." Cilla closed her eyes, remembering. She and Ratha and the now-dead Giri had spent many hours playing games in the mountains near their Tel-ner, learning the ways of the rocks, and through that play learning the skills of their ancestors.

They had learned that it was necessary to find a rock that was willing to be shaped and included with others. Some rocks would become difficult to handle, their songs darkening, even their colors changing. The children had learned to seek out those that wanted to be part of a childhood playhouse.

"That is something the Bozandari never understood about us," she said.

"What?"

"That the rocks speak to us, and we do with them only what they wish. They insisted we force what *they* wanted, and that is why their buildings have never been as good as what we built for ourselves. They misused us in many ways."

"That they did. But it is important now to focus on correcting the wrongs of the past."

"Most definitely. But I am speaking of our youth, when we learned our most important lessons on the mountainsides."

"Lessons? In masonry, you mean?"

Cilla shook her head. "Lessons in cooperation and respect. For without that, the rock would resist us. And then, when we had the cooperation of the rocks, we needed to cooperate among ourselves, to respect one another's ideas, in order to complete a structure."

"All you say is true." He smiled faintly. "I recall all the fun we had. I did not think of it as learning."

"Nor I, at the time. Yet still we will need those lessons in the days to come."

"Aye, that we will. I hope the Bozandari who are fighting with us have learned them."

"I think they have, at least within their armies. Somehow we must bring that to the fore."

"'Twill not be easy. They are accustomed to thinking of us as little more than animals."

Cilla's mouth curled. "They treat animals better than slaves, I have heard."

Finally Ratha chuckled, the first truly relaxed sound Cilla had heard from him since Giri's death. "Again you speak truth."

"You are a great man, Ratha Monabi."

He looked away, embarrassed, but Cilla would have none of it. She placed her hand on his cheek and turned his face back toward her. "We have little time. Very little time. Are we to waste the opportunity within our grasp?"

"Opportunity?"

She leaned forward and kissed him gently on the mouth. "I feel as if I have longed for you forever, cousin. Have you not felt even a little of the same? There is so little time left in our grasp that I don't want to waste it on games. Mate with me, Ratha Monabi. Mate with me now."

Blood thundered in his veins, and there was no hesitation as he reached out for her and drew her close.

This, he thought, was all that mattered in life, and if they were to have only one day of love, it would justify everything else. For this night, he could live in a world removed from the blood and cries of battle. For this night, he could celebrate life rather than spreading death. For this night, he could dare to surrender to the love of a woman who had waited for him through all of his grief and pain and doubt.

Tomorrow, perhaps, battle would return and his blood would be spilled onto the earth. But for this night, he was alive. And it felt good to be alive.

Chapter Twenty-One

Throughout the next days, Tom watched as escaping Anari slaves were passed through the combined army. Here, the administrative efficiency of Tuzza's and Alezzi's officers proved itself in abundance. The wounded and sick were quickly transferred to Tess and her sisters for treatment. Those unable or unwilling to fight in the coming battles were formed into columns and assigned guides to lead them back to Anahar. Those who were able and willing were assigned to Anari units and provided with training on the march.

On the morning of the fifth day, they mounted a forested hill and looked down on the gleaming sea of Enalon, and for the first time Tom looked down upon the shining city of Bozandar.

From the heights of the mountain, the view was breathtaking. By this time the fleeing slaves had painted an all-too-clear picture of what lay in the streets, but from this distance that was hidden. Instead there were gleaming walls of sandstone, sparkling with crystal, all hewn by the hands of the Anari. While it was hardly the gloriously organic and living city that was Anahar, Tom still felt his heart leap at the sight of the city he had longed to see since his childhood days in Whitewater. The stories told by the traders were not wrong. Bozandar was truly a wonder.

The Bozandari troops grew restless and uneasy as soon as they set eyes on their capital city. The stories of the slaughter that had happened within those walls were fresh in their minds, and the officers had to work hard to keep the troops in order. Fear of reprisal, second thoughts at their new loyalty, and anger at the thought of family members killed in the Anari revolt, combined in a volatile mix that could explode at any moment and shatter the army.

Archer turned to Tuzza and Alezzi. "We walk on a thin ledge right now. It would not be good to bring the army any closer to the city."

"I agree," Tuzza said immediately. "Nor do I suspect that anything we may say will get a favorable hearing in Bozandar."

"I will go," Tom said.

His voice seemed to surprise them. For most of the march he had remained in the rear, with Sara or Erkiah, but now he stood among the commanders, mounted upon a sturdy mare, his leathern mask shielding his eyes.

"Why you?" Archer asked.

"I have longed to see Bozandar all my life," Tom said. "But more than that, I am a legal neutral. Whitewater is neither a client nor an enemy of Bozandar. Our traders and citizens have always been welcome there."

"You will not go alone," Sara said, riding up with Erkiah

to join them. "If Whitewater is neutral, then I, too, should go. And Erkiah. He will be our guide."

"You should have an escort," Tuzza said.

"Yes," Alezzi agreed. "I fear the people of Bozandar will be suspicious of any outsider right now. It is better if you have protection."

"No," Tom said. "To arrive with Bozandari soldiers would make us seem either prisoners or invaders. This is a mission of peace, Lord Archer. Let me go in peace."

Erkiah smiled at Tom. "We will never get close to the emperor as mere visitors to the city, my son. You are right that we cannot come in the company of an armed body. And yes, I can be our guide. But we do require an escort. Overmark Alezzi should accompany us."

"We will go together," Tuzza said.

"Nay," Ratha said, his dark eyes flashing. "That would leave our Bozandari without leaders. If we are forced to fight, they will be lost."

Tom put a hand on Ratha's shoulder. "My friend, if we are forced to fight, then all is lost regardless. We have not the strength to lay siege to the city, and even less have we the strength to conquer it. This must be a time of councils and not of swords."

"He speaks truth," Jenah said, looking at Ratha.

"Perhaps," Ratha said. He turned to Tuzza. "But I still fear for the peace of our own camp if you and your cousin are not with us. Already the tension is high, as Bozandari soldiers look upon their homeland and wonder if they have chosen well their new colors. I say this not to insult you or your people, my brother. Any man would feel as they do."

"Aye, brother," Tuzza said. "But my men are loyal to the Weaver."

"Your men are loyal to you," Ratha said, his eyes deep and earnest. "And justly so, for you have led them through much hardship, and in the end you have given them back the pride they lost in defeat. Do not misjudge your own worth, my brother. For rare indeed is the commander who inspires such devotion."

"Tom is right," Alezzi said. "Cousin, we cannot both be gone. But one of us must be with Tom if he is to secure an audience with the emperor."

"My men have spent more time with the Anari," Tuzza said. "They march under the banner of the Snow Wolf. They would be less likely to cause a disturbance in my absence. Thus, I should be the one to accompany Tom."

"No," Erkiah said. "It must be Alezzi. Overmark Tuzza, you must remember that you very likely stand in some distrust in the court, owing to your suspected captivity. And surely by now spies have reported that your men march with the Anari under a new banner. You are more likely to be arrested than to gain an audience at court."

"Let us not forget the Enemy," Archer said. "He must have agents, if not hives, in the imperial court. And he certainly knows of your new allegiance, Tuzza. Erkiah is right. It must be Alezzi."

"My men know that you are no traitor," Alezzi said to Tuzza. "Great was your reputation before this campaign in the Anari lands, and greater still among my men as they see you walk with the Weaver. You have served with many of my officers before. They know you, and you them. I feel no reluctance in entrusting my legion to you, cousin. Where you lead, they will follow."

"Trust your cousin," Tess said to Tuzza. "He is an honorable man. He would not betray us, nor would his men betray you, Overmark."

Alezzi smiled. "Thank you, Lady Tess. Then it is decided."

"Yes," Archer said. "I agree."

Ratha squeezed Tuzza's shoulder. "I would not see you arrested, brother. Your place is here, with your legions, and where our council may profit from your wisdom while Tom and his companions are in the city."

Tuzza finally nodded. "Yes, so it must be."

"Then let us prepare," Tom said, excitement in his voice. "If I am to be our emissary to Bozandar, I must be worthy of that task."

Archer chuckled. "Young Tom Downey, you were worthy of that task from the day I first saw you as a child. 'Tis my dismay that you have not yet realized this. Go forth and state our case, Prophet. Trust your own wisdom, and in the wisdom of those with you. The world could ask for no better ambassadors than the good people of Whitewater."

Alezzi watched as Tom squeezed Sara's hand. The nearer they had come to Bozandar—its walls gleaming white and silver, even in the cold winter sunshine—the more excited the lad had become. The guard eyed them warily until Alezzi rode to the fore and announced himself and the company. Whatever suspicions might exist in the imperial court, they had not filtered down to this man, whom Alezzi remembered from their service in the north years ago.

"You and any in your presence are welcome in the city of Bozandar, Overmark Alezzi."

"Thank you, Filemark Varlen," Alezzi said, dismounting to take the man's hand. Searching his memory, he recalled that the man had left his legion when his wife died while bearing him twin boys. "And how are your sons?"

"Always into mischief," Varlen replied with a laugh. "They drive my new bride to the edge of her wits and beyond almost daily."

"If theirs were the only mischief in this world, we would be blessed indeed," Alezzi said.

"Aye, Overmark," Varlen said. "For theirs is the innocent mischief of children learning their way in life."

"Perhaps," Tom said quietly with a dip of his head, "the same is true of all of us. In the eyes of the gods, we must all seem like children."

Alezzi noted the guard's quizzical look and smiled. "My friend is a great prophet, Filemark. We should all heed his words."

"It is my honor to welcome you, Prophet," Varlen said. "And I will pray that we children can all be as forgiving as my sons. For while they may squabble, they still sit together at dinner, and only a foolish man would dare to come between them. Walk in peace and freedom in my city."

"Thank you," Tom replied.

As they walked through the gate, Alezzi heard Tom gasp. While Alezzi had grown up in the city, he knew that this first view of the wide boulevard that gently sloped down to the sparkling imperial castle compound could take the breath from many a man.

For Alezzi, the sight was quite different, however. He did not see the usual bustle in the streets. All but absent were the brightly painted carriages that were usually abundant, passing in calm but brisk procession, bearing men both high and low to their daily tasks. In any other time, Alezzi would have hailed one for their journey, for in Bozandar no free man need tire his feet to travel this city. On this day, there was no carriage to be had.

"I am not accustomed to walking this city," Alezzi said, still on foot and leading his mount by the reins. "Truly the people are troubled."

"We need not walk," Tom said. "We have our mounts."

"Nay, my son," Erkiah said gently as he climbed down from his bay mare. "We must stable our horses. Such is the law of the city."

"And a good law it is," Alezzi said. "It helps us to keep the streets clean. And though these are not ordinary times, still we should follow the law. I have walked many leagues in my life. It will not harm me to walk today."

"But what of Erkiah?" Tom said.

Erkiah laughed. "Worry not for me, my son. These legs have borne me far. I am not so old that they cannot bear me farther."

Alezzi paid their stable fees and led them into the heart of the city. It was nearly a two-hour walk, for the city was larger than any his Whitewater guests had ever encountered, and many were their pauses to ask of this or that statue or monument. Erkiah knew the history better than he, and Alezzi listened to the tales that painted his city in a glory he was not sure it deserved.

Too much of that glory had been built on the backs of Anari. Anari who would have no choice but to walk as Alezzi was walking this day, for they would not have been permitted to hire a ride, even had they money to do so. It was, he thought, good that they were walking as common men. It reminded him of why he was here.

For to Alezzi, Bozandar was as seductive as she was beautiful. He had earned a reputation as a man who shunned the trappings of the court, trappings to which he was fully entitled by right of birth. But he knew that reputation was more a matter of necessity than moral standing. For whenever he had been in the city, whenever he had allowed himself to be drawn into discussions of politics, he had felt a pull that filled him with shame.

Though others may not have known it, Alezzi did not hate the intrigues and schemes of the palace. Rather, he loved them too much. And he knew it.

Now he was walking into precisely the nest of vipers that he had worked so hard to avoid, even to the point of taking distant assignments in the provinces when he was entitled to administrative postings in the city. And this time he would have no opportunity to place himself on the list for such a self-imposed exile.

Into the viper's nest it would be, and he hoped his fangs were up to the challenge.

Chapter Twenty-Two

Sara felt the nagging, insistent presence she had sensed so strongly in Lorense. The Enemy had a hive in Bozandar. She was certain of it. *If I can feel them, they can feel me,* she thought.

Yes, Tess replied. *But Cilla and I are with you, sister. You are not alone.*

Was that enough? Sara wondered privately. But even while she shielded the details of her thoughts, she could not shield the feelings.

Do not fear, Cilla whispered through the tendrils of Ilduin thought. *For nothing is more crippling than fear, sister. Rather, learn what you can. Open yourself to sense all that is happening around you. We will not leave you to fight alone should it come to that.*

The words were comforting, and Sara had no doubt about the sincerity of her sister's promise. The question was whether her sisters' combined power would be enough to make good on that promise. She and Tess had battled a hive in Lorense, but they had done so by attacking the hive leader, Lantav Glassidor. And while Sara's and Tess's Ilduin blood had judged Glassidor to a horrible, fiery death, the price of victory had been the death of Sara's own mother, whom Glassidor had abducted into his service years before.

The memory of her mother's last breaths still brought tears to Sara's eyes. If they met another enslaved Ilduin, and if there were no other means by which to break that thrall, could Sara slay her? For that woman would be no more than Sara's mother had been: someone's wife, someone's mother, enslaved and coerced into the dark service of an Enemy who saw the Ilduin only as weapons to be employed in his evil designs.

The Enemy would see Ilduin. Sara would see a captive sister yearning for a freedom that might only lie in death.

"You are troubled, my love," Tom said.

Sara tried to shake off the thoughts. "I will not fail you, Prophet Tom Downey."

"I know that," Tom said quietly. "But still your hand trembles in mine. You walk in memories, Sara."

"Yes," she said.

"Do not," he replied with a gentle squeeze of her hand. "There is no surer way to defeat than to refight the last battle. Our present foe may be far different. Your sisters are right. Open yourself and learn."

You can hear their thoughts, too? Sara thought.

Only when you do, he replied, *and only while we touch. For then I can feel your full heart.*

Ilduin milk, Sara thought suddenly.

Tom looked at her in surprise.

"When you were most ill," she whispered. "I nursed

you, my love. Eisha, the Anari woman who was with us, said that while Lady Tess saved you from death, it was my milk that restored your health."

Tom gave her a playful wink. "I wish I remembered. For I know no milk has come from you since."

"Shame on you, Tom Downey!" she hissed mirthfully. "Take not a blessing of the gods into your trousers!"

He kissed her. "Ah, love, but I do that whenever we are together."

It was not the Prophet who lightened her spirits. It was the husband, the boy who had once been tongue-tied in her presence. That tongue, now loosed and perhaps too much so, brought her out of the darkness of her thoughts.

"I do love you so, Tom," she said with a sigh.

"And I you," he replied.

"And true love is beautiful indeed," Erkiah said, "but lest the two of you slip into the poetry of songbirds, let us not forget our calling here."

"Not even for a little while?" Tom asked, the tone of his voice so ambiguous that not even Sara could tell if he was serious until the smile slowly crinkled the corners of his mouth.

"No, lad," Erkiah said, arching a brow in mock sternness. "Not even for a little while."

"Oh, to know young love again," Alezzi said to Erkiah. "Would it not be a delight?"

"My legs can bear me through the city," Erkiah said, laughing. "I am not sure they could bear me through that."

"Nor mine," Alezzi said. "Nor mine. Perhaps it is good that such things are left to the young, lest the rest of us find ourselves barely able to crawl."

"Enough," Sara announced with a gentle smile. "You

boys may have your fantasies at your leisure, but for now we must keep our wits about us."

"Yes, m'lady," Alezzi said with a mock bow. Then, his eyes more serious, he added, "You are right. But still it is good that we find such laughter as we can in these days. There will be far too little to savor."

Tom turned to Alezzi. "Now who speaks as a prophet?"

"Not a prophet," Alezzi replied, his face sober. "Merely as a man who has spent much of his life grasping at such laughter as he could find between the tears."

"I meant no offense," Tom said.

"And I took none, my friend," Alezzi said. "But I have spent my life avoiding this city, and now I walk into its grasp more fully than ever before. It is that, not you, which clouds my heart."

"But how?" Tom asked, looking around. "This city is…majestic. Even in winter these grassy expanses in the center of the avenues are green with life."

"They are green because the sea warms us," Alezzi said. "And however beautiful they may be, however many mothers and children may play in these parks, their true purpose is war, my friend. The main boulevards of this city are wide so that our legions and their horses can form and move easily if the city is attacked. If you look past the green, you will see something else."

As if guided by his words, Sara saw the blotches of dried coppery brown. "Blood," she whispered. "But it is not blood that you fear, Overmark."

Alezzi shook his head. "No, Lady Sara. Blood I have seen, and more than most. Mine has been shed and, sadly, I have shed that of others. But I would gladly bleed from a wound in battle rather than from the wounds we now face.

For the blood extracted in the palace is, too often, not the blood one can wash from one's hands. It is the blood of the soul itself."

"That is why you have avoided Bozandar," Erkiah said.

"Yes," Alezzi replied. "The palace is filled with men who would sell their mothers for a seat nearer the emperor. Or, even better in their minds, sell the mother of the man whose seat they wish to claim. They speak of an honor they do not practice and make promises they would not keep even if there were no need to break them. They catalog one another's vices and whisper of one another's failures, but of course always neglecting their own roles in nurturing those vices or ensuring those failures."

"You despise them," Sara said, studying his face.

"Yes," Alezzi said, pain evident in his eyes.

"Because you would beat them at their own games," she continued. "You think you would be the best and the worst of them all."

He shook his head. "No, fair lady. I do not think I would be. I know I would be. I have both the skill and the taste for it. It is the stomach for it that I lack."

"And therein lies your honor, Overmark," she said, recalling the trials she and her companions had faced in the past months. "It is not what we could do that damns us, nor even what we would do. It is what we do, or too often what we fail to do, that the gods judge. If I have learned nothing else in this war, I have learned that."

"Then you have learned truth," Erkiah said, nodding. "And grave indeed will be their judgment if we fail in the task we now face."

"I pray that the price of victory is not too high to bear,"

Alezzi said. "I have too many memories I would like to forget. I seek no more."

And then, as if by magick, they were at the outer palace gate, a huge structure of metal that looked as deadly to overcome as it was beautiful. Two guards in full dress scarlet and brass stood there, and stiffened watchfully.

"Who approaches the emperor's gate?" one demanded.

"Alezzi Forzzia, cousin and member of his royal house, Overmark of the Legion of the Black Lion."

"State your purpose, Overmark."

"I have brought two prophets and an Ilduin who seek to give my cousin the emperor their foretellings and warnings so that he may continue to protect his empire from all threats."

One of the guards bowed stiffly and called to someone inside. Another guard approached the gate and received the message. At once he turned and trotted into the depths of the palace compound.

"That was easy," Tom remarked quietly.

Alezzi shook his head. "Trust me, the word will pass through many other ears and mouths before it reaches my cousin. We will not find it easy to gain audience."

"But he's your cousin."

"He has more than a few cousins, Tom. More than a few. And many are within those walls already."

Sara suddenly reached out and grabbed Tom's forearm. "The hive," she whispered, her face pale. "There is a hive very near."

Tom nodded and looked at Alezzi and Erkiah. "We may face grave danger."

Before the men could acknowledge the remarks, Sara swayed a little. "Inside. They are already inside."

At once Alezzi's hand fell to the hilt of his sword. "Then this may become far more difficult than I imagined."

Mihabi sat close to his mother on the hillside, near the Anari army, not far from the Bozandari who also marched under the banner of the White Wolf. The combination amazed him, and he experienced an increasing sense of guilt over what had happened during the uprising. He had killed. He had seen his brother Ezinha, a Bozandari, killed. The senselessness of war had never been more apparent to him.

Yet armies had gathered, speaking of a greater Enemy than Bozandar, and of another war to come. If it was that important, he would take up a sword and join them, but for now he could only hope that another fight wouldn't be necessary.

Beside him, his mother still occasionally wept for Ezinha. Mihabi felt responsible for that, even though he was not responsible for the decisions his nursing brother had taken. As for his blood brother…neither he nor his mother Ialla had any idea where Kelano had gone. Probably to linger among the Anari soldiers.

Anari soldiers. That idea still amazed him. His people had always been so proud of their peacefulness. Now they had taken up arms, not only in a slave revolt, but now against a greater Enemy. He wished he knew what this greater Enemy was. Perhaps that was why Kelano had disappeared, to learn what he could about this strange alliance.

His mother began to sob again, and Mihabi reached out to put an arm around her shoulders and offer silent comfort, though he knew there was nothing that would fill the hole in her heart.

It was then that he noted a stirring among the nearby armies. A murmur arose, and with it the soldiers of the White Wolf.

Looking down the hillside, Mihabi stared in shock, then, too, rose to his feet, feeling for the blade he had used during the rebellion, little use though it would be.

From the shining city below emerged a legion under a flag bearing a large red symbol. He could not immediately identify the sign, but he would have wagered that it was the red panther of Owazzi's legion. He had heard they were marching toward Bozandar in the days immediately preceding the full revolt. They had apparently arrived, though too late to prevent the slaves from escaping. Now, perhaps, they were coming to take the slaves back.

Mihabi turned and looked at the hillside. Since he had arrived, very little of the armies around him had been visible. Now, as one, as if they had received silent orders, they formed up, making their numbers clear to the legion in the valley below.

The Red Panther was outnumbered by the Snow Wolf and the Black Lion. But a distinct uneasiness filled the air, and men looked at one another, as if they were not certain they could trust their allies.

It was then a woman garbed in snow-white stepped onto a ledge slightly below them. The murmuring among the soldiers changed at the sight of her.

"Be strong," she said, in a voice that seemed to carry over the entire hill and the mountains beyond. "Stand fast. They will not attack."

How could she know this? Mihabi wondered. How could anyone know this?

But then a man clad completely in black stepped out

beside her, and with them a Bozandari and two Anari. Ranged together they seemed to be a wall, a wall with its back toward the threat below.

It was as if the five scorned the Red Panther. As if they knew the legion below was no true threat.

Slowly Mihabi sat and stared at the five. Beneath him, for the first time in his life, he felt the rocks come alive. He gasped and turned to his mother. In her teary eyes there was a smile.

"The mountains are with us, my son," Ialla said. "And now you know your true heritage."

It was as Alezzi had predicted. They passed the outer gates, but then the layers of people who surrounded the emperor began their own interrogations. Everyone wanted to know what this was about. Everyone wanted to find a reason to prevent Alezzi from seeing his cousin, for their positions might be at risk.

But Alezzi knew the ways of the court. He refused to describe the threat except that it was bigger than any Bozandar had ever faced. He suggested, and sometimes said outright, that anyone who hindered him would later pay for it when the emperor learned that important information had been kept from him.

Still, Sara remarked, "Water runs faster uphill."

Tom smiled and squeezed her hand, but felt that her impatience arose more from nerves than time. "Do you still feel it?"

"It is here," she said again. "So far none we have seen are part of it, but it lies within these walls somewhere."

"Then it is a direct threat to my cousin," Alezzi said. "You must let me know the instant we face one of them, Lady Sara."

"Trust me, I shall probably deal with him or her before you can."

Tom looked at Sara, feeling a sudden, deep concern for her. The things she had sometimes been required to do as an Ilduin gave her nightmares, yet the set of her features said she was prepared to do those things again. And more, if necessary.

Tom felt a shiver of apprehension and looked at Erkiah. The old prophet shook his head. "An angry Ilduin is beyond description, my boy. Those who oppose her had best tread lightly."

The last man who had questioned them, then gone off to speak with someone else, now returned with two guards.

"Alezzi Forzzia," he said, "I arrest you in the name of the emperor."

"For what?" Alezzi asked pleasantly.

"Your legion opposes the Legion of the Red Panther just beyond the city."

"My legion has opposed no one, nor has a sword been lifted. We have come in peace to alert the emperor. Do you stand in my way?"

"You are guilty of treason."

"I am guilty of nothing except dealing with idiots like yourself who don't care enough about the empire to pass me through to my cousin."

The man waved a hand at the guards. "Arrest him!"

At that Sara lifted a hand. "Touch him not."

The official sneered. "Who do you think you are?"

"Uh-oh," said Erkiah. "You had best watch your step."

But it was too late. Blue fire sprung from the tips of Sara's fingers, and the guards dropped their weapons with cries, as if they had become molten hot. The official gaped.

"Now," said Sara, "you have wasted enough of our time. I suggest you take us to the emperor before I decide this entire building is in my way!"

"We have Ilduin, too," the official squawked.

"And if they will oppose me, they threaten the empire. And if they threaten your empire, my blood will judge them, Ilduin or not. Now take us!"

As they followed the official down a winding hallway, Erkiah winked at Tom and whispered, "Got yourself a bit of a firebrand there, boy."

Tom merely smiled.

Chapter Twenty-Three

Standing with his back to a Bozandari legion made Ratha's neck prickle, but he refused to obey the urge to look over his shoulder. Watching the armies above, noting their restlessness as they looked down on the legion below, especially among Alezzi's Black Lions, he wondered if their cobbled-together army would hold.

Then he saw Cilla making her way down the slope to join them. With authority arrayed like this, backs to the potential attackers, he thought it would be hard for the armies to do anything but stand as Tess had ordered. And except for the Black Lion Legion, everyone up there knew Tess's power and her importance as the Weaver.

They would stand, he decided, and felt a surge of pride in his fellow Anari who were mere babes in the game of war. Their numbers had greatly swelled with those slaves who had fought their way out of Bozandar, most of whom appeared to have already been bloodied.

His race could be trusted. And he could, he supposed, be forgiven for a bit of doubt about the Bozandari. They were the ones who now looked down on a fellow legion and had to argue with themselves about whether they would attack their brothers. He didn't envy them. In all honesty, he wasn't sure he could stand firm against an army of Anari.

But Tess and Cilla stood between the armies, and he believed they would do anything necessary to prevent a clash. If their intervention was needed, he hoped it would be enough.

The walk through seemingly endless, winding halls soon had Tom utterly confused about where they were. It seemed the palace was built as a maze, and as soon as he thought that, he knew he was right. In its every curve and bend it was built to keep invaders at bay.

He hoped the man leading them was leading them toward the emperor. He hoped that Alezzi knew his way through these labyrinthine corridors. He hoped, as the guards behind them steadily grew in number, that Sara could handle them if necessary, because it wasn't long before he was quite convinced that even the experienced Alezzi would be unable to get them out of trouble.

"Not much farther now," Alezzi murmured, answering one of Tom's silent questions. "We are approaching the audience chamber."

"Is that good?"

"Ordinarily my cousin would receive me in his private chambers. He probably made this choice because I bring strangers with me."

"Or because he doesn't trust you or us."

Alezzi smiled mirthlessly. "I am well aware of that possibility, Prophet. Well aware."

Shortly thereafter, they emerged into the audience chamber, a room large enough to hold hundreds of people. Given its size, Tom would have expected there to be advisors or nobles everywhere. Instead there were just the three of them and their expanded escort. With a glance to the rear, Tom estimated they were now accompanied by thirty or so fully armed palace guards.

Centrally located near one wall with a door on either side, a golden throne sat on a dais. Sparkling jewels of every kind studded it and made it glisten in a rainbow of color. Beside it sat a smaller throne, less ornate. Tom wondered who would sit there. Wife? Or heir?

They waited a short while, then a trumpet sounded near one of the doors behind the throne.

"Bow," said Alezzi, so all four of them did, bending forward until they stared straight down at the floor.

A rustle and the sound of many footsteps echoed in the room, then a surprisingly pleasant voice said, "Rise."

They straightened to find the Emperor of Bozandar seated on his throne. He was dressed in cloth of gold and a gold coronet crowned his head. He looked much like Alezzi and Tuzza, his features as fine cut, his eyes the same color. And he, too, appeared somewhat worn by his cares.

Scattered around now were other elegantly garbed men and women, perhaps a dozen of them. Courtiers or advisers, perhaps. Tom wished he knew more about these matters, then realized that knowing nothing meant anything he said would be untainted.

He tried to stand as straight as he could, feeling suddenly very young in the face of all this power and nobility. Then he felt Sara's arm brush his and realized that she must be feeling much as he was. Like him she was basically a simple girl from a small village who had been thrust upon a stage larger than either of them could ever have imagined.

An innkeeper's daughter and a gatekeeper's son might dream of adventure, but never would they have imagined standing in a palace facing the Emperor of Bozandar, planning to tell him what he must do.

He decided right then that he had best stop thinking about these things before his knees began knocking together.

"Alezzi," the emperor said at last. It was the same pleasant voice that had told them to rise moments before.

"My royal cousin," Alezzi said, bowing again. When he straightened, his face was grim. "I wish I came before you bearing glad tidings, Maluzza."

"So I wish as well, cousin." The emperor, who had been sitting firmly upright, now leaned forward a bit. "You would never betray me."

"I would die first."

"Then tell me why you have come before me without my cousin Tuzza, whom I sent you to rescue. I sent you out to bring him back to me, alive or dead, so that I might honor him. I set you forth to bring back the sons of my people, who weep heavily from recent events. The only reason I did not call you back to defend this city from the rebellion was because my people wanted their sons returned, dead or alive. And you have come empty-handed."

Alezzi bowed his head momentarily, then raised it and met the emperor's gaze directly. "Maluzza, my cousin, you know full well that the clan of Forzzia has forever been willing to make any sacrifice necessary for the empire."

"'Tis true," the emperor agreed, and waved aside a man who tried to lean over and speak into his ear. "Let me hear my cousin out, Izza. There will be time enough for your words after I have heard from Alezzi's lips."

The man stood back, frowning but obedient.

"My cousin," Alezzi said, raising his voice as if to be heard by all. "I set out as you bade me, and my only purpose was to accomplish your wish. To serve you and my people in their hour of trial. I cannot express how hard it was for me to press forward when I learned of the slave troubles in this beautiful city. But my orders were clear and I continued toward the Anari lands."

The emperor nodded as if he approved.

"My scouts warned me that an army approached us, an army of Anari and Bozandari together under a single flag. They were described to me as being only slightly larger than my legion, so I felt no fear, only curiosity at what had caused this treasonous alliance. For so I thought of it when I first learned of it."

"So you should have," agreed the man at the emperor's shoulder. Maluzza himself, however, appeared more intent on hearing the full story and waved his adviser to silence.

"When we came within sight of one another across a valley," Alezzi continued, "they requested a parley. To my astonishment, I thought I spied Tuzza among the party who came forth for the parley. So I agreed and went down to meet them, certain there must be some explanation for what I was seeing other than treason."

The emperor nodded again.

"Our beloved cousin indeed was there, and the story he told me and the sights I then saw caused me to return to you immediately with a warning and a proposal."

"What did you see?"

"My cousin Tuzza indeed had allied with the Anari army that had fought his legion."

A gasp went up from all around.

"They now ride under the flag of the White Wolf."

The emperor straightened again. "The White Wolf? The foretelling…"

"Exactly, my emperor. The White Wolf. But it proved to be more than a banner, for the white wolf came down out of the mountains while we parleyed, and placed himself beside an Ilduin. This Ilduin was attacked by one of my officers, and when her blood fell on him, he burned. Her blood judged him, and there was no way to save him. What is more, when her blood dripped on the ground, flowers sprang from the desert."

Murmurs passed through the room as this news was absorbed.

"My cousin," Alezzi continued, "the Ilduin and Tuzza informed me that a greater enemy than any we have ever faced is bearing down on us. These are the prophesied times coming to pass, and it is our duty to protect the empire and all our allies. The unnatural winter that killed so many in the northlands was sent by him. He has powers I can scarce imagine. He controls the hives we have all heard about."

More murmurs, louder this time, until the emperor waved for silence.

"How can you be sure of this, Alezzi?"

"Because, Maluzza, I have met the Ilduin who is the Weaver. And I have met Annuvil."

Now the gasps could not be silenced. The emperor bowed his head and let the sounds bounce around the room, let all the listeners talk among themselves until at last the noise tapered off. Only then did he raise his head and speak.

"You are sure it is the Firstborn Son of the Firstborn King?"

"Aye," said Alezzi. "I saw his sword, Banedread, and he offered to let me kill him with it if I did not believe what they told me. But I believed. How could I not believe when the White Wolf walks with the White Lady?"

"So it is true," Maluzza sighed. "True. I had hoped that it would not be in my time, but my seer has warned me that the day of prophecy fulfilled was not far away. Who are these you bring with you?"

"Erkiah, a prophet of Bozandar."

Erkiah stepped forward and bowed. "My emperor."

"And the youngsters?"

Alezzi almost smiled. "Not so young, cousin. The Lady Sara is also an Ilduin. Her companion is her husband, Tom Downey."

"And the mask he wears?"

Tom spoke. "I was healed by Ilduin fire, Emperor Maluzza. The price was paid with my sight. Light is painful to me."

"Healed with Ilduin fire? I have heard of that, but only as something from the mythical times of the Firstborn. And did it not only happen once?"

"I believe that is true," one of the men in the room said. "'Tis said that the price of such healing is high."

"In my case," Tom said, "it helped open my inner eyes."

"Aye," said Erkiah, leaning on his staff. "The lad is a prophet of the new age we are entering. He is the one foretold. The Foundling."

More gasps and murmurs ranged around the audience

chamber. Tom glanced about and saw that even more people had joined them.

"So you are here to prophesy for me?" the emperor asked.

Tom stepped forward boldly. "My lord, no prophet is needed to tell you that the Enemy, he who is known as Lord of Chaos and as Ardred, Secondborn Son of the Firstborn King, threatens all that you hold dear. All that every one of us holds dear. He has brought the terrible winter down on the northland to weaken us not only by diminishing the numbers of those who might resist him between his fortress and this city, but also to empty granaries and food stores so that we might have little to rely on as the winter lengthens. Indeed, I can tell you with greater certainty than prophecy that spring will not fall over the land again until the Evil One is defeated!"

His voice rang through the room, but then he began to rock gently from side to side. His voice became monotonal yet rhythmic as he fell sway to his vision.

"If we do not act soon," Tom continued, "I see a blighted world where even the most important and wealthy scrabble among bare rocks and struggling plants to find food, where children cannot grow, and their mothers weep for lack of milk."

He lifted an arm, swaying even more, seeming to include the entire room in his gesture. "All of this will fade away as the Firstborn faded, to be nearly forgotten except as stories the poor tell one another around paltry campfires as they try to keep warm. All that you cherish will be stripped from you, and only by serving the Lord of Chaos will you survive at all. You must join with us in the fight!"

"And Annuvil?" asked Izza, the emperor's adviser. "I suppose he wants to be king over all."

Tom stiffened and turned slowly, looking directly at the adviser. "He wishes to be king over nothing. He wishes only to atone for the past. Can you say the same?"

"Hive!" Sara whispered, and suddenly she was wrapped in blue flame that hissed and crackled.

"Where?" Alezzi demanded, reaching for his sword.

Before he could act, Sara pointed at Izza and a ball of blue fire flew from her fingertip to hit the adviser right between the eyes.

Izza's eyes widened and he sank to his knees. At the same instant, the soldiers who had followed them drew their weapons and pointed them at Sara and Tom.

"Stop!" Alezzi shouted at them. "Stop if you love your lives!"

The soldiers hesitated. Sara turned slowly, still a tower of sparkling blue flame, and faced the soldiers. "Put away your weapons," she said gently. "That man belonged to a hive. You are safe from me. And he is no longer part of the hive."

Indeed, even as she spoke, Izza was struggling to his feet, looking dazed. "I…where….?" He shook his head. "Oh, no! I was…I was…"

"'Tis no matter," the emperor said to him. "Apparently you could not help it. Go and rest, old friend. But take someone with you to protect you."

Two of the soldiers immediately detached from the group guarding the visitors and moved to aid Izza. The man was still stumbling as he was led away.

Maluzza, the emperor, rose and stepped down from the dais. Soldiers immediately repositioned themselves to protect him, but he motioned them away. He looked at

Sara, who was beginning to return to normal, and at Tom, as if trying to peer through the mask, then at Alezzi.

"So, cousin, you bring dire warning indeed. But how can I be sure this Ilduin has really released Izza from a hive, and not merely injured him through some minor magick? After all, I have heard of only one hive, and that was destroyed by some strangers."

"We were those strangers," Tom said boldly. "The Lady Sara judged the hive master with her blood, and in the final moments of his life, Ardred spoke through him."

"The notion of hives troubles me," the emperor admitted, looking at Tom. "You say there are more?"

"There is one in your palace," Sara said. "I sensed it when we reached the gate."

The emperor eyed her skeptically. "I have felt betrayal from none around me."

"Nor will you until it is too late. If you play *shefur,* do you let your opponent know where you place your pieces before you are ready to use them?"

Alezzi nodded grimly. "'Tis a basic principle of war, as you know, my emperor."

"Aye, 'tis so. And thus it is difficult for me to know what to believe."

Sara stepped apart and looked around the audience chamber. "The hive knows of my presence since I freed Izza. It knows what we came to tell you. The danger is thus magnified."

"Perhaps," agreed the emperor.

"But it is not yet time to show their hand," Sara said. "Emperor, if you had heard of what is happening here in this audience chamber, would you come to see for yourself, or would you stay at your work?"

At that the emperor stiffened. He turned to the soldiers. "Close and seal all doors. Let none enter. None!"

Armor and swords clanked as the soldiers hastened to do his bidding.

"Now," said the emperor, eyeing Sara, "are we imprisoned here in this room?"

"Not for long." She began to walk around the room, her eyes nearly closed. As she passed, people drew back as if afraid of merely brushing against her. The silence, however, was so deep that the swish of her riding skirt could be heard.

Finally she stopped and lowered her head. When she spoke, her voice was quiet. "Soon will come a spy. She is already on her way. She will seek to gain admittance through a sweet lie."

"Will you release her, too?"

Sara nodded to the emperor. "She comes on fleet feet, sent because the hive master is concerned about our secrecy. She is young, so young, helpless against the power that controls her...."

Sara's eyes closed. "She is born to be Ilduin, though has not yet come into her powers. That will happen soon, which is why the hive wants her. Her mother was not Ilduin. The talent skipped a generation...." Sara paused. "Emperor, she is your daughter Lozzi. And she comes now."

"Lozzi!" Emperor Maluzza spoke the name with shock and anguish. "My Lozzi!"

"Let her enter," Sara said kindly. "But you must let her come with me to the Weaver. For only the Weaver can save her now."

"You want to take my daughter?" The ruler was horrified.

"Only for a brief while," Sara said.

"I cannot believe this!" Anger replaced anguish and the emperor turned on Alezzi. "This is an attempt to steal my child! How could you have betrayed me so, Alezzi? How?"

Before Alezzi could even attempt a response, there came a knocking at the door to the rear left of the throne. The emperor froze, then nodded to the guard.

The man opened the door a crack and looked out. A small voice could be heard and the emperor closed his eyes. The guard turned toward his master. "Princess Lozzi, my emperor. She begs a word, for she says one of the maid-servants slapped her."

Maluzza drew a startled breath. "Never," he whispered. Anger gave way again to horror. "Never," he said again. "Let her in."

Into the room ran a girl of about twelve or thirteen, clad in a beautiful gown, her hair twirled and twisted into a high pile of golden braids. She ran straight for her father, a tear running down her cheek.

"Nona hit me!"

The emperor took her by the shoulders. "Nona has loved you since birth, and never once has she struck you, no matter what trouble you got up to. Why should she strike you now?"

Lozzi gasped. "You don't believe me, Father?"

The emperor searched his daughter's face, pain in every crease of his. "Why, Lozzi? What did you do?"

The girl's lower lip trembled. "Nothing. At least nothing that deserves being struck."

"Let me be the judge of that. What did you do?"

Lozzi stepped back, her lips trembling, her face piteous. "You have always believed me."

"I want to know why Nona should do such an awful thing. The transgression would have to be terrible."

"You support Nona and not me?"

"I support no one until I get an answer."

When none was forthcoming, his shoulders sagged sadly. "Ah, Lozzi, what is wrong with you?"

All of a sudden, Lozzi turned and pointed at Sara. "She is making me do it! She is the problem!"

Chapter Twenty-Four

As the hours drew on, men waiting on the hillside began to grow restless. The army below, ranged before the city, looked as if it had no intention of moving. Perhaps its orders were simply to prevent anyone from entering the town.

"It is possible," Tuzza said when Archer suggested that. "It would be a wise move. Other legions are likely even now headed this way from their outposts to face the threat we represent. If I were in command, I would guard the city like a hen guards her eggs until reinforcements arrive."

"So our greatest fear," Tess said, "is that the emperor won't listen to Alezzi, Tom and Sara, and the other legions will arrive and strike at us."

"Of course." Tuzza looked at her as if he were surprised that she should state the obvious.

"How long?" Tess asked.

"A day at most. Perhaps two. It depends on when the

calls went out to them, but I suspect it must have been right before the uprising for at least several of them. Or perhaps right after. They may have believed the Red Panthers alone could have quelled the uprising."

"Could they have?" Archer asked.

"Most likely. Every legion is trained to defend the city single-handedly, and with that kind of organization, 'tis possible the slaves might not have succeeded."

"'Tis very difficult," Archer remarked, "to defeat an enemy who won't hold still and can hide in every nook and cranny."

"True, but Anari are easily identified."

Archer nodded grimly. "My feeling is that we should tell our armies to break out and feed themselves, making fires if they wish to."

Ratha raised a brow, his blue-black face glistening beautifully in the afternoon light. "Is that wise?"

"It will certainly glean for us some information about the intentions of the legion below."

"Ah." Ratha slowly smiled. "I am slow."

Archer shook his head. "No, my brother, you have simply not had the experience I have had. Count yourself blessed not to know these devious ways."

"I think the times require me to learn, my lord."

Tuzza nodded sadly. "I have devoted my life to the defense of my people and my empire. I am glad to say that I was never called upon to engage in conquest, though others have been, including my cousin Alezzi." He turned a little to look out over the valley toward the city. "The lessons are bitter, Ratha. Every one of them. And while some acts may be genuinely justifiable, that does not mean they won't return to you in the dark and solitude of night."

"That is one lesson I have already learned," Ratha said.

"I as well," Jenah added. Cilla and Tess remained silent, though both looked down as if sharing the feelings.

"'Twas this awareness," Annuvil said quietly, "that led me and others to believe we could create a peaceful race. That I have lived to see the Anari need to take up swords…" He trailed off and shook his head. "Bitter indeed. Bitter beyond the bitterest of my life."

Tess immediately reached out and gripped his arm. "You tried to mend a problem. War is seldom just or justified. Indeed, whatever the cause, it is ugly and brutal. And were we not facing the terrible threat I have seen in the encroachment of an early severe winter and the deaths of thousands, were I not able to imagine worse deeds and outcomes, I would declare we must not shed blood.

"This time, my lord Annuvil, *he* gives us no other choice. And perhaps, he didn't give you a choice in the past, either."

Archer closed his eyes, then looked at her. "Thank you for your faith in me. I wish I shared it."

The others fell silent, pondering sadly that which lay ahead, each locked in his own thoughts and memories. But then Ratha stirred. "We must tell the armies to break out. How do you want the fires built, my lord? As they would for camp? Or another way?"

"Keep the fires to the front of the lines. If we are attacked we can regroup behind them more easily than if they are everywhere."

Ratha nodded. He, Jenah and Tuzza climbed away from the ledge toward the waiting armies. The Ilduin flanked Archer, and he turned to look on the valley below. They turned with him.

"Could you?" he asked them. "Intervene if they begin an attack?"

"We will certainly try," Cilla answered.

"Aye," said Tess. "I would not like to see bloodshed between armies that need to ally. 'Twould be a terrible waste."

Archer nodded. "I agree. Without purpose. Do you have any sense of what is happening with your sister Sara?"

"They are in the palace," Tess answered. "Before the emperor. But her mind is busy, and I cannot discern any one thing."

"I feel the same," Cilla agreed. "She is not trying to reach us."

"I hope that is good," said Archer. His hand fell to the hilt of his sword and he sighed. "By the gods, I am sick unto death of war."

Sara and Tom stood amid a ring of spear points. The instant Lozzi had accused Sara, the soldiers had sprung into action. Only Alezzi, an overmark and of royal blood, escaped the threat.

"Alezzi," the emperor said sharply. "How could you have brought this danger to me? How could you have betrayed me so?"

"If I have betrayed you, I will gladly sacrifice my head," Alezzi said. "But I have not. And Lozzi lies."

"Lie?" the girl shrieked. "I never lie."

"You lie all the time," Sara said calmly, ignoring the painful tightness with which Tom held her hand. "You began lying some six months past, when the hive took you in."

"Lies!"

Sara smiled faintly. "You are pure, then?"

"Except for what you do to me."

"I do nothing to you and you know it."

Alezzi spoke. "Maluzza, my cousin, we played together as children. We stood side by side through many trials. I have always served you well and with pride. I tell you, I am serving you now, this very instant. Does my young cousin Lozzi ever scream at anyone?"

A frown knit the emperor's brow and he looked at his daughter.

"She's making me do it," the girl said, pointing at Sara.

"And," said Alezzi, "we are to believe that Nona, who has never laid a finger on you in anger, whatever your misdeed, has now hit you."

"It is so!"

"I think not," said Alezzi.

"Of course not," said Sara. Gently she freed her fingers from Tom's clutch. Then, almost quicker than the eye, she brought forth her small dagger. An instant later, she had cut her palm and blood began to drip steadily to the floor. "I am Ilduin," she said calmly. "My blood judges. Those of you who know the old stories know that my blood will judge those who are evil or possessed by evil. It can judge no other."

Turning, she let her blood fall on Tom. Nothing happened. "Alezzi?"

He hesitated a moment, then held out his own hand. Blood fell harmlessly upon it.

"Who else in this room will stand for judgment?" Sara asked, holding up her hand. "How many of you have only the emperor's best interests at heart?"

No one moved, and Sara's lips curled. Then she looked

at Lozzi. "My child, you are so young no evil could have taken root in your heart or mind. So my blood will not harm you. Step forward and prove the truth of what you say. For you see, I cannot choose who my blood judges. It is beyond my control. So this blood cannot possibly harm you, can it?"

"No," the girl said, wide-eyed, backing up a step. "No!"

Sara moved toward her and not even the guards dared step near her or her blood. "But it cannot harm you. And what better way to prove the truth of your accusation?"

"No!" Lozzi backed up even more, cowering. "Keep it away from me!"

The emperor reached out a hand, catching Sara's arm and holding her. "Do not hurt my child. You are Ilduin, and I cannot prevent you. Not all my armies could prevent you. But do not hurt my child!"

Sara looked at him. "I told you she came with lies. I warned you of her approach. There is a hive in your palace, and it has taken your child. There is within these walls an Ilduin who works for the Enemy. She betrays you every day, every hour, and she has taken your child into the hive. Her minions are working to weaken you and weaken your empire, for in the days to come, when Ardred marches on you, he wishes to find little opposition. You will waste your legions fighting the wrong enemy. You will curse your people by listening to lies and by trusting the wrong advisers."

Sara shrugged. "If you do not believe me, lock us all away. But before I leave this room, my blood will fall on your daughter."

"You threaten me and mine!"

Sara's eyes sparked. "There is more in the balance than you, your child and your empire. You have heard the words of the prophet. Erkiah has vouched for him. Would you ignore the warning because a child lies to you?"

Slowly the emperor released her arm and turned to his daughter. "Lozzi, why did Nona strike you?"

The girl, staring at the blood that still dripped from Sara's palm, seemed suddenly lost and confused. "I…she…." Her voice trailed off and she dragged her gaze from the blood to her father. On her face there appeared a monumental struggle, and all who could see could not doubt that some battle raged madly within her.

"She…she did *not* strike me!"

With that, the girl collapsed into an insensate heap on the floor.

The emperor knelt beside her and cradled her gently. "My child, my child…"

"She is strong," Sara said gently. "On the cusp of finding her Ilduin powers. She will be fine. And you should be proud, for she battled and won freedom, however brief, from the hive."

The emperor looked up at Sara. "You can heal. Help her."

"Healing is not what she needs. And I alone am not strong enough to battle another Ilduin for her mind and heart. I will need my sisters."

"Then send for them!"

"You must let them pass safely."

"They shall."

"And you must let Lord Annuvil come with them."

"He is here?" The emperor looked both amazed and stunned.

"He leads us," Alezzi said. "He will lead us in the fight against Chaos. He and the White Lady."

The emperor nodded and looked down at the daughter he cradled in his arms. "She is so pale. I will send a messenger."

"That is not necessary," Sara said. "I will tell them. You will ensure that they meet no obstacles of any kind on their way."

The emperor nodded, rocking Lozzi as if his heart were breaking.

"I never thought I would see such a day," Cilla murmured to Tess. Astride their mounts, she, Tess and Archer were passing among the orderly ranks of the Bozandari legion. The soldiers watched them with the greatest suspicion, but the order had been given to pass them through unhindered, and these soldiers obeyed their orders.

Tess nodded. "It feels…strange."

Cilla looked at her. "Strange in what way?"

"It is as if…" She shook her head. "I think I have done this before. It stirs a memory I cannot quite reach."

She lowered her head, reaching for the slippery wisps of something from her forgotten past. Part of her feared what she might find there, for she must have forgotten it for a reason, and the one full memory she had recovered had been of holding her dying mother in a strange world.

But this somehow seemed important, and she struggled to grasp the slippery threads of thought as they rode between the orderly ranks toward the gates of the beautiful city.

But then the memory opened into something entirely different from orderly rows of soldiers into a scene more like that battle the Anari had fought against Tuzza's legion. Every bit as bad. Worse.

Doc!

She was crawling on her belly, dragging a heavy bag. Around her explosions shook the world, making the ground heave beneath her. Dirt and other debris, some of it human flesh, rained on her as she lowered her helmeted head.

Then forward again, urgently squirming along the ground. *Doc!*

She reached two men huddled together behind the shelter of a ragged hump of ground covered by the husks of dead foliage. The one who had been screaming for her held his hand tightly on the leg of another man, who writhed horribly.

Jumbled words filled her ears, but then the man lifted his hand from the wound and she saw the horrific spurt. *Pressure!* she heard herself yell over the surrounding roars and chattering bursts of deafening noise. *Keep it on!* Then she pulled the bag up to eye level and began to rip open a dark green package....

Tess blinked, returning to the here and now with a near sense of shock.

The orderly rows surrounding her were so far removed from the mayhem she had just seen that it seemed surreal.

Archer's voice reached her. "Are you all right, my lady?"

"I just remembered something from my past." She looked at him and found his strong face furrowed with concern. "It was ugly. It was a battle. But it was not here."

His brow creased even more. "Not here?"

"Not in this world."

His lips suddenly compressed into a tight line. "Will the gods never stop toying with us?"

"Will I never escape war?"

"I often wonder the same thing." Then he utterly astonished her by leaning over in his saddle, grasping her hand and carrying it to his lips. "May we be facing our final battle," he said, then squeezed her fingers and let go.

The flutter in Tess's heart totally distracted her from the ugly memory that had returned to her.

The final battle. How good that would be.

But first they must survive it.

The emperor kept the audience chamber locked. Everyone had settled, waiting for whatever lay ahead of them. The guards remained on full alert, and periodically one would come to the door to give a report on the advance of Tess, Cilla and Archer.

Lozzi remained unconscious, her father hovering over her as she lay on a bed hastily contrived of pillows. Once he looked at Sara and asked, "Will she recover?"

Sara nodded. "Aye. She is strong. Stronger than the hive. But the effort to break their hold exhausted her. She needs the rest. And 'tis better she remain this way until my sisters arrive, for if she wakes, the hive will again take control."

"I want this hive exterminated from my palace," Maluzza said, his voice cracking. "I want every one of them destroyed like the vermin they are!"

"Patience," Tom counseled, speaking for the first time in quite a while. "When the three come together, no hive will withstand them."

"And there is one who can be saved apart from your daughter," Sara said. "We must try very hard to save her."

"Who?" Maluzza demanded.

"Your seer."

He looked aghast. "She is part of this?"

"Not by her will. We must free her."

"By Adis!" The emperor looked like a man from beneath whom the very earth had been yanked. "Lies. I have been surrounded by lies and betrayal, and yet I trusted."

"Those who betray are evil," Sara said gently. "Those who trust are good at heart, and cannot be expected to look for evil in others."

The emperor rose from the floor beside his daughter and looked at Alezzi, Tom and Sara. "I was born to this. The moment I drew my first breath, I was fated to sit on that throne and bear its burdens. Not once in my entire life have I thought of doing otherwise. Nor would it have been permitted. My daughter, too, faces the same fate. One day she will sit on that throne."

He shook his head, as if clearing his thoughts. "I have always cared for the people of this empire as best I could. I have not always been right. Nor have I always done good. The slave revolt—I should have seen it coming before anyone died. I have failed so many, both slave and free."

Tom spoke, surprised. "You care that slaves died?"

"Of course I do," the emperor answered sharply. "They are in my care as much as any Bozandari!"

"Then how can you endure that they are slaves? Are they not people to you?"

"Slavery began before my time. And to remove it too quickly would result in the collapse of the empire I have sworn before the gods to protect. *You* try sitting in that chair, young man."

Tom flushed. "It is an evil beyond almost any."

Alezzi spoke. "I have never owned a slave. Nor has my cousin Maluzza. Every Anari in this palace is free. But my cousin is right, Tom. Because of what happened in the past, change must happen at a careful pace."

"Then why," demanded Tom, "do you still allow the slavers to raid the Anari villages? Why do you let your armies march on defenseless towns and seize the prized youth of the clan? Why do you allow this evil?"

The emperor lowered his head. "Then perhaps I had best not let Ilduin blood fall on me."

"I think not," said Tom irately. "You claim to protect all your people, slaves included, yet you have not even ordered your armies to stop stealing men and women from the Anari. You have not ordered that no more slaves be sold, so the raids will stop and those who depend on slaves will have to care for them as irreplaceable. You talk of seeing slow change, yet you have let the cusp of change slip through your fingers throughout your reign!"

Soldiers edged closer but the emperor held up his hand. "The young prophet is right."

"You have cared more that your wealthy classes not be angry with you than you have cared that Anari are being stolen, sold and chained as if they were mere cattle. You have recognized a wrong, yet have done little if anything to correct it. That makes you more evil than most."

Out of Tom's mouth, those words emerged as a judgment spanning ages rather than the moment it took him to speak them. He reached up, removing his leather mask with one tug of the string that held it in place and revealed his strange eyes, eyes with a clear iris so that the pupil appeared to fill the whole space. As the light struck his widely opened eyes, like an animal's at night they shot back red light.

Those who could see him gasped and fell back.

"Ilduin fire not only heals, it purges and cleanses. Before you face the evil we must battle, you must cleanse yourself, Maluzza Forzzia, for evil draws evil to itself. If you are to protect your people and lead them in this fight, you must be free of true evil yourself!"

Tom's finger had risen and pointed at the emperor. "The Ilduin will cleanse the hive from the palace, but who will cleanse the throne?"

Alezzi looked as if he wanted to step forward and silence Tom, as if he feared what the emperor might order after being treated in this utterly unprecedented way. Sara, too, appeared poised to protect her husband.

But after a few seconds, it became apparent it would not be necessary.

"No one has spoken to me so truly in a long time," Maluzza said heavily. "Alezzi, you have stayed away too much."

Alezzi sighed. "I could not bear to be here."

"So you, too, realized."

Alezzi bowed his head slightly.

"I have been receiving poor counsels." The emperor looked around the room at all the gathered people. "How can I govern well if no one tells me the truth? If no one reminds me of what is good and true?"

No one answered. Not a single voice.

"Scribe!"

A man bearing a tablet and pen hurried forward. "My emperor?"

"Write me a law this very instant. Free all slaves and ban the ownership of slaves, under penalty of prison. And add that any of my soldiers who enrich themselves by engaging in the slave trade will forfeit their lives and their property."

The gasps and murmurs that filled the room then could have grown to a deafening crescendo quite quickly as the scribe began to write.

"My emperor," a guard announced. "The Ilduin have arrived along with the man who is called Annuvil."

Chapter Twenty-Five

Ardred leaned closed to the old hag and listened to her muttered words. It seemed she could no longer tell what was happening in the audience chamber of the Bozandari emperor. The hive had been attacked in some way, though she was not clear on the details.

He restrained an urge to hit her, so that if she was deceiving him in some way she would stop. He'd possessed her for too long, he reminded himself. She no longer resisted any whim or request of his. Long since had she learned the anguish resistance brought her.

She turned her wrinkled, skeletal face toward him, her eyes white with blindness. "I cannot learn anymore, my lord. The girl is unconscious. Izza has been freed and until one of the hive is allowed to approach him again, he will be useless."

"And the rest?"

She closed those hideous, sightless eyes. "They are

making a plan to enter the audience chamber. But they are not that many in number."

"No." No, that had been his doing. He had wanted key people in this particular hive, but not so many that they might be noticed. Other hives were larger, but they were intended for very different purposes, weakening the empire's defenses in every direction by collecting larger and larger numbers of obedient members. But in the palace, a mere handful who truly claimed the emperor's ear. Until now the plan had worked splendidly.

He sighed and tapped his toe impatiently. "Try harder. There must be something you can learn."

"Aye, my lord."

"Send for me if you do."

"Aye, my lord."

He strode from the room, and he did not see the faint, bitter smile cross the woman's lips as she sat back in her padded chair and allowed sleep to come to her.

Sara watched as Tess, Cilla and Archer walked through the audience chamber toward her group and the emperor.

She was struck, suddenly by how different they looked. Archer, who had once been a weary-looking traveler who rarely cared to be noticed, who had always been soft-spoken, courteous and nearly invisible when he stopped at her father's inn over the years, now strode with purpose and confidence that made him seem yet taller and more powerful. No one could ignore him now, or find him invisible.

And his sword, usually well hidden under his cloak, peeked out, its intricate, jeweled hilt visible to everyone. His companion quiver and bows were absent, however. He was no longer Archer, she realized with a jolt. This was Annuvil, the man who had paid a price beyond imagining for his failings, a man born to be a king.

Beside him, Cilla, too, seemed transformed. She had always borne herself proudly, but battle had affected her in some way that made her look older, sterner, less of the young woman Sara had first met in Anahar.

Sara supposed she herself had changed in just such ways, given the journey on which life had taken them since Whitewater. None of them was truly young anymore.

But then came Tess, and Sara not only noticed the change, she was shocked by it. The young, frightened woman who remembered nothing of her past, who had awakened amid the gore of a slaughtered caravan, had been more transformed than any of them. Why had she not noted the change before? Had she really been so self-absorbed, or absorbed in Tom? Or was it merely the venue that made her so aware now?

The blond-haired, blue-eyed woman garbed in perfect white entered the room with the Weaver's sword hanging from a brown leather belt at her hip. The sword itself was in no way remarkable in appearance, but in Tess's hand it had come to life far beyond the mere ability to slash and cut. Only once had she removed it from the plain leather scabbard, and that had been in battle. Those who had heard it sing in her hand, who had seen it flash with inner light, would never forget.

But now Tess herself shone with an inner light. Gone was the lost and frightened woman, replaced by an Ilduin who walked with confidence and head high into the presence of the most powerful man in the known world as if he were no more important than anyone else.

But, Sara thought with a catch in her own breath, had she not done the same thing herself earlier this day?

They had all been changed. *All* of them. When she felt Tom's fingers against hers, she reached for them and held them.

The emperor faced the new arrivals, his face a mix of consternation, fear, anguish and controlled anger. He was not pleased with the things that had been said to him, that much was clear, yet he was the kind of man who would stand and take criticism. That alone marked him as well above average.

Alezzi hurried to make introductions. The emperor, for the moment, however, was only interested in Cilla and Tess. "Can you help my daughter?"

"She fought free of the hive," Sara said quietly. "But I alone can do nothing to rouse her or heal her."

Tess nodded and knelt beside the girl. With one hand she touched the smooth young forehead. "She has gone far away to hide from the hive." She looked up at the emperor. "You daughter is strong. She will become a great Ilduin."

"I only care that she survive this."

Tess nodded. "So it is for all we love. Greater battles lie ahead of us, but at this moment none is greater than saving this child."

She looked at the other two Ilduin. "Join me, sisters."

They knelt with her, creating a circle around the girl, and linked hands.

Tess closed her eyes, reaching inward. Those watching saw nothing for a long time except three women kneeling around the emperor's daughter, but then, slowly, a rainbow arced between the three of them and over the girl who lay between them.

It grew in brilliance, scintillating and sparkling in every color the eye could see. Then slowly it lowered until it touched Lozzi's forehead.

An instant later a soft cry escaped the girl, then her eyes snapped open. At once the rainbow vanished.

"Can I?" the emperor asked, reaching for his daughter.

"She is well now," Tess said. She rose and drew back to stand beside Archer and Alezzi. Cilla and Sara joined her. It seemed to those gathered around that Tess looked paler than when she had entered the room, but she still stood strong and straight.

The emperor hugged his daughter, tears running down his cheeks for a few minutes until the strength of his relief eased. Then he rose and faced the party, his cheeks unashamedly wet. "Thank you," he said to the Ilduin.

As one they bowed to him.

"And you." The emperor turned to look at Archer. "Should I bow to you?"

Archer shook his head. "No man need bow to me. I am here merely to serve my purpose."

"I admit I am having trouble believing what I am told, that you are Annuvil, the Firstborn Son of the Firstborn King."

A half smile curled Archer's mouth. "You need not believe it. It matters not. All that matters is the threat this world faces from Ardred."

"I have heard the old stories and prophecies," Maluzza conceded, "and a seer warned at my birth that I should play a part in the prophecies, but I cannot understand why anyone at all would wish to do to this world what the young prophet here foresees. What would it profit him?"

"I do not know. I have never understood this part of him. I suspect we are but pawns in a game the gods play. But of this I know one thing for certain—this game will not end until he and I finish the business between us."

"And that is what?"

"One of us must die."

"And into this the entire world must be dragged?"

"So it seems. Ardred will have it no other way and never would. It was not enough to hate me and kill me. Instead he involved the entire race of Firstborn, first through building his own faction, then through causing my father to build one for me. Out of this came wars beyond imagining. You have seen the plain of Dederand? 'Twas there the last blow was struck in the war. You have seen league after league of black glass where nothing can grow. Not even that seems to have stopped him."

The emperor frowned, trying to absorb the meaning of all this.

"And it is across that plain that we shall have to march to meet Ardred, for he is ensconced in the mountains near Earth's Root."

"'Tis a dangerous way to travel," the emperor said. "'Tis slippery and there are many sharp places. We will lose men simply by crossing it."

Archer nodded. "I believe that is what he intends. But I will go alone, if need be. I only wish I could guarantee your safety and the safety of the rest of the world if I face him alone. But I cannot. He builds hives, which will become armies. Only those who serve him will survive and prosper. Always has he been thus."

"Then," said the emperor, decision clearly made, "we must make plans. Together. For the sake of our people."

Archer nodded. "For the sake of our people."

"But first," said Sara, "we must deal with the hive inside

the palace, for if we do not, the Enemy will know every detail of every plan we make."

"Then let us go, sisters," Cilla said. "It is time to show the Enemy that we are not without teeth."

Tess walked with her Ilduin sisters on each side. The news of their arrival had already spread through the palace and even Bozandari nobles seemed to flatten themselves to the walls as the women passed. She didn't like being the object of fear. On the other hand, she made no effort to comfort the dread she saw in the eyes around her. If they wished to fear her, let them. Others had certainly quailed from these people often enough.

"You have been here longer than I," Tess said to Sara. "Have you any idea where the hive is hidden?"

"We should go to Lozzi's nanny," Sara said. "The nanny is the girl's primary caretaker. That was obvious from the emperor's reaction. She will know who else the girl has seen regularly."

"You do not think she is in the hive?" Cilla asked.

"We will soon find out," Tess said, her eyes grim and determined. That someone could use a mere child in this way drew forth a wrath that burned in the pit of Tess's belly. For the first time, she did not quail at the thought of meting out Ilduin justice. If ever there was a time for justice, that time was now.

Tess barked questions at palace guards and officials as they passed, seeking and gaining directions to Lozzi's private chambers. If any of those she questioned had been reluctant to give her the information she sought, that had quickly given way under Tess's fierce gaze.

Be not too led by anger, Cilla cautioned in thought.

If we cannot be angry at this, when would be the right time? Tess thought back. *The Enemy was going to turn that beautiful girl into a burned-out Ilduin husk. His evil knows no bounds.*

Then she walled off her mind. Something, some memory she could not reach, fueled her anger like an unseen but volatile gas. She did not attempt to plumb that memory. There would be time for that later. For now, she simply drew strength from it.

Lozzi's nanny was a half-Anari woman named Nona. When she saw the three Ilduin enter, her dark eyes widened in surprise and then narrowed in caution.

"Where is Lozzi?" she asked.

"She is with her father," Tess said. "You are her nanny, yes?"

Nona nodded. "And more her mother than the woman who birthed her. How is my child? If you have harmed her…"

"We have not," Tess said. "We have freed her from the dark bonds that lay on her mind, and she is well. If you truly love her, you will accept my solemn promise of that, and help me find those who enslaved her. If you do not, I warn you, hope not for another sunrise. For your life will end this day, in this room."

"I would never harm her!" Nona said. "Aye, she has changed these past months. But I thought it simply that she was entering womanhood, and later that she had heard of all that was happening in the city, and feared for me."

Tess studied the woman. Her face was Anari, but her eyes were Bozandari. And while her face was as impassive as any Anari, her eyes shielded nothing. She was telling the truth.

Tess permitted the briefest smile on her lips. "I believe you, Nona. Now tell us, please, who else Lozzi had seen of late.

For it is nigh certain that one of them had enslaved her mind."

Nona drew a slow breath. "Please understand that I do not wish to accuse the innocent."

That was a lie, Tess knew. "I need names."

Nona shook her head. "If I were to give you ten names, not knowing which is the one you seek, what of the other nine? Do you think they will not know who gave you their names, who cast them into suspicion? Do you think they will forgive me that indiscretion? If so, then you know nothing of this palace or these people."

"If it is your position and safety that concerns you," Tess said, "consider the danger that I pose. I am here now, Nona."

"If you are truly Ilduin, you would not harm an innocent," the nanny said. "Not even to punish an evil. Not unless you yourself were possessed of the very evil you claim to fight."

Tess fell silent. The woman had called her bluff, and it had indeed been a bluff. She was not going to torture this woman to get information. And in truth, she saw well why Nona was reluctant to talk. That she had also turned over the name of the guilty person would not matter to the innocent. And they would work their revenge on Nona, who would be helpless to prevent it.

"We will need Lozzi's help," Sara said, as if reading through the wall Tess had put around her thoughts. "Nona, Lozzi will be coming with us in the coming campaign. She will doubtless want you at her side, and we would want her in no other arms. So you will not be staying here at the palace, regardless. There is no need to fear retribution, for both you and Lozzi will be in our care."

"You cannot protect me from her," Nona said, shaking her head. "Not even Ilduin power is that strong."

"Who?" Tess asked, stepping forward.

But Sara put a hand on Tess's arm. "She doesn't have to tell us, sister."

"She must!" Tess said. "Someone tortured and used a young girl. They must pay for that atrocity!"

"No," Sara said, her grip tightening. "Sister, she doesn't have to tell us. For I already know."

"What?" Tess asked, looking at Sara.

Something in Sara's eyes said *let me in*. Tess did, and in an instant, she knew Sara was right.

Chapter Twenty-Six

Tess looked down at the captive Ilduin. She wondered how long the emperor's mother had been enslaved. And, more important, by whom. She suspected she would never know the answer to the first question. But if experience was any guide, she would soon know the answer to the second.

Fetzza had once been a beautiful woman. That much was obvious. She had high, patrician cheekbones and green eyes that must have once fetched many a man's gaze. Now she lay on a sumptuous bed, surrounded by every creature comfort a son such as hers could provide. Yet, Tess saw, she was hardly comfortable. And if ever she had known true happiness, those days had long passed.

"You cannot win," Fetzza said, scorn in her eye. "My master is far stronger than you will ever know."

"You are enslaved," Tess said, trying to reconcile this woman's behavior with what she had seen of Sara's mother in Lorense. Surely Fetzza must be as innocent as Mara had been. "Your mind is hostage to evil, sister."

"Sister?" The woman nearly spat out the word. "You are no sister of mine. I would not share blood with such... weakness!"

"Surely you recognize Ilduin kin," Sara said.

Fetzza shook a bony finger at the three of them. "You are but pale shadows of what Ilduin should be! Afraid to claim your birthrights as daughters of the gods, and mothers of the world. For it was through us that the gods birthed all life! You were born to rule, and instead you cower behind kindness."

"I cower not before you," Cilla said, stepping forward. "I do not fear those who have been spoiled by power. And I will not fear those who have enslaved my own brothers and sisters."

"We birthed you for slavery!" Fetzza shouted at her. "Your kind are sheep and were always to be thus. Your illusion of freedom will not long last. Your army will be crushed. And you will wipe the pus from my bedsores as I serve the one, true Power."

"Step back, Cilla," Sara said. "She seeks to goad us into rage. She wants us to fall with her."

"And you," Fetzza said, fixing Sara in her icy gaze. "Your mother was pathetic, a village cow whose udders could nurse no one better than Lantav Glassidor. You thought you won a victory when you freed her. But look now at what lies in the north."

Suddenly Tess's mind was flooded with images. In the town of Derda, famine still ruled the land, the frozen dead were stacked like cordwood outside the city gates, their bodies raided in the night by those who could find no other sustenance. And in Whitewater, the Deepwell Inn filled to bursting with the cold and the needy under a shoulder-deep layer of snow. Bandylegs withered as he parsed out the last of his food with eyes that knew there was not enough.

"He's dying!" Sara said, hands quaking.

"By his own weakness," Fetzza said. "If he were to care for his own needs, he might have enough to endure. But no. His own kindness will kill him."

"Enough!" Tess said, now restraining Sara.

The woman was playing on their anger, tempting them one by one to fall into the abyss that was her home. Tess tried to probe the woman's mind, to search out the identity of Fetzza's tempter, but it was like battering herself against a wall.

"And there is the Weaver," Fetzza said, turning to Tess. "Trying to learn who seduced me? No one! I merely see the truth, and I am not such a fool as to align myself and my son with the weak and the sheep. And I certainly will not bow to the nameless spawn of a whore."

"I do not fear your lies," Tess said, meeting her gaze, unflinching.

"Then fear the truth!" Fetzza said.

The bitter waves of memory crashed through Tess like the surge of a raging storm. Watching her mother dress for the evening in a short leather skirt and obscenely high heels. Sitting in their filthy apartment, with nothing but the scent of decay and the wails of sirens to rock her to sleep, until her mother came home in the wee hours, reeking of sweat and men. The sound of her mother showering, furiously scrubbing herself, trying to wash away the stain on her soul. And then her mother slipping into the small bed that they shared, Tess's tears falling as she tried not to let her mother know she was awake, her mother whispering to whatever gods might care that soon, soon, she would get them out of here.

Tess saw clearly the day when her mother moved them into the new, clean house. The day her mother walked with her to the new school and signed the papers and explained that she and Tess did not have the same last name, handing over Tess's birth certificate as proof that she was in fact her daughter. That night Tess had asked why her last name was Birdsong when her mother's name was Palmer. She was born in early spring, and her mother had listened to the birds singing as she had made her way to the hospital to give birth. Only years later had Tess learned that her mother never knew which of her tricks had spawned her.

In all of these months, Tess had never remembered a father, and now she knew why. She had never had one.

Fetzza was no longer broadcasting the memories. There was no need to, for now they flooded unbidden. Her mother had worked as a receptionist after she had gotten off the streets. The table had been spare and the larder lean, but her mother had scraped every dime to hold on to the house and keep Tess in a school where everyone else seemed to despise her because she was from the wrong side of town. Tess had taken their spite and turned it into a fiercely competitive nature, throwing herself into her schoolwork with a fanaticism that even her teachers sometimes found daunting. She had been determined to exceed everyone's expectations, to prove her worth in the world.

All of that had changed on the cold autumn day that her only friend, Gail, had undressed to shower after gym class. Tess had seen the cigarette burns on her belly, and had immediately known what they were. Her mother had more than once come home with bruises and burns, back when she had been on the streets, and a tiny Tess had helped to tend them. Tess had not quailed from the horror as a child, and she had not quailed from it as an adolescent.

She had pressed Gail for answers, long into the evening as they sat in the grass on a hill outside of town, looking up into the sky, watching the clouds redden as the story poured out. She had taken Gail home with her that night. The next day she and her mother had walked Gail to the police station, where Gail had begun to describe the horror of her life at home.

Gail had been inside, telling her story to the young female detective, when Tess's mother had suggested that she and Tess get lunch at the small diner across the street. The diner was a special treat, a place Tess had always looked forward to, for they could only afford to eat there once a month.

She had not eaten there that day.

She had never eaten there again.

For they had never reached the far side of the street. The truck had come out of nowhere, and in the time it took to hear the screech of tires and the blare of the horn and the sickening thud, Tess had found herself looking at her mother's limp body, then kneeling beside it, trying to tend wounds that could never be tended.

Instead, she could only hold her mother's hand as she died, tears falling onto her mother's bloodstained face, a face that finally knew peace.

Tess came out of the reverie slowly, realizing she had sagged against her sisters, tears once again rolling down her face. She was Tess because her mother had once prayed to Saint Theresa. She was Birdsong because the birds had been singing as her mother walked to the hospital. She had no father, save for whatever man had paid to deposit his seed in her mother's body.

But if she was the nameless daughter of a whore, she was also the daughter of a mother who had fought her way out of a depth Tess had never imagined, and who had chosen for her names that captured the few good memories she had.

And it was the memory of that woman that had caused Tess to get the tattoo of the white rose on her ankle. Roses had been her mother's favorite flower, and white represented purity.

But there was more, much more. Tess understood with blinding clarity that her mother had chosen that life to protect her daughter. Had chosen, as an Ilduin, to raise Tess in the comparative safety of a different world until the moment came for Tess to assume the prophesied burden. Her mother had chosen that hardscrabble life for no other reason than to ensure that Tess would not be discovered by Ardred.

Tess lifted her head and looked at Fetzza. "If you think that memories of a mother's love will enrage me, you know nothing, old woman. My mother was more worthy than you could ever be."

Fetzza's eyes flared with the knowledge that she could not win this battle of wills, and her hand reached beneath her pillow for the dagger. Ilduin Bane dripped from the blade as she drew it back, taking aim for Tess's chest.

"*Sha non!*" Tess cried, glaring at the woman.

The woman's hand froze in midair, the dagger slipping

from weakened fingers, tumbling once before falling blade down through her nightclothes and pricking her pale belly. A scream rose from her throat as the poison went to work, her skin peeling back in gray ash, blackness spreading through her innards.

"No!" Maluzza said, bursting into the room, rushing to his mother's bed.

"Touch her not!" Tess said. "Let not her poison work on anyone but herself."

He froze, hands pressed to his ears to close out her screams, eyes squeezed shut to keep away the horror of her body rotting right before them. Only when the last scream had echoed through the palace halls could he bear to look up at the sooty stain that had once been his mother.

"She…she…" he stammered.

"She was once your mother," Tess said. "But that was long ago. For far too long she was the Enemy's mistress."

"Perhaps," he said, wiping tears from his eyes. "But I cannot remember her thus."

"No," Tess said. "You cannot."

"Let us leave here," he said. "I will close up this room. No one will enter it, ever again."

Tess nodded. It was a grander crypt than the woman she had seen deserved, but a fitting resting place for the woman who had been Maluzza's mother.

"Aye, let us leave here," she said. "The Enemy must be stopped. No other mother should bear this stain."

"We must find Lozzi," Cilla said. "She will now come into her powers and will need guidance."

"And there is another in the palace," Sara announced. "I sensed her earlier. She was not the focus of the hive, but she was most certainly part of it."

Cilla answered angrily. "She will certainly become the focus *now.*"

But Tess, who had given up trying to measure her powers or the growth of them, or to even figure out how she was using them, closed her eyes a moment and pointed toward the left. "She is that way. And she has been struggling."

She reached out and dared to touch the emperor. He did not appear to mind. "Go to your daughter. You and Nona keep her safe, for now that your mother has died, the Ilduin power in her will begin to emerge. If she was a target before, she will be even more so now."

He nodded, looking almost relieved to have someone tell him what to do. The shock of his mother's horrific death, and possibly of her betrayal, had shaken him to his core. When he walked away toward the audience chamber, his posture lacked some of its earlier confidence.

"Can we find our way through this warren?" Sara asked. "The corridors are a maze and I doubt I could find my way back out the same way I came in."

"Can you not sense her?" Tess asked. "We have merely to follow that trail."

"I get only a general feeling."

"I, too," Cilla said.

"Then follow me." Because, in some corner of her mind, Tess had seen the warp and woof underlying reality, and on the fabric she could not only see the blackened area to the northwest where Ardred awaited them, but much closer, she could see the frail light of another Ilduin, a light that was surrounded by distorted threads of reality like a trap.

She needed little else to guide her. Striding down the corridor, she heard her sisters follow.

Even in its interior, the palace sacrificed none of its security. Corridors wound, then turned sharply, branching off into other winding corridors. Yet somehow there was a plan to this seeming madness or no one would ever be able to navigate this place.

Reaching for the pouch at her neck, Tess poured the stones into her palm. The amethyst one glowed brightly. Returning the others to the bag, Tess held the amethyst out before her. Each time she prepared to take a turn, it acted like a guide, fading when she started to go the wrong way, brightening when she chose the right path.

Her unknown sister was aiding her. Tess's heart beat more strongly with hope. "She is not utterly lost. She calls us."

"Or is being used to call us," Cilla cautioned.

The warning weighed heavily on Tess as she followed the beacon in her palm. With her sisters beside her, she ought to be able to withstand a single Ilduin. And it certainly seemed that whatever powers Ardred might retain he still needed Ilduin to work his worst.

At least for now.

Finally they reached a door.

"She is here," Sara said. "I can feel her."

"As can I," Cilla agreed.

The amethyst in Tess's palm shone brightly with the same message. Slowly she closed her fingers around it, concealing it.

Sara reached out and rapped on the door. There was no answer. Glancing at the other two as if in question, she then reached out and pushed the door open.

They saw a middle-aged woman rocking rapidly in a rocking chair beside a narrow bed. She stared blindly into space, her face contorted.

"Sister," Sara said quietly, and stepped into the room. "Sister, can you hear me?"

The woman's head turned, her eyes seeming to reflect the blackness of evil. "Help me," she whispered.

As soon the words escaped her, she contorted with pain and screamed. Ardred's attempt to fully possess her threatened to tear her apart.

Sara, Cilla and Tess quickly gathered round her and linked hands. With heads bowed and eyes closed, they sought the power their birthright had given them.

But this time was not as easy as before. Before they had been dealing first with a child who had not attained her powers and then with an old woman who, Tess suspected, had been on her way to being discarded by Ardred.

This time Ardred didn't want to let go, and the Ilduin who controlled his hives for him fought hard to retain control over this woman.

This struggle, Tess realized with dawning horror, as she felt chill, oily fingers in her mind, could entrap any one of them.

Or it could end in death.

Chapter Twenty-Seven

Ardred leaned near the ear of the old crone, crooning softly. Ignoring the stench of rot that forever rose from her was difficult, but he had far more important things in mind.

"Do you see her?" he asked quietly. "My Tess? Can you pick her out?"

The Ilduin who had spent much of her adult life honing her powers under the boot and prodding of Ardred, nodded slowly, her sightless eyes seeing what he could not.

"She stands with the others around Yazzi. They have joined as one to fight me."

"All you need to do is make a little distraction," he murmured softly in her ear, almost like a lover. "Enough that you can slip into Tess and command her."

"She already resists my touch."

"She is joining with other Ilduin," he said more sharply. "That leaves her open to you."

"It would," the crone said bitterly, "if *your* stamp weren't all over my touch."

Enraged, Ardred reared back and slapped the woman on the side of her head. "Find a way! Disguise yourself! Invite yourself into the circle she creates! Do it."

"Or what?" the crone demanded. "What will you do? Kill me? Then who will you have to do this work for you?"

"There are others."

"Oh, aye, there are others," she retorted. "But none as powerful as I. No other could do what I do for you."

"My Tess could."

She laughed, a sound as dry and brittle as old leaves tossed by the wind. "You need me to control her. No other can."

"Defy me, old woman, and I may decide to wait to correct the evils of the past. After all, I have all eternity. You have only as long as I choose to give you."

"I pity you," she said. "Nothing could induce me to live forever."

He raised his hand to hit her again, then thought better of it. Reining his temper, he gentled his voice, turning on every bit of the charm that had swayed thousands.

"You forget," he said softly, "why we do this."

"Do I? I have created blight at your behest, and thousands have died. How will that reunite the world and restore the glory and beauty of the Firstborn?"

Gently, gently, he touched her bony shoulder. "I have told you," he said patiently. "Many died because of my brother. 'Twere there any other way, I would use it. But the gods exact their due, Hesta. They are still angry over my brother's arrogance. And they are still angry that I failed to deal with him in time to save the first world. I need to flush him out, bring him to me on the plain of glass. I need to face him on the ground he destroyed, on the graves of the thousands he killed. A balance must be maintained."

The crone lowered her head. "Balance is always needed."

"What we do now restores balance. And it brings my brother to me that I may smite him as I should have done so long ago. He must come to me to defend the people of this world, in order to atone for his past evils. And I must exact the penalties set by the gods."

"You will kill your brother."

"It is ordained."

"And you will take control of the Weaver."

"That is also ordained."

"And you will kill me."

"Not if you help me."

The old woman sighed. "Kill me," she said. "I have no desire to live. Promise me that when this is done, you will set me free."

He agreed, his tone leaden with reluctance he did not feel. He had every intention of ridding himself of this Ilduin as soon as Tess, the Weaver, belonged to him in mind as well as body.

"As you wish," he said. "But 'twere a pity if you miss seeing her reknit the worlds."

"I have known only one world, and 'tis bitter enough." She sighed, then bowed her head. "Leave me. I cannot bear distraction while I do this thing for you."

Ardred hesitated only briefly, then took himself from the room. Outside he had other matters to occupy his attention, including overseeing the final distribution of Ilduin Bane to his hives who were gathering for the confrontation before his keep. This poison alone could kill Ilduin, but his armies were quite clear on its use. The poison-dipped daggers were only to be drawn if Ardred himself ordered it.

And that, he thought with a smile, would depend on who decided life under his control was better than death.

As for Tess…he knew in his heart that the gods were at last granting him the gift of which he had been deprived so long ago. Theriel had refused to come to him. But Tess would not.

No, Tess was *his,* and with him she would rule over the reunited world.

The future, he thought with pleasure, would be as glorious as the distant past.

For those who agreed with him.

The cold dark touch recoiled, and Tess drew a long, relieved breath before plunging herself into the circle she was creating with her sisters.

Sara and Cilla became comforting presences within her once again. In these moments, they ceased to be three distinct entities, but instead melded into a place somewhere between three and one. And in their midst now, surrounded by them, lay the tortured mind and heart of the Ilduin they sought to free.

With eyes closed, Tess watched the rainbow grow among them and around them, scintillating light so pure that even when seen only with the inner eye it inspired an awe near pain.

But then, slowly, she began to see what lay behind it. Gradually her mind revealed to her the golden fabric underlying reality, the warp and woof of the world. There she could see their circle, a brilliant golden light dancing along the threads around a tiny dark spot.

And then she saw the black streak that stretched away from them toward the inky, distorted part of the web controlled by Ardred.

Fear made her heart leap uncomfortably. The darkness was so great, so enormous compared to their small area of golden light. How were they to withstand such a blight? How could it possibly be mended?

With every ounce of energy she possessed, she willed the darkness back from them. It almost seemed to recoil, then stiffened again. Yet it came no closer. Little by little she could almost see it shrink. Part of her wondered if the shrinkage was real or merely an artifact of her wishful thinking.

But as it pulled back, the dark spot in the golden fabric that represented their sister Ilduin shrank. Then, with a pop, it vanished.

At once she felt relief from Cilla and Sara, felt their awareness that the evil had fled from this room. Before Tess could react, the other two grasped the hands of the freed Ilduin and drew her into their circle.

For an instant, they were utterly open in welcome.

And then she heard a voice cry out in her head, "Save me, Sister!"

At once her attention was drawn to the blot of darkness that sullied the golden fabric. Again she heard the cry. Then, in the instant before her sisters could close the circle, she felt the other Ilduin connect with her.

Oily. Cold. Repellent. In trouble. The shock struck her like an ice bath, causing her eyes to fly open and her entire body to stiffen. With every ounce of strength and will she possessed, she tried to drive the presence away, tried to close the connection.

Then her entire world turned black.

* * *

Into the blackness emerged the most beautiful man she had ever seen. His hair looked like spun gold, and his eyes were the blue of a summer sky. Garbed all in white, he stepped slowly toward her.

"My love," he said, his voice as smooth and golden as honey. "I have waited so long for you."

She felt as if she knew him, yet had never met him. His pull was incredible, drawing her closer to him even though part of her remained uncertain. "I don't know you."

The closer she drew to him, the bluer his eyes seemed to grow. He smiled, an expression of such warmth that she ached to know more of it.

"You will know me," he promised. "We are destined, my love."

Then his arms closed around her and she felt peace, such peace....

Everyone gathered around Tess, who lay on a bed hastily arranged for her: Archer, Tom, Erkiah, Cilla and Sara. Even the emperor and his daughter stood nearby looking concerned and the Ilduin who had recently been freed, a woman named Yazzi, sat weakly in a chair, clearly drained by all that had just happened.

"She's gone," Sara said, anguished. "I cannot feel her!"

"Nor I," said Cilla. She frowned so deeply her entire face sagged.

Archer sat beside Tess on the pallet and leaned over her, cupping her cheek with one hand. "Tess," he murmured. "Tess, come to me. You must come back to me."

"It happened when we opened the circle for Yazzi," Sara said to Cilla. "Did you feel it? I think the other one joined us."

"The evil one," Cilla agreed, nodding. "I think you are right. Something cold touched her then."

Archer looked up. "Something cold has been trying to seep into her from the beginning of our journey together. So far she has fought it back. What changed?"

Yazzi spoke for the first time since thanking them with all her heart for freeing her. "You opened the circle to welcome me, and at that moment any Ilduin could join. It was then the other one made her move. And my feeling is that she knew exactly who she wanted to take."

Cilla scowled. "I fear you are right, Yazzi."

"I have had some months to get the measure of this one. She is powerful, very powerful, else I could have held her off. The most powerful of all Ilduin."

Sara shook her head. "I don't believe it. I can't believe it. The Weaver *must* be stronger."

Tom spoke for the first time. "Safe shall she come to Arderon, unmolested, she who holds the warp and woof."

All except Archer turned to look at him. Tom's mask once again covered his eyes, making him difficult to read.

Sara reached for his hand. "Are you sure?"

He turned his head toward her. "The gods will not be cheated of their game. We must take her with us."

"My lady," Archer murmured. Reaching out, he lifted Tess from the pillow and cradled her close to his chest. "He shall not have her."

"That is part of what lies in the balance," Tom said. "And I fear that is beyond prophesy." His gaze settled on Archer. "All is beyond the reach of prophesy now, for the outcome lies within you, within all of us. But you... Archer, take care. For I can feel that the gods care not whether you live or die."

"Nor do I," he said simply. "Nor do I. I care only for you, my companions and Tess."

"But," said Lozzi, speaking for the first time and stepping forward from beneath the protection of her father's arm, "he will not harm Tess while he thinks he has her, nor will he harm those who bring her to him. So she will come safely as the prophet has said. When we arrive…"

"You are not going," the emperor told her sternly.

The girl faced him. "I am, Father. I have been touched by what the Enemy would do to us all. I cannot stand by and watch while others fight him. If I can help at all, then I must."

"She can help," Yazzi said. "I was brought here to train her. Little did I know it was a ruse to capture me. But it is a ruse no longer."

Sara nodded. "We shall *all* train her. And help one another through the days to come."

Archer finally looked up from Tess and scanned all their faces. "Regardless what else may happen twixt now and then, we must march on the morrow at dawn. He has done enough damage."

He looked sternly at the emperor. "If you cannot make your legions join the Anari in this fight, then we shall go alone. But go we will, before he exacts another toll, one higher than any of us can pay."

Chapter Twenty-Eight

Another legion arrived overnight, and messengers had been sent for two others. At dawn two days later, fully three Bozandari legions stood in formation on the plain north of the city. Approaching from the hills came the combined army of the Snow Wolves, banners held high like the signal of a new age.

Those among the Bozandari who might have refused to believe their orders stopped grumbling and arguing when the emperor rode forth in battle splendor, his renowned armor and his personal flag of a gold coronet on a blue background unmistakable to even the lowliest ranks.

Soon displeasure was replaced by amazement, for under the red sky of dawn, the emperor rode forth to meet the Snow Wolves, and he rode with only his cousins Tuzza and Alezzi.

Tuzza introduced the emperor to Ratha and Jenah. Maluzzi was more than polite to them. He gripped hands with them both. "So you are the generals who defeated Tuzza," he said, a wry little smile on his mouth.

Ratha and Jenha exchanged looks. It was Ratha who spoke. "With the aid of Annuvil and the Weaver, aye."

"I shall look for their aid as well as yours in the days ahead. I am sure we are all equally sorry to be living out the days of prophecy."

"'Twould not be *my* choice," Jenah said boldly.

The emperor cocked his head to one side. "I am proud to ride beside you. And rest assured, I am not proud of what my people did to yours. There will be no more slavery from this day forth, and those who engage in it will face death. This is my promise to you. I wish only that I had had the courage to act before so many died."

After a moment, Ratha cleared his throat. "It speaks highly of you that you have acted at all."

Maluzza shook his head. "It speaks poorly of me that it took so long. Now we ride forth to face an evil that would make slaves of us all. And we ride under greater burden than you imagine."

"Why so?" Ratha asked.

"Tess," said Tuzza before the emperor could speak. "Tess. The Evil One has claimed her. She comes with us, but she cannot wake from his hold."

Ratha lowered his head, and his hands tightened. After a moment he said, "Then we must save her. And the others?"

"Cilla, Sara and Tom are with her, along with two other Ilduin. One is the emperor's young daughter. You must keep an eye on her, Ratha," Tuzza said. "Please. She is only a child."

"I will. I will ensure that all of them are protected."

"They will come up behind the rest of us," Alezzi said. "With the rear guard. Perhaps some of the newly freed Anari can help there, until they learn more battle skills."

Jenah nodded. "They will be glad to be of use. Many have already asked me what they can do, but little enough they know of battles. They have no training. But there is also another group."

"There is?" Maluzzi was clearly curious.

"Aye. After our first encounter in battle, the lady Tess healed a great many wounded. Thirty of them swore themselves to her service under Topmark Otteda. They have kept watch over her since as her bodyguard."

"Good," said Maluzzi. "The Weaver must be protected at all costs."

"They will do so with their lives."

"I would expect no less of a soldier of Bozandar."

Then he turned his mount and followed by Alezzi and Tuzza, he galloped toward his own assembled legions.

With raised hands, Ratha and Jenah motioned the Snow Wolves to follow.

Otteda accepted the trust from Annuvil with a great deal of solemnity. He was surprised at how much it hurt him to see the Lady Tess lying silent and as still as stone on the pallet in the covered horse-drawn cart. The four other Ilduin walked on either side of the cart, making a protective phalanx of their own. Annuvil, he who had been a king yet would not wish to be a king again, rode behind them. Otteda wondered why he did not ride at the front of the army where he belonged, then decided it was none of his business.

With a few sharp orders, he brought the thirty men of the

lady's sworn bodyguard into position around the carriage and the Ilduin. Annuvil nodded to him, a mark of appreciation.

Otteda dared to approach him. "What has happened to the lady?" he asked.

"The Enemy has attacked her. I know not if he has taken her mind, or if she fights him. None can tell. The veil has been lowered, Otteda."

"What do you mean, my lord?"

Archer looked at him from gray eyes too old and too sorrowful to be merely mortal. "We are walking into the times where none can see the future, for everything depends on the outcome of what we do or fail to do."

Otteda compressed his lips and squared his shoulders. "I have never been able to see into the future so nothing changes for me. I know only that I must do my duty."

Archer reached over and clapped his shoulder briefly. "'Tis as much as any of us can say, I suppose."

"'Tis the most important thing to say. Our duty is clear. I have listened. We will fight the Enemy for the safety of our peoples, our families, our homes. Ever has it been thus. For each man alone, nothing is changed. For the world, the price is higher. I understand that. But for each soldier, what has changed?"

One corner of Archer's mouth lifted. "You are wise, Otteda. Each can only do what is in his own power."

"Aye. Still, I would feel much happier if the Weaver were awake."

"So would I. Indeed, so would I."

Otteda fell silent, the Lord Annuvil's sorrow a palpable thing to him. He couldn't imagine the trials this man had suffered, couldn't imagine what his life must have been like. Couldn't imagine having endured it for so long.

Yet he supposed there were those who couldn't imagine living Otteda's life. At fourteen he had entered the Legion School, and spent the next four years training to become exactly what he had become: an officer in the empire's army. Thence he had gone straight to his legion and had stayed with the same legion ever since. He enjoyed the times when he could find a woman to keep him warm, or could spend a night in a town drinking at a tavern, but he rarely sought more. He had his duty, and seemed to need little else other than the companionship of his fellows.

In short, he was ideally suited to the life his family had chosen for him. For that alone he was grateful.

His days were ordered, his path straight. Until he had sworn allegiance to the Lady Tess, he realized now as he glanced over at her motionless form. At that moment the neat and predictable order of his days, though he had not seen it at the time, had been forever changed.

The Lord Annuvil was right, he realized. They were truly marching into the unknown, to a place where there would be few signposts to guide them.

As they marched northwest toward Arderon, toward the mountains, the terrain became increasingly more forbidding and more difficult to traverse. They were skirting the southern edge of the Deder Desert, long the province of cutthroats and thieves. While such were no threat to an army, the officers took care to ensure that foraging parties went out in strength. Even so, their gleanings grew leaner, for even the dry plains surrounding the Deder seemed desolate as compared to the Anari lands. They were not helped by the fact that Arderon was more a rumor than a place. If anyone had ever gone there, he had never returned.

Rumors of its existence had existed since time out of mind, but not even Archer knew its location.

The Ilduin assured the army's leaders that it did indeed exist, but only Yazzi seemed to have a clear idea of where.

"While I was possessed," she said on the second night of their march, "a memory was impressed upon me. Not my own, I am sure. It must belong to the Ilduin who imprisoned me. But *she* was in Arderon, and she knew its location."

Annuvil, who sat on the cot beside Tess in the huge tent that served as headquarters and residence to the Ilduin, spoke. "You can guide us there?"

Yazzi hesitated. "I think so. I would feel better if I draw it on a map."

Maluzza, the emperor spoke. "But you believe we are so far headed in the right direction?"

Yazzi nodded. "Though I have never been there, I know that it lies beyond the Plain of Dederand, beyond the Sea of Glass."

"No one ever goes there," Maluzzi remarked.

Tuzza nodded his agreement. "Which is perhaps why Arderon has remained nothing but a rumor all these years. Past the Sea of Glass, the mountains become nearly impassible. To my knowledge, no one has ever crossed them or dwelt there."

Yazzi spoke. "They can be crossed. There is a way."

Maluzza rubbed his chin and leaned back in his chair. He looked at Alezzi and Tuzza. "What say you? Will it be a trap?"

"It is likely," Tuzza responded. "Would he put his city in a place easy to attack? We will need to draw him out."

"You may draw his army out," Annuvil said, "but you will not draw *him* out."

"Then what?" demanded Maluzza. "You say we must be rid of him, yet it appears we cannot reach him."

"The armies may not be able to reach him. But a small party can."

"I like this not," Maluzza said.

"It remains, we must defeat his hives and armies as well as him."

"Aye," said Tuzza. "I have no argument against that. Mayhap we will proceed one step at a time."

At that moment, a dusty messenger entered the tent and stood at attention, waiting to be acknowledged.

"What is it?" the emperor said.

"Two more legions join us by dawn, my emperor. And behind them come two more."

Maluzza nodded. "Good. Excellent. Go rest and eat."

The messenger bowed, then slipped from the tent.

"We will be strong enough then," Alezzi observed.

"For the first part at least," agreed Annuvil. He lifted Tess's hand and gently stroked the back of it. "For the rest…for the rest we need her, or all is lost."

Uneasiness lay over the armies camped in the foothills of the craggy mountains: uneasiness about the morrow, uneasiness about their alliance. The Snow Wolves camped apart from the others, not as much through their own doubts as because they were made to feel unwelcome by the other legions. And yet, as acceptance and understanding began to filter through the ranks of the Bozandari officers, the atmosphere began a slow but subtle shift.

Ratha and Jenah were astonished by a visit from the overmark of the White Tiger Legion. He stepped through their open tent door boldly enough, the cold air turning his breath into an icy cloud. For long moments he did not speak as he stared at the two Anari sitting at the folding camp table, a map spread before them. They stared back, watchful, distrustful.

Finally the dark-haired Bozandari officer spoke. "I am Overmark Suzza of the White Tiger Legion," he said.

Ratha rose. "Ratha Monabi, co-commander of the Snow Wolves. This is my second, Jenah Gewindi." He inclined his head respectfully, and Overmark Suzza answered with an equally respectful bow.

"It seems we have become allies," Suzza said after a moment's hesitation.

"Aye," Ratha agreed. "Necessity makes for odd companions."

A faint smile lifted the corners of Suzza's mouth. "I am cold," he said. "You have a warm fire. Perhaps, if you do not object too much, I might bide with you a little while. It seems to me that if we are to fight a common enemy, we would do well to get to know each other."

Ratha nodded slowly and motioned to a chair near the fire pit. A column of smoke rose from the burning logs and vanished through the vent above that revealed the brightest of the night's stars.

The overmark bowed again, then took the offered seat.

"Would you like hot ale?" Jenah asked. "We were about to pour some ourselves."

"It would delight me," Suzza said with a friendlier smile. The tankards were filled, then the chair moved so that the three men sat around the fire pit facing one another. Suzza offered a silent toast, and the other two responded.

"This is difficult," Suzza said. "I am certain it is as difficult for you as it is for my soldiers. For so long you were our prey. You must loathe us. And some among my soldiers lost loved ones in the recent slave rebellion. So they are rather hardened and bitter."

"So it is," Ratha agreed. "Tuzza killed my brother. After my brother killed his cousin."

Suzza nodded and swigged his ale. "I cannot pretend I come with clean hands. But unlike my men, I have heard from the lips of my emperor why it is we unite. Why we *must* unite. And why, in the end, we must learn to live together."

Ratha lifted a questioning brow.

Suzza held out his tankard and thanked Jenah for the refill. "Among my studies in my youth, before I trained in soldiering—which was required of me as the younger son of nobility and the cousin of our emperor—I was taught some philosophy. I believe you know my teacher, Erkiah."

"Indeed!" said Ratha. "He travels with us."

"I have heard. With the Foundling and the Weaver, is that not so?"

"Aye, it is."

Suzza nodded. "Erkiah taught me many things, some of which I was later taught to scorn. Building an empire hardens men, Ratha Monabi. It hardens hearts and minds and perhaps even spirits." Abruptly he shook his head. "No perhaps about it. It hardens the spirit. Since the age of sixteen summers, I have carried a sword, and I can no longer remember the faces of all I have slain, though they sometimes come to my dreams to remind me. This was my duty. I have been awarded many honors."

Ratha nodded, his face expressionless.

Suzza sighed. "I cannot say, however, that fulfilling my duty has made me proud. Blame Erkiah for that. He attempted to make me see a different way. Some of his teaching remained with me through it all."

Ratha nodded. "I was not raised to fight."

"No." Suzza looked into his mug, nodding. "But for me and my ilk, you would have been left peacefully in your villages creating the beauty from stone that was our first reason to take you into our cities." He looked up, smiling crookedly. "I have always suspected that your people never built as well for Bozandar as they did for themselves."

A sly grin crossed Ratha's face. "Perhaps their hearts weren't in it."

"Most likely." Suzza shook his head and gave a short laugh. "However it happened, we are here now. Erkiah told me all those many years ago that if I didn't get myself killed in some battle or other, I would live to see prophecy fulfilled. And here I am."

"Aye," Jenah said, pouring more ale all around. "Here are we all. An uneasy alliance against a threat I doubt we even begin to understand."

"I fear you are right," Suzza said. "As a youth, Erkiah's words thrilled me. How much more could a lad ask for than to be involved in the fulfillment of a prophecy. Now…" He shook his head ruefully. "I would say I wished we were already past it, except that there is no way to know what awaits us on the other side if we fail."

"We will not fail," Ratha said firmly. "We will not because we must not."

Suzza nodded agreement. "Is the Weaver as powerful as I hear?"

"In truth," Ratha said, "I am not sure that even she knows the limits of her power yet. She forever seems to find it within her to do greater and greater magicks."

"That is good." Suzza took another swig of his ale. "Well, my new friends, I came to promise you something."

"Aye?" Ratha questioned.

"Aye. Regardless of the difficulty my soldiers may feel in joining with your army, regardless of how they may feel about Anari, they *will* follow their orders. You need not fear them."

"Then they need not fear us."

Suzza nodded. "Right now, I think that is all we can hope for."

Chapter Twenty-Nine

The armies followed the Panthea River for nearly two weeks, climbing steadily through rolling hills, before they reached the foothills of the Panthos Mountains. Another three days' march north brought them to the Aremnos River. Now the army turned west into the broken foothills of the Panthos range, following the river toward the place where Yazzi claimed that Arderon lay.

With each step forward toward the saw-toothed, towering peaks ahead, the armies drew closer to the place where the glorious city of Dederand had long ago existed. The upper two-thirds of that mountain had been hewn off in the firestorm, and what remained was now known as the Ardusa Mesa, but to Archer it would forever be engraved on his mind and soul as the Plain of Dederand, and the Sea of Glass. With each step, Archer's heart grew heavier. When he had come to this mesa in the past, it had been to visit his own failings and his ghosts.

This time his ghosts did not await his arrival. Already they rode his neck and shoulders like the blast of an ice storm, reminding him.

Reminding him.

Almost without realizing it, he began to talk, a quiet murmur that probably most around him could not hear, not Otteda's bodyguard nor the other Ilduin who walked behind Tess's pallet, apparently to give him privacy with her.

Any other time, he would have been amused. But with Dederand up ahead, little could amuse him. He scanned the surrounding rock formations, pointed spires that were the lone remnants of what had once been lush green hills.

"I used to love to ride this way to Dederand," he said quietly, his words for Tess's ears alone. And had he thought she could hear him, he might have spoken other words entirely.

"Once there was a wide avenue through here, frequented by tradesmen and travelers. All around the hills blossomed with trees and flowers. The beauty of these hills was in large part the reason so many Samari decided to build a city here, rather than below on the water. First there were a few villas, small ones, used as retreats by those who sought the quiet of the country as a relief from the bustle of the city. But within a few years, the villas grew in number, then the trades they needed followed them, and then, one day it became a city named Dederand. Second City. It seemed like a great thing when our father chose to name Ardred as king of Dederand. The residents of the city celebrated with such joy, for they felt they had taken their place as equals with Samarand."

He sighed. "An odd thing, surely since all came from Samarand to begin with, and many still had homes there."

He closed his eyes, remembering the day of Ardred's coronation, when rose petals had strewn the entire avenue between the cities, when flower petals had seemed to fill the air and the people of two cities celebrated with unadulterated joy the coronations of Ardred and Annuvil as lesser kings of their cities.

To Annuvil, at the time, it had seemed more like an excuse for a celebration than anything more. His father, the High King, had managed to rule quite well without assistance other than his council for many, many years. Neither of his sons had needed a coronet, nor had both cities needed their own kings.

But he had not questioned, for it had been his father's will. Besides, he had been too busy mooning after Theriel and wondering if she would ever cast her eye his way.

But as the way steepened and he rode closer to Dederand, it now seemed to him that it was that day, that decision, that had set the Samari on the course of destruction.

Perhaps the love of power had always been part of Ardred's makeup, or perhaps he had learned it as king of Dederand. However it was, the coronation had been the beginning of the biggest changes in him.

"I should have seen," he murmured now to the unconscious Tess. "I should have seen that Ardred was in trouble, instead of seeing only that he grew into a nuisance. Somehow I should have averted the course of the horrible things to come. Instead I was preoccupied and unaware, and by the time I saw the truth, it was too late to stop anything. I have only myself to blame."

How could he have failed to see the changes taking place in his younger twin? Even a man falling in love with the most enchanting woman ever created by the gods should surely have seen beyond the end of his own nose.

He could only lay it to willful blindness. He had not wanted to see. He had not wanted to be distracted from Theriel.

His selfishness had led to the tragedies as surely as anything else that had happened. Even thinking of it made his chest tighten with pain. He had betrayed them all, his brother, his Theriel, his people.

Out of mere selfishness.

"I am so sorry," he murmured to the ghosts that crowded his memory and mind. "I am so, so sorry."

He must not fail this time, he reminded himself. He must save these people who had grown in the place of the Firstborn, must protect them against evils they really couldn't begin to imagine. Even when they looked upon the plain of Dederand, and the Sea of Glass, he doubted they would grasp the evils that had been unleashed. That could once again be unleashed.

"It is so dark."

Startled by the sound of Tess's voice, he glanced down at her and saw that she still slept. At once he slipped from his saddle to walk beside her litter. Not caring who might see, he reached out and grasped her hand. "We approach Dederand," he said.

"So dark," she murmured. "Everything here is blighted."

"Aye."

"So dark," she repeated as if unaware of him. "The scar…the scar…the darkness here reaches deeper than reality. What? What?"

Then she fell silent again, and a small sigh fluttered past her lips. Her hand in his had remained slack the entire time.

He swallowed, squeezing his feelings back into the box inside his chest, which was the only safe place for them. If he ever let them out, he did not want to think of what he might be capable.

Deeper than reality. Her murmured words returned to him and he felt a jolt. *The darkness here reaches deeper than reality.*

He looked around, noting the rock spires, seeing that in some places burn marks still survived. "Cilla?" he called out.

"Aye, my lord?" She was walking with her sisters, and now she strode faster to catch up with him. Despite being an Ilduin, she was still a soldier, and she carried a quiver and bow over her shoulders, and a dirk at her side.

"Cilla, Tess is murmuring in her sleep. She said the darkness here reaches deeper than reality."

Cilla opened her mouth as if she would answer, then quickly closed it. "A moment, my lord."

Gripping the edge of the litter for steadiness, Cilla closed her eyes. Archer watched her from the corner of his eye, noting that after a moment her dark features were suffused with an almost rainbow glow. It shimmered and glowed, and moved in gentle waves over her and about her. Truly, he thought, the Ilduin bore a remarkable beauty. To one with eyes to see, they could never be otherwise.

Slowly Cilla opened her eyes. "I think she is beginning to awaken, Lord Annuvil. A little. There is a struggle."

"But can you tell what she meant? Or was it mere dream rambling?"

Cilla lowered her head. "What our forebears did here left a permanent scar, my lord. It burned through the warp and woof of the world to whatever lies beyond it. I think it will never go away."

Archer's mouth tightened. "I fear not."

Cilla lifted her face, and something very like awe shadowed it now. "I had no idea such was possible."

"The eleven who formed the circle did," he answered grimly. "They sought to retaliate for the murder of Theriel, but this…this is beyond that."

"I agree."

His smile was bitter. "They helped birth the world. I suppose they thought they had a right to unbirth part of it."

"I am glad I know this."

He lifted a brow. "Glad to know this ugliness?"

"Glad to know I have the ability to commit such an atrocity. I will be wary now not to repeat it."

"Good." He walked a few more paces before he spoke again. "You think she may awaken?"

"It feels more likely now. Whatever took her seems to have weakened a bit. Or perhaps she is fighting free. I cannot tell."

He nodded. "Let me know if you sense anything else."

"I will."

She dropped back, leaving him to walk between his mount and the litter, and to wonder if he was equal to the task before him.

Perhaps, he thought, it did not matter which brother died. Perhaps all that mattered was that one of them did. Whatever sport the gods sought in their conflict would then be gone.

And if he died, he could not be responsible for whatever mischief they might devise next.

It was as if the legions came up against a great, invisible wall. Once they emerged from the desolate hills and negotiated the slope of the Ardusa Mesa, they halted. To a man they stopped in their tracks and stared.

Before them lay the Sea of Glass, the place where an entire city and most of the mountain on which it had been built had vanished in a heat and fire so intense that all that remained was black glass, whipped into wavelets as if it were water, frozen for all time.

All had heard of this place, but none had ever dared come here. It was known from earliest childhood that this was a place of unmatched evil, that nothing could grow here, that those who had ventured to cross its vast expanse never returned.

But now they were being asked to march across it, this black sea that devoured the unwary. Not a soldier budged.

Annuvil had ridden to the fore to join the commanders when the army came to a halt. They were all conferring, trying to decide whether to let their armies balk, or order them to march ahead.

"Let them camp here," he said. "'Twill take more than a day to cross the mesa and 'tis better if we start the journey at first light. They are less likely to be unnerved."

The emperor agreed. "The men need time to overcome childhood warnings. Let them rest and accustom themselves to what they see. And send men out among them to remind them that this evil occurred in the distant past. The powers that caused this are no longer with us."

If only that were true, Archer thought, but he remained silent. This time, however, the Ilduin were divided. Five marched with him. Ardred might have taken the other seven. His brother's ability to charm and persuade was in itself a form of magick. Although it was possible, he supposed, that some Ilduin still remained free and unaware of events. Some might not even be aware of their potential.

Even though the ground near the plain was bare of all comfort, rocky and uneven, the soldiers seemed glad not to have to venture out onto the glass yet. They lit fires with what brush they could find, and cooked quick meals. Then they huddled as close as they could get, for the breath of winter, which seemed to have lessened for the past few days, began to deepen again.

Ardred, Archer thought, knew they were here. The cold and snow that had killed so many at Derda was about to be inflicted on this army.

As the temperatures steadily fell, the seasoned troops began to deal with it. They found sheltered places out of the wind, built large fires and surrounded themselves with horses if they had them, transport mules, and every bit of clothing and blankets they carried.

They arranged themselves in circles two deep around their fires, those outside switching with those within often enough to prevent the cold from endangering them.

The Anari, who had until recently never known such cold, were happy to take instruction from the Bozandari members of the Snow Wolves, and soon, light-skinned and dark, they gathered together against the cold. Any distance they had maintained because of past conflicts vanished in the basic need for survival.

A sardonic smile lifted Archer's lips as he watched the transformation take place from the very edge of the plain. "So, brother," he murmured, "did you imagine your winter would tear us apart? For you certainly did not imagine that it would draw former enemies together."

But the cold alone was not enough for Ardred. No. As

darkness blanketed the world, snow began to fall, at first
with gentle beauty, but then with increasing fury. The flakes
turned to icy pebbles, striking with a sting, and the wind
picked up even more, finding its way even into the protected crannies the soldiers had found or built and blew
hard on the flames of their fires as if trying to extinguish
them.

Ignoring the bite of the blizzard, his cape blowing out
behind him, then wrapping around him as if it wanted to
bind him, Archer walked out on the plain. Alone.

He didn't go far, for the glassy ground was treacherous
at the best of times, and the wavelets that covered it were
often as sharp as razors. Here, however, the snow could not
stay. For whatever reason, the flakes melted the instant
they touched the ground, although behind him he could
have seen it deepening on the ground where the men
camped.

In all the years he had walked this world, in all the times
he had come here to brood and remember, he had never
seen anything of life on this plateau, not even the snow.
Tonight was no different. The icy pellets melted, and even
the water they left behind vanished quickly.

Sometimes he wished he could do the same thing. Sometimes he wished he could come out here, lie down and be
absorbed into the glass that was the mark of his shame.

Never had it happened.

Now the moment had come. The moment he had yearned
for and dreaded ever since this plain had been blasted into
reality. The time of his reckoning. The time of Ardred's reckoning. He must face the brother he had not seen since the
beginning of the Firstborn Wars, and there was no doubt in
his mind that both of them could not survive the meeting.

It filled his heart with grief and anguish, not because he cared whether he died, but because two brothers should not come to this end. Because if two brothers had not come to this to begin with, thousands would never have died, Theriel wouldn't have died, and this plateau wouldn't have been blasted in the world as a reminder of arrogance and evil.

He dropped to his knees, ignoring the harshness of the glass poking into his leathers, and let the tears fall down his cheeks, not caring if they froze there. He had failed his brother and his people, and quite frankly he was not certain that he would not fail them this time.

The wind bit harder but he ignored it. He was not certain he had grown enough or changed enough to avoid failing again. He might be cursed with immortality, but he was also cursed with the same weaknesses and failings of men everywhere. He had been arrogant enough in the past to think he was doing the right thing, and now he knelt on the results of all his mistaken decisions. How could he possibly be certain of what was right now?

The anguish of all that had happened and all that was to happen overcame him then. He bent over, ignoring the press of his sword hilt in his side, until his head nearly touched his knees.

He had been born to such privilege and beauty, and all he had managed to do was create a darkness that spanned the ages.

Death was too good for him.

Chapter Thirty

Tess stood somewhere beyond time, somewhere that appeared to be nowhere. Above, darkness ruled, with not even a star to pierce the void. At her feet lay a featureless, colorless plain that stretched as far as she could see in any direction. That she could see at all when there was no light surprised her.

The beautiful man had long since vanished. He had not achieved whatever he had wanted from her. How she knew, she could not say, but gathered that she had been banished to this place where nothing lived, nothing moved. A prison.

For an eternity, or perhaps two, she neither moved nor really thought. It was as if her mind had been utterly emptied and left as barren as the plain around her, as void as the sky above.

No memories. No wishes. No wants. *Non-being*.

The last thought frightened her, and with the fright

came the first glimmers of memory. Who she was. Who she had been. Where she sought to go.

Not much. Like fireflies the memories darted around her brain, appearing and disappearing, only to reappear in another place. She began to struggle with all her might to grasp even one of them, sensing that if she could hang on to some part of herself, the rest would follow.

Then a voice reached her, seeming to rise from the deepest part of her being. She knew that voice. And she knew that he needed her.

Closing her eyes to banish the prison that held her, she focused on the anguished voice, and formed his face in her mind. Then his name came to her.

Annuvil!

Her eyes popped open, and this time she knew exactly where she was. Knowledge flooded into her and she felt her strength grow.

The wind whistled about him, bitter and clawing, the sleet battered whatever exposed skin it could find. Lost, alone, always so alone, Archer battled his own doubts, his own guilt, his own anguish, for much as he deserved to die, despite how much he had failed, others depended on him now.

Then, barely audible above the wind, he heard a gentle woman's voice. Startled he turned and saw Tess, arrayed in her usual white riding garb, a hooded white cape billowing backward over her shoulders.

"The past is not a prison," she said. "It is a map and a star toward a new path."

Relief at seeing her awake hit him so hard it drove the wind from him, but only for a second. Then her words penetrated, sending a shaft of warmth into his long-riven heart.

"My lady," he said hoarsely. "Thank the gods you have returned."

"Just in time, it seems." She stepped closer, then bent a little as she touched his shoulder. "From somewhere out of my poorly remembered past comes a saying. The only true mistake is the one we do not learn from. You have learned. I know you have learned. And you will not repeat your errors."

"I thought I acted rightly before."

"I know." She lifted her hand and brushed some long strands of dark hair back from his face. "My lord Annuvil, you were young then. Much much younger. Barely a man even in terms of your immortal people. The young are prone to error and arrogance. When I look at you now, I see no arrogance at all. You are not the man you were then. Do not doubt it."

He still knelt on the painful ground before her, and nothing could have prevented him from what he did then. Straightening on his knees, he took her hand in both of his and brought it to his lips, warming her chilled skin with a kiss.

With her other hand, she smoothed his hair back, only to see it tossed again by the wind.

"Come with me," she said gently. "Back to the tent I share with my sisters. 'Twill be a sad day indeed if you freeze out here."

He rose easily to his feet in a single movement. "I will not freeze. I cannot."

She started to smile then, and her impish expression surprised him. "Are you so sure?"

Then she grabbed his hand and tugged him back toward the camp. "Come. My sisters and I will warm you, and we will talk about what lies ahead."

* * *

In the tent of the Ilduin it was as if the original party, lacking only Giri, were together again as they had been at the outset of their journey. What had begun as a quest to find the thieves who had so brutally slaughtered a trade caravan had turned into something so much greater, that if any of them thought back to the day they had departed the village of Whitewater, they could scarce believe what they had come to.

"It is ironic," Sara said as they sipped mulled ale around the central fire, the tent walls billowing with each gust of the killing wind, "that it was this very winter that sent Tom and me along with you on your journey to find those who had slaughtered the caravan."

"How so?" Cilla asked.

"We were facing starvation in Whitewater," Sara explained. "Our fields had been blighted by snow and ice just before harvest, and little enough we had remaining from the year before. I insisted on accompanying Archer and your cousins Giri and Ratha in hopes of finding trade to the south so that I could bring food home to my people. My father's ale is usually good coin. Instead…instead I found no food. I found starvation in Derda, and the storm that killed so many. From that point on, I knew my path lay elsewhere."

"Aye," said Tom. "It was then we realized we faced more than unusual weather."

"So, aye," Sara said, "it is ironic, for it was the Enemy's attack by means of weather that led us all to this moment where we will now face him."

Ratha, holding Cilla's hand, cracked a smile. "He may have set his own downfall in motion."

"Let us hope," said Archer. He sat on the ground near the fire, near Tess who sat just behind him on a camp stool.

"He is cunning," she said quietly. "He came to me while I was held in thrall by his Ilduin Hesta."

Archer turned his head immediately, looking at her. "I feared that."

Her small smile held little humor. "I now understand how he could have created such havoc in the past. He is quite beautiful, your brother, and silver-tongued. Had I not known of him already, I would have found it easy to believe that he is all goodness."

"How did you escape his Ilduin?" Cilla asked.

"'Twas not easy. She is very powerful, this one. What is more, unlike me she is very much in command of her powers. However, just as the storm created an irony, I believe his attempt to capture me may have done the same."

"How so?" Archer asked.

Her smile deepened a shade. "While I was held in thrall, I learned from his Ilduin. I am not certain if that was by chance, or if it was what she wished to happen. I certainly felt that she was not entirely happy to be Ardred's pawn. However it may be, I learned much. I think I shall be able to control and use my powers better now."

Sara spoke. "You must teach us, Tess."

Tess bowed her head a moment. "I will teach you what I can. All of you, including Lozzi, for you will need it to protect you. But I sense that in the end…" She trailed off briefly, then lifted her head and looked at her two sisters. "Yazzi is teaching Lozzi, and I must teach her as well. But in the end I believe Annuvil and I shall have to face him alone."

"Alone?" Ratha appeared appalled. "Never!"

"You do not understand," Tess said gently. "It is the Enemy's obsession that drives him. He is obsessed with his brother, and with me. It is the two of us he most wants. While the rest of you can deal with his armies and his other Ilduin and the hives, only the two of us can deal with him. Else he will never cease."

"We can kill him," Ratha said, his hand instinctively falling to his sword hilt.

"You cannot," Annuvil said. "He must be struck with Banedread, or Ilduin fire."

"If I cut off his head—"

"You will not get close enough," Annuvil interrupted. "Trust me on this, Ratha. You will have other tasks of equal importance. If I should fail, at least you can deprive him of his teeth by defeating his armies and hives. That alone will save the world for a while. Indeed, if I fail, his obsession may pass."

"'Twill never pass," Tess said with certainty. "He thinks he must right wrongs of the past. He is blind to his own lust for power."

Annuvil frowned. "Is that indeed how he understands it?"

"It is." Tess sighed and leaned forward, holding her chilled fingers out to the fire and feeling them sting as they warmed. "He is righteous in his own mind."

"Then perhaps he *is* righteous." Annuvil shook his head. "How am I to know? After all this time, I have still not sorted all the threads that came together to create our downfall. I am still not entirely certain which of my actions were mistaken and wrong. Yet I know for certain that many of them *were*."

Tess laid a hand on his shoulder. "You must cease this constant self-reproach. In the days ahead you must be strong and certain. You know Ardred's intentions."

"Aye," said Tom. "There is no good ahead if he triumphs. In that you have always been correct, Archer. Always. I have seen it. Ask yourself what good could he intend when he causes the deaths of thousands through cold and starvation."

Annuvil nodded. "True."

"Simply because he convinces himself he is the right and his goals are good does not mean it is so," Tom continued. "The means by which he achieves them are the truest indicator of the man he is. Even with all of Tess's powers beside you, you have never sought to harm anyone needlessly. You have never asked her to do a single thing for *your* benefit. To me that is the best measure by which to judge you and your brother. It answers any question anyone might have."

A round of "ayes" answered Tom's words.

Archer lowered his head a bit and stared into the flames. For a long while he did not speak. Where his thoughts traveled none could guess, for his face revealed nothing.

At last he sighed and reached for his tankard. "'Tis fated that this comes to pass. All any can do is his best." He looked around the group he had traveled with these months. "I have faith in all of you. I could ask for no better companions and comrades."

"There it is, then," said Ratha. He raised his mug to the others. "May we all live to meet again when this is over."

Later, when all slept, it was Tess's turn to walk out to the edge of the Sea of Glass and stare across its black, glittering expanse. The blizzard had given way to stillness, a stillness so cold she found it hard to draw in a breath. Overhead the stars shone again, their light illumination enough. All around the black glass the snow clung whitely, turning the hills and spires into ghostly shapes. On the glass alone it did not cling, and Tess wondered at that.

The Ilduin who had gathered not far from here to focus their powers on the destruction of Ardred, and consequently Dederand, had created a magick so great that after all this time it still clung.

Closing her eyes, she let herself feel the tattered remnants of the power her sisters had unleashed here. Anger. So much anger. They, too, had believed in their righteousness. They believed they would end the wars that tore the Firstborn apart, but more, they were angry that Theriel had been murdered. The Ilduin were inviolate, but Ardred had violated one of them.

It was that anger, she realized, that had caused the worst of this destruction.

A saying from her other life wafted through her mind, "The road to hell is paved with good intentions." She nodded to herself in agreement. They must take care, she realized. She and all her sister Ilduin must take care not to act from anger. They must enter into this confrontation with the purest hearts they could imagine or their magicks would turn wild as they had here, and who could then anticipate the destruction?

Squatting, she laid a hand upon the glass and drew into herself as much as she could from the remnants of power and rage that lingered here. Then, closing her eyes, she sent the knowledge and awareness to all of her sisters, including Lozzi and Yazzi, with clear warning.

Feeling their acknowledgements, she reinforced the images, then allowed them return to their slumbers.

Continuing to stand there, buried deep within the folds of her woolen cloak and hood, she meditated on all she had learned during her brief captivity by the Ilduin Hesta. Meditated on the strands of memory the plain of glass still harbored, meditated on the past she had only recently reclaimed, meditated on her purpose in this world she had been brought to.

The worlds had been rent by the jealousy of a brother and the rage of eleven women like herself. The black glass before her was a scar on the warp of reality itself.

And it was up to her to heal that scar.

Chapter Thirty-One

Every soul greeted the rising sun with gladness and relief. Even the first touch of its warming fingers felt miraculous after the bitter cold of the night. While they had lost no one to the cold, all were stiff and tired from a night spent fighting it.

Fires were fed fresh fuel, giving them new life and warmth. Rations were heated and tea brewed. To the vast relief of the rank and file, they were given time for breakfast before being ordered to form up for the march, while their commanders met with the emperor and the man they were all coming to know as the fabled Annuvil. Joining them were three of the Ilduin who traveled with Annuvil. Yazzi and Lozzi remained in the emperor's tent.

"We must have some idea of what we face on the plain," Alezzi said. "All of us need to know how best to plan and guide our legions. We must send out patrols."

"And we must patrol in strength," Tuzza said.

Annuvil nodded. "This is not a place for small bodies of men to be caught out. As for the terrain ahead, I can tell some. The glass itself is treacherous. As it cooled, the winds blew fiercely. This is why it looks so much like a black, frozen sea. Many of those ripples are still as sharp as a finely honed blade, despite the centuries of weathering. A fall may cause a serious wound. The surface itself is not as slippery as one might expect. It is not like walking on ice, for there is no water to slicken its surface. Carefully placed feet will find purchase on it."

Everyone nodded.

"If all goes well, it will take us a day and a half to cross it on foot. I would advise no one to ride."

"Can we bring our supply trains?" Tuzza asked.

"We must," said Alezzi. "We do not know what awaits us. If we face a long march before we meet the Enemy, then we will need every bit of food we carry."

"I agree," said Archer. "The supply train must come. But care well for our mounts, and watch their steps more carefully than your own. If it slows us down, so be it. We will need our provisions, for we will find no more along our journey."

"The Snow Wolves should form the patrol columns," Tuzza said. "I have seen how Anari can move silently and invisibly. And my men have marched with them long enough to have learned some of their skills."

Tess thought for a moment. On the one hand, the Snow Wolves might indeed be better at the patrol actions. On the other hand, their special tactical skills, operating as a legion, made them better suited to serve as a reserve, ready to unleash their deadly efficiency at a key moment.

"No," she said. "Tuzza, I know you are a brave man, and

I have no doubt that the Snow Wolves could serve well as the army's scouts. But the patrol columns will suffer attrition in detail, and the tactical value of your legion relies upon your Anari and Bozandari regiments working in concert."

"Attrition in detail?" the emperor asked. "I am not familiar with these words."

"Tess comes to us from a different world," Archer said. "She sometimes still speaks from that world."

"Aye, Emperor," Tess said. "I apologize. The patrols will take casualties in the skirmishes along the way, as they contact enemy patrols and try to identify his main body. The Snow Wolf legion has trained to combine Anari and Bozandari tactics. It is our only such legion, and as such we should not divide and winnow it before we are ready to engage the Enemy."

"And Bozandari lives are less valuable?" Topmark Crazzi said. His Golden Eagle legion had joined them outside Bozandar, and while the other legions seemed to have adapted to the alliance with the Anari, the Golden Eagles and their commander had done so only reluctantly. "Whose legion would you volunteer to suffer 'attrition in detail,' as you put it?"

"Mine," Alezzi said. "We have marched alongside the Snow Wolves long enough to learn some of the Anari skills in stealth. And there are still those who look at my men with suspicion because we marched under Annuvil before the emperor declared the alliance. Let no one doubt our honor now. We will form the patrols."

"Your men have no dishonor for which to atone," Maluzza said. "You did not betray me, cousin. You simply had the opportunity to meet the truth before I did."

"Aye, Emperor," Alezzi said. "And that is kind of you to

say. But you cannot command the hearts of men, Emperor. When this is over, my men do not want to take dark glances from other Bozandari. Allow us to redeem ourselves in the hearts of our countrymen."

Maluzza seemed to consider the argument for some time before he nodded. "Aye, cousin. And as you said, your men have learned some of the Anari stealth. May it protect you in the task before you."

Alezzi bowed. "By your leave, my emperor, I will go to brief my officers and organize my men."

Tuzza reached out and grasped Alezzi's hand. "Do not be so bold that I lose you, cousin."

"I would not permit you to be rid of me so easily," Alezzi said with a short laugh. "We shall toast each other when this is over."

"And soon may that be," Tuzza said.

The sun was near midday when the first two columns of Alezzi's legion marched out. Each brought its own supply train, allowing it to move and fight independently. If Yazzi's map was accurate, it would take four days to reach Arderon after they had crossed the Plain of Glass. After the Black Lions had departed, the main body set out, with Suzza's White Tigers and the Golden Eagles under Crazzi marching on parallel courses. Between them and slightly to their rear marched the Snow Wolves in two columns, with the Imperial Guard at their van and the supply trains in their midst. Tomorrow, once the army was well under way, Alezzi's last two columns would follow as the rear guard.

By nightfall, Alezzi's patrols were at the south rim of the mesa, with the army spread out behind. The lead elements of the Snow Wolves had barely reached the center of the

Plain of Glass, and Tuzza's rearmost units had made only a few hours' march before the army huddled down for another frigid night.

As he listened to the reports arriving at Maluzza's tent, Archer felt a growing sense of unease. Each regiment had taken casualties from men who had lost their footing on the razor-sharp edges of rippled glass. An Ilduin had been assigned to each legion, and their healing arts were much in need both during the march and throughout the night, as for every man who was injured there were at least two horses who had sliced open hooves or broken legs on the jumbled ground. If such continued, their Ilduin would be exhausted long before they had closed in on Ardred's army and his lair.

Yet neither Archer nor Maluzza could bring himself to order the Ilduin to conserve their energies. He could not abandon good men to the cruelty of this evil place, and the army could spare no mounts if they were to have adequate provisions for the battle ahead. Once again, Archer hated himself for what he had brought on the world, for on this day its cost was driven home, almost minute by minute, with the cries of those for whom a simple stumble could be a death sentence.

The next day offered no improvement, for the men were growing weary of having to watch every step. By the time the army had descended the south slope of the mesa, every man had reached the end of his tether. Grumbling had risen in the ranks, and Archer knew they would need a full day's rest before they could press on.

But that rest was not to be, for no sooner had the sun began to set than a rider returned on a frothing horse to report that one of Alezzi's columns had come upon an enemy outpost. The Enemy position was well fortified, and the Black Lion patrol had withdrawn before it became fully and inextricably engaged.

But Archer had no doubt that their approach had been reported. At this moment, his brother would be devising his strategy for the destruction of the approaching army. And Archer still had no idea of the strength or composition of his brother's forces.

It was no way to fight a battle, and each of his officers knew it. When the council of war formed at sundown, their eyes were hollow with fatigue, their faces dark with frustration.

"Your brother planned well," Crazzi said, sarcasm almost dripping from his words.

If Archer scowled at the disrespect, he knew it was justified. For Ardred had sited his lair well. Any enemy would be tattered and worn by the Plain of Glass, at the very moment that it reached his outposts. Were Archer in his brother's place, he would have disposed raiding parties to attack the Enemy camp when they were at their lowest ebb, before they could rest.

"He did," Archer said. "And every regiment must be ready to repel an attack tonight."

"We cannot," Suzza said. "My men are too tired to stand, let alone to fight."

"And Ardred knows this," Archer said. "Would you not have plans to strike a tired foe, were he approaching you?"

Suzza nodded sadly. "Aye, I would. You are right, my lord. But how I can impel my men to forego sleep and stand ready in ranks, I do not know. A body can bear only so much, and my men have borne that and more in crossing that damnable plain."

"Then they must stand watch by shifts," Maluzza said. "The night will be long. Divide your legions into thirds, and give each third a three-hour tour at ready. The others can rest, but must remain dressed for combat and keep their weapons at hand."

"Aye, Emperor," Crazzi said. "We can do that. But if the Enemy strikes in strength…"

"He will not," Tom said, walking into the council, his face flushed from his journey from the White Tigers, where Sara had spent another day and would spend another night healing the wounded from the Plain of Glass. Tom bowed to the emperor. "I apologize for my tardiness, my lord. I remained behind to help Sara set up the aid station, and to tend what wounds I could without need of magick."

"Do not apologize for so noble a task," Maluzza said. "So, young prophet, why do you say the Enemy will not come in strength on this night? What have you seen?"

Tom spoke quietly. "I have heard it said that in some quarters of Bozandar, men fight fierce boars for sport."

Maluzza nodded. "Aye."

"I have never seen such sport, nor would I wish to," Tom said. "But often traders in Whitewater spoke of it. The fighter does not wield his sword against the boar at the start of the fight. Instead, he jabs it with barbed daggers, to weaken it."

"This is done to prolong the contest," Crazzi said. "No one would pay to see a single strike."

"Perhaps," Tom said. "Though I once met a trader whose brother was a boar sportsman. You will pardon me if I trust in his brother's understanding over yours. A boar is very dangerous, and its tusks can hew through a leg or a belly in an instant. Only a foolish fighter would risk such until he had taken the measure of his boar, and in the taking, brought him to exhaustion."

"Aye, he is right," Alezzi said. "By the end, the crowd yells for him to kill the boar and put it out of its misery. I watched this…sport…only once. I would never wish to see it again."

Maluzza raised a hand to silence any argument. "Young prophet, you say that we are the boar?"

"Aye, Emperor," Tom said. "The Enemy will tempt us with barbed daggers, this night and every night as we draw nearer to the place where he means to deliver the killing blow. We must not surrender to that temptation. No boar can fell a fighter when the fighter chooses his own place."

"Alezzi," Archer said, "your men must find each of his outposts. They will be sited so that each can support the others. We must know his strength that we can find his weakness. Only then will we show him our teeth."

"My men will do so," Alezzi said. "By sunset tomorrow, we will know his dispositions better than he knows them himself."

"I pray not for that great a success," Maluzza said. "But by the least we will know where to search next."

"Aye," Archer said. "Mark my words, sirs. We face great trickery in these coming days. Make each man rest when he can, for my brother's guile is beyond measure, and any man who is not at his peak will be easy prey. Even those who are ready will be at risk. Let there be no weak men among us. Even one could be the death of us all."

Archer left the tent to look up at the stars. For in his heart, he knew there was a weak man among them. And he was that man.

Chapter Thirty-Two

Cilla had never been so exhausted. For the past two days, she had spent more of her Ilduin powers than she had ever believed might exist. And those efforts—throughout the days and long into the nights—had come in addition to the exertions of her own trek across the Plain of Glass. Now that she had cared for the last of the injured men and horses, she was ready to search for a vacant cot in·the aid station or, failing that, a vacant spot on the ground. She knew she should eat, but she could not summon the energy to find the cook tent. She simply wanted sleep.

It was not to be.

She had only just found a cot that was not too blood-soaked when she heard the cries of the sentries on alert begin to ripple through the camp of the Golden Eagles. In minutes, men were pouring out of tents to the cries of their officers, falling into hasty formations as the sounds of battle began to filter in from the perimeter.

Despite the leaden feeling in her limbs, she began to walk among the men, moving those whose earlier wounds had been sealed and bandaged onto the ground. While there was some grumbling, most of them understood what she was doing and why. There were not enough fresh coverings to spread on the cots, and she found the four least seriously wounded men and drew them together.

"We cannot have men lying in the blood of others," Cilla said. "Find me something to cover these cots. Cut up tent cloths if you must. And do it quickly."

The oldest of them nodded, and they set out at once. Within minutes they had returned with enough fresh cloth to cover every cot in the aid station several times over. As Cilla changed the covers on the now-vacant cots, they piled the remaining tent fabric in a corner, except for two tents that they began to cut into strips for bandages.

The work was hardly under way when the first of the casualties began to arrive. Unlike the wounds caused by falling on the Plain of Glass, these were savage, gaping tears deep into the flesh, exposing muscle and sinew, bone and innards. Cilla could remember a time when such a sight would have turned her stomach. That time had long passed.

She treated with poultices and bandages all that she could, preserving her Ilduin energy for the worst cases, moving steadily, woodenly, ignoring the fatigue that sapped her spirit with each step. The four men she had sent for tent cloth had remained behind to help, boiling herbs into poultices, handing her fresh bandages, changing the covers on cots as men were moved off and new men arrived, and giving water to those who could drink.

She had barely finished tying a poultice into a gaping wound in a man's thigh when another was brought in. Every eye in the tent went to him at once, and Cilla looked up to see Crazzi, the overmark of the Golden Eagle legion. His face was twisted in agony, though he refused to scream as two of Cilla's assistants pulled his arms away so she could examine the wound in his belly. Only when she drew his trousers down and away from the wound did his first scream pierce the air.

The blade had cut from above, entering just below his navel and slicing down along the side of his crotch and into his thigh. Blood geysered into her face, its coppery taste cutting through the haze of fatigue that had gripped her. She knew he had only minutes to live, unless she could find some combination of skill and gift by which to heal him.

Ignoring his wails of agony, and calling for her assistants to hold him still, she plunged a hand into the wound, following the pulsing wet trail until she found the slick tube of tissue from which his life was leaking. She squeezed it tight and held on, whispering a silent prayer to Elanor, hoping that she had something left by which to channel the healing touch of the goddess.

Her fingers felt warm and then hot, the burning more intense than anything she had ever felt, and her screams soon joined those of Crazzi. When she finally forced her eyes open, she had charred and sealed the artery.

But the cost had been severe.

Her obsidian skin was now a pale gray ash. The pain she had tried to shut aside earlier now slammed her with the force of a boulder, and immediately she plunged her hand into a basin of water. But the burning did not stop, and when she drew her hand out strips of skin hung off it in flaky gray-black ribbons.

In an instant, she felt the presence of Tess and Sara, and their horror as they shared the awful pain that surged through her. They drew on what strength they could find from their fellow Ilduin, but Cilla could feel that it was not enough, that it could never be enough to overcome the shrieking nerves in her ruined hand.

And it was not. For even while new skin began to appear over the red, raw flesh, it was not the whole, smooth skin she had once borne with such vanity. Instead, it was gnarled and shiny, a hand that filled her with such revulsion that she emptied her stomach onto the ground. And still the pain did not stop, for with every attempt to move it, the nerves remembered and screamed out again and again.

"You must rest, Ilduin," the oldest of her assistants said. "We have watched closely how you treat the wounds of most of our men. We can do it. You must rest."

"I will rest when the battle is over," Cilla said, trying to rise and only then realizing she had fallen to the ground. "Help me up."

"No, Ilduin," he said, placing a hand on her chest. "You have done what you can, and more. Let us care for our own, and for you."

"There are other wounded…" she began.

"Aye," he said. "And there will be more after them. And yet more on the morrow, and the day after. We will have more need of your Ilduin gifts, but for the nonce, lie still and sleep, Lady Cilla. We have sent a runner to the camp of the Snow Wolves to fetch your cousin."

"No!" she said, shaking her head. She knew how Ratha would react when he saw the ruined remains of her hand.

He had seen the destruction of too many whom he had loved. She did not want him to fall again into that dark rage of the warrior. "He cannot see me thus."

"Shut her up," Crazzi said weakly, moaning as he tried to roll onto his side. He seemed to give up and spoke to the man who knelt over her. "Tell her that I have cursed her kind for the last time, but that if she does not rest, I will order her bound to a cot."

Her assistant looked down at her and smiled. "You heard him, m'lady. And we will obey his orders. Now let us get you onto a cot."

Cilla knew they would force her to rest, if need be. But her will was not broken. "No. I can lie here. I will not take a cot from a wounded man who needs it more."

He seemed ready to argue the point, but then simply shook his head and laid a blanket over her. "So be it."

Crazzi's hand seemed to fall off of the cot above her, but she realized it had not fallen. Instead, he took her hand in his and held it as she fell asleep.

Denza Gruden lifted his sword and cried "Follow me!"

His battalion, normally part of Tuzza's First Bozandari regiment, had been held as the legion's reserve. Now he was leading them into the thickest of the action, where the line of Jenah's Anari regiment threatened to crack under the unrelenting pressure.

It was not that the Anari lacked courage. Never had Denza seen men fight so valiantly. But the Enemy's attack had continued through the night, always on Jenah's section of the perimeter. So far they had held firm, but now the exertion of two days' marching on the cruel glass and an all-night battle were taking their toll.

Denza's men moved swiftly, passing through the lines of the Anari, a danger in itself given the threshing line tactics the Anari employed. Now he was grateful that they had rehearsed such maneuvers countless times on the march from Anahar. As his men emerged, they were faced with an enemy that seemed to be everywhere and nowhere, barely more than a milling mob, yet each man fighting with a fanaticism that made the whole more than the sum of its parts.

These must be the hive tactics of which Annuvil had warned, for these men were utterly dismissive of danger, rolling forward in swarm after swarm, like sword-bearing locusts. Within minutes his men were fully engaged, and he wondered how the Anari had borne this pressure all night.

Thrust. Step. Push with his shield and withdraw his sword. Then repeat. The rhythm, drilled for endless hours through his years in the Bozandari legions, was as natural as breathing. But it was different now, for every thrust struck flesh, and every step was through the squirming, wet remains of those who had fallen.

Denza glanced to his right and left. His men were holding their formation. As wounded men fell back, the men of the next rank filled their posts and those behind passed the wounded to the rear. He had begun with his men in six ranks of fifty. Now, in many places, only four ranks were still standing.

They had pressed the Enemy back fully a hundred paces, buying time for Jenah to rally his shaken men. When Denza glanced over his shoulder, however, the Anari behind him had disappeared into the night.

For the merest instant he felt the pain of betrayal, but

then the deep, thrumming Anari battle cry came from his left front. Jenah had circled his men around to take the Enemy in flank, the hammer upon Denza's anvil.

"Hold!" Denza cried.

The command rippled down the line, and now the Bozandari switched to a defensive posture: one half step forward with the thrust, then a half step back with the push of the shield to withdraw their swords. The forward progress of the line stopped, though its strength and savagery were undiminished.

Denza was shocked to see that the Enemy hive did not react to the threshing lines of Anari who fell upon its flank and rear. Instead, they continued to press forward, oblivious to the swirling death that was consuming them with an awful, mechanical precision. His sword glistened black in the moonlight, and his arm was slick with blood, yet the killing would not end.

Never before had he seen slaughter such as this. These men were not fully human, blinded by the control of their hive master, until steel bit deep into flesh and the shock of pain and death made them aware of their mortality. And then they were all too human, their screams and cries burning themselves into a part of Denza's memory that he could only pray might be locked away forever, knowing all the while that it could not.

In the end, it was not the firm Bozandari anvil that crushed their spirit, nor the swirling Anari hammer. Only the pale pink tendrils in the eastern sky brought relief, for only then did the Enemy suddenly break and flee into what remained of the darkness. Many would not make good their escape, for Jenah's men pursued them hotly and took no prisoners of the laggards.

Denza sank to his knees and heard a moan from beneath him. He looked down and saw that he had knelt on the belly of an enemy soldier, the man's eyes wet with fear and pain, his breath coming in short gasps.

He raised his sword, ready to slash through the man's throat, to punish him for the horror that Denza had seen this night, to put him out of his misery, to rid Denza of the hollow, sinking feeling in the pit of his belly. But then he stilled his arm and moved his knees.

"I will get you to our healers," Denza said, sheathing his sword.

He took the man's arm and began to lift it over his shoulder, but the man let out a shrill moan that froze Denza in place. The act of lifting the man had opened the wound across his chest, and a bubbling wetness spilled out over Denza's knees. No healer could save this man. He would be dead long before Denza could get him to an aid station. And to move him only tortured him more.

"Kill me," the man said.

Denza shook his head. "I have killed enough for one night."

"I will die regardless," the man said. "You know it to be true. Spare me the pain."

He was right. But try as he might, Denza could not bring himself to draw his dagger. "I am sorry. I cannot."

The man gripped his tunic fiercely. "I would do it for you. Does it matter that I die of a wound you gave in the heat of rage, in battle, or of a wound you gave later, in mercy? Which will lie better on your conscience?"

Denza nodded. This was no longer a locust in a swarm, nor a man whose mind was bent by the dark magick of a hive. He was a man in pain, knowing his death was near, and only seeking to end the pain more quickly. Denza would have done it for a wounded dog. Was this man less than that?

He drew his dagger. "I am sorry, soldier."

"Be not sorry," the man said, closing his eyes. "Only be quick and sure."

Denza plunged the dagger in, closing his eyes as soon as he was certain of his aim. When he opened them, the pain had melted from the man's face.

He wondered if it would ever melt from his own.

Chapter Thirty-Three

Ratha knelt beside Cilla, watching her sleep. The man who seemed to be running the aid station told him little of what had happened, and Ratha had found it difficult to look at her hand. The fingers that had caressed him with such tenderness were now gnarled and curled, shiny, covered by a patina of wavy ripples. Through the night, he had forced himself to look at it again, and again, hoping that with time his stomach would not lurch when he looked upon it.

"I know not whence the power of these women comes," Crazzi said, looking at Ratha. "But in these past days, we have seen the horror they can wreak, and the good that they can do. I pray that yours will do only good."

"She will," Ratha said quietly. "She can do no other, for her soul is pure."

"I would that we were all thus," Crazzi said.

"Do you know what happened?" Ratha asked.

Crazzi shook his head. "Not in full. I was wounded in

one of the early attacks of the night, and brought here. Then I felt an awful burning, and passed out. But I knew when I was struck that I could only die, and still I live. I can only say that she saved my life. If not my leg."

Ratha had been so focused on Cilla that he had not examined Crazzi's wounds. Indeed, where his leg had been there was now only a short, thick stump, tightly wrapped in an herb-soaked bandage.

"That was my decision, sir," a man said, moving over to them. "She stopped the bleeding, but your leg was cold and blue. I knew it was dying."

"And you are?" Crazzi asked.

"Tende Kanholt," the man said. "Of your Third."

"You did well, Tende Kanholt," Crazzi said. "You, also, saved my life. And many others here, it seems."

"We did what we could, sir," Tende said. He bit his lip before continuing. "There were too many that we could not save."

"I could have," Cilla whispered.

Ratha looked down. "You wake."

Her eyes found his. "Aye, cousin. I wake. If I had not slept…"

"You would likely have died," Crazzi said. "And how many more would we have lost for lack of an Ilduin?"

"You cannot know that," Cilla said.

"Nor can you, m'lady. The stain of those who fell last night is not on your soul." Crazzi looked up at Tende. "Nor on yours, soldier. Torment not yourselves for that which you could not do. We are all grateful for that which you could."

"Those who can still feel gratitude," Cilla said, her eyes dark.

"Do not go to that place," Ratha said, leaning over her. "You will find only darkness and pain, cousin. But you will never find redemption. Not in that place. This truth I know in my soul."

Finally she nodded. "Yes, cousin. You know."

Ratha took her good hand in his and kissed her fingers. Then, steeling himself, looking into her eyes, he did the same with her other.

"You need not pretend, cousin," Cilla said softly, tears in her eyes. "I know it is horrible."

"I have seen worse," Ratha said. "And Overmark Crazzi suffered worse. You still have your hand."

"Aye," she said. For a long moment, she seemed to almost sink into sleep again, but then opened her eyes. "What of the others? How badly were we hurt last night?"

Ratha drew a breath before he answered. "We lost many, Cilla. Though not as many as we would have had we not Ilduin among us. Jenah's regiment suffered the worst of it, along with Crazzi's Golden Eagles."

"How many?" Crazzi asked.

He had no need to finish the question. "Nearly one hundred, sir," Tende said. "Almost all of them from the First. Topmark Langen said that, along with his wounded and missing, he lost nearly a third of his strength."

Crazzi shook his head. "One night of fighting this enemy, and already one of my regiments is shattered. We cannot endure four more nights of this. Not and have any army left to fight at Arderon."

He tried to roll into a sitting position but quickly fell back onto the cot. Tende put a hand on his chest. "I am sorry, Overmark, but you are not ready for action. Like the Ilduin, you must rest, sir."

"While my men are hacked apart in these night battles?" Crazzi asked. "I cannot allow it. There must be another way."

Ratha nodded. "Aye, Overmark. There must. And even now, Annuvil and our commanders are in conference, seeking that other way. I would be with them were I not tending my cousin. But you cannot be, sir. We will have more need of your services once you have rested."

Crazzi nodded. "Have you a regiment in the Snow Wolves, Ratha Monabi?"

"I had," Ratha said. "I have delegated command to one of my cousins, that I may serve as Lord Archer's second."

"I have seen what your family can do," Crazzi said, looking at Cilla. "I have no doubt that you share her courage, if not her Ilduin blood. I would like you to command my Golden Eagles."

Ratha looked at him. The Golden Eagles had been the most reluctant to serve alongside Anari. Now Crazzi, their commander, was asking an Anari to lead them. "Are you certain of this, Overmark?"

Crazzi gripped Ratha's hand. "None of my topmarks would do better, and I need them where they are. Have no doubt of my men. They will follow you…Overmark Ratha Monabi."

"I will carry your wish to the war council," Ratha said. "And I ask you to take care of my cousin, lest her courage overcome her common sense."

"I will watch her as I would my own daughter," Crazzi said, smiling at Cilla. "Or perhaps I should say, as I would my own mother, for she bore me back into this world last night."

"Your mother would be proud of you, Crazzi," Cilla said, smiling weakly. Then she turned to Ratha. "Go now, my cousin. There is much to do, and there are many here to tend me until I am ready to tend others. Do well the duty before you. And return to me whole."

"I will do my best, my love," Ratha said, kissing her lips softly. "Soon we can be together."

"Yes," she said, returning his kiss. "Soon."

"We cannot bear another three nights of this," Tuzza said. "We killed ten of the Enemy for every one we lost, and yet they came on, unrelenting, until the dawn."

Archer nodded sadly. His brother had bent his army into hives, or at least that portion he had sent out to probe Archer's positions last night. All told, that had numbered perhaps four thousand, less than a legion. Three in four did not see the dawn, lying in windrows around the camps they had charged so blindly.

But they had taken more than three hundred Anari and Bozandari with them, despite the best efforts of Tess and her sisters, men who died where they fell or bled out long before they could reach an aid station. Jenah's regiment of the Snow Wolves had taken the worst of the attacks, though not a single regiment had met the dawn unscathed.

"Your Anari fight well," Maluzza said, nodding to Jenah. "How many did you lose once you turned his flank?"

"Fewer than a dozen," Jenah said. "But that was near to dawn. Most fell in the early hours of the night."

Maluzza thought for a moment. "And you say the Enemy took no note of you on his flank?"

Jenah shook his head. "No, sir. They kept pressing the attack on the Bozandari that Overmark Tuzza had sent to my aid. It was as if each man could not see us beside or behind him, until we struck him down."

"And that is their weakness," Maluzza said.

"Aye," Archer said, nodding. "To control a hive takes great power, but it can be only a blunt instrument, aimed and loosed at a single objective. This is what we saw in Lorense as well. Complex maneuvers are beyond their ken."

"Then every legion, every regiment, must learn this maneuver you used," Maluzza said. "What did you call it, a hammer and anvil?"

"Yes, sir," Archer said. "But we spent weeks learning this on the march from Anahar."

"My men must learn it in a day," Maluzza said. "This day. We will march no farther today. Alezzi's men are out scouting the Enemy. Today, our men will drill on this new maneuver, this hammer and anvil."

"And rest," Tuzza said. "The men must rest, Emperor."

"Not until they have drilled," Maluzza said firmly. "I am sorry, cousin, but it cannot be otherwise. We cannot bear another night like the last. We must stand ready for these…hives. And we must crush them, completely, and prove to the Enemy that such raids will do naught but to drain his own blood. One such night will buy us passage to Arderon."

"Aye," Archer said, nodding. "It will be done."

"Now," Maluzza said, "what of prisoners? I have heard no reports of them."

"We took none," Jenah said flatly. "Those who fought died. Those who fled escaped."

"And likewise with those who fought the Golden Eagles," Ratha said, stepping into the tent. "Emperor, Overmark Crazzi will live, but he has lost a leg. He must rest and heal. He has asked me to take command of his legion, and by your leave, sir, I will do so."

Maluzza arched a brow. "It seems the healing touch of an Anari did much to change his heart."

"It seems so, sir," Ratha said.

"Then lead his men well, Overmark Monabi. They are brave and disciplined. Where you lead, they will follow. You have my word."

"I do not doubt it, sir," Ratha said.

Archer briefed Ratha on the plan to train the troops in the tactics they had practiced on the road from Anahar, and Ratha quickly agreed. "Yes, Lord Archer. And Crazzi will be glad to hear that we will not suffer another night like the last. The loss of so many of his men saddened him greatly."

"He is a good officer," Maluzza said. "Tell him that his legion is in safe hands, and we will return it whole to him when he is ready for duty."

"Have we anything else?" Archer asked, looking around the tent. "If not, there is much to do by nightfall. Let us make ready. Tonight the locusts will not swarm us. We will swarm them."

Tess lifted her head from a pile of bandages, shocked to see that the sun was high overhead. Her body still felt as if every limb were bearing the weight of the world, but she roused herself, finding her way to her knees and then to her feet.

"Are you hungry, Lady Tess?" Odetta asked, walking over to her. "We have kept some stew warm for you."

"Why did you let me sleep so late?" Tess demanded.

"You had not slept for more than two days," Odetta said calmly. "Lord Archer ordered that all of our Ilduin be allowed to sleep undisturbed. You, they, had less sleep than any of us on the march across the Plain of Glass, and then with last night's fighting…"

Tess did not need a reminder of the previous night. She had seen what a hive could do in Lorense, but that had been a small hive and they had not struck in mass. Last night, the horror had been multiplied a thousand-fold, and the stream of casualties had been endless. The sun had been well above the horizon when finally she had found no more whom she could treat, and had thought to lie down for a moment's rest. She had slept much longer than that.

"Please, Lady Tess," Odetta said. "You must eat now."

Much as the memories of last night revolted her, she knew he was right. "Aye. But please ensure that the wounded have been fed first."

"They have been, m'lady. I knew you would expect no less, and thought to save myself the argument."

Tess smiled. "You are a mother hen, Odetta. And a wise one at that."

Once she had eaten, she began to feel her energy return. And none too soon, for many of the wounded were in need of further tending. Most of the men were in good spirits as she changed bandages and replaced poultices, though some were still reeling from the shock of the last night's battle.

"They wouldn't stop," one Anari said, tears in his eyes as he stared at his hands. "We killed so many, and they wouldn't stop. They wouldn't stop."

He repeated the words over and over, barely aware as she changed the bandage on his thigh. The wound had not been deep, and it was healing well. His gaze never left his hands, and Tess grew concerned that she had missed some wound there in the bustle and fatigue. But as she reached for them, he pulled them away, looking up at her in fear.

"No," he said. "Too much blood. They wouldn't stop."

His eyes were on hers, but it was as if he was looking through her into eternity. *Thousand-yard stare*. The words came from her military service in her previous life. The eyes of a man who has seen and done and borne more than his mind can handle.

"Fetch me some water," Tess said to Odetta. "And a clean bandage."

"We are short of bandages, m'lady," Odetta said.

"Find me *something*," Tess said. "Something clean. Do it now, Odetta."

Minutes later, he returned with the water and a scrap of pale gold fabric. When she took it in her hands, it was as soft as fleece, yet seemed to slide through her fingers like liquid silk. She looked up at Odetta.

"It is from my bedroll, m'lady," he said. "My mother is a master weaver. She fashioned this for me when I joined the army, and I have carried it with me since."

She nodded and paused a moment, wondering whether to use so precious an heirloom in this way.

"She would be honored if it helped him," Odetta said softly.

Tess dipped the cloth into the water and then met the Anari's eyes. "Let me wash your hands, my friend."

"They wouldn't stop," the man mouthed almost silently.

He nodded, whether to her or to some scream he was hearing from the night before, and Tess gently took first his right hand and then his left, stroking them with the smooth, damp fabric. There was no blood on his skin, and only the small cuts and scrapes that they all bore by now. Still, she continued to draw the cloth over his wrists, palms, and fingers, in a slow, soothing rhythm.

Focus crept back into his eyes, as if his mind were

fighting to swim to the surface of a thick sludge. When he looked up again, Tess knew he saw her.

"Why wouldn't they stop?" he asked.

"It was not their fault," Tess whispered, still holding his hands in the warm, damp cloth. "The Enemy took over their minds and their wills."

"I did not hate them," he said, blinking back a torrent of tears. "I promise I did not hate them."

"No," Tess said, feeling her own eyes prickle with moisture. "You did not kill in hate. You are a soldier, and a brave soldier. You fought to save your kin."

His chest began to heave as sobs burst forth. His head shook and his hands squeezed hers. "I do not want to be a soldier again. Please."

A callous soul might have thought this cowardice, Tess thought. It was nothing of the sort. This man's soul bore a weight that not even her Ilduin gifts could lift. It was not courage he lacked, but the cold, implacable spirit that allowed a man to kill without remorse. She could not condemn him for that, and yet she knew he would not feel whole until he could return to his unit.

"You saved many of your cousins last night."

"Did I?" he asked. "So many fell."

"And how many more would have fallen, had men like you not stood bravely?"

The words seemed to sink into his consciousness, like water into finely spun wool. He drew his hands from hers and looked at them, turning them, curling and releasing his fingers. He closed his eyes and brought them to his nose and inhaled slowly, wide nostrils flaring.

Finally his eyes opened.

"This war must end," he said.

Tess nodded. "Aye. It must."

He stood, wincing from the obvious pain in his thigh, and flexed his hands. "I must return to my cousins."

"You can rest here today," Tess said. "Your leg…"

"Will heal as quickly in their camp as here," he said. "Too many of us lie here. My cousins will need as many as can return. And I can return."

"As you wish," Tess said. "But if you cannot keep up on the march, return to us."

"I will keep up," he said, testing the leg gingerly. "I will do what I must."

As he walked away, Odetta shook his head sadly. "He will have to kill again, m'lady."

"Aye," she said, nodding.

"You cannot heal those wounds," he said.

"No, I cannot," Tess said. Even the Weaver had limits, it seemed. And cruel limits indeed. She dipped the cloth into the basin, rinsing it, then wrung it dry and offered it to Odetta. "This is yours, I believe."

He started to reach for it, then paused. "Another will need it, m'lady. Perhaps the time for keeping such things has ended. You have sacrificed all of your past. I can sacrifice this remnant."

Tess nodded silently.

In the distance, she saw the Anari soldier limping back to his cousins. He had surrendered a past of peace and an innocence he would never regain. She could only hope the sacrifice was worthy of its cost.

"Can any victory pay such a debt?" she asked.

Odetta did not answer.

Neither could she.

Chapter Thirty-Four

Tom looked up as Archer strode into his tent. With Sara busy tending to Alezzi's wounded, his mind had been occupied with a little known verse of prophecy that he had come upon in Erkiah's scrolls. But its vague references to cloud and vapor, sunlight and fire seemed impenetrable. If there were any deep meaning, it lay hidden behind a curtain of fatigue, frustration and fret.

The military arts that now occupied the army and its leaders were beyond his knowledge, and he had little to contribute to the daily councils of war. Nor could he remain at Sara's side, for she was moving quickly between Alezzi's regiments as they scouted the terrain ahead. Both Erkiah and Maluzza had insisted that Tom could not be so close to the action that he would be unavailable if needed. Twice already, Sara had barely escaped capture as she and a small personal guard made their way from one patrol column to another. It was impossible not to worry about her, and impossible to accomplish anything else while he did.

"Good afternoon, Lord Archer," he said, grateful for the interruption. "Are the preparations going well?"

"As well as we could hope," Archer said. "There is too much to teach and too little time to teach it, but has it not been thus for us all along?"

"Aye," Tom said, nodding to a chair. "Your brother did not afford us leisure."

"No, he did not," Archer said. He sat and drew a breath before he spoke. "And now the time has come to meet him. We must prepare."

"We?" Tom asked.

"Aye."

Archer was obviously uncomfortable, and for a moment Tom thought back through what he had said, wondering if he had said something untoward. But he could find no cause.

"What burdens you, m'lord?" Tom asked.

"What does not?" Archer said, shifting in the chair, as if his legs wished to be propelling him to whatever fate may lie ahead, rather than resting idle. "But for the present, the greatest burden is my own weakness."

"The *Eshkaron Treysahrans*," Tom said.

"Aye, Foundling. While my pen birthed those words, I fear my mind did not. Now I must turn to you for guidance of my destiny, lest I misstep and fail us all. Again."

"Lord Annuvil did not fail the world…." Tom began, but Archer stopped him.

"I have made my peace with that mistake, and a grave mistake it was, Tom. It is not one I wish to repeat. So I come to you, not as a teacher but as a disciple. I come to you and I ask you to teach me. Please."

This was a different man than Tom had ever known. Gone was the stout heart, which had guided them for these past months. For a moment, it seemed as if Tom were looking at the Annuvil of the First Age, and not the Archer Blackcloak who had walked this world throughout the Second. Tom realized that he had never imagined Annuvil, a young man in a contest with his brother, love turning to anger, anger to rage, rage to hate, consuming them bite by bite until they shredded their world and themselves.

"You know you must go to your brother," Tom said.

Archer nodded. "Aye. I have known that moment would come. Had I been able to face that confrontation in the first age, we might not have come to this."

Tom drew a deep breath. "I am not certain it would have been so simple."

"No? I am. I let factions play out their games, the one raised by my brother, the other raised on my behalf by our father while I dallied with my lady love. Had I ever spent the time to speak to Ardred, to learn his disaffections, I might have found some way to avoid the pitfalls. I certainly could have spared Theriel's murder and the revenge of the Ilduin, which rent the world."

"You underestimate yourself. Or perhaps overestimate what you should have been."

"Do I? I think not, Foundling. I have long had to live with my failings and weaknesses, longer than any mortal man. If I have not learned, then the years have been sorely wasted. So, aye, now I must finally face my brother. And instead of facing simple disaffections and jealousies, I will face a heart hardened by ages of bitterness."

He rubbed his chin, staring off as if to some distant place, then his gray eyes returned to Tom. To the younger man, it seemed they had become shards of ice. "My brother has always built well. I have no doubt that Arderon will be too strong for our army to storm."

"Lady Tess must accompany you," Tom said. "For your brother will not open his gates to you."

"But he will to her," Archer said, his face sagging with understanding. "For she is his true desire, as once Theriel was. Once again he has fixed his yearnings on the one thing that he cannot order. And I must use her as bait, that I can slay him and end this."

"She is not bait," Tom said. "Search your heart and you will know that. You may be the Firstborn Son of the First-born, but Lady Tess is the Weaver. Let her weave."

Archer shook his head. "The last time I permitted Ilduin to weave, I left that blighted black glass. That I cannot allow again."

"They were Ilduin," Tom said. "But they were not the Weaver. All that has gone before has led to the moment we now face. Even the destruction of Dederand and the rending of the worlds. This path was set for us by the gods, Lord Archer. For all of us. Even you. Even Lady Tess. We but merely set our feet on the path they have made for us."

Archer sat silent for a moment, staring at the ground between his feet. When he looked up, his eyes were wet with tears.

"I love her, Tom."

Tom put a hand on Archer's shoulder. "We need no prophet to know that, my friend. Though perhaps she does."

"I have not told her," Archer said. "I dare not. For in the final moment, I must be ready to let her go."

And suddenly the painful truth lay open before Tom's

eyes. This was the true agony of soul that underlay the *Eshkaron Treysahrans*. The ultimate betrayal.

"Aye," Tom said. "You must. For to grasp her at that moment would be the end of all."

"How can I tell her that I love her," Archer murmured, as if to himself, "when I know I will betray her thus? Is it not better that she never knows?"

"There is much wisdom that I cannot plumb," Tom said. "The human heart is such an abyss. I cannot tell you what you must do here, my friend. I can only tell you what I would wish for, if I were Lady Tess."

"And that is?"

Tom smiled. "I would wish to know that I am loved."

Cilla was taking her supper when she found Ratha standing at the back of the line before the cook tent. The men ahead of him offered to defer to their new commander, but he shook his head firmly. He would not eat until all were fed. It was a tradition among Anari fathers, and in the Bozandari legions as well, it seemed.

When finally he had received his rations, she realized he had seen her as well. He came to her with a measured, purposeful stride, pausing to whisper a word into the ear of an officer, then sitting at her side.

"If he means to lead," Ratha said quietly, "he must first learn to serve. He took his meal before his men, and they noticed."

"He is young," Cilla offered.

Ratha nodded. "And he will be young in four days, when we stand before the gates of Arderon. We have no time to wait for age to mature us."

"He cannot lack for much maturity," Cilla said. "He took your words well."

"Aye, that he did. They all have, thus far. We will see what four days of hard marching and the specter of the final battle do for their wills."

"These are good men," Cilla said. "They are hardy and courageous. Most are not from Bozandar itself, but from the northern lands."

"I have seen that, cousin," he said. "In many ways, they remind me of our friends from Whitewater. They take care of one another in the manner of those to whom life has often given hardship, and who learned to rely on one another from the cradle."

"Like Anari," Cilla said.

He took her gnarled hand and kissed it. "Yes, cousin. Like Anari."

A quiet murmur spread through the men, and when Cilla looked up, she realized Ratha's kiss had drawn attention.

"We should perhaps be discreet," she whispered. "Your men do not need to see their commander acting like a schoolboy with a crush."

"Their commander is with the woman whom he hopes to take as a wife when this is over," Ratha said.

Cilla's breath caught. For a moment, her heart leapt, and then it sank. "This is not the time for such thoughts, Ratha. Not with what lies ahead."

"It may well be the only time we have," Ratha said. "And if we cannot speak of hope in such a moment, we have naught left but fear."

Fear. It had been her constant companion for so long that she had forgotten its name. But the word brought it all forth. So many had fallen. Ratha was a good man, but those who fell had also been good men. Why would the gods spare him? For her love? That did not seem to count for much in this age.

Yet he was right. If they forsook hope, there was nothing left to cling to. Not even each other. She kissed his hand softly.

"Yes, Ratha Monabi. I mean to be yours when this war ends. We will marry in the Temple of Anahar, and we will raise children in our Tel. They will listen as you tell stories of all that we have been through."

Ratha laughed. "They will pretend to listen."

She squeezed his hand hard. "No, Ratha. They will listen, and they will learn what it means to be Anari, and the price we paid to live free and in peace. They will honor you and all of those who paid that price."

"Like Giri," he said softly, his stomach turning to lead.

Her grip on his hand softened. "Yes, cousin. Like Giri. We will want to forget these days, to forget the pain and sorrow, the fear and hardship. But we cannot forget. And we cannot allow our children to forget, or their children. These days must be marked forever, that we shall never fall into them again."

Ratha smiled. "You speak to a soldier, cousin. I am no scribe."

"Not yet," she said. "But who among us is all that he will ever be?"

"You would make me a scribe and a priest," Ratha said.

"And a father, forget not that!" Cilla cut in.

"And when will I make time for this?" He leaned in and kissed her lips.

She was about to respond when the murmur around them grew to a chorus of whistles. She was certain her cheeks were a deep crimson when their lips parted, and to her greater horror, Ratha stood and lifted her to her feet, then bowed to the men.

The whistles grew to a roar of applause, and despite her embarrassment, she felt as light as she had since the first time she kissed him. Lighter, even, for now she had no doubt that their hopes ran side by side in the river of time. To her surprise, she could feel that a smile had broken out over her face.

More to her surprise, that same smile was mirrored in the faces of the men around them. They were not making fun of her and Ratha. They were sharing the moment, marking the memories of times with their own lovers, long leagues away and months or years past. For that brief flicker of the day, as the sun set behind the mountains, they were no longer in a cold valley, in the shadow of Arderon and a battle many of them would not survive. They were back at home, in a world where it was safe to think only of the pleasures of the moment.

The moment passed as quickly as it had come.

No sooner had the long shadows fallen over the valley than the cries of sentries split the dusk. Ratha set her on her feet almost before Cilla recognized the sound.

"To ranks!" he cried, although the men were already in motion, grasping shields as they stuffed last morsels of bread into their mouths. "Fly, Golden Eagles. Fly!"

In moments, the area around the cook tent was deserted save for men who were unable to return to their units. They ushered her back to the aid station, carrying food and water for those who could not rise from their beds. There were far too many of these for the few cots she had.

And tonight, she knew, there would be more.

Chapter Thirty-Five

The night's fighting had been a series of brief but bitter skirmishes. At various times, the Enemy had probed at nearly every point along the army's perimeter. At each point, the new hammer-and-anvil tactics had been employed to take advantage of the hives' weaknesses. When the sun rose, the Enemy dead once again numbered in the thousands, but this army had fewer than a hundred of its own. Now the army's vanguards were on the march, the Snow Wolves falling into formation to take their place in the center column.

Tuzza had not been comforted when Lord Archer had announced that he and Lady Tess would be leaving the Snow Wolves in Tuzza's hands.

"We have a private mission that we must fulfill if the army is to have any hope at all," Archer had said.

"Your brother," Tuzza had replied.

Archer had nodded silent agreement, apparently neither

wishing nor intending to give a more complete explanation. Of course, Tuzza had some idea of the task Archer and Tess faced, because he had listened to the many conversations that had floated around over the weeks since they had left Anahar. Perhaps all of his men had heard the same talk in the wind, and knew what was afoot. But he feared for morale if his men began to suspect they had been abandoned in their time of greatest need.

"Take not counsel of your fears," Tom said, seemingly appearing at his side, eyes concealed behind the leathern mask he wore.

"You startled me, Prophet."

"My apologies, Overmark. Though perhaps it is for the better that I did. Your face was dark with worry."

Tuzza feigned a smile. "There is a reason they speak of the burden of command, young friend."

"Perhaps," Tom said. "But take not upon yourself an undue burden. It rests upon each of us to do what he can, and trust that the gods will grace our efforts."

Tuzza compressed his lips. "You will pardon me if I say that is easier to do when one's decisions do not leave one's men dead and bleeding on the field. Please, I mean no disrespect, Prophet, but my men are walking into battle, a battle I know they cannot carry themselves. This ending will be written by Annuvil and the Weaver. If they cannot triumph over Ardred, we can but die in the trying. Are my men not mere fodder in their game?"

Tom seemed to think for a moment before he spoke. "Have you ever built a house, m'lord?"

"No," Tuzza said. "I have not."

Tom nodded. "I have, back in Whitewater. When fire or

storm would claim the house of someone in the village, we all came together to rebuild it."

"In Bozandar, a man would pay a builder to do that," Tuzza said. "I am not saying that we are better, nor that you are. It is simply a different way of doing things."

"Aye," Tom said. "When I build a house, perhaps my hands touch only the beams of a single wall, or lay only a small portion of the tar and thatch on a roof. Are my hands not fodder in a larger effort whose outcome is beyond my control? Have I wasted my sweat and my blisters if my neighbor does not perform his part of the task well, or if a windstorm destroys the house before we can finish it?"

"But it is your sweat, and they are your blisters," Tuzza said. "You bear personally the cost of your action in helping your neighbor. Whatever cost I bear pales beside the cost borne by my men and their families and loved ones. I may choose to help build this house, but these men—" he drew a hand around, pointing to the ranks of the Snow Wolves "—these men will suffer the blisters. Or worse, they will never see their own homes again. It is easy, far too easy, for us to say that the promise of light is worth the wax of the candle. If indeed we do prevail, we will see that light. But too many of them will be the wax burned away for a light they will never see. And those who do see that light will have not their own victory to credit for it, but their having fought and bled to lay the table upon which Annuvil and Ardred could settle their age-old blood feud."

"Do you believe in our cause?" Tom asked plainly.

For a moment, Tuzza wondered if Tom were questioning his loyalty. But perhaps that questioning was not wholly unfounded.

"I do," Tuzza finally said. "And if we can do naught but

to keep Ardred's army occupied so that Annuvil and the Weaver can deal with him directly, that must be our task. But I grieve for these men, Prophet. Every one that falls is a weight against the balance of my soul. When finally I meet the gods, I pray that weight will not be so great that I am cast out. For I fear I will deserve no less."

"Let the gods weigh those measures, m'lord," Tom said, grasping Tuzza's shoulder. "We lack the wisdom to do thus for ourselves."

"Aye," Tuzza said. "And for the want of that wisdom, the world was torn."

"Many will think we have abandoned them," Tess said quietly.

She and Archer had left the valley of the Aremnos River, climbing up into the deep pines that blanketed the shoulders of the Panthos Mountains. The terrain looked very like what she had first seen of this world, on the banks of the Adasen River outside of Whitewater. However, when they crested a ridge, they could look back down the valley to the mesa, two days behind them and still seeming as if it were hard on their heels, an ominous, shimmering black abyss. It was as if its desolation was mirrored in the emptiness of what lay ahead.

"There is no other road that leads to victory," Archer said. "Were we to stay and fight with them, all would die. Worse, all who have died thus far, and who will die, and who would die if we fail, would have died for naught."

"Aye," Tess said.

It was obvious that two people alone could travel more stealthily than an entire army. Even with Ardred's scouts in these hills, there was no way to guard every trail that wound through these forests. And, far more often than not, Tess and Archer followed no trail at all.

For Tess found that she had an instinct for how the terrain ahead would flow, where box canyons or ravines that would block their paths lay. It was not Ilduin magic, she knew. It was yet more of the knowledge she carried from a past that had been scarred and shaped by war and training for war.

War and death had been the organizing focus of her entire life. She hoped that would end with this coming battle. With each passing day, she longed more for a life of peace, of the ordinary tasks that carried one through the rising and setting of suns, the passing of seasons, the cycles of dream and thought and breath and pulse.

"You are weary," Archer said.

"Aye," she said. "I am."

He pulled up his mount. "Let us rest, then."

She shook her head. "The weariness I feel will not pass with an hour's rest, nor even a day's. We must press on, for the rest I need cannot come until all of this is finished."

He nodded silently.

Too much of their time had been spent in silence. In part that was so they could listen for the telltale sounds of followers, or the preternatural quietness that presaged an ambush. But the greater weight of the silence seemed to lie in burdens each carried within and alone, unwilling to share lest they only add to each other's trial.

Hours later, when they had found a mountain cave large enough to bear themselves and their mounts, after they had brushed, watered and fed the horses and tended to their tack, after they had measured out and shared a portion of their provisions that seemed far less than either of their bodies needed, only then were they still enough to speak.

"By this time tomorrow night," Archer said, looking up at the canopy of stars, so bright in the thin mountain air that they seemed near enough to touch, "we will be at the gates of Arderon."

"Aye," Tess said. "We should find shelter outside the city for the night and approach it in the daytime."

He nodded. "We cannot come as thieves in the night, lest the city guards fall upon us with their black swords dripping Ilduin Bane."

"You are certain they will be thus armed?"

"I have no doubt of it," Archer said. "Nor do I doubt that Ardred has reserved those men bearing Ilduin Bane for this final battle. He knows he must slay a Firstborn to win the Weaver. He will be ready to do so."

"You told the others that only your own sword could claim your life," Tess said.

"Aye, I did. Ilduin Bane will not kill me, but even the Firstborn are not wholly immune to it." He held up an arm. "It would take only a slash here to render my arm limp. And while I would heal from it in time, if Banedread falls into the hand of another..."

He did not need to finish the sentence.

"I will not let that happen," Tess said.

"Be careful how much you expose of your powers," Archer cautioned. "He will try to turn them against you. And he knows what you can do, better than you do."

Tess nodded. She drew a breath and tried to quiet the feelings of futility that rose like bile in her stomach. "That is the worst of it. Too often I feel as if all I can do is draw and loose the arrow, half blind. More than once has he then steered that arrow to a target of his choosing, and not of mine. When I have done great good, it has come as much a surprise to me as to those around me."

"Is that not true of all of us, Tess? We step out with one intention, and find that intention turned this way and that along our journey, and often find ourselves at a place we had not intended to go."

"Aye," she said. "But that makes it no less disquieting. Perhaps if I were a painter, I would feel blessed when my creation emerged in ways that were not strictly my original vision. I would have no worry of creating a new Plain of Glass. Instead, I am the Weaver, and yet I cannot set myself to weave with confidence."

"We are all cast into roles that we could not foresee," Archer said, his voice tinged with sadness. "It is as if we came onto this earth bearing secret orders that not even we could read. It is a cruel fate, to be the subject of myth, the object of prophecy, the engine of destiny. We live in that awful shadow, Tess. All of us. More than once have I wished for hearth and home, planting and harvest, wife and children. A life in plain light, however dreary and ordinary that light may seem."

Tess looked away, hearing her own thoughts echoed. Tears stung her cheeks. *Let this cup pass from me.* Words she had learned in the religious beliefs of her childhood. Thoughts she had harbored for so long she could not recall a time when she lived "a life in plain light," as Archer had described it. If ever she had.

Had she ever been in love? Had she ever known that most basic human experience, of looking into the eyes of another and seeing the light that Sara saw in Tom, or Cilla in Ratha? If she had, the memory of it still lay locked in the missing filaments of her past.

She felt Archer's hand on her shoulder, steadying her, and realized she was sobbing.

"What is it, Tess?"

She turned to face him. "I have never known love."

If she had kicked him in the stomach, he could not have looked more ashen. "Oh…Tess."

"What did it feel like…to love her?"

Tess had expected his eyes to turn that deeper gray that they did when he sank into memories of the First Age, but they did not. Instead, they stayed on her.

"I can speak only of what I feel now," he said.

For a moment, she thought he would avoid the subject, but then his own eyes began to leak star-glistened tears.

"My life is only complete when I am with you, Tess."

Her heart thundered. She closed her eyes, unable to meet his, lowering her head. Did she? Could she?

"Archer…I…"

"I felt it the first time I held you, on the road to White-water. When you emerged in white robes, it was as if my heart would burst. The first time I heard you speak the Old Tongue. You were her. You were Theriel, my long dead love. But—"

"I have no wish to be the incarnation of another," Tess said softly.

"No," Archer whispered. "You were not Theriel. She is but memory, a wisp of smoke I could no more clasp than I could sit astride the wind. Whatever I felt with her, the emptiness in my heart when I lost her, the sorrow that lay over every day I spent walking this land…she is gone, Tess. She is gone and will never be again. But you are here. And if my heart lifts when I see your eyes, it is not the memory of her that lifts them, but you and your presence here. Whatever shadow cloaked our paths, it has brought you into this world, into my life. If in shadow I must walk, that shadow is lightened when you are beside me. And, for an instant, I can see that plain light."

The words seemed to melt in the tears that flowed on her cheeks. She felt as if she could not pull them in fast enough, that her anguish and confusion might sweep them away before her heart could receive them and let them seed.

His arms enveloped her, pulling her to him. She was limp in his embrace, a tiny child again, lost in a world she could not fathom or master, sleep torn by a dream that haunted her waking, and the only safety lay in this moment, with his arms around her, at once shielding her from the world without and the world within.

Every safe moment she had known had been when she had lain in his arms. From the first moment when she sagged against him astride the horse on the road to Whitewater, a dead child in her arms. Time and time again, the world had rent her as completely as her forebears had rent the world, and the only security had come in a moment like this one, when in weakness she found what strength she could in him, in his arms, in his broad, firm chest, listening to his heartbeat, her head rising and falling with his drawing of breath.

And she knew.

"Please do not let go," she whispered between sobs, her fingers knotted between her breasts.

"Aye, Tess," he said.

"Is this…?"

"This is what is given us," he whispered.

She looked into his eyes and put a finger to his lips. "Just for now," she whispered, "pray do not speak of what *is*. Just for now, let us be two ordinary folk. Please."

Rachel Lee

After a moment's hesitation, he nodded and drew her deep into the cave, away from the cold's deepening bite.

"I will build us a fire," he said as he helped her settle into a protected niche. "Then I will see to our mounts and we shall eat something to warm us against the night ahead."

With sodden eyes she watched him work his magick of fire, building a small smokeless blaze that bathed her with welcome warmth. Then she heard him bring the horses within the opening of the cave, listened to him talk in his deep voice as he soothed them and spread feed for them.

Finally he returned to her, carrying the extra blankets and the pack full of their food.

Her eyes began to dry as the warmth stole into her bones, but the ache in her heart did not ease. Not one whit. This man, this immortal, this king who was the son of a king, had come to mean much to her. Much more than she could put into words. Yet, he had spoken true: this was what had been given to them, and in it she could see no prospect of happiness, no prospect of an ordinary life in the plain light. He was Annuvil and she the Weaver, tools of destiny. Not even the death of Ardred would change that. They were forever doomed to live in the Shadows of the Gods, both greater and far, far less than ordinary mortals.

Grief for all that could not be, and grief for all that had been stolen from them, savaged her heart. Unendurable pain filled her, and her heart cried out to do something, to seize this moment, to make of it something special, even if nothing else in her life ever brought her joy.

But silent she remained, eating what he fed her though she tasted it not, listening to the bitter wind whistle past the cave entrance.

This journey would end in death, though whose she

could not say. Perhaps all three of them would die and leave the world to its own devices, ending forever whatever game the gods played with them.

However it ended, she was sure of only one thing: She was entitled to this night. This one night.

If only he would have her.

Together they lay on the pallet he made, blankets beneath them, their cloaks over them, and huddled together against the encroaching night. From time to time he murmured something, and then for a while the fire burned brighter and hotter.

She told herself to sleep, but a tension deep within her persisted in growing. When his arms tightened around her, she knew what it was.

Eager hands met eager flesh, eager mouths joined, then bodies came together in a cataclysm of need.

For this little while, though the frigid wind howled just a few feet away, though death awaited them just over the next mountain, they found warmth and life together in a paradise where not even the gods could touch them.

Chapter Thirty-Six

"Lord Ardred, we cannot afford such losses," Ras Lutte said. "Even under the guidance of the crone's hive magick, my men are but wheat to be hewn and sheaved. We must pull back to Arderon and hold behind these stout walls."

His liege did not answer, lost in thoughts that Lutte dared not interrupt further. Instead, Lutte stood and waited for Ardred to come out of the abyss that claimed his mind more and more each day. It was if a vortex were claiming Ardred, its suction growing ever more irresistible. Lutte knew it was the looming battle. Archer had matched Ardred step for step thus far, and with the Weaver and four other Ilduin among them, the Enemy was no lot to be discounted.

Nor could Lutte honestly claim that he had done all he could in his master's service. He had given his full skill to training the men, but he had despaired of training good officers to lead them. Perhaps he might have found among their number a handful who were capable, had he been more attentive, had he been more receptive to Ardred's strategy of laying out a cordon of fortified strong points to hamper the Enemy's approach. In truth, he had never thought it a viable plan for the campaign.

Thus, he had focused on rudimentary training, on the premise that this would be sufficient to hold Arderon when the Enemy broke upon the carefully woven layers of *abatis*—sharpened stakes implanted securely at an angle almost level with the ground, their tips pointed outward—that surrounded the moat of the fortress. A hail of arrows would greet the Enemy as he tried to force the *abatis,* and cauldrons of pitch were already mounted on the walls, ready to pour down upon the few who might cross the moat itself.

Any enemy that somehow survived this gauntlet would then face the task of scaling walls studded with shards of black glass that Ardred's men had harvested from the remnants of Dederand. The basic training his army had undergone would have been adequate to deal with the lucky few who made it into the city itself.

But Ardred had insisted on a forward defense, and Lutte had carried out those orders as best he was able. The early results had seemed promising, but Archer's army had reacted with alarming speed. In the course of a single day, the Enemy had learned to counter Lutte's hives and had slain his men by the hundreds.

"He comes," Ardred said, his voice rumbling like an angry mountain.

"Aye," Lutte said. "The Enemy army is no more than four days' distant, m'lord. And our army cannot contain them. Not in the open. I beg you, m'lord, let us withdraw to the city."

Ardred waved a hand as if Lutte had been speaking of a fly circling the castle's sewer. "It will not matter. He comes to me, and he brings the Weaver with him. The rest of his army…"

Lutte waited for him to finish the sentence, until it became apparent that he would not. "Shall I give orders to withdraw into the city, m'lord?"

"Do as you wish," Ardred said. "Only I say, do not attempt to detain my brother or the Weaver. I will deal with them myself. Once I have done so, their army will fall, whether at the gates of Arderon or in the valleys beyond."

"But m'lord—" Lutte began.

"You have never understood this," Ardred said. "You and the men who served you were but bait. If my brother thought I had no army at hand, he would have dismissed me again, as he did in our youth. He has not. You and your men have served your purpose. Now the moment is mine."

"So many dead…" Lutte said, shaking his head in disbelief.

"And I would have given ten thousand more, had it been necessary to draw out my brother!" Ardred thundered. "Go, Lutte, before you speak that which you should not, and I count you as yet more chaff for the fire. Go and issue your orders. Make yourself feel worthwhile. But leave me now, lest my wrath be diverted from more worthy aims."

Lutte bowed and left without a word, betrayal bitter in his belly. His considered surrendering his army, but he had no doubt what would become of captured traitors. No, he and his men would hold Arderon. Not for its founder, but for themselves.

"The Enemy has fled," Alezzi reported at the evening council. "It would seem our new tactics shattered the will of the hive leader."

"How many have you captured?" Maluzza asked.

"Only a few stragglers," Alezzi said. "They melt into these forests and it is impossible to follow in strength. I do not wish my men to fall into one ambush after another chasing a beaten enemy."

"I do not think he is beaten," Maluzza said. "If he were, we would be capturing deserters, not stragglers. No, Overmark, he is not beaten. He is withdrawing of his own will and to his own plan."

"Into Arderon," Tuzza said.

Maluzza nodded. "Aye. He means to hold us at the city walls."

"And well he might," Alezzi said, his eyes dark and lips drawn tight. "If my scouts are to be believed, the city might be impregnable. They speak of walls of jagged glass, bounded by a moat thirty paces wide, ringed with layer upon layer of *abatis*. A dozen legions could crash and break against such defenses. And we have but four."

"Then four will carry them," Maluzza said, obviously in no mood to brook doubt.

"Waste not your men upon those fortifications," Tom said, speaking for the first time. "We must go to Arderon. But that outcome will be decided for us, by Lord Annuvil and the Weaver."

"But…" Alezzi began, his face incredulous.

Tuzza nodded to Tom before speaking. "The Prophet is right, cousin. Who can know what further sacrifices might have been called for, had we not safeguarded Lord Archer and Lady Tess thus far, or had we not crushed the enemy's hives in battle these past nights."

After a moment the emperor nodded and sighed grimly. "The Prophet is correct. We have laid the table for the brothers. Now we can but march to Arderon and stand at the ready for whatever lies ahead. But we will not waste brave men upon that fortress, unless the gods permit us no other fate." He turned to Ratha. "Bozandar and Anahar have marched and fought side by side. Let no Bozandari ever again doubt the mettle of your people, nor your title to liberty."

Cilla extended a hand to Maluzza, clasping his firmly. "If that be the final glory of our armies—that our great peoples may live in peace—then it is glory indeed. But if you will excuse me and my sisters, Emperor, we must now retire together to our tent and focus on Lady Tess. As we speak, she is nearing the time of greatest need. They are at the gates of Arderon."

"He was always a great builder," Archer said as they knelt in the tree line and looked at the fortress city.

It lay on a broad plateau, partway up the side of a steep mountain, shimmering black in the moonlight. And while it had been built as a fortress, there remained a subtle beauty in its crenellated walls and the soaring spires within. Where Anahar sang of the beauty of stone, and Bozandar boldly whispered its wealth, Arderon brooded in silence. If there were within its walls people busying themselves with the ordinary tasks of life, tucking their children into bed and finishing the last bites of cooling dinners before banking their fires for the night, there was no outward sign of it.

But neither did it have the look of a city abandoned. Far from it. Along the tops of the walls, soldiers stood, wrapped in cloaks, shivering against the nighttime chill, eyes darting as if they had been alerted. Which, Archer reasoned, they probably had. His brother was doubtless as aware of Archer's presence as Archer was of his. They had always shared that connection of knowing when the other was near, even when they could not see each other.

"He knows we're here," Archer said.

"Aye," Tess said. "But strangely, for the first time since this began, he is not reaching out to me."

"He has no need to," Archer said. "He knows we will come to him, and that is what he has wanted."

"His Ilduin is weakening," Tess said, sadness on her face. "I am not sure if we can save her."

He studied her eyes, and saw the hollow hope deep within them. "Tess, we cannot look for her. Once we are within those gates, my brother will be our focus."

She nodded, blinking away tears. "Aye. But you were not in the chambers of Lantav Glassidor. You did not see how your brother had desiccated Sara's mother. The shell of a woman who had once shone with the love of a wife and mother. The woman he holds in thrall there now is surely no different."

"Tess—" he began, but she pressed on undeterred.

"You fight an old evil, Archer. Whatever past I have is mostly lost to me. I fight a battle in the present, a battle for the souls of my sisters. You have your personal reasons for walking through those gates tomorrow. Do not doubt that I have mine as well."

He had not realized the depth of her anger until that moment. Somehow, he had gone from distrust to an uneasy truce, then to admiration and finally to loving her, and all without knowing the wellspring that had driven her through all of the hardships they had faced.

"You were a good soldier," he said quietly.

"Aye," she said. "That much I remember. Perhaps that is why I respect the Anari so deeply."

The comment seemed out of place, and he studied her, arching a brow.

"We were not supposed to fight," Tess said. "Women. In the world I came from, in the army I served. We were not frontline soldiers."

"But it did not work thus," Archer offered. She had found another memory, that much he could see, and he sought some way to coax her into letting it find words.

"I was a medic," she said. "A healer in this world, though there was no magick in what I did. In that world, such things were not known."

He nodded. A world without magick? Had the gods been so cruel as to create a world without such a light? Yet he knew Tess would not lie. "How did you heal, then?"

"We had medicines that would relieve pain or stifle the spread of infection. We had bandages and tourniquets, but much different from what we use here. Our doctors could replace a man's blood, or even his heart itself. We could rebuild a shattered knee or hip, or give a man a new arm or leg."

"And you claim you had no magick?" he asked.

"It must seem like magick to you," Tess said. "But we called it science. It was sterile and precise and answered to the language of numbers."

Archer shook his head. "I cannot imagine it."

"And perhaps that is better," she said. "For we had weapons that would make your heart quail with fear. They, too, were science and answered to the language of numbers. They could tear a man to pieces in a single blinding flash of fire and flying metal, leaving nothing but his boots on the ground and a pink mist settling out of the smoke. We imprinted our names on metal tags, for too often there was nothing else left by which to identify the dead."

"You saw this," he said. It was not a question, for there was no doubt in the look on her face. She had lived in a world more horrific than he could imagine.

"I was not supposed to fight," she said. "I was to tend to the wounded, save those lives I could. We saved many, but we could not save them all. We treated friend and foe alike, for the wounded have no flag save that of life itself. And that was how they came into our aid station that night."

He sat, silent, watching her eyes, listening to her breath, waiting for her to continue.

"Children," Tess said. "They brought children. Boys and girls torn open by our bombs. I…we…did not pause to question their motives. The children needed care, and care we began to give. One of our doctors reached into the belly of a wounded child, and that is when the grenade—the bomb—exploded. It tore the doctor's arm away. I had bent to pick up something from the floor, and the blast went over my head. Parts of the child, the child whose life I had just been trying to save, fell on me like rain."

"Tess," he said, reaching out to squeeze her hand, but she withdrew it and shook her head.

"Five of the adults who had brought the children in drew weapons from beneath their robes and began killing. One of our own wounded had come in with his weapon, and it was on the floor beneath the stretcher. I picked it up. I heard nothing. I felt nothing. I squeezed the trigger and watched the red splotches appear on their chests, watched them twitch and fall to the ground. My weapon held thirty rounds and was set for three-round bursts. I fired exactly as I had been trained. I did not miss. When they were all down, I went around the tent and put another bullet into each of them, right through their heads."

He did not understand the details of her weapons, but he did not need to. The truth of what she had done was not in her words, but in her eyes. Eyes that were more haunted than he had ever seen.

"The other children also had bombs inside them," Tess said. "Our sentries had heard the gunfire and they called for our bomb disposal teams to disarm the bombs. They sent us out of the tent, bringing those of our wounded that we could move. The man whose weapon I held, we could not move him. He died before we could get back in to treat him. My commander said more of us would have died had I not reacted so quickly. He said he would recommend me for an award. I never received it."

"Why?" Archer asked.

"Because that night, I awoke in the caravan outside of Whitewater." She fixed her eyes on his. "Yes, I was a good soldier. I survived on instinct. I killed as I was trained to kill. I saw death. I dealt it. But never did I—never could I— torment someone as Lantar Glassidor tortured Sara's mother, as your brother surely tortures his captive Ilduin even now. A soldier lives in darkness. Your brother *creates* that darkness. Do not question my resolve, Archer Blackcloak. You must settle your accounts with Ardred. And I must settle mine. I have been at war for too long to stop now."

He drew her into his arms. "It will end tomorrow, Tess. I promise."

He wished he could promise that it would end well.

Chapter Thirty-Seven

The dawn came with a cold cruelty, light without heat, the light itself flat and comfortless, stripping the air of depth and almost of color itself. When Tess looked across the plain at the gates of Arderon, they could have been at her fingertips or a thousand leagues distant. She pulled her woolen cloak tight around her shoulders and examined the Enemy, her eyes flickering along the tops and bases of walls, pacing distances in her mind, calculating the steps she would take as she and Archer walked up to those jagged walls, counting how many archers would have them in their sights, how many eyes would be looking upon them with hate.

"It is time," she said to Archer, aware without turning that he stood at her shoulder.

"Aye," he said.

They broke camp and loaded their mounts in silence, and this time Tess did not find the silence uncomfortable.

They had said to each other all that needed to be said. The time for words had ended. It was now a time for action.

As they mounted their horses and left the tree line, she watched the reactions of the Enemy soldiers. A few notched arrows, only to be stilled by commands she could not hear. Their eyes bored into her, wrath transmitted by a science her old world would have denied, a magick that she no longer questioned.

Let them stare, she thought.

She no longer feared this day. Everything in her life had prepared her for these moments. She would prevail, or she would die. Regardless, she would not bend. Terror had plagued her for far too long, but in these past days she had pushed it into a box that she now nailed shut. Ardred wanted her to fear, but he was not her lord, and she would not give him that duty.

Beside her, Archer gripped the pommel of his saddle tightly, as if the uncertainty she had carried for so long had been taken from her heart and placed into his. But if he doubted his resolve, she did not share that doubt. The man beside her had endured too much to get to this place, to this bleak morning. He would not waver. She would not allow it.

As they neared the gates, a uniformed man stepped in front of them, his hand on a sword. Tess's senses tingled with the presence of Ilduin Bane on his blade, but she did not hesitate to meet his eyes.

"We come to see my brother," Archer said, his voice betraying none of the uncertainty Tess felt in his heart. "Stand aside, or die."

"I am Overmark Ras Lutte," the man said, "commander of the army of Arderon. Though I am under orders to let you pass, know certain that I would slay you where you stand if it were permitted me."

"Your courage is not in question," Archer said. "And if it be a fool's courage, you cannot be faulted for that. Now show your final act of loyalty, for you owe him no more than that."

Tess saw the man's eyes shift with Archer's words. Whatever thrall Ardred had once held over this man, it was now broken. They were eyes that foresaw no victory and no reward for faithful service. They foresaw only death. Yet he stepped aside and withdrew his hand from his sword to usher them through the gates.

She barely registered the stout grace of the city's inner buildings, which seemed to rise from the ground as if they had been birthed by the mountains, though not the beautiful act of birth she had witnessed in Anahar. Everything here spoke of defiance, defiance of the mountain on which the city rested, defiance of the gods who had shaped that mountain. Defiance of the fate Ardred had been dealt. The city was a statement of will, not of beauty.

She understood that defiance. She, too, had been cast into the fates of this moment. She, too, bore scars that no science or magick could erase.

This place fit what would happen here.

Beside her, Archer stiffened in his saddle, and she followed his eyes to a face she had seen only in dreams.

Ardred sat on a gleaming black throne, it doubtless, too, hewn from the Plain of Glass. Yet he wore no dark robe, and there was nothing in his visage to proclaim the evil he had wrought. Instead, his pale golden robe seemed to shimmer in the bleak dawn light, and his face was that of an angel. Tousled blond locks rimmed eyes that simmered with inner strength.

She could well imagine how this man had taken her sisters in thrall. Only after one knew him would the cruelty of his heart be apparent.

"Brother," Archer said as they drew near.

"Brother," Ardred replied, rising as they dismounted. For a moment, it seemed they might embrace, but then their eyes hardened. Ardred's gaze shifted to her. "And you are the Weaver."

"I am Tess Birdsong."

"A name that whispers of springtime," Ardred said, smiling.

She did not return the smile. "My mother chose it as she heard birds singing on the day I was born. It is in her honor that I bear the white rose."

He nodded. "I remember."

And then she knew. Every step in her life had been taken under the gaze of his hateful eyes. He had taken her from that world and into this one, as he had taken Ilduin before, as he would take them again.

"Release my sister," Tess said quietly. "You have wrung from her all that you can. Let her die in peace."

He lifted his hands as if weighing his thoughts. "I would do so, Tess Birdsong, if I could. But you know as well as I do that, if I did, you and my brother would tear me and this city apart. He and I weigh equal in the scales of the gods. Neither can overwhelm the other alone."

"It was never their will that we do so," Archer said. "That was your choice, brother. And heavy has been the price for your folly."

"My choice?" Ardred said. "My folly? I did not act alone, brother. I did not cause the rain of fire. You, too, chose this struggle. If it be our folly, then it is a folly we shared together. Now let it end. For only one of us can prevail this day."

Tess stepped between them. "Release…my…sister. You have no rightful claim on her. The Ilduin are the daughters of Elanor, and belong to no man."

Ardred laughed. "And has not my brother wielded you like a flaming sword? Have you not other Ilduin with your army, pledged to Annuvil's will, laying waste to those who oppose you? I watched your blood burn Lantav Glassidor, Tess Birdsong. Do not claim to be a daughter of the gods, when you act at the will of a man, a man with whom you lay, not as an Ilduin but as a woman."

Fire raged in Tess's belly as he spat out the words. Nothing she had done was hidden from him, and nothing was sacred. Not even love itself.

"Your jealousy is undimmed, it seems," she said, stepping closer to him, her eyes fixed on his.

"Tess," Archer said, reaching for her arm. "He seeks to turn you. Do not let him."

"He would turn me?" Tess asked, shaking free of Archer's arm. "He would turn the Weaver? He has not the power. Not in his spent Ilduin, not in his army, and not in his beguiling eyes. Ilduin are born of sacrifice. Those he has taken gave themselves in the will of gods, even if they knew it not. As will I. But he will not turn me."

She looked through his eyes and into the dark cell where a woman sat on a bed, old and frail, her heart long since devoid of light, her eyes hollow, only her soul left to burn with the chains that bound it.

"*Ertalah versahmnalen!*" she cried.

Ardred recoiled at the words, and in his eyes she saw the

woman smile her last before her soul fled, leaving only the detritus of a human form sagging to the floor.

The sword appeared in his hand as if by conjuring, though he had drawn it from the folds of his robe. The blade gleamed with a cold, golden light. The metal seemed to bleed, and as each drop fell, the gold turned to an impenetrable darkness before hissing on the ground.

Behind her, Archer drew Banedread, but she shook her head. "Sheath it, Annuvil! Your time is not yet come."

Archer met her eyes. His brother's face no longer bore the guileful openness it had only moments before. He knew he could not possess her, and now Ardred meant to kill her. Weaver or no, Archer knew his brother's prowess with a sword, and now his brother held Banegeld…a sword he had forged in the depths of a time long forgotten, tempered in the emerald fire of jealousy. The sword that had slain Theriel. The sword that would slay Tess.

He could not let it happen again.

Yet as he tried to lift Banedread, it was as if his sword bore the weight of the world itself. For a moment, he wondered what dark magick Ardred had conjured, but when he looked into Tess's eyes he saw that it was not Ardred who stilled his hand. It was Tess herself.

"Sheath it, Annuvil!" she commanded again.

The sword of the Weaver sparkled with blue light, yet she made no move to draw it. Ardred meant to kill her, and she meant to let him.

Their eyes met, and suddenly he was cast back into a scene from the First Age. Theriel, too, had carried the blade of the Weaver. Theriel, too, had kept it sheathed as Ardred stole up on her with Banegeld held high. His wife could have spared her own life, and yet she had let herself fall with the blade that bit deep into her breast.

Tess was willing to do the same.

Why? What gain could come from such empty courage?

Theriel's blood had spilled forth onto the ground, and for a moment he had looked in horror at what he had done. But then his face had hardened and he had hewn through a heart that he knew would never have beaten with love for him.

Archer's breath caught in his throat as he watched his wife's murder, painted in his mind's eye by the magick of the Weaver. He saw Theriel's face twist with the pain of the blade within her. The face he had kissed. The breasts he had nuzzled in the quiet sunset after their marriage, now torn and red as blood fountained from her chest. In her last instant, her eyes softened, and Archer saw his own reflection in them. And then she had fallen still.

And he knew.

Theriel had died on the wings of a promise that Archer had never seen. Her last thoughts had not been of fear and pain, but of hope and love.

Hope for this moment.

Love for him.

His heart squeezed as he slid his sword back into its sheath. Tears rolled down his cheeks as he watched Tess turn to face his brother. The next moments seemed to pass as if time itself had all but stilled.

The rage in his brother's eyes.

The firmness in Tess's face.

Banegeld lifted.

Tess's arms spread wide.

Banegeld falling.

Tess never flinching.

She uttered only the smallest cry as the sword drove into her breast. For a moment he thought the Weaver's magick would cast the blade aside, tear it from Ardred's hands, or allow it to pass right through the fabric of reality without harming her.

But no.

She could have, he realized. The Weaver could have cast his brother into eternity with the merest whisper of her mind. Instead, she tried to suck in breath, gurgling, her chest heaving, her arms falling limp at her sides.

And then Ardred withdrew the sword.

Tess's blood poured out, blue flame licking its way down Ardred's blade, spilling at his feet, creeping toward him, engulfing him. His first cries split the air as she slumped to the ground.

His body did not burn as had the others her blood had judged, for it was not given to even the Weaver's blood to slay a Firstborn. But it could still judge, and Archer watched as Ardred fell to his knees, crying out with the agony of a thousand souls. It was as if every man, woman and child who had fallen in this dark winter now clawed at his soul with teeth as sharp as knives.

Banegeld fell to the ground.

"Kill me!" he cried to Archer. "Kill me, brother! I beg you!"

It would be so easy, Archer thought. Banedread would slice through his brother's body as a hot knife into butter and still forever the evil that had grown there. It would wreak vengeance for Theriel.

It would wreak vengeance for the frozen dead stacked outside the walls of Derda.

It would wreak vengeance for Tess, who now lay pale and still between them.

It was his moment.

Archer drew his sword, but now it did not sing.

It wept, as he wept.

"Do it!" Ardred said, his face contorted in an agony that went beyond the physical pain of the blue flame that now crawled onto his face. "Spare me this, Annuvil. Slay me!"

Archer lifted his sword, and then from the corner of his eye he saw movement. The white wolf approached, its golden eyes fixed on him. Mesmerized, Archer watched as it drew nearer, now standing over Ardred.

To slay his brother, he would have to slay the wolf.

As if in a dream, he watched the world blacken and die around him, shriveling not into glass but into an ash that would leave nothing in its wake but debris floating in the night sky.

He had raged once. And vengeance he had wrought. But it had not cleansed the world. Nor would it now.

The wolf looked at him, impassive, unblinking, eyes fixing first on his sword and then on his arm.

Archer extended his arm and lay Banedread across it, drawing it slowly back, the razor-sharp edge cutting deep through skin and sinew. He did not need the wolf to tell him what to do next.

He stood over his brother, letting his blood flow. Everywhere it touched, the blue fire first burst anew and then flicked out. Ardred twitched and screamed with each drop, his cries growing weaker until the last of the flames had been extinguished.

Archer felt the dark ash recede, replaced by a warmer darkness that seemed to well up within him. He saw that he was face-to-face with the wolf, and realized he had fallen to his knees. The world seemed to sway before him, and his head felt too heavy.

As he let it droop, he saw that he was kneeling beside Tess. He tried to slip his arms around her, to lift her to him for one last kiss, but he could not find the strength. Instead, he bent to kiss her.

Her lips were softer than he had ever felt.

And cool.

He went to her.

Chapter Thirty-Eight

Sara wept as they approached the gates of Arderon. Tom had spoken to her for two days as the army had marched, and she could not recall a single word he had spoken. She moved numbly, an emptiness in her heart, a leadenness in her limbs.

She had felt it the moment it happened.

As she looked to her side, Cilla's eyes mirrored hers. They were walking into an abyss that would never release them. An abyss that had opened in the moment their sister was torn from their souls.

Even Maluzza's daughter felt it. More than once had she fallen into Sara's arms, tears flowing down her cheeks, seeking a comfort Sara could not offer.

Not even the warming sun had softened her grief. The trees no longer seemed to fight a dark cold. At the tips of their branches, flickers of bright green had begun to sparkle. With each step, it became apparent that winter had yielded to spring, and yet Sara could not greet that springtime with joy.

It had been purchased with death.

The fortress of Arderon now seemed an empty shell of itself. Men and women wandered aimlessly along its walls, as if in a daze. As they passed through the gates, there were neither rains of arrows nor cheers of liberation. If anyone spoke, Sara could not hear it.

They came to the center of the city, where a black throne was now overgrown with thorn bushes.

But not just thorn bushes. Each branch bore a white rose.

Sara reached out and picked one, determined to place it on the grave of the woman who had given herself to end this winter.

If only she could find the grave.

She turned to a woman in the square, mouthing words, asking where the Weaver lay. The woman spoke back, but no sound came from her lips. Sara wept again, and the woman took her hand and pointed to the palace.

Sara nodded, emptiness denying the smile she would otherwise have offered. Tom guided her, his hand gentle but firm on her arm, and they passed through a door that had once given in to the darkest heart of the world. Now it was set as a dining hall, three rows of tables laden with food that, much as Sara's stomach desired it, her heart had no desire for.

Then her heart stopped in her breast and her jaw dropped. Standing at the head of the hall were three people, two of whom she recognized. Her legs weakened beneath her and Tom had to steady her.

Archer and Tess. But a refined Archer and Tess. No longer the heavily burdened victims of fate and prophesy, but alive and beautiful. Never had she seen Archer look so tall or proud or so happy. It was as if all the years, miles and sorrows had been lifted from him.

And Tess…Tess was radiant. She smiled and her smile deepened when she saw Sara and Tom. "Dear friends," she called to them, and Sara hurried forward with Tom in her wake.

"You're alive," Sara said, her words breaking on a sob. "Oh, dear Elanor, you're both alive! The link severed and I thought…I thought…" She couldn't finish the words as she fell into Tess's embrace and through her tears looked into Archer's smiling, noble face.

"It is over," Tess murmured. "The Weaver is no more. We are free. We are all free. We are no longer the tools of the gods, and it was that fate which joined our minds. The need is gone."

Sara stepped back, dashing away her tears of joy with one hand. "We are no longer Ilduin?"

"We will always be sisters, Sara. We will always be Ilduin. But our gifts have been changed. I think you will find you can still heal, though not quite as powerfully." Tess stepped to one side and indicated a seated man. The man's skin seemed to have been stretched over what had once been perfect features. Thin tufts of almost-white hair lay scattered about a scalp that was pink and raw. He looked weak and pained, but even he had begun to smile.

"The Firstborn are gone as well," Tess said. "This is Ardred. Like us he is now mortal, and sadly I could not completely heal him. He is blinded."

"Ardred!" The name escaped Sara's lips on a gasp.

"Yes," Tess said. "Whatever good or evil will be of our own doing."

Slowly a group had been gathering around them, a group that included Cilla and Ratha, Tuzza and Alezzi, Jenah, the emperor and his daughter.

The change seemed to be affecting them all. They looked around and blinked like dreamers awakening until their gazes again settled on Tess and Archer.

"It is over," Archer said. "Over. And the gods have granted me my dearest wishes, for I am no longer Firstborn, but merely a mortal man, as is my brother."

As he spoke, he laid a hand on Ardred's shoulder and his brother smiled again.

"And Tess," Archer said, "has granted me her hand in marriage. From now on all will be different. The shadows no longer hang over the world. It will be up to all of us to build anew, the best kind of world we can."

Many heads nodded in agreement. Then Ratha said, "My lord?"

Archer shook his head. "I am no longer anyone's lord. Nor am I Annuvil. I am Archer Blackcloak until the end of my days."

Ratha smiled. "To me you will always be my lord."

"And to me," the emperor said. "For all who have fallen in this battle, I have a request to make."

Archer cocked his head to one side.

"I ask you, Archer Blackcloak, to become my adviser, for I think you have seen more than anyone, and perhaps understand better what we must avoid." The emperor then chuckled. "Of course, this will make you a lord all over again!"

Everyone laughed, but only Tess noted that Archer hadn't yet answered one way or the other.

But then he spoke. "If I am to advise you, emperor, then I have two suggestions."

"Aye?"

"Amnesty for Ardred's armies, for they were not in control of themselves."

"They seem harmless enough right now. Agreed."

At that a cheer went up from around the hall, and Ras Lutte, who had been sure he would die this day, stepped forward.

"I am Overmark Ras Lutte of Ardred's armies. I accept the amnesty. I have already ordered my men to lay down their arms." Then he bowed deeply.

The emperor's brow creased. "Ras Lutte? I remember you. When you were younger and less wise you made a mistake with the wife of one of my commanders."

Lutte stiffened. "Aye. And I was put out of the army."

The emperor waved a hand. "Youthful indiscretion. You are pardoned, Lutte. None shall lay a hand on you."

Lutte's eyes widened. "Truly you are merciful!"

Maluzza smiled. "I am learning. High time." Then he turned again to Archer. "Your second suggestion?"

"Tens of thousands died as a result of the severe winter. There are nothing but abandoned farms between here and the northern mountains, farms that will need to be tilled and planted and harvested if we are to have a crop in this autumn. I suggest you offer these lands to the men who fought on both sides. For it is my hope we will never again need so large an army."

The emperor nodded thoughtfully. "I like it." He turned to his scribe. "Write it down and organize a group to parcel out the land to all who want it."

Then he looked at Archer. "Anything else?"

Archer smiled. "Only time to enjoy my bride and our new lives."

"And your brother?" Maluzza asked.

"I shall care for him for the rest of our days together," Archer said firmly. "He, too, was but a tool in the designs of the gods, and the evil has been driven from him. I wish only that I could offer him a better life."

At that Ardred rose and reached out blindly for Archer. "Brother," he said. "Forgive me."

Archer embraced him. "My brother. Always."

"Always," Ardred echoed through his tears.

And it was done.

Epilogue

Autumn had come to Whitewater again. Preparations for the Harvest Festival were well under way. Tom and Sara had virtually taken over management of the inn from her father, Bandylegs Deepwell, who declared himself ready to step aside in favor of the younger generation and spend his days brewing his famous ale and talking in the public rooms with his friends.

This year the farmers had reaped the best harvest in anyone's memory, a harvest that would become woven into the tales that were shared in the public rooms through the cold winter months.

But along with those tales there were other new tales, tales brought home by Sara and Tom of strange lands and beauties beyond description. Tales of adventure and triumph. It would have been a lie to say that everyone in town was not waiting for the festival in hopes of hearing the two give a retelling of their travels.

Sara was growing large with child, and she smiled a great deal. Jem Downey had accepted that his son would not follow him as gatekeeper, and had chosen a likely lad from another family. Not that the gates often needed to be closed these days, for there was so much abundance even the animals had no desire to venture into town to hunt for chickens or scraps.

But on the day of the harvest festival, early in the morning, Sara began to grow jumpy.

Tom kept questioning her about it, for he feared for her health. It was too soon for the birthing, but something might be wrong.

She merely shook her head and smiled, assuring him that everything was well with their child—a son she had told him months back. Apparently her Ilduin powers extended to that knowledge as well as healings.

"No," she said finally when his concerns began to overwhelm her. "I just have a feeling that something very special will happen today."

"What?"

"I know not. It is just a feeling."

With that he had to be content as he strung lanterns and helped make mounds of bread and huge pots of stew. They would eat tonight as they had not been able to eat at all last winter. The land again blessed them with its bounty.

The festival was in full swing, children running everywhere underfoot, the men telling their tall tales to various audiences, the women gossiping in happy groups, when a small mounted party passed through the gate.

Jem Downey, who had just been about to abandon his post for the night, looked up and his eyes widened. "My word!" he said in amazement.

A gold coin flipped through the air and landed in his

hand, while a familiar voice spoke from beneath a dark hood. "Buy something nice for your wife, Jem Downey."

Jem nodded and stepped back to watch. Never had he thought to see so much splendor at a Harvest Festival. Or ever, for that matter.

The first two passed him by, the familiar man in the black cloak, only this cloak wasn't worn but was made of the finest black wool. Beside him rode the lady, garbed all in white, a smile dancing in her blue eyes.

Behind them came two of the dark folk from the south, Anari he thought they were called. Two of their men had always traveled as part of this party, but this night it was a man and a woman. Beautiful people, he thought. Wisdom seemed to sit on their shoulders.

Behind them came two more lords, to judge by their dress. From Bozandar, perhaps. And in the rear a shrunken, scarred man who nevertheless smiled as if he were enjoying himself greatly.

When they had passed, Jem stood staring after them. The world had indeed changed, he realized, when such a party could ride together. His son's stories had apparently not been exaggerated. Then with a shrug, he looked up the road, saw that no one else approached, and swung the gates closed. Tonight with everyone having such a good time and probably drinking a little too much of Bandylegs Deepwell's famous ale, he did not want a fox to slip in and get into someone's coop.

The party reached the inn and the ostler came running up to take their mounts. Around them a pool of silence grew as people forgot their chatter and stared in wonder.

Then Sara emerged from the inn's front door and cried out with joy.

"Tess! Archer! Tom, come at once!"

Tom scrambled out the door, his hands full of mugs, and then a big grin split his face. He was still obliged to wear the leather mask, but it concealed nothing of his joy in this moment. Behind it, it seemed, his pale eyes shone with delight.

Alezzi and Tuzza were there along with Ardred. They threw their hoods back and joined in the happy exchanges of embraces, which even included Ardred.

Soon places were made for them in the public room, and when Tess removed her cloak she revealed her own swollen stomach. Soon she and Sara were whispering happily about their hopes for their children.

But before long, as the ale and food flowed freely, Tom asked how things were in the south.

Cilla smiled, holding Ratha's hand. "Anahar is beautiful, more beautiful than ever. And Ratha has taken his position as priest. Our priests have always been women, but when Ratha and I returned to Anahar, the clan mothers quickly recognized that our former soldiers had need of the quiet wisdom of one of their own, to help them through the memories of the war."

"I listen more than I talk," Ratha said, waving a hand. "There is little I know that those men do not know for themselves, somewhere in their hearts."

"Tch," Cilla said. "He is wise, and people seek his wisdom, that is all."

"And what of you?" Sara asked Tuzza and Alezzi.

"We spend a lot less time on the march," Tuzza said. "Bozandar maintains a small army in case there should ever be a problem, but Alezzi and I are getting fat and happy. We have wives now, and we husband the family estates we have so long ignored in our service to the army."

Alezzi chuckled. "It is fair to say we are enjoying our retirement."

"And you two?" Sara asked of Archer and Tess. "How are you?"

Tess smiled at Archer, the expression conveying more than words ever could. He returned the smile, his eyes full of peace and love. "We are happy," he said. "Do we need any more?"

"You will not return to your old world?" Tom asked.

Tess shook her head. "That doorway has been closed, and I do not regret its closing. The life to which I would return...is no life I wish to revisit. I pray daily that I have seen the end of war. And in this world, perhaps, I have."

Sara turned to Ardred, who had been sitting quietly amidst the group, listening, and laid her hand on his. "You look as if you are healing."

"Tess works at it." He bowed his head a moment, then raised his face, showing a hint of the beauty that had once been his. "I am learning," he said, "to live with my regrets, and to live with what I have become. I have learned that a brother's love and mercy knows no limits. I have learned that the most important thing in the world is the arrival of a new life. I have found that I love working with the farm animals, especially the horses."

"And do not forget," Tess said proudly, "the lute. Before we leave you must beg Ardred to play the lute for you. His fame as a lutist grows rapidly."

Ardred shook his head. "Helping a foal into the world is more important. But I do love music."

He sighed and lowered his head, then said quietly, "The blindness I suffered before was far worse than the blindness I suffer now."

Tom reached out and touched Ardred's shoulder. "I understand. I truly do."

"I believe you do." But then Ardred brightened. "Mortality is a beautiful thing."

Those among the group who had always been mortal looked at him in surprise. Alezzi spoke. "You don't miss being immortal?"

Ardred laughed. "How could I? You have no idea what a sweet beauty mortality lends to each and every day. Joys I would have missed before now leap into my heart. Thank the gods for this gift."

Tess took his hand and picked up his thought. "We were born into shadows. Myth and prophecy and destiny hovered over our days, weighing our souls, binding our paths, blighting our hearts. Now we live in the light. The light of ordinary lives. Waking and sleeping. Planting and harvest. Winter and spring. And aye…birth…and death."

"To the light of ordinary life," Archer said, lifting a mug of Bandylegs's ale.

The others joined in the toast, and then Tess raised her mug to theirs. "Aye. To light."

For on this night, the shadows were gone.

Imagine not knowing if your next meal may be your last.

This is the fate of Yelenda, the food taster for a leader who is the target of every assassin in the land. As Yelenda struggles to save her own mortality, she learns she has undiscovered powers that may hold the fate of the world.

LUNA™

Visit your local bookseller.